The Swan Road

Angeline Hawkes-Craig
Scars Publications
America

The Swan Road

Angeline Hawkes-Craig
ISBN# 1-891470-46-9
$7.50

scars publications and design
http://scars.tv

first edition
with the assistance of *Freedom & Strength* press services
printed in the United States of America

writings copyright © 2002 Angeling Hawkes-Craig
book design copyright © 2002 Scars Publications

This book, as a whole, is fiction, and no correlation should be made between events in the book and events in real life. No part of this book may be reproduced or transmitted in any form or by any means, graphic, electronic, or mechanical, including photocopying, recording, taping, or by any information storage or retrieval system, without the permission in writing from the publisher.

Table of Contents
chapter, page

Chapter	Page	Chapter	Page
Chapter 1	9	Chapter 11	137
Chapter 2	23	Chapter 12	151
Chapter 3	39	Chapter 13	167
Chapter 4	51	Chapter 14	183
Chapter 5	63	Chapter 15	195
Chapter 6	73	Chapter 16	209
Chapter 7	83	Chapter 17	223
Chapter 8	95	Chapter 18	237
Chapter 9	109	Chapter 19	251
Chapter 10	121	Chapter 20	265
		Chapter 21	279

Bibliography 293

To Rob and my babies:
You are my sun, my moon, and stars.

Of living strong men he was the strongest, Fearless and gallant and great of heart. He gave command for a goodly vessel Fitted and furnished; he fain would sail Over the swan-road to seek the king.... And his bold retainers found little to blame In his daring venture, dear though he was; They viewed the omens, and urged him on.

-- Beowulf I. iii. 159-167.

chapter 1

Tore shivered as she opened the door to let out some of the smoke that had curled around the wood beams of the ceiling in a desperate attempt to hang on and choke the inhabitants. She waved her arms, trying to get the smoke to leave. She had burnt the stew...again. Her brothers constantly ribbed her cooking saying that it didn't matter how pretty she was, once a man tasted her food they would never look at her again. Tore frowned. She propped the door open with a log from the wood pile, and turned to scoop the charred and foul smelling remnants of meat and vegetables from the great iron pot that hung over the fire.

Tore grimaced. It smelled so bad, even the dogs wouldn't eat this! Tore went outside, and dug a hole in the snow and dumped the burned stew into it, careful to cover it up afterwards. Tore looked around to make sure that all of the other holes she had dug and covered up were still concealed. She didn't like being the brunt of the bad cooking jokes, but as the years went by, her skills in cooking never improved.

Nordahl, Tore's father, had often said that Tore spent far too much time play fighting with her brothers and not enough time learning to develop the more womanly skills such as cooking and weaving. Tore could hunt better than any man Nordahl had ever seen. Her skill with the bow was remarkable. His only unfulfilled wish in life was that Tore could've been born a man. She was far more skilled with the bow and knife than any of his three sons. She would've made him proud on the battlefield; but a battlefield was no place for a woman. So cook and clean she must.

Tore put new ingredients into the pot and tried hard to keep from day dreaming this time. She stirred the contents, trying hard to remember how her mother had done things when she was alive. Life seemed much simpler when her mother had been there to instruct her. She never burned food in her mother's pot. Now that it was her cooking pot, she was concerned for the health of her brothers and father. Her cooking had taken its toll, and she could see that they weren't as hearty as they should be.

Tore sighed. Father was right; she should concentrate more on domestic life. When she was busy with the household chores, she found herself fantasizing about sea voyages and fighting with iron battle-axes; but none of this would ever be for a woman. The meat began to sizzle in the pot, and Tore stirred more vigorously than before. She wouldn't let it burn this time!

Ubbe and Arne, inseparable as always, came panting into the house from the fierce cold of the outside. The foul reek caused by the earlier pot of stew had almost vacated the room. Arne smiled at Ubbe as he shook out his goatskin robe and tossed it onto his sleeping mat in the corner. "How many pots of stew did you cook before this one, little sister?" Arne laughed loudly.

Tore flashed him an angry look.

"Ah, Arne! You've got the fire up in her now!" Ubbe smiled and pulled the long bench closer to the table as he sat down on it.

"What makes you think I didn't get it right the first time?" Tore ladled the stew into wood bowls and passed them to her brothers.

Both brothers laughed. "The smell!" Ubbe said looking at Arne, who nodded in agreement.

Nordahl came grumbling from behind a skin divider. He sat on the bench across from his sons and hacked a body-racking cough. His health continued to decline and Tore grew more worried with each hacking cough.

"What is that stench?" Nordahl rumbled. Arne smiled and nudged Ubbe in the ribs.

"Tore's trial run, father!"

Tore dipped the big wood ladle back into the pot and dished up a bowl full of stew for her father. She sat it in front of him on the table.

Nordahl sniffed at his bowl like a dog. "By the Gods, girl, I believe a man who eats your cooking and survives should go straight to the halls of Valhalla!" Nordahl took a bite of his stew. "Ah, but you are improving." Tore smiled. She sat down next to her father and made a face at her younger brother, Ubbe. The brothers ate their stew hungrily, and didn't seem to notice that the bread was as hard as a rock on the outside, and rather sticky and wet in the center.

Tore hadn't realized how hungry she had been until she began to eat her own bowl of stew. In her attempts to make an edible meal, she had totally forgotten to eat her noon meal. The evening meal had taken her entire afternoon. There still was some weaving to be done, and some wood to be chopped. Her chores were endless. As soon as she completed one there was another waiting to be finished also. Tore sighed.

"What is it, sister?" Arne looked at her with a concerned look.

"Just tired." Tore smiled back and took a bite with her wooden spoon.

"I thought you might be worried about the family problem." Arne said.

Nordahl grunted from his seat at the table.

"Father?" Arne frowned.

"I specifically told you not to discuss that matter in front of your sister!" Nordahl was visibly angry.

"What matter is that, Father?" Tore knew to ask was risking sparking her father's temper further, but they had made her curious now.

"No matter that concerns you, girl." Nordahl held out his bowl, signaling that he wanted more. Tore flashed Ubbe a look that said 'you will tell me later', and got up to get her father a second helping. Ubbe rarely crossed his older sister. He was almost a man, true, but his sister could still beat him in physical combat. Being beaten by a woman was not a thing to be proud of, so Ubbe avoided it at all costs.

Tore fiddled with the oval shaped pin on her shoulder that secured her blue apron. The pin was gold. Most women wore pins of copper or bronze. Not Tore. Her father's family was wealthy and their women wore pins and jewelry of gold or silver. She absently picked at the engraving of a dragon's head, and sat trying to figure out the expression on her father's face. She decided to go ahead and risk her next question.

"Father, why must every issue of importance, be no matter for a girl? Am I any less intelligent than my brothers?" Tore trembled as she defied her father's earlier commands.

Her father pulled at his beard in thought. Slowly, he smiled and as he did so a thousand little wrinkles rippled out from his mouth over the rest of his face. He never could deny a woman anything. He had been a stern man, but women had always been his soft spot.

"No, no, my girl. Not less intelligent." He smiled again revealing little pieces of meat stuck in his teeth. "Than what is it, father?" Tore resented being treated differently than men. She refused to sit passively by a fire for

11

the rest of her life, serving as the docile wife and mother. She was just as good, if not better, than most men she knew.

"You are a woman." Nordahl laughed. "I have known that for all my life." Tore smiled at him lovingly.

"Ah, yes, you have; but, you also know a woman's place and you refuse to accept it." Nordahl shook his head slowly and looked at his sons.

"It is an unjust place, Father." Tore knitted her brows close together.

"But, nevertheless, it is your place. You can't change what the Gods have ordained." Nordahl could understand his daughter's restlessness, her mother had been very much the same at Tore's age; but time and motherhood had tempered that rebelliousness.

"What about Sif? She is a woman, and she is a warrior. Does she sit quietly by the fire making stew for men?" Tore hit the table with her fist. Dishes bounced up and hit the table again under the force of her fist.

"Always Sif. I'm sorry, Tore. You'll learn, in time." Nordahl smiled and took his daughter's hand and kissed it. He reached into his pocket and pulled out a new ring, slipping it on her finger.

Tore looked down at her finger and smiled at her father. "It is beautiful, Father. Thank you."

"But, it does little to calm that storm in your heart, I imagine?" Nordahl laughed softly.

"How can you understand so much, yet understand so little?" Tore asked smiling.

"I understand too much. I am an old man. I grow weary of this conversation. Ubbe, help me lie down." Nordahl unsteadily pushed himself up from the table. He had drank one too many cups of mead again this meal. Ubbe rushed to his side and helped his father to his sleeping mat. Tore sat studying her new ring.

"Father thinks that trinkets will appease you, sister." Arne laughed.

"What do you think?" Tore asked her brother honestly. "I think that Father is an old man, who doesn't realize how much fire he gave to his daughter." Arne laughed. "You think that I should be content with my lot though, don't you? You think that I should do my womanly duties without questioning the ways of men, don't you?" Tore cocked her head and spoke to her brother like she couldn't speak to her father, or any other man.

"Yes. I think after awhile you'll see how foolish you're being. Look at Aelfgife. She never complains! She's been married for four years now! Two children, and she's still just your age." Arne pointed towards their cousin's home.

"I am not Aelfgife." Tore said simply.

"Lucky for you. She has a face like a dog!" Arne laughed boisterously, spilling his mead down his beard and over his tunic.

Tore laughed at his folly. She never did understand men and their excessive drunkenness. She preferred to keep her senses at all times.

Arne staggered outside muttering the whole way towards the door about how badly he needed to piss. Tore laughed. Men! They forever told the world what was on their mind!

She scraped the dishes into a large wood bowl and set it outside for Gunlod, their dog. After awhile, she heard Gunlod sniffing around and hungrily lapping up the food in the dish. Tore cleaned up the dishes, and wiped up after her brothers and father.

When Ubbe came to the fire to get warm, he found Tore on her hands and knees retying the stone weights on the loom. The weights were too heavy for the yarn, and kept snapping the thread and falling to the ground.

Ubbe sat on the bear rug and poked at the central fire with a stick. He watched his sister working at her loom. She seemed annoyed.

"Need any help over there?" Ubbe asked jabbing at the fire.

"No. I'm nearly finished. Did father go to sleep?" Tore looked up from tying her weights.

"Yes. He was talking a lot of nonsense about Freya and you and having children. You worry him too much, Tore." Ubbe rubbed his hands together over the licking tongues of the fire.

"Death worries him, not me. He's afraid of dying in his bed instead of with a sword in his hand." Tore tugged at the strings securing the new weight.

"Still, you should try to be more..." Ubbe paused. How could he phrase it so Tore wouldn't fly into a rage.

"More what, Ubbe? I'm interested in how you're going to say what I know you're going to say." Tore laughed and came over to the fire. She sat down beside her brother.

"More womanly." Ubbe closed his eyes tight as if expecting to be hit by his sister.

Tore laughed. "And, what do you know of women, Ubbe?" Ubbe frowned. He didn't like being insulted by his sister. Anyone else's sister wouldn't dare say the things that Tore said to him. Ubbe shrugged, anyone else's sister wasn't Tore. She was in a class all by herself. That's what Arne always said anyway.

"I know plenty." Ubbe tried to sound convincing. "Do any of the women you know so much about, know how to do this?" Tore darted her arm over and before Ubbe knew what had happened, he found himself face down on the ground, with Tore's knee planted firmly in the small of his back, and his left arm twisted uncomfortably upward and behind him at an odd angle.

"No." Ubbe said shortly, gasping for breath. Tore let him up, laughing she brushed the dirt from her dress. She pushed the white blond hair from her face and sat back down where she had been sitting a few moments before. Ubbe looked at her half mad, and half amused.

"Ulf shouldn't teach you things like that." Ubbe smiled at last.

"He said it was for my own protection." Tore smiled slyly.

"I doubt he thought you'd use it on your brothers while he was away." Ubbe laughed, snorting as he did so. He had a good sense of humor. All of the men in her family had good senses of humor. Tore supposed it was fortunate for her that they did; few men would tolerate a woman like her.

"Are you going to tell me the big secret?" Tore said after a few minutes of silence.

"I don't know. Arne told me not to." Ubbe said quietly, running his hand over the blond fuzz that had begun to appear on his chin and cheeks. Tore remembered how proud Arne had been when his beard came in. She noticed how alike Ubbe and Arne were growing the older Ubbe got. She had always looked more like Ulf. Ubbe and Arne resembled the soft, kind look that their mother had about her. Ulf and her own face tended to hold a more somber expression most of the time. She looked fondly at her younger brother.

"Does Arne do your thinking now?" Tore took a jab at his ego.

"No, I do my own thinking." Ubbe sounded hurt. "Then are you going to tell me or not?" Tore knew that she would have to wait until later if she couldn't manage to get Ubbe to tell soon. She didn't want to make him feel like he had no choice. She wanted him to feel like they were allies, not like there was some kind of chain of command due to their ages.

Ubbe found the stick he had cast aside earlier, and thrust it into the fire furiously. "You shouldn't make me tell these things." He said grumbling.

"I'm just a woman. How can I make you tell me anything?" Tore feigned innocence.

Ubbe glared at her. He knew as well as she did that she could physically make him tell if she wanted to. Why did he have to have a sister who was so damned strong?

"If you'd rather not tell me, I'll leave it alone." Tore said at last. She didn't want her brother to tell her something if it was so important that he not tell her.

"I think you should know." Ubbe said softly.

"But Father and Arne don't?" Tore questioned.

"It's not just them. I mean, it's all of the men. They don't want any of the women to know." Ubbe said hesitantly.

"You mean Father's brothers?" Tore asked, realizing now that this was a much larger problem than she had thought if it involved the rest of their kin.

"Yes. There was a meeting." Ubbe looked over his shoulder to make sure that they were alone. He wasn't supposed to tell a woman the things men speak of in private.

"The other night when father asked Arne to help him to Athelwold's fire?" Tore whispered.

"Yes. All the men were there." Ubbe poked the fire sending little sparks flying.

"And the meeting involved this problem only?" Tore was anxious to find out the problem.

"Yes. It is a big problem." Ubbe was slow in delivering his banned information.

"Big enough not to tell women." Tore snorted. "They think it is for your own safety." Ubbe said softly and with much concern.

"I'm not like the other women! I am strong! I can fight like a man and think like one too! The other women, they are sheep!" Tore felt insulted that her father would lump her in with the other women of the family.

"It wasn't father's decision. It was Athelwold's. He is the eldest." Ubbe's head nodded up and down furiously in his attempt to be persuasive.

"I can keep a secret." Tore sharpened the small knife that hung from a chain at her waist with a whetstone.

"You know how father feels about following rules." Ubbe shrugged. "When Athelwold says don't tell the women, Father pretty well much thinks that includes you too. You do consider yourself a woman, don't you?" Ubbe laughed.

"Just because I don't have teats that brush my knees like an old cow, doesn't mean I'm not a woman!" Tore spat at him.

"But you do have teats somewhere under there?" Ubbe took his stick and poked her chest.

Tore snapped the stick in half with one hand. Ubbe raised his eyebrows and smiled.

"What is the secret?" Tore blurted.

"You won't tell?" Ubbe looked around again.

"You know I won't." Tore frowned.

Ubbe sighed. "Some mead maybe?" He decided if his sister wanted this information badly, he should make her play the servant like she usually made him.

Tore smiled and pushed herself up from the floor, brushing the dirt from her behind. She crossed the room and poured a horn cup full of mead from a gigantic earthenware pitcher. She handed the cup to her brother and then sat next to him eagerly.

Ubbe took his time drinking his mead. He would stop and smack his lips, looking over the rim of the cup at his sister to make sure she was still waiting captivated for his next words. Ubbe let out a loud burp and handed the cup back to Tore.

Tore took the horn cup and sat it next to the stones around the fire. She glanced at the ceiling at the dried meat hanging there, and then over her shoulder to make sure no one was around. The she nervously looked back at Ubbe.

"You'll tell me now?" Tore tried to coax the excitement from her voice. She didn't want Ubbe to know how badly she wanted to know.

"Yes." Ubbe stretched his arms and then lowered his voice. "There is a family that has accused Athelwold of killing one of their kin, a very important person, in a drunken rage. For your own good, I do not tell you who this family is. It is better you do not know. Don't fight me on this issue, Tore."

"Did he do it?" Tore moved closer to her brother and she could smell the mead on his breath mixed with his breath's usual stench.

"Athelwold says no. It seems that they don't want to wait for Hablok Bloodaxe's return from sea to settle this dispute." Ubbe paused.

"A wergild?" Tore whispered.

"Yes. This family is afraid that Hablok will rule in favor of payment rather than in blood. They want vengeance, and they want it now." Ubbe coughed.

"But, Athelwold says he didn't do it." Tore said.

"But, this family does not care. They want revenge for the death of their kinsman, and they want it now. Ulf and Hablok and the others have been gone nearly a year now. No one can say for certain when they will return." Ubbe said slowly.

"What of the other families?" Tore asked.

"They refuse to get involved until Hablok's return." Ubbe said angrily.

"Surely someone knows when Hablok will return. What of his family?" Tore thought about the other voyages that their oldest brother Ulf had been on, some lasted two years or more.

Ubbe shook his head sadly. "No one can say for certain. The real problem is that this family wants their vengeance now. Our kin are afraid they will cause an all out feud." Ubbe cast another nervous glance over his shoulder.

"But, they have to wait for Hablok's decision." Tore said innocently.

"You think like a woman." Ubbe laughed.

"Why do you say that?" Tore asked, somewhat wounded.

"This family is mad with revenge. They care not for the decision of a chieftain who isn't even here to be chief! Hablok spends too much time at sea on his strandhoggs when he should be home." Ubbe argued.

"But the shore raids provide many necessities that we wouldn't have otherwise!" Tore raised her eyebrows. It seemed almost cowardly to hear a man talk bad about raiding.

"They provide more slaves for Hablok and little for anyone else." Ubbe grumbled.

"You shouldn't say such things. Not at your age." Tore suddenly grew afraid for her brother at his expressing such bold statements about their leader. Usually only men who wanted to challenge the chieftain's position spoke like Ubbe was doing now. He shouldn't make a habit of it.

"Most of what you say, Tore, shouldn't be said. Not from a woman." Ubbe smiled crookedly. "Do you know how I feel now?"

"Of course I know how you feel. Just be careful whom you say such things around. You don't want people to get the wrong idea." Tore stared into the fire.

"And who are you to worry about people getting the wrong idea? You have been spouting off at the mouth for years without regard to your future, and now you warn me of my words?" Ubbe actually sounded angry.

"What future do you mean? Slaving away over the fire and swatting at sniveling brats that cling to my ankles and squall? Is that a future?" Tore laughed.

"A safe future." Ubbe nodded to himself.

"Safe, until the man gets himself killed. Safe. Who wants safe? Certainly not you, I hope! Not one of my kin, I pray!" Tore blushed from shame to think her younger brother a coward.

"You think you know so much!" Ubbe snorted.

"And, tell me, what have your thirteen years taught you, Ubbe the Grown?" Tore laughed.

"Nearly fourteen!" Ubbe protested.

"At fourteen I could swing a sword double the weight you now carry!" Tore laughed again.

"You shouldn't be swinging swords at all!" Ubbe grunted.

"Now you sound like Athelwold!" Tore laughed and pushed herself up.

She had work to finish before it was time to go to bed.

"Athelwold is a coward!" Ubbe whined.

Tore suddenly sensed that there was more to the story than what Ubbe had told her.

"Why is Athelwold a coward, brother?" Tore leaned over, her hair falling across Ubbe's face as she whispered the words close to his ear.

"He will not fight." Ubbe said shortly.

"And father, and the rest, want to?" Tore asked.

"Yes." Ubbe said. "But, Athelwold says we wait for Hablok Bloodaxe's return."

"What if he doesn't return soon enough?" Tore frowned.

"Then someone dies." Ubbe said bluntly.

"One of us?" Tore's voice sounded raspy in her throat as she whispered.

"One or many." Ubbe said solemnly and then got up and went towards the door. "Do not repeat what I have told you."

"You have my oath." Tore stood still where Ubbe had left her. Why would she tell anyone? To do so would only get Ubbe and herself in trouble. Besides, whom was she going to tell? Women? Her aunts, cousins, grandmothers? Her circle was a limited one. She was lucky if she saw something more than an iron pot and the weaving loom in a day! Tell someone! Women had no secrets in their world. Only men had secrets.

Tore smiled to herself. Except in their dwelling. Her brothers knew she was their equal if not their superior. Ulf had always said she was too smart for a woman's own good, but the Gods must have thought otherwise. Tore picked at her teeth with her fingernail. The gods must have their reasons for making her strong and intelligent – even if she was just a woman.

Tore finished tying the weights onto the loom, and tended to her weaving. Ubbe stayed outside longer than was good for him in this cold night air. Tore poked her head out of the door and cast a quick look around in the front of their home. The biting wind nipped at her face, making her nose grow numb in seconds. Ubbe was standing looking out over the land towards their uncle's dwelling. Tore called out his name.

Ubbe turned as if suddenly slapped from a dream, and staggered through the snow back to the house. He closed the door behind him with a loud thud, and closed and barred the wood door.

"Lost in thought?" Tore asked.

"Guess I better not do that too often, if I don't want to freeze to death, huh?" Ubbe laughed.

Tore was glad to see that Ubbe's somber spirit had lifted. He was much too young to worry about such things. Tore wished that they didn't let the younger boys join the family meetings. Not that they were family meetings, family meant men. Women belonged to the men. They were baby makers and decorations, not real people.

Tore watched Ubbe head towards his sleeping mat. She finished her duties, and then slipped off her apron and jewelry.

Tore pulled the thick goat pelt over her, and lay down on her mat. The soft glow of the fire lit the walls to a hazy orange, making her rather sleepy. She had had a good day today. She had learned the men's secret! With that thought in mind, she drifted off to sleep.

The next morning, she stretched her arms high above her head. She got up, and tossed some logs onto the fire. Wrapping herself in her goatskin, she hurried outside to relieve herself. As she squatted beside the house, she could make out the other faint forms of the other women doing the same before the busy day full of activities ahead. It was cold, and most of her piss froze before it hit the snow. She pulled the fur tighter around her and rushed back into the house.

Tore brushed her hair quickly, and put on her red apron. It was one of her favorites. It was embroidered on the ends with a diamond shaped pattern in blues and greens. It had been one of her mother's and now it was hers. She fastened the clips at the top and slipped her chain with the little knife over her head and around her waist. Picking up a bronze plate, she examined her own distorted reflection. She was ruggedly handsome. Not beautiful, but finely chiseled out of fine white ice. Every feature was perfect. She had an angular face, strikingly Nordic, with steel blue eyes trimmed in white blond lashes peering out from under fine blond eyebrows. She looked enough like Ulf to pass as Ulf. If she was taller and broader, of course. Tore stretched herself to her full frame of five feet seven inches and studied her figure too. She was too tall for a woman. Her father made that a regular point of conversation. It wasn't as if she could change it any, even if she went around stooped over; she still stood taller than some of her kinsmen. Not all of them though. Her family grew tall men. Ulf was a head taller than Hablok Bloodaxe. Ulf was a head taller than most men. She missed Ulf.

"Stop dawdling, girl!" Nordahl bellowed from the table where he sat waiting for his morning gruel.

Tore glanced one last time at the tall, sinewy figure with its muscular arms that stared back at her in the platter, and then sat it down in the chest from which she had taken it from. She ran to the pot and began to make the morning meal. Usually, her father didn't awake this early. She felt bad for keeping him waiting. She was used to waiting for her brothers to come in after their morning activities to serve the first meal, but if her father was hungry now then she had to hurry to get it made.

Tore smiled weakly as she put her father's gruel before him in a wooden bowl. He didn't say a word, but began hungrily scooping the mush in with his spoon. Tore sat down and ate her own quietly. Nordahl didn't like to make conversation in the morning. Mostly, during the morning meal, everyone would just eat as quickly as they could so that they could be off taking care of whatever chore lay ahead.

Tore had a lot to do anyway, she was glad she didn't have to make small talk. She finished her food, collected the empty bowls and cleaned up. She had to go over to Elfled's to learn a new weaving pattern. Weaving was another task that Tore wasn't especially fond of, but unfortunately was necessary. Elfled was her father's youngest brother's wife. After Tore's mother's death, Elfled had appointed herself the mother figure in Tore's life. Nordahl didn't seem to mind. He was glad that someone was willing to step in and guide his daughter in the ways of women. The only problem was that none of the women had the strength to keep his daughter in check.

Tore trudged through the snow towards Elfled's home. Children ran to greet her, pulling her clothes and limbs every which way in their excitement. Tore had long ago decided that Elfled would be fertile enough to have children until she was an old hag. By the Gods! Tore thought to herself, she had never seen a woman with more children than Elfled. Some of Elfled's children were even older than Tore herself, and there was one or two still sucking from Elfled's breasts! Tore entered the dwelling, eager for the warmth of the fire. Elfled stood amidst her throng of noisy children, plump and red-cheeked. Despite all the work she must do, she was always cheerful. Tore envied her good nature. No matter what mistakes Tore made, Elfled always had an encouraging word for her. Sometimes Elfled's encouragement bordered on the nauseating side. Too much good spirit was too much for Tore to handle. She wasn't one of those sweety sweety types, and it was hard to tolerate those who were all of the time.

Elfled shooed all of the children who weren't busy with various chores into the back part of the dwelling, and started showing Tore the weaving technique. Tore sat near by on a roughly hewn wood bench, attentively watching Elfled's fat, chapped hands fly in and out of the yarns on the loom. It wasn't Tore's idea of a fun time, but she didn't want to upset Elfled. Besides, Elfled must think highly of Tore if she took time away from her own tasks and children to devote so much effort to demonstrating weaving patterns.

Tore found her mind jerking back and forth from the weaving to her usual daydreams of fancy swords and hidden dirks. In her dreams, she was always a man. Tall and strong and feared by all. Tore stifled a laugh. Here she sat weaving. How fearful did she make others, she wondered.

Before too long, it was time for Tore to return home. She promised to practice the weaving and bring something to show Elfled the next time she came over. Elfled smiled and smoothed Tore's long gold hair over her shoulders.

"How you look like Ulf!" Elfled laughed. "Your father must miss his son more each time he looks into your face!"

"Father says he doesn't miss Ulf as much, because he can look into his face each time he looks into mine." Tore smiled.

"Ah, yes. It could go either way, I imagine!" Elfled kissed her on the cheek and opened the door.

Tore waved her farewells and hurried across the swirling snow. The wind was howling and she could tell tonight wouldn't be one to be out in. These winter storms had grown fiercer this year. Tore prayed to Sif, and to Thor for her brother's protection. She had no way of knowing if Ulf was at sea, on land, or lying dead somewhere on a foreign field. She had faith that her gods would bring him safely back to her though.

Tore went inside and hung her fur on a wood peg on the wall. She had a lot of things to do before it was time for her to cook again. There was no time for daydreams now.

Chapter 2

Thick smoke choked the room, and made it difficult to make out all that were there. It hung around the room like a foggy curtain, so thick it couldn't be slashed with the sharpest dirk. Angry shouting could be heard even outside of the dwelling, so loud it surmounted even the angry shouts of the cold wind.

Men of all ages surrounded the blazing fire that popped and hissed and spit furiously. The fire itself seemed to mimic the atmosphere and the charged energy of the men in the room.

In the center of the great hall sat one man. He was old now, but once had been a mighty warrior. That he was still alive was a miracle in itself, as he had suffered numerous life-taking wounds in his lifetime; but none of them had taken his life. For this he often felt ashamed. No man wanted to die an old man. All men wanted to go out in a ferocious battle screaming and bleeding all the way into Valhalla. For Thorvald, this had not happened; but there was life in him yet.

Thorvald scratched at his greasy gray speckled beard. He pulled on the long whiskers listening to all the ranting and raving that surrounded him. They could scream and curse all they wanted, but the fact of the matter was that only he could make the final decision. He was the head of his family until he died and more importantly, he was Jarl.

Thorvald looked over toward his sons. They were strong, wise men. They remained in their seats calm and calculating, not yelling their passions for all to hear. They sat like he did, and soaked up the feelings of the others. A wise man didn't let others know his every thought. Five brave sons he had. Thorvald imagined he felt his feeble body grow stronger when he peered at the five of them: Jens, Brock, Havelok, Claus, and Johan. They were good men, and would be great warriors in their own time.

Thorvald felt it was time to create some order in this madness. He slowly raised his left arm. His right arm hung limply at his side, sometimes useless due to severe pain from an old wound caused by a mighty cut to his upper arm that should have taken his life as well.

The room slowly grew quiet as one by one the men realized that Thorvald wished to speak.

"I have heard all of the anger and the cries for justice in this room tonight." Thorvald began.

"We want blood!" A cry rang out.

"Vengeance for our kinsman!" Another cry followed. Thorvald raised his arm again, hoping to quell the possible tide of commotion that could rise up again. "I have heard your anger." Thorvald repeated himself. "And, I, too, want justice. It is an awful thing that has happened. That one man could kill another and then like a coward deny his deed!" Thorvald's booming voice filled the hall and echoed from its walls.

Thorvald paused as someone opened the door allowing a gust of freezing wind to purge the hall of the foul odor of piss and mead that had accumulated in the thick straw at their feet. He coughed to clear his throat. Hummings and murmurings of the word 'coward' buzzed through the room and then grew silent again. "The question at hand is what are we going to do about this crime?" Thorvald raised his hand before any shouts could begin. "Do we wait for Hablok Bloodaxe's return from his latest Strandhogg? Or do we demand blood now?" Jens looked intently at his father and listened with as much devotion. To not demand payment of some form would be cowardly. No man wanted to be labeled a nithing - the worst kind of coward - for not avenging his kin.

More angry murmurings rose up. The tension in the room was growing. Soon, Thorvald wouldn't be able to quiet it as he had before.

"Every day I watch from the cliffs for the Drekar of Bloodaxe to return. I look for the sails, for the many oars of Bloodaxe's langskip! But, no longship appears. No Hablok sees my waiting. It has been a year now, and still he doesn't return to us. Is he dead? Is he alive? Will he return before the spring? Before the summer? Before the fall? I ask myself these questions everyday as

I argue with myself and our Gods over what we should do." Thorvald took a great gulp from his mead cup.

"If we wait for Hablok to return, he may demand that the coward, Athelwold and his kin pay us. Yet, you want blood." Thorvald paused. "So, even if we wait the many months or possible years for Hablok's return we face the possibility of not being pleased. What then do we do?"

As if something snapped, the room burst into another roar of excited and furious shouts. Thorvald knew the decision that he would be forced to make. He didn't want the violence they demanded, but there was no other way. Hablok's return was too far off, too unknown. The time for sensibilities was past; action was required now. Thorvald felt an awful gnawing in his gut. There hadn't been a wergild for many years. Hablok had decided justice with monetary compensation rather than bloodshed. There was no point losing a good warrior in family disputes. At times it seemed there weren't enough able-bodied men how it was; but this time Thorvald knew his family would not wait for Hablok's return. Blood would be spilled.

Thorvald watched the angry exchanges around him. He turned to his sons. He would let them make the decision. He wanted his family to recognize the position of his sons and now was a good time to let them demonstrate their finely honed senses and abilities.

He turned to his youngest son, Johan. "Johan, my son?" Thorvald raised his voice above the many others. Silence came over the room in a staggered sort of way.

Johan looked at his father. "Yes, father?" Thorvald leaned closer to the fire and tugged at the gray braids that hung at either side of his face. "My son, how would you settle this matter?"

Johan nearly gasped. Why was his father asking him? Johan looked nervously at his brothers and then back at his father. "I would decide with the majority." Johan felt that that was a somehow safe response.

"Ah, but you wouldn't voice your own opinion?" Thorvald was a little disappointed with his son's eagerness to please and compromise.

"The majority should be listened to." Johan nodded again.

"And Claus and Havelok? How would you decide?" Thorvald knew that they would concur on whatever decision they made. Claus and Havelok were so close; sometimes Thorvald forgot that they were separate human beings.

The two men looked at each other. Expressions of knowingness crossed both of their faces as if they were reading each other's minds. Almost in unison they replied, "We would entreat the Gods for a decision." Thorvald slapped his knee. He found this answer mildly amusing. He realized that he must have been striking more terror into his sons than he had imagined. He made a mental note to encourage them to voice their opinions more often. "My boy, what if the Gods are busy?"

A roar of laughter rumbled through the hall. Claus' rosy cheeks grew a darker shade of red, and Havelok looked as if he might just crawl under the bench he was sitting on. Thorvald looked at Jens, his oldest son, who looked as if he was growing angry at the other men's taunting of his younger brothers.

"Jens!? My son, you aren't happy by the men's reactions?" Thorvald was still chuckling. Jens jumped to his feet unable to contain himself any longer. "You fools laugh! Laugh some more! All three of my brothers have given adequate answers to my father's question. Deciding with the majority, ja that is good. Asking the Gods for help, no man should mock that. But, my brothers lack the thirst of blood that can only be gained through battle. They haven't been in the midst of a blood soaked field, and heard the last blood-choking gurgle of a dying man. They take the safe way out." Jens paused and cast a look at his father that said he cared not what an old man thought. "In battle there is no safe way out. You must kill or be killed." The room echoed with the nods and agreements of the men around them. Thorvald noticed how devotedly the men hung onto Jens every word. Jens would make a good leader someday, though now he was still too impetuous and rash.

Jens, like a natural born speaker, waited for the noise to die down before continuing on. "My father asks us what shall we do about this problem. I say we take what is ours. Not only do we kill Athelwold, but we slaughter his entire family."

A stunned hush blanketed the room.

"We must make it clear that our family will not tolerate cowards. Cowards should not be allowed to live. I say death to them all!" Jens raised his fist high with a frenzied air.

The men cheered him loudly and waved their knives, dirks, swords, and axes in the air. Thorvald shook his head. These men needed a good battle to release some of this pent up hostility. They were too blood thirsty for their own good. Too much anger clouds the judgment of a good warrior. Thorvald noticed his second son, Brock, sitting quietly beside his brothers. Thorvald turned to Brock.

"Brock. You are so quiet." Thorvald stated.

"There isn't much to say, father." Brock said slowly as if he had already contemplated his response beforehand.

"You think this matter trivial?" Thorvald raised an eyebrow.

"Not at all." Brock answered shortly. The man was just like his mother,

Thorvald couldn't get anything out of him even when he tried.

"Then what is it that makes you so silent?" Thorvald noticed that the room had come down from its hyped up frenzy courtesy of Jens.

Brock fiddled with the embroidered band that held his flaxen hair away from his face. "I think that laws were meant to be followed."

"What do you mean, brother?" Jens hissed.

"We have a chieftain for a reason. Why have a chieftain if we decide to make our own rules and codes?" Brock shrugged.

"You do not agree that we should demand blood for the blood of our kin?" Jens roared as if insulted.

"I do not agree that we should kill women and children for something that hasn't been proven yet." Brock's voice was clear and strong. He didn't hesitate to contradict his brother.

Angry shouts burst forth. Jens leaped to the top of a nearby roughly hewn wood table. He looked down on his brother who was at least a head taller than he was, and shook a fist at him.

"You are afraid to fight!" Jens roared.

Brock laughed. "You forget yourself, brother. You and I have fought the same number of battles. I have done my share of killing."

"You fight like a woman!" Jens tried desperately to provoke his brother. Brock remained calm and unmoved. Thorvald felt that this rivalry was interesting to say the least. Brock was by far the smarter one of the two; Thorvald reasoned that would keep him alive much longer than Jens.

Brock smiled revealing two prominent dimples on either side of his full lips. He looked up into the angry face of his brother who was trying so hard to win the hearts and faith of their father's men. Finding the humor in every situation, Brock laughed loudly. "Well, brother, I wouldn't know. I haven't fought many women!"

The angry shouts suddenly turned to boisterous laughter. Thorvald chuckled at this besting of Jens by his number two son.

Brock suddenly grew serious and frowned. Jens was red faced and very obviously trying hard to control his temper. He knew that if he were to challenge his brother that Brock would win. Brock was bigger and stronger than he was and there would be no contest.

Brock stood up and faced Jens. "I do not agree with these men, father, nor do I agree with Jens." Whispered murmurs hissed through the air for a moment. "However, Jens is my eldest brother and I am sworn to follow him. If it were up to me, I would say wait for Hablok Bloodaxe's return, but it is not up to me." Brock faced Jens who had stepped down off of the table and now stood squarely before his brother. "Jens, I swear by the Gods that I would follow you into Valhalla if you were to ask it of me."

Jens stared at Brock too stunned to speak. He grasped his brother's forearm in a brotherly lock. Thorvald smiled to himself. He had raised good warriors. He knew that it would be Brock who ultimately would lead this family. He just didn't let any of them know that. Jens' days were numbered. He was too hasty to live long.

Thorvald sighed. Now it was his decision. He thought long and hard as he gulped his mead. Rapping the horn cup nervously with his fingers he reached his decision. The crowd sensed he was about to speak and grew quiet once again. "I have decided." Thorvald said slowly. "Since it is agreed that no one can be certain of Hablok's return, we will take justice into our own hands." Thorvald sighed heavily for this was not an easy task. "I agree that the evidence shows that Athelwold did in fact kill our kin regardless of his cowardly claims. I concur that payment should be exacted."

Whispers circulated through the room once more. Thorvald raised his good arm for silence. "However, I do not agree with my son Jens' position. We shouldn't slaughter an entire family. I do believe that more should be done than just taking Athelwold's life. Because his family didn't demand he account for his cowardly crime, I believe more than Athelwold should be punished." Thorvald hacked up a wad of mucus and spit into the fire then continued. "I have decided that the families of the two eldest brothers should be killed. The families of Athelwold and Nordahl will be killed as revenge for the cowardly act against this family." Thorvald stood up slowly. "Go now. I have spoken."

Jens helped his father stand as his brothers helped herd the drunken men from the hall. Brock sat by the fire. He still didn't agree with his father's ruling. Their family was much larger than Athelwold's. To take the lives of the families of two brothers seemed extreme to him, and he knew that Hablok wouldn't agree with such a decision either. Then again, Hablok shouldn't be gone so long.

Claus spotted Brock sitting alone by the fire. "Father's decision troubles you?"

"Yes, it does." Brock said slowly poking at a log.

"But you'll do as he says anyway?" Claus probed further.

"As always." Brock said quietly.

"Why do you do things that go against your own judgments?" Claus said simply.

"It is not my place to make the decisions, only to obey them. When structure isn't followed, chaos rules." Brock said sadly.

"By acting on our own we are breaking rules." Claus looked at Brock.

"I fear that our god Forseti will be angered. This is not justice, brother." Brock shook his head forcefully.

"Justice or no, we shall soon see the face of the goddess Hel riding on her white horse of death as she claims the lives of Athelwold and Nordahl's brood." Claus almost whispered as if to say Hel's name too loudly would invoke her presence here.

"I do not have an easy feeling about this brother. I shall pray to Tyr for comfort. If there is another path to follow, perhaps Tyr will reveal it to me. He is still the God of law, if he desires for our laws to be followed maybe he will stop this carnage and send Hablok home soon." Brock got up from where he had been seated.

"Will Tyr intervene?" Claus asked anxiously.

"If I knew that, wouldn't I be in Asgard with the gods?" Brock laughed and slapped his younger brother on the back. The force of his blow nearly knocked his brother off balance and onto the floor. Claus smiled weakly and rubbed his shoulder blade slowly.

Brock drank another cup of mead before heading through the narrow hall to his room. There was so much to think about, none of which he could really do anything about. He hated having to go along with actions that he didn't agree with, but that was the way of things.

Brock thought of Hablok Bloodaxe and what might happen upon his return. Hablok might rule that their family had acted harshly and penalize them in some way. Then again, Brock thought as he stared at the splintery wood beams that hung overhead, Hablok might never return. There was one thing that deeply troubled Brock. Nordahl's eldest son, Ulf, was with Hablok. In fact, he was very close to Hablok it was said. If actions were committed in Hablok's absence against one of his closest warriors, might Hablok be angered even more than he would be in just finding out that a wergild had been settled without his judgment? Brock knew Ulf. Ulf was a few years older than Jens. He was a brave warrior.

It was even known that Ulf had gone into battle much younger than the usual eighteen years of age. Ulf had been bigger and stronger and during a crisis where men were short and boys were plenty, Ulf had been loaded onto a ship with a battleaxe and a lot of motivation. He had proven himself the mighty warrior finding favor with the chieftain quickly. And now...now, Thorvald had decided it was best to kill Ulf's immediate family and the family of his uncle. Brock felt apprehensive about this decision. Ulf wouldn't stand for such actions. There would be retaliation of some form, Brock could feel it. Brock rolled over and faced the wet, stonewall. Then again, there was the slight possibility that Ulf, like Hablok, might never return. Killed in battle, lost in a storm on that angry whale road, sickened along the way, the possibilities were endless. After all, it had been so long now --- was there any hope that they would return? Brock shut his eyes. Tomorrow the decision would be hammered over and over again until a plan was agreed on. Brock decided he would rather not be there for that meeting. He would just do what he was told, and pay for his actions later. For he knew there would be a payment someday. He wasn't as rash as Jens, or as foolhardy. All actions have their consequences. Brock struggled to sleep, haunted by dreams of an angry Hablok and a much angrier Ulf Nordahlsson.

The next morning, Brock was awakened by the wet nuzzle of his dog's nose. He stumbled from his bed and stretched. He could smell the morning meal and lumbered out of his room and towards the cooking pot eager to get his bowlful.

Johan stomped in from the bitter cold of the outside. He laughed loudly as he smacked at his pants and sleeves trying to knock off the great clumps of snow that had gathered there. "If anyone is talking with the Gods this morning, " Johan called out loudly, "Let them ask Uller to ease up on this snow!"

Brock smiled widely and laughed at his brother. He passed Johan a bowl of gruel and then commenced eating his own. The door swung open once more as Havelok came through, already Brock could see the men gathering outside.

Brock cast a quick glance at his mother who frowned as she stirred the pot. "Always there are men here shouting and pissing on my floor!" She grumbled.

Brock laughed softly. "Ah, but it is your good mead that makes them piss so, mother!"

His mother, Ymma, was a good woman. She wasn't really his mother. His mother had died in childbirth with a baby girl a few years after he was born. He barely remembered her now. Ymma had been his mother ever since he could remember, and a good mother she had been to he and Jens despite the fact that they were not her own sons. They were Thorvald's sons and that was all that mattered to her.

Ymma laughed at Brock's compliment. "Maybe if my mead was not so good, there would be less piss on my floor, ja?"

Brock and Johan laughed again, but soon grew quiet. Today was a day for serious thinking. Today the deaths of many people would be well planned out.

Ymma sensed their heavy spirits. "There is something important on my sons' minds?"

Brock nodded slowly all the while looking at Johan who just sat looking back at Brock.

"You wish to talk about it?" Ymma tried not to sound eager, she knew they wouldn't tell her.

Johan laughed again. "It is nothing, mother. Father will take care of everything."

"Your father is a good man, a strong man." Ymma said in agreement with Johan. Brock ate his gruel in silence, all too aware of his brother and mother's stares at his nonresponsive and disagreeing expression.

Brock handed his mother his empty wood bowl and pulled on his cape. He swung open the door and pushed his way through the crowd of men that stood huddled and shivering outside of the door. Thorvald wasn't even awake yet; these men were going to freeze to death waiting for him! Brock laughed. Idiot bastards were so eager to do some killing that they were willing to lose a few toes waiting for it.

Brock's thoughts raced through is mind in a blurred fashion. There was no point in mulling it over and over. The vote had been cast, and his input had been thrust aside. It was within his father's right as a Jarl under their chieftain, Hablok Bloodaxe. That was how their legal system worked. First the chieftain, then the Jarls, and then the Hersirs. Brock shivered and pulled his cape closer. As Jarl, his father had the right to administer justice; however, technically, he should wait for Hablok in this matter since he couldn't decide what justice was with an unbiased mind. Unfortunately for him, his family had never developed much of a conscience. Brock somehow got a sensitive gene that required thought before action. The rest of the bloodthirsty mob that he claimed as kin had no such gene. Basically, his family were a bunch of thieving pirates who took what they wanted and exacted revenge as they desired, regardless of the laws.

Brock wished he did not think so much. He wished he could be more like his brothers and fit in with the rest of the family; but he wasn't.

Brock stomped through the snow to his sister's house. He had no desire to be present for the meeting. His father would be enraged of course, but Brock didn't care. He would do his duty and carry out the plan of action, but he didn't want to see the exhilaration of the crowd and how pleased they were about the grim task at hand. Geira, Brock's sister, would have a warm place by her fire for him.

Brock called loudly at Geira's door. Her husband, Ingolf, would be at the meeting with the rest of their clan. Geira opened the door and smiled at the shivering figure of her brother.

"I thought maybe you'd come here." Geira laughed.

"I didn't want to go to the assembly." Brock came inside and huddled over the fire to thaw his hands and body out.

"Is it that bad, brother?" Geira smiled slightly.

"It is bad." Brock accepted the cup of steaming liquid that his sister passed him.

"Ingolf seemed to look forward to this assembly of yours." Geira returned to her weaving and talked over her left shoulder in Brock's direction.

"I am not Ingolf." Brock said simply.

Geira laughed. "You are so much like mother was."

"What's that supposed to mean?" Brock looked up from the fire.

"You don't remember, but she hated anything bad. She liked to pretend the world was only good. She learned later that it wasn't." Geira said sadly.

"I know the world is not always good. I don't have to learn the hard way like our mother." Brock looked back into the tantalizing flames.

"The men need to see you as a leader, Brock. You and I both know that father will probably outlive Jens." Geira didn't give advice very often, but this time she took a more motherly tone with her younger brother. She studied his expressionless face before the fire and decided to lighten the mood. "If a battle fails to get him, some woman's husband or brother will soon enough!"

Brock chuckled at this. "He does carry on with the women, doesn't he?"

"Too much for his own good. Half the time he isn't even drunk!" Geira laughed and checked around to make sure none of her children were listening in on their conversation.

"Jens sleeps with a sword under his mat for fear of some woman's father killing him in his sleep!" Brock laughed again.

"Jens would try to kill you for telling me that!" Geira smiled and pointed at Brock.

"Jens couldn't kill me if he tried. Few men match my strength." Brock stated and then mentally ran down a short list of men he knew could best him. He shuddered when he ran across the name of Ulf Nordahlsson.

Brock stayed until he could hear the voices of men stomping by outside, and then determined he should go back home. He kissed his sister on the cheek and dreadingly turned towards home.

Thorvald waited for him before the fire.

Brock opened the door and looked down the hall to the very end where Thorvald sat wrapped in fur. He expected anger. He deserved anger for defying his father like he had. Brock shook the snow from his cape and made his way to the end of the hall. Thorvald didn't look up, but continued to stare entranced at the fire before him. Brock sat down across the fire from his father.

"My son." Thorvald stated in a form of greeting.

"Father." Brock replied.

There was stony silence where there should have been shouts and curses. Brock was somewhat confused by this change in his otherwise stern father.

Finally, Thorvald spoke. "You were not present this morning."

"No, father." Brock answered.

"It is because you do not agree with my decision." Thorvald looked at his son who was busy studying the fire.

"Yes, father." Brock answered.

"But, you will do as I tell you anyway?" Thorvald knew his son would he just wanted to hear it from Brock's mouth.

"Yes, father." Brock said again.

"Next time make sure you find your way to my fire during an assembly." Thorvald said and then snorted. "I have told Jens to tell you what has been decided."

Brock still waited for the severe reprimands and curses, but none came. He looked up puzzled at his father.

"You are not angry with me, father?" Brock finally asked.

"No man should be angry at another man for standing by his convictions." Thorvald smiled. "I was proud of you."

"But, I defied you!" Brock almost begged for punishment.

"And that took courage. I would be angrier if I saw you sitting passively at my fire despite your feelings. Instead, the men saw that you refused to listen to something you didn't feel was right." Thorvald put a grizzled hand on Brock's knee, "But my men will also see your loyalty when you do as you are bid."

Brock looked into his father's wise eyes. "Is it age that makes you wise, father?" He asked.

Thorvald roared with laughter. "The only thing age makes me, Brock, is old and crippled! Even my mansword doesn't fight like it used to!"

Brock laughed.

"It is this…" Thorvald rapped sharply on the top of Brock's head, "That makes a man wise. Some men have it, most men don't. You, my son, will be wise in time."

Brock smiled at his father. "I hope you are right."

"I am already right." Thorvald spit into the fire more for emphasis than for necessity.

Brock waited for his father's orders.

"Go find Jens. He will tell you the plan." Thorvald pulled his fur pelt closer to him. Age had made him perpetually cold.

Brock got up silently and sought out Jens.

Jens was not as forgiving, nor as wise as his father had been. Brock was aware of Jens' sneer as he sat down beside him.

"Father said you would tell me what it is that we must do." Brock leaned forward, his hands on his knees, waiting for the details that he wished he didn't have to hear.

Jens sneered awhile longer. Brock sat patiently by waiting for Jens' little display of contempt to wind down.

"The coward wants to know what happened this morning, ja?" Jens said while chewing at the leg of some roasted fowl.

Claus sat nearby, and suddenly got up and moved to the other side of the room.

Brock sat still observing Claus' move, and Jens' chewing.

"You speak strong words, brother." Brock nearly whispered.

"What words do you not like?" Jens laughed.

"Do not make me repeat them, brother." Brock stared Jens hard in the eyes.

"All cowards fear the word, coward, Brock. You are no exception." Jens laughed and continued gnawing at the bird leg.

In a whirlwind flash, Brock was atop his brother. Benches and straw flew about in a dirty gust. Claus retreated even further into the shadows. Jens was easily penned beneath the massive frame of Brock. Brock spit in his brother's face and let the spittle slide over Jens' cheek and into his matted hair.

Jens tossed and kicked to no avail. "Let me up! Let me up, do you hear me?"

"Yes, I hear you, brother!" Brock held him firmly down and laughed. Suddenly, Brock's mood changed, he whipped out his dirk from its sheath and pressed it up against his brother's throat. "Now, you hear me. If ever I hear you call me a coward again, be it to my face, or behind my back, let it be known this day, that I will kill you." Brock pushed the dirk more firmly against Jens throat, causing a slight trickle of blood to appear against the creamy whiteness of Jens' complexion. "I will kill you." Brock released the dirk with a jerk and jumped to his feet.

Jens lay there for a moment, and then leapt up as well, wildly slapping straw and filth from his clothing and hair. Jens growled at Brock who now stood watching as he groomed himself. Brock grabbed a bench and righted it again. He sat down and looked at Jens.

Calmly and evenly he said, "Now, you will tell me the plan."

Jens retrieved the other bench from its overturned position and sat on it. He touched the wound on his neck. He glared at Brock who sat motionless before him. Jens ego stung as fiercely as did the cut on his throat.

That night it was bone-chillingly cold. The wind blew snow and ice in frenzied swirls over their fur-covered bodies as they trudged to the place where Athelwold and his brother, Nordahl lived. The dark and cold provided them the cover needed for the ambush.

Brock tried to push his thoughts to the back of his head. A sneak attack on sleeping women, children and old men. Some attack this was going to be. More like mass slaughter.

They hit Athelwold's home first. The children were easy, one quick slash across the throat. Athelwold fought courageously, but was no match for the twenty men who swarmed him. Athelwold's wife was another matter. She had been in a dark corner pissing, and the element of surprise was taken away when she spotted them before they spotted her. She let out several blood-curdling screams before she went down in a pool of warm blood and gore.

Over in Nordahl's home, Arne, Ubbe and Nordahl heard the screams. They knew it would take their attackers several minutes to make it through the snow to their dwelling. Ubbe dragged Tore from her bed and pushed her towards the huge sea chest in the corner of the room. It had a false bottom large enough for a woman. Nordahl had made it to hide their mother back when roving bands of Danes plundered their lands. Ubbe pulled the secret panel away, pushed handfuls of valuables at Tore and ordered her into the chest.

"I will fight! I'm not going to cower in a box while you and father and Arne fight alone! Give me a sword!" Tore tugged her arm away from Ubbe stubbornly.

Nordahl saw the squabble. "For the God's sake, girl! For once in your fucking life get your arse in that box and shut your mouth!" Nordahl picked her up with renewed vigor and tossed her kicking into the chest. Ubbe slammed the false bottom over her and threw the original contents of the chest back as they were.

Tore knew that she could release the bottom and push her way out, but to do so would be in direct violation of her angry father's order. She lay there holding her breath, listening to the blood swishing in her ears and the thump thump of her heart beating against her breast. The chest was cold and cramped. Her mother had been a much smaller woman than she was and her legs were bent at awkward angles in order to fit. She lay there listening through the thick walls of the chest for whatever was coming.

And come it did. Brock and the rest of the men stormed through the door. Nordahl and his sons were armed to the teeth. Arne managed to take out a few of Thorvald's men before four or five cut him to pieces with their swords and axes. Ubbe went down sobbing like the child he was, crying out for his brother, waving a dirk weakly in front of him. Brock turned his face as blood squirted up from the wound he thrust in Ubbe's chest. Brock wiped at the sticky blood that covered his arm; this killing wasn't right. Ubbe was only a boy.

Nordahl, for an old and enfeebled soldier, fought like a man twenty years younger. He fatally wounded three men, and killed two outright, before someone crept up behind him and took his head with a mighty swing of a battle-axe.

Tore felt the tears roll down her cheeks as she envisioned what she knew had taken place. She could hear the screams and curses and swords clashing from within her hiding place. She listened, as the men in the room grew quiet.

Jens looked around. "There's a girl."

"Where?" A man said.

"Not here. There's a girl missing." Jens said again. The men began searching the room for the missing family member. Tore heard someone lift the lid of the sea chest and she drew in a great gasp of air and held it in, afraid to breath for fear of discovery.

"Maybe she's not here, tonight." Someone said.

Brock felt relieved. He wasn't too keen on killing women or children. "We can get her another time. What is her name?"

Jens gave up the search. "Her name is Tore Nordahldatr."

"Then we kill her when we find her." Brock said simply. "For now, we go."

Tore let the air out slowly. She listened as the men left the hall. She lay there for what seemed like hours, for what was an hour. She had to be sure that they were gone, and that they were not waiting for her to crawl from her hiding place to be butchered like the rest of her family. Tore dreaded opening the chest. She didn't want to see what she knew she would have to see. It was up to her now. She had to stay alive until Ulf came home. She had to find out who had done this to her family, and stay alive to tell Ulf.

Tore pushed the false bottom up and over the top of the chest. Luckily, one of the men had left the heavy sea chest lid off, so it made her ascent from the deep chest somewhat less difficult.

Tore climbed out of the chest slowly. Before her in the straw and dirt, illuminated by the fire, lay her family. Straw soaked up blood quickly; it was everywhere thick and slick beneath her bare feet. She leaned over Ubbe and felt for the heat of his breath. He was the only one that was whole enough to have the slim possibility of survival. Arne was butchered into more pieces than she cared to count. His limbs and head no longer attached. And her father, her beloved father, lay headless in a heap near the wall. His gray old head upside down under the table. Tore sat in the bloody puddle that once was a comforting floor. She held Ubbe's young head in her lap and allowed herself to cry.

It was something she rarely did. It would be the last time she would ever do it for them.

Soon, sorrow was replaced by rage and Tore vowed to stay alive until Ulf returned bringing with him Hablok Bloodaxe and all the fury of the great goddess, Hel.

Chapter 3

Tore sat like that for quite some time. Her dress was soaked with blood and her hair too was matted with the sticky stuff. She knew that she had to leave. She couldn't take the risk of letting the rest of her family discover she was alive. They might give her over to whoever did this. They might reveal her identity or her whereabouts. She couldn't trust anyone until Ulf came home from sea. Ulf was the only one she could trust. He was her brother. He would take care of her. Until then, her job was to stay alive. How was she going to do that?

Tore thought hard as she dragged buckets of snow in from outside and melted them down in the cooking pot. She stripped naked and peeled the offending bloody clothes from her body. Taking time to drape fur pelts over the dead bodies of her brothers and father, she then washed herself of all the blood. She knew her family would give them a proper burial, and so she tended to her own plan for survival. She could not help her brothers or father now. She had to think of herself and how she would survive.

Tore wrapped herself in a fur cloak to dry by the fire.

She knew that whoever these men were they had killed Athelwold's family too. Could these be the same men that Ubbe had told her about so secretly? She also knew that they knew that she was a woman and missing. They would be looking for her.

Tore drank some mead, something she didn't do too often for she disliked the taste. They would be looking for her, Tore, a woman. Tore smiled. She had an idea, but did she dare try it?

Tore held up a gold platter and looked at her reflection. That was it. They would be looking for a woman, but they wouldn't find one. For Tore was going to disguise herself as a man. At age seventeen, she still remained narrow hipped and somewhat gangly; she could pass as a young man, perhaps around age eighteen. She had the features, but no beard. Tore frowned. How would she explain that?

She had time to think about that one, but for now she had to concentrate on getting away before sunrise. When the rest of the family awoke, the sights they would see here would scare them into doing whatever necessary to preserve the lives of their own families. Tore could only imagine the horrors that awaited her kin at Athelwold's. She thought about the children for a moment, then shrugged it off as she saw again the bodies of her own brothers and father covered up on the ground where they had fallen. The Gods would take care of the dead, for now she must take care of herself.

Tore, dry and warm again, stood naked in front of the fire. Her knee length hair was much too long for a man's. Some of it would have to go. She picked up a cooking knife, and hacked off handfuls of her gorgeous flaxen hair until it was a shaggy shoulder length mass. Tore looked down at the ground where she stood. Her feet were barely visible beneath the piles of platinum hair that had fallen there. She couldn't leave the hair behind; it might give her plan away. She scooped up the tresses and tossed them onto the fire. The smell of burnt hair filled the air for a moment or two and then faded away. Tore plaited two braids into the hair at the front of each side of her head and secured the rest of her hair with an embroidered band that had been Arne's. Her mother had made it for her father years ago, and Arne had worn it proudly. So now would she.

Tore stood with her hands on her hips. She had taken care of the hair, now for the clothes. Fortunately for her, Ubbe was nearly the same size. She went to his chest and rummaged around until she found a suitable wardrobe. His pants were too short. She went to Arne's chest and dug around until she found some pants. They were slightly too long. She decided she didn't have time to fix them, so she hitched them up a few inches with a finely decorated leather belt of Ubbe's. Tore felt odd standing there in her brother's clothes. The smell of them that clung to the fibers of the cloth, caused an empty, sick-gnawing feeling to swell up inside her. Her brothers would never wear these clothes again. Poor Arne! How he loved his clothes too! He was a handsome, conceited young man who loved fine clothes almost more than he loved women! Tore smoothed the wrinkled fabric of the billowing, baggy pants. She was grateful for Arne's exquisite taste.

Tore held out her arms and studied her wardrobe from top to toe. She looked down at her chest. Damn! She, in her haste, had forgotten about her breasts! Granted, she was small busted, but any bust at all would give her away. Tore stripped off the tunic and stared at her bare chest. She couldn't very well cut the damn things off. What was she going to do with them? Tore thought about a woman she had once known who had some form of breast ailment and had bound her breasts tightly with strips of cloth. It just might work, Tore thought to herself.

Tore found an old shirt and ripped it into strips. She wound them tightly around her until her chest was nearly flat. She smiled to herself. Thank goodness she didn't have an ample bosom! This was uncomfortable enough; she didn't want to imagine trying to conceal large breasts! Her once thought curse, now was a blessing from the Gods. She knew that somewhere Ubbe and Arne were watching her now and laughing. Let them make jokes about her not having teats now. Now, it might just save her life!

Tore put the tunic back on and tossed another looser vest over it. She could barely make out the small bumps on each side of her breastbone. Another cape and nothing was visible. Tore laughed. It was as if all of her daydreams were coming true. She half expected someone to nudge her into reality and she'd find herself sitting before a burning cooking pot with foul food burnt to a crisp and clinging to the iron sides. Now, she looked like a young man. She gathered some extra clothing and found a bearskin bag to put her belongings in. She also found a pair of Ubbe's old shoes and tossed them into the bag as well.

Tore had no idea where she would go. She reasoned that she should go into the next shire and find lodgings somewhere. The next shire was about six hours walk from here in good weather, longer in bad weather. She wasn't sure how much longer as she wasn't accustomed to being out in bad weather she was just going by reports she had heard before. The next shire was ruled by a Jarl named Thorvald the One-Armed. Tore stopped for a minute. There was a slight chance that this was the same family that had a grievance with Athelwold. What if it was that family that had killed her kin? No. It had to be somebody else for some other reason. She didn't even know if they were North men. They could be some band of foreigners who were out pillaging and looting before setting sail or traveling somewhere else. Surely, the family that had complaints against Athelwold would wait for Hablok Bloodaxe's return to settle their dispute. That was what Hablok was for! Tore wished she had gotten a look, even a faint glimpse at her family's slayers; but, she hadn't and until Ulf came home there was no point in her trying to discover who it was. That would only mean more trouble. She didn't need any more trouble than she already had for herself. These men spoke her language, which didn't necessarily mean they were native or foreign. Lots of different people spoke different languages for trade purposes. The land was full of merchants these days. It was getting hard to distinguish the foreigners from the natives of Norway.

Tore knew that she had to maintain her new identity. That meant not doing anything rash or stupid. Just stay alive until Ulf came home. If Ulf came home. Tore frowned. Now, why did she go and think a thing like that for? She hated those little torturous thoughts that crept in unexpected like that and managed to dash all of her confidence in a single moment. She couldn't let herself think things like this! Ulf would come home, and when he did Ulf would make everything right again. Tore just knew he would.

Tore scurried through the house searching for various weapons and other valuables that she might need. She tossed them into the bag. The only thing she couldn't seem to find was a sword. It seemed that whoever had attacked her kin had taken all of the swords. Could they have been after the swords? One didn't hear of plundering for weapons that much anymore. She had heard of it mentioned that it had happened frequently in the old days, but not in her lifetime. Why would they take the swords then? There were so many unanswered questions and pieces to this riddle and it frustrated Tore horridly. She wished she were a man so that she would know more about the things she needed to know now. She laughed again. To mortal eyes, she was a man now.

Tore made a mental note to acquire a sword from somewhere. She knew that she would need one. If not to use, to have. Every man had a sword. Some preferred the axe, but everyman had a sword just the same.

Tore took down the strips of dried meat from the ceiling and wrapped them in a thin piece of hide. She tied it securely with a bit of leather cord and tossed the bundle into the bag.

She rolled up a fur and tossed it in along with all of the gold and valuable items that were small enough to take with her. Hopefully, her family would just assume that whoever had killed their kin also had stolen from them as well.

She had everything she thought she might need. After all, she didn't anticipate traveling long. If the next shire wasn't to her liking, she could always pick up and go to the next seaport along the way. She wasn't sure which one Ulf would pull into anyway. She didn't worry about how she'd find out if Ulf were home or not. She knew that he traveled with Hablok Bloodaxe, the chieftain; and everyone would know when Hablok returned. When she heard Hablok had returned she would make her way back to her kin and tell Ulf all that she knew.

Ulf would be displeased with her for masquerading as a man, she was sure of that; but she also knew that Ulf would be proud of her courage to undertake such a feat.

Tore wrapped herself in a fur pelt, put on a helmet of Arne's, and slung the heavy bag over her shoulder. She put the bag back down to retie her fur boots, and to stick a dirk in her belt. Pulling her fur mittens on, she slung the bag back over her shoulder and opened the heavy wood door leading to the outside.

A freezing blast of snow and icy wind slapped her in the face, shoving her back a few paces. She staggered to keep her balance. She had to be insane to go out in weather like this! She grunted as she tried to close the door behind her. The wind was too strong. Something lay in the snow in front of the door. It was Gunlod, their dog. The men had killed her too lest she bark and wake up the rest of the men. Tore sighed. She turned around and took one last look at the covered figures of her loved ones lying there on the bloody floor. She would allow herself to mourn when she was safe. Right now, she owed it to them to keep herself alive. She was the only one that could tell how bravely they had fought before Hel had whisked them off on that great horse of hers.

Tore trudged in the direction of the nearest shire. She had to cross through a great forest and walk beside the steep cliffs before she'd reach it. She knew that it would take her much longer than six hours. Tore stomped through the snow, through the dark, and through the icy wind. She had been smart enough to bring a torch and a wineskin that she had filled with whale oil. The other wineskin was full of wine. Fire or wine would keep her warm. She decided she was far enough away from the rows of dwellings of her kinsmen to light the torch undetected. The great wood and stone houses were growing smaller and darker with each step she took. She was going uphill, a task hard enough to do under the pounds slung on her back. Nearly impossible against the cold wind; but, she had to do it.

Tore stumbled many times, but each time she would haul herself up with renewed vigor and strength. Somewhere deep inside of her she was able to find the spirit she needed to keep herself going: to face the challenge that would be her life until her brother's return.

Tore stood against a huge tree and stared down into the circle of dwellings that belonged to her kin. It would be morning soon. She knew that her brothers and father wouldn't lay there undiscovered for long. She hoped that her kin would just assume that she had been taken to sell on the slave block with all of the foreign girls that got sold everyday in the port towns. She took a long look. She didn't know when she would see these familiar dwellings with their warm, inviting fires again.

Tore sighed and pulled the fur up over her nose so that just her eyes peeked out above the fur. As she trudged along in the knee-deep snow, careful to avoid the much deeper drifts, she began to form the complete identity that she was assuming. Her only major drawback was her voice. Though low for a woman, it was still higher than a man's. She must try not to speak often. She also had to have a new name.

Eirik. She had had a brother that was named that once. He had died while still a baby. She had always liked the name. Eirik what, though? Tore thought. Eirik the silent! That would tell people that she rarely spoke, and men would think it was because of her, or rather Eirik's silly sounding voice!

So, Eirik the Silent she would be. Tore suddenly looked around her and realized she no longer knew where she was. Sometime in her daydreaming, she had veered off of the path, if it might be called that, and now was heading towards a part of the forest she had never been to.

Tore stopped. She knew that she couldn't just stand out here for long or she'd freeze to death. She would have to make a quick decision as to which direction to head and do it quickly. Her feet were beginning to feel the cold and she would need to find shelter soon. Tore's eyes searched the scraggly tree line and tried to find a clearing, but the snow was getting deeper and everything looked alike. The snow swirled with a passion, and she could almost envision the goddess Frigga blowing with all of her might and causing the snow to dance and leap. Tore shook herself. Daydreaming was what got her lost in the first place. She had to concentrate now. The storm was growing worse, and she hadn't found any sort of shelter yet. This trip was going to take much longer than she had first planned.

Tore strained to see before her. Not too far from where she was there was the wall of a mountain close behind a line of great trees. If she could make it over there perhaps she would find a cave or a crag to crawl into. She struggled against the wind, painfully aware of the biting coldness in her toes and feet.

Fighting against the elements, it suddenly occurred to her that she might not be alone out here. Out here, in this frozen expanse of land, Frost giants and Storm giants could live! Tore shuddered. She had never seen a giant of any sort, but she had heard the terrible tales of how giants would catch a human and roast him on a spit and then eat him for dinner! Tore looked behind her, just to make sure she wasn't being followed.

"That's great." Tore thought to herself. Now, not only did she have to contend with a hoard of unknown men who wanted her dead, but with human-eating giants besides! What had she done to anger the Gods! Maybe her father had been right all along. Maybe she was too outspoken and man-like for the Gods' liking. Tore scowled. No! She wouldn't accept that. She had been loyal to Sif all of her life. Had she not prayed to her every night? Did she not make sacrifices to her when the need called for one? Sif would not desert her, not now, not ever. She had been courageous and brave, and Sif would protect her now just like she had protected her back in the dwelling when the men came. Sif had a purpose for her, and she would be protected. Tore imagined she saw Sif before her now, clad in silvery white with her long, beautiful golden hair flowing down her back and billowing against the wind. Tore reached down to feel her own hair, and grimaced at the memory of it burning away on the fire. Sif would take care of her until Ulf could.

Tore neared the stony side of the mountain. She touched the frozen, ice-covered rock delicately. She stayed close to the mountain wall, and trudged along using it as a guide. There would have to be some form of indention eventually. No mountain was without its secret places. That brought another horrid thought to mind. What about Stone giants then? If she found a cave, might there not be a Stone giant bedded down and waiting to pop her into his mouth like a roasted bit of fish? Tore felt her heart beat from fear now, not just from exhaustion.

She would just have to take her chances with the giants. If she didn't find a cave soon, she'd be joining her brothers and father a lot sooner than she had planned; and, Tore knew that Sif would not be pleased with her for freezing to death like an idiot out here.

Tore felt a rock fall. She stopped. It was a cave. Not a large one. It was only about four feet high; she'd have to crawl in. The good thing was that Tore knew no giant could fit into this cave! Tore pushed her bag and torch before her. She kicked a pile of some indiscernible animal bones over to the side, and kept crawling back. She wanted to get far enough back that the wind and snow couldn't touch her. Finally, she came to a good point to stop. It widened out a bit and there was enough dragged in pieces of wood that some chewing animal had left before her that she might be able to make a small fire. The wood was dry. She piled it up, and poured a small amount of her precious oil over it. Lighting it with her weakly lit torch, Tore put the torch out, and huddled close to the fire. She only had the few scraps of wood. It wouldn't burn for long. Tore thought about going back outside, but the only thing she'd probably find were branches on the trees. The snow was much too deep for her to find wood on the forest floor. However, her fire would burn too low soon, so she must go look before the storm grew any worse.

Tore left her bag in the small cave and crawled out with her torch newly lit. As she suspected, she didn't find wood on the forest floor. Instead, she had to hack off some bare branches with her knife and hope they would burn sufficiently enough for her to keep warm.

She pushed the branches in front of her until she came to the part of the cave where her fire was waiting. She could almost sit up straight here if she leaned against the cave wall. Tore broke the branches into smaller pieces and stacked them in a pile beside her. She was hungry.

Digging around in her bag she came to the bundle of dried meat and untied it. She put some in a small iron pot she had packed and scooped some snow in with it. She set it in the burning embers on the outskirts of the fire and stirred it occasionally with her knife. After drinking the broth and eating the meat, she had a little of her wine and then pulled out the extra fur to sleep on. She didn't know how long she would be here; it all depended on when the weather let up some. For now, she was tired and it was nice to be warm and still for a little while. Tore lay down with her arm under hear head, conscious once again of the absence of hair beneath her back. She sighed.

It was safe here. She wished it could stay this way, all quiet and warm. Tore watched the fire closely. She knew it wouldn't stay burning forever. Though she had no idea of what the future held for her, she was almost certain the road wouldn't be easy or pleasant. Every minute from now on would be dangerous, but exciting. Exciting? Tore laughed. Here she was embarking on a totally insane venture and she was anticipating excitement? What would her father say to her now? Tore didn't foresee her having to huddle over any large cooking pots for awhile. If anyone doubted her masculinity, all she would have to do is prove herself with her cooking. No woman cooked as horribly as she did; and, no woman could wield a sword like she could either!

A sword. Swords were very expensive items. She only hoped she had enough to trade for one. She had never actually seen a sword being purchased, though she knew they were sold. It just seemed to her that everyone always had one. How the sword had been obtained had never crossed her mind before. Now, it did. There was so much she was going to have to learn. So much that before she had simply taken for granted. In her charade as a man, she would have to acquire this knowledge as quickly as she could, or else act as though she already possessed it.

Ubbe better be glad she was as stubborn and inquisitive as she always had been. All of that improper behavior might just save her life now.

Tore closed her eyes. She knew she shouldn't sleep too deeply because her fire might go out, but her journey through the snow and storm had exhausted her. Sleep waved its magic hand before her and beckoned her to follow it to the land of dreams. The days were short in the winter. Nights were long, nearly seventeen hours. When you're wedged into a small cave, what is there to do but sleep?

Outside the cave a snorting sounded, followed closely by the shuffle of feet digging in the snow. Tore's eyes shot open. Dreams had taken her back to her own warm bed under the same roof of her father's house…but then, she remembered her father was dead, her house no longer safe, and her bed was a fur laid out on a cavern floor. What was that sound outside of the cave? Could it be horses? Tore drew her knife out and waited. Surely, men wouldn't bring horses out in this weather! Horses were much too expensive. Her father had always said that the foreign merchants asked far too great a price for even an old horse. Tore crept to the entrance of her small cave. She leaned close to the wall trying to stay invisible. Poking her head around the rocky opening, she peered out into the blinding white snow.

Reindeer!

All of that snorting and sniffing had been a solitary reindeer that somehow must have gotten separated from the rest of his herd. He must have smelled Tore's dinner earlier and made his way to the cave.

When the reindeer spotted Tore he dashed off in a blur. Poor creature had scared her, now she had scared him! Tore laughed and crawled back into the heart of her cave. She didn't need any more excitement for the time being!

Tore sighed. There wasn't much for her to do in here. She pulled out her dirk and whetstone and aimlessly began sharpening the blade of her dirk. Tore found herself almost longing for the monotony of her everyday chores and "womanly" duties at home! Being caged up in here like an animal was driving her crazy. The dense trees obscured the sun, which caused Tore to loose track of time. She wasn't sure what part of the day it was, but it was light out now. For how long was another question.

It was clear to Tore that she would have to remain in the cave for at least another night. The weather wasn't any worse, but it hadn't improved either. Here she was protected from the winds. If she tried to continue her journey not knowing what time of day it was, and not knowing if there was any other type of shelter on down the line, then she could find herself in a very grave situation. She thought it best just to bide her time here until things looked better than they did now. At least until the wind stopped howling so loudly. Tore cupped her hands over her ears. She hated the sound of howling wind. It had always sent shivers up and down her arms. There was just something eerie in its sound. Before, the wind always seemed distant outside of the thick wood and stonewalls of her home. Here, the wind roared and howled right up next to her, swallowing her up in its loudness.

Pulling the fur up and over her head, Tore continued sharpening her dirk. She also found time to hem some of Arne's pants that she had brought with her. At least she wouldn't have to hitch them up so high now!

Tore went over her plan again. She had thought of a new last name while she was sleeping. She would be Eirik the Silent Graafell. She had heard the name somewhere before, but couldn't remember where. She liked the sound of it.

Tore had everything down. Her story would be that she had been traveling across Norway with her mother, when her mother caught fever and died. Leaving her, or rather him, an orphan. Everything she owned was in her bag. Her father had been killed while she was young.

Nearly every detail had been ironed out. Tore knew there were a few kinks in her plan. The first one, she had already encountered at home while dressing. Her breasts ached from being bound so tightly, but it was the only way. The second being her voice, but she thought she would be able to dismiss that as a quirk of nature. She could act offended and pissed at anyone who commented on its womanly tone. The third kink in her otherwise, she thought, solid plan was what to do about her womanly matters. How would she take care of her moon flow when constantly in the presence of men? She would have to devise some scheme of Eirik being overly private, who preferred being alone most of the time. That shouldn't be too hard!

She had known a berserker named, Galarr the Victorious, while she was a small child. He stayed off by himself always. He even preferred taking his meals alone. Tore could remember an occasional glimpse of him off somewhere in the shadows. He didn't like people it was said, and the ones he did like he lived in constant fear of accidentally killing one day. Everyone left him alone because everyone knew that Berserkers were a strange and frightening breed.

Tore laughed. She couldn't go around claiming to be a Berserker. She didn't look like one. Every Berserker she had ever heard of wore only furs or loose hides, and smelled badly. Their hair was unkept and wild. Essentially, they were an animal-like breed; fearful of hurting innocent people…but turn them loose on the battlefield and it was said that one Berserker could do the fighting of fifteen men! They were worth the danger of keeping around. She was no Berserker. She would have to have a more plausible explanation for wanting her privacy.

Tore examined her dirk and found it satisfactory. She put it back into the scabbard on her belt and put her whetstone back in her bag. The slim patch of sunlight penetrating the thick trees above that shone down into her little cave had long ago gone away. Tore crawled out of her cave to go relieve herself. She took care of her business quickly. It was thirty-seven degrees at the most out here and she wasn't one to be sticking her arse out in the snow to freeze off! Tore hiked up her pants and scurried back into the cave.

Hopefully, tomorrow the weather would wind down enough for her to travel some distance...perhaps even make it to the next shire.

Chapter 4

When Tore awoke the next day, she brewed some tea in her small pot and drank it heartily. Sticking her head out of the cave, she could see that the winds had died down, and the snow had hardened a bit. If she hurried she might be able to gain more ground before nightfall than she had yesterday.

Tore packed her belongings in her bearskin bag, and put out the fire. She tucked her extinguished torch into the side of her bag, and gathered up the firewood that she hadn't used during her duration here in the cave. She tied the wood into a bundle with a bit of leather cord and pushed it out of the cave along with her bag. Outside she tossed both the bag and the bundle of wood over her back and began hiking off in the direction that she hoped would soon take her to the nearest shire.

She was grateful for the break in the wind. It was so much easier to walk in this snow when one wasn't fighting the strength of the wind. Tore marveled at the height of some of the trees she was passing under. She stayed close to the side of the mountain, occasionally having to veer away from it to avoid crags and crevices. Wherever she was, and she wished she knew, at least the snow was hard and easier to walk in then the snow had been when she had left her home.

Tore buried her face in her fur and tried to think of riddles and songs to pass the time away as she walked. Even though the weather had improved, it didn't seem as though she was making much progress in getting anywhere!

Tore wished she had a live animal so she could make a sacrifice to Sif and ask for her direction; but, she only had her dried meat. Tore had an idea. She had seen a number of foxes darting between the trees and over rocks. If she could kill one, she could sacrifice it to Sif and have some fresh meat to eat as well.

Tore headed over to where she had seen the foxes earlier. She found a suitable tree with a strong, but elastic branch hanging low enough to stretch back and secure. The trees were close enough together that it was possible for the branch to impale the fox against the trunk of a neighboring tree if stretched back properly and fitted with her dirk. She pulled out some leather cord and fastened her dirk securely to the branch. Then she fastened the leather securely to the branch and pulled it back, releasing it in order to test her trap. The branch shot forward with a great whooshing sound and the dirk stuck deeply into the tree trunk. Tore smiled.

She found some of the dried meat in her bag and scattered a few pieces of it around the base of the tree trunk. Next, she made a little trail of the dried meat shreds towards a thicket of snow crowned trees where she had seen the foxes dash into.

Tore hurried back to her hiding place behind the thick boughs of the tree and stretched the branch back and held it tightly. Now all she had to do was wait.

She knew it wouldn't take long for at least one fox to smell the meat. It was the dead of winter and food was scarce.

Tore crouched on the ground. She held perfectly still and tried to breathe shallowly and quietly. Soon, she spotted the auburn fur of a fox creeping slowly and cautiously her way. She watched it look around and smell the trail of meat. It inched forward eating a piece at a time.

Steady. Steady. Tore thought to herself. She didn't want her anticipation or excitement to make her miscalculate or give her away.

The fox crept closer to the deadly tree trunk. All at once, Tore knew the fox was where she wanted it. She let go of the branch and it slashed through the air, stinging her ears with its cut. The fox only had time to look up and raise its ears before it found itself impaled on the blade of her freshly sharpened dirk. Tore sat still as the dying fox writhed and wiggled in a vain attempt to free itself from its life taking trap. Tore whispered a prayer of thanks to Uller, the god of hunting, and stood up. The fox was dead, hanging limply from the dirk and stuck to the tree. Tore grasped the fox and freed her dirk from deep within the animal's flesh.

"Forgive me brother fox for taking your life. The goddess Sif will thank you for your sacrifice." Tore said aloud as she laid the fox on the ground and removed the leather cord from the branch and from her dirk. She put the cord back into her bag, and picked up the dead fox by the scruff of his neck.

Tore built a small fire next to the wall of the mountain. She skinned and cleaned the fox, saving the fur to cure later. Tore cut off a chunk of the meat and stuck it on a stick to roast over the fire. The rest of the fox she placed on a large jagged rock for Sif.

She hoped that her goddess was listening and that she would tell her which way to go soon. At least provide her with another cave to spend the night in. Without one she would freeze to death out here in the open. Tore ate her meat hungrily and packed up her belongings again. She was starting to feel as though her entire life would be spent packing and unpacking a few items at a time. Tore kicked snow over her fire and prepared to leave. She looked back checking to see if the fox was still on the rock and smiled when she saw that it was now gone. Sif had claimed it. She had listened to Tore's prayers.

Tore smiled and asked Sif for her direction. Standing perfectly still, she listened to the soft whooshing of the moving branches and the loud beating of her own heart. Sif would tell her. Tore closed her eyes and breathed deeply.

She turned to her right and began walking again. Sif had shown her the way. Like most gods and goddesses, Sif hadn't revealed every detail to Tore. Just a push in the right direction. That was how the gods operated. Men were here for their amusement. It wasn't very much fun for them if one god or goddess provided too much help. Half of the entertainment that man offered was to see how much man could accomplish by himself using his own ingenuity and skill. Sif had helped Tore just enough to let her help herself.

Tore sat her bag down in the snow and sat on top of it to rest for a few minutes. She knew the right direction now. The next question Tore asked herself was how far was the nearest shire from here? Sif wouldn't tell her that of course. Tore would just have to wait and discover that fact for herself. And, it was a fact that she wished she would soon stumble across. Traveling had never appealed to Tore, and it certainly didn't now. She was cold and her feet ached from walking, not to mention the stinging ache in her shoulder that came from carrying her heavy bag all this way. She was strong and fit, but the elements and the lack of proper sleep conspired against her causing her to feel pain in parts of her body she never knew she had. She was grateful for the strength she did possess; a weaker woman would have died from cold by now.

Tore staggered back to her feet. She resumed her journey with thoughts of her brothers and father. Her family must have been discovered the rest of her kin by now. What wailing and cursing would be heard! Tore sighed. She wondered if her disappearance would stir up any trouble, or if her kin would be content to just let her suffer whatever fate was in store for her. They may have reached the conclusion that, whoever had murdered her family, had taken her for their sport and profit. Many a young girl was kidnapped and sold into slavery. There were always men who would pay for sex with a virile, young girl. The marketplaces were full of such traders in human flesh and misery. Once a girl disappeared into this realm, it was unlikely she would be heard of again. She knew her kin would take it up at the assembly upon Hablok's return; but, then again, that didn't matter much to her because when Hablok returned all of her troubles would be taken care of anyway. Ulf would protect her and they would be a family again. Vengeance would be swift and great and she would never have to live in fear for her life again. All would be well with Ulf's return.

Tore watched a hare leap through the forest. She wondered absently where a hare could be running off to so quickly. Tore smiled as she imagined him having a little hare assembly to go to with all of the other male hares who were holding little hare-sized swords and squeaking in their little hare voices. Tore shook her head. Her daydreams were dangerous. Maybe the cold was starting to affect her brain. Tore laughed. Who was she trying to kid? Her daydreams had always been a bit on the insane side. Look at what she was actually up to right now! Trudging through knee-deep snow in the middle of an unknown forest, dressed in man's clothes, and going off to the god's only knew where. Why were her daydreams any more insane than her actual life itself!

Tore looked around her. The sun was starting to set. During the winter the days were so damn short that there was hardly any day at all. Tore sighed. She hoped that Sif had a cave waiting for her somewhere close. As soon as the sun went down, the winds would pick up again and it would get quickly get even colder than it was now.

Tore slowed down as she approached a large fallen tree that was directly ahead of her. She grasped the side of the trunk and swung her legs up and over the icy obstacle. Looking up she spotted a small cave and looked skyward with an expression of thankfulness.

Tore ran as best as she could in the knee-deep snow towards the cave. Sif had provided a cave much better than the previous one she had slept in. This one was large enough for her to walk into if she bent over at the waist. Tore went through the same motions that she had the other night. It seemed as if she could do it all from rote memory now.

She had been traveling for at least two days now. From her best recollections, she knew that she had strayed way off course. It wasn't as if she was a navigator or anything, so she didn't hold herself personally responsible. She was, after all, a woman who was used to be accompanied by a male relative nearly everywhere she went outside of their own walls. Tore thought that if she got anywhere near the next shire that it would be a worthy accomplishment. She especially didn't expect the weather to take such a turn for the worse. She wasn't really worried about her food supply. There were enough small animals to last her for a while in these deep woods, and plenty of water from melted snow.

Loneliness was another thing. Already she longed for the familiar warmth of her family's fire and the laughing, loving banter and chitchat that went along with it. She knew she would never have that again. Not with her family. Tore smiled, maybe someday she would have her own family with her own sons to talk to around her fire; but that was a long time off. Tore frowned. An unpleasant thought had worked its way into her mind. Maybe she wouldn't ever have any sons to talk to around a fire. Maybe she wouldn't even live to see her brother Ulf again. She was playing a dangerous game now. Not only did she not know who wanted to kill her, but she was also masquerading as a man in a man's world that had rigid rules for women to follow.

Tore angrily punched the fur she had wadded beneath her head. Yes, she was playing with fire, but she had Sif on her side.

When day broke, Tore struggled out of her cave eager to be on her way. She was anxious to find people and people would mean a shire.

Tore walked for hours. The weather had let up finally, and only a few gusts of strong wind blew over the snow periodically. She didn't have to struggle to walk at all.

Tore found that she was getting hungry. So she looked around for a spot to sit and eat some dried meat. Looking to the right of her, she thought she could see a clearing through the wall of trees that surrounded her. She cautiously pushed the branches aside and made her way towards the clearing. Once there she observed a large area that had been cleared of trees. Stumps stuck out from under the snow, revealing that someone at sometime had chopped down these trees and cleared this small spot of land for a purpose.

Tore saw that it was almost perfectly round, and the trees that had been chopped had been stacked neatly in a pile near the side of the mountain. Tore stood there just looking for a moment. Why would someone clear a spot of land out here in this dense forest? There was no evidence of there ever having been a dwelling here, and no burial mound of any sort. Those kinds of things would be obvious and not easily hid. So, why the clearing?

Tore shrugged. Maybe someone had planned a dwelling here. A criminal perhaps? Tore dug around in her bag for her dried meat and made a small fire to brew some tea, all the while romanticizing her escaped criminal who had planned to build a house here in the dense trees and hide out with his lover from the men who wished him harm. Her daydreams kept her mind off of the cold and kept her from giving up on her quest for the nearest shire. Tore waited for the water to boil in her little pot. Hot tea would be just the thing to warm her up right now!

She sat on a stump and stirred the tea leaves into the water. She sipped cautiously, and pulled her mouth away upon realization that the water was too hot. She scooped up some snow from the ground next to her, and crumbled it into her cup.

"There." She said out loud, surprised to hear how scratchy and stiff her own voice sounded. She sipped her tea and continued to stare around her.

Suddenly, between bitefuls of her meat, she noticed that over towards the edge of the clearing, something was sticking out of the white snow. It wasn't a tree or a stump, but something metallic. The few dim rays of sun that were out today, bounced off of the object half buried in the snow. Tore sat her cup down on the stump, and curiously went over towards the object.

From what she could see, it looked like the hilt of a large sword. Tore dropped to her knees, and began scooping the snow away from the object. It had been buried for a while, and some of the snow had hardened into ice along time ago. Tore whipped out her dirk, and began chipping away at the ice-covered sword. It was a very large sword, and she found herself amazed at the depth that she had to continue to dig in order to reach the end of the blade. As she dug, she noticed that alongside of the sword was a scabbard as well. The ice had wedged the two pieces into one.

The scabbard came out first. Tore examined it closely.

It was wrought out of steel and silver. It was plain, undecorated, and efficient. The inside was fur-lined and the whole thing was in rather good shape for being buried for so long out in the elements.

Tore chipped away at the ice around the sword, occasionally jerking the sword back and forth in an attempt to loosen it. Finally, the sword slid from the ice with a crunch. Tore grasped the hilt, and pulled up the sword. The unexpected weight of the blade caused her to drop the blade downward, plunging the blade into the snow she had just freed it from, and nearly dropping it.

"That's one big sword!" Tore exclaimed.

She braced herself and heaved the sword upward. It was a large warrior's sword. The man who had commissioned this sword must have been extraordinary in stature and girth. Tore found that she could barely even lift it, thrusting it was nearly impossible. The sword blade was of quality steel and undecorated. The hilt was simple too. It was bronze wrapped with leather. The workmanship was of high quality and superior to any sword that Tore had ever seen. It was a good sword, not gaudy or over decorated as some men's swords were. There were no flashy jewels embedded on this sword, and no gold encrusting the scabbard. This was a warrior's sword. A battle sword. It wasn't meant for impressing; it was meant for fighting.

Tore took the sword and scabbard back to her fire. The inside of the scabbard was full of ice. Tore laid it near her fire hoping that the heat would cause some of the ice to melt. She threw out her tea, which was too cold to drink, and refilled her cup with water from the little pot that she had wisely left sitting in the embers of the fire. She put a pinch of tea leaves into the boiling water and watched as each leaf floated to the bottom and then back to the top again. Tore propped the sword up against a rock, and drank her tea, all the while staring at the sword she had just discovered. All at once, Tore spit on the ground.

"Agh!" She spat again. Mesmerized by the sword and thoughts of its former owner had made her oblivious to the dregs at the bottom of the cup. Tealeaves, thick and wet, refused to leave the softness of her mouth. Tore spat again.

Tore looked up from her stump and noticed that there was a small cave, really more of a crack in the mountain to the side of her. She picked up her belongings and went to inspect the cave. Once inside, she started another fire and placed the scabbard next to it, then went to extinguish the fire near the stump. While outside, she tried relieving herself with her legs akimbo male fashion. Most of her urine ended up on the legs of her pants and on her boots. Somehow she would have to go off by herself whenever she had to piss. She would never be able to fake the steady arched stream that men so casually produce.

Tore scooped up some snow and wiped at her pants legs and boots with it, trying to get the urine off. She didn't want some wild animal stalking her by her scent and eating her for dinner.

Tore went back to her fire, and lifted the scabbard. Some of the ice was trickling away. Tore picked up her dirk and chipped at the inside of the scabbard. A few larger chunks managed to fall out and onto the stone beneath her. Tore was careful not to cut the fur lining. If it had lasted this well preserved for this long, she surely didn't want to be the one to damage it now.

Tore decided to take the sword back outside and practice using it. She had been lucky enough to find a good weapon; she must honor it by being able to use it well. Her father used to tell Ulf and the boys, and reluctantly, her as well, that a man could have a thousand swords, but he might as well not have any of them if he could not use them properly. A warrior's best friend is his sword, her father would say; honor that friend by using it well.

Tore first studied the sword from the hilt to the tip of the blade. She felt its weight in her hands. She raised it slowly upward, aware of the strain of every muscle in her arm, back, and chest. Gripping the hilt with both hands, she bent her elbows and drew the blade in towards her. It was heavy, but she would learn to fight with this sword. She had to swing a sword like a man, to be a man.

Tore thrust it sharply and cried out. Over and over again, she swung the blade as if in mortal combat. With each violent thrust, she grew increasingly aware of the ache in her muscles, and the sweat rolling from her brow. Finally, she collapsed sore and tired.

Gasping in the snow, Tore remembered happier times when Ubbe and Arne would both scowl at her with envy at her skill with the sword. She saw her father's knitted eyebrows and words of condemnation, but also she saw the glint of pride in his eye and the glimmer of longing that Tore could have been a great warrior, if only she had been born a man. Tore breathed raggedly, exhausted. She fondly caressed the blade as if caressing a lover. She would master this sword.

All of her days of chopping wood, hauling water, and swordplay with her brothers would reward her now. Her arms were strong and muscular. Her body endured pain and strain just as well as any man's did. Tore laughed. She would master this sword. This massive sword. She would prove that a woman could be a warrior.

For now though, Tore thought to herself, she just had to concentrate on getting herself in the vicinity of the nearest inkling of civilization. All of the sword skill, grit, and determination would mean nothing to a dead woman. Or a dead man, Tore thought. For if her bones were discovered, and they probably wouldn't' if some animal had any say in the matter, the men's clothing that would be hanging from shreds from her poor, unfortunate bones would label her as an unknown man. She wanted to escape for a while as a man, not for eternity.

Tore staggered back inside to her fire. She was tired now. The scabbard was nearly ice free. She put it back in its place near the fire in hopes that the remaining ice would thaw and the fur would dry out.

Her sacrifice must have pleased Sif more that Tore had originally thought. Not only did Sif point her in the right direction and provide her with shelter; but also, Sif had saw fit to reward her with the greatest gift of all: a sturdy and reliable sword. Tore smiled and hugged her knees to her chest, she had never doubted Sif and now she was glad for it. Her father used to laugh at her loyalty, to a point anyway. No man laughed too much at any man's god or goddess no matter how trivial he might think the deity was, after all, gods were gods and men were men.

Tore felt warm now, from the fire and from an inner glow brought about by a feeling of protection from evil. Sif was watching over her now. Sif was watching over this motherless, fatherless girl. Tore knew it. She could almost sense Sif's presence near her. Lying down to sleep, she felt keenly aware of her warrior goddess' blessings, but she couldn't help but have an ominous foreboding as well.

Tore shook it off. She was only tired, that was it. Sleeping on edge and barely warm had pushed her to the limit of human endurance. All was going to turn out well Tore knew it. Hadn't Sif helped her, protected her, saved her? All would turn out well. Tore only had to pray.

Dreaming that the spirits of her father and brothers were high in the court of Odin, watching over her, guiding her, she fell asleep with a smile on her face, and her hand grasped firmly around the hilt of her newfound sword.

An achy feeling of stiffness greeted Tore when the first ray of sunlight crept into the cave. She moved her arm sluggishly, every muscle tense and tight.

"Good morning, my friend, Sword." Tore said to the sword, which still lay beside her. She smiled and sat up still swaddled in her warm fur. "I wonder if your steel muscles are as rigid as my flesh ones are today!" Tore laughed and reached for her scabbard. The ice was gone, and the fur was nearly dried.

She hated to leave her little nest. She had slept better than the previous nights. She felt safe and protected for the first time since before the slaughter of her family. Now, it was morning, and she hated facing the unknown that lurked beyond the cave walls. She wished she could stay here forever, safe and warm; but she knew she couldn't. She had a destiny to fulfill; the gods had so deemed it. She would do her best to fulfill that destiny, whatever it would be.

Tore drank some tea, ate some broth and dried meat, and packed up her things. She pulled her warm fur over her head and pulled on her reindeer skin mittens. She took one last look around the cave, and kicked the now dwindling fire until it died out.

Another day had dawned.

Tore decided that each morning she should practice with her sword. Regardless of the biting pain that screamed at her from every inch of her body, she sat her bag down against the mouth of the cave, and went through the practice drills she had watched her father and brothers do every day of her life. Gone was the violent slashing that she had raged out of herself the day before. Stern steadiness had replaced her desperate need to prove her skill to herself. Tore felt the hilt in her hand and realized that already it was beginning to feel comfortable.

It was time to get going. Tore slung her bag over her shoulder and threaded the scabbard onto her belt, thrusting the sword into it. She lurched off through the snow, feeling the dull banging of the scabbard against her thigh. Again, she thanked the gods for blessing her with the height that had often been scorned by her kinsmen. She had always been derided for being so tall, flat chested, strong, and unwomanly. Now, all of her worst qualities were her best assets…and her salvation.

Tore trudged on. The landscape didn't change much. Acres and acres of dense forests, jagged rocks, and deep crags. Cliffs loomed about dangerously, and the path she walked seemed to never have known the touch of human feet. Tore sat down near a cliff, but far enough away to feel safe from the treachery it posed. Below her was spread the majestic sea, waves crashing on rocky shores, and wind blowing salty coldness up and over the cliffs towards her. She scanned the horizon for the welcome masts of a ship, but none could be seen. She felt the yearning her brother and the safety he could provide.

Tore pushed herself up. She turned from the cliff and continued in the direction that Sif had given her. Surely, she would reach a shire by nightfall. She had traveled closer to the sea, and where there were fjords, there were ports, and where there were ports, there would be people. She had to keep going. She had to persevere.

It was hard trying to keep her mind on the task at hand. She found herself wanting to think of what she would do once she found a shire, on how she would survive, how she would tell her tale of her fiction based life. All of this was frightening, and Tore knew that she must not dwell on that for now. For now, she had to concentrate on surviving and getting to that unknown shire…the rest would fall into place somehow. She had money and valuables that could be sold if need be. She wasn't poor. There was no need to worry about shelter or food once she made it to a shire. There was a need to worry about whoever killed her family, and maintaining her new identity. But, for now, her only need was to continue on the path she was now making for herself through these deep woods, and reach the shire that Sif would lead her to. That was what she tried to keep her mind focused on.

Tore became aware of the gusts of cold air that had eased up on her slowly. The gusts were also growing stronger with each passing second. Tore suddenly grew afraid. This was the beginning of a storm and she was out here with no shelter. No shelter meant death. Tore looked up through the trees that even immense as they were provided little in the way of protection from the snow that began to fall steadily, and more heavily.

She pushed on, each step growing more difficult to put her foot up and out of the snow and back down again in front of her. She had to find shelter quickly, the snow was growing blindly and soon the limited vision she had now would be gone leaving her with no hope of finding a safe haven.

Holding her arm in front other to block the thrusting snow and wind, Tore plunged onward. Her eyes frantically searched the stony walls of the mountainside for any indention, crevice, or crag she could crawl into. There was nothing. The snow was mounting.

Tore struggled to maintain her balance in the tugging wind. It blew her in one direction and then yanked her back again. the bitter cold made breathing increasingly more difficult. Tore could feel the snot that was running from her nose, freezing and clinging to her face like icicles off the eaves of a dwelling. Tore pulled at her bag that shad somehow slipped from her shoulders and was now being dragged behind her. She struggled to return it to her shoulder, but to no avail. Tore was vaguely aware of a tingling sensation in her feet, and of no sensation at all in her toes.

She was running out of time.

A huge blast of icy wind knocked her on her arse, sending her legs flying and her bag tumbling beside her. She was running out of strength, and the cold was sapping her alertness. Tore shook her head. She couldn't' go to sleep, not now, not here. She struggled to get up. She scrambled to her knees and hoisted herself up with the scabbard at her side. Looking skyward, Tore called out,

"Sif! Save me!" Her cry had the ring of a frightened and desperate child, and the agony and terror of a dying man.

Tore struggled to walk, collapsing again in exhaustion. She wanted to cry, but it was too cold. She breathed sharply. Then, suddenly and sharply, as if an invisible hand had reached out and grasped her chin and thrust it forward, Tore saw what lay before her...a giant, hollowed out tree deeply embedded in the side of the mountain.

Sif had heard her prayer...again.

Chapter 5

Tore stumbled towards the tree. It was deeply embedded in the side of the mountain as if the mountain had consumed the massive trunk eons ago. The inside of the tree had long ago rotted out and was now just a hollow shell…a thick, hollow shell. The tree was so gigantic that Tore could nearly walk right into it. She pushed her bag in before her and struggled into the protective clutches of the fallen tree. Crawling over pine needles, piles of rocks, and other natural debris, Tore scurried to the back of the trunk where the mountain had grown over it. The back of the tree trunk was a firm wall of stone. Tore sat there for a moment, breathing a little easier now that the wind wasn't knocking the breath right out of her.

Slowly, she moved the fur around her face away enough that she could survey her surroundings. The storm outside was quickly swallowing up the daylight, so Tore dug around in her bag for her flint and struggled to get her numb, cold hands to obey her mind and start a fire.

Tore struggled with getting that fire started for what seemed like forever. At last, she had a flame and she lit her oil soaked torch and waved it around in the trunk to see what she had crawled into this time. The pile of rocks she had crawled over could be spread out and a fire built on top of them. She gathered smaller pieces of wood and added some of her own she had collected along the way to the top of the pile over the stones…and lit the fire. The stones should protect the aged wood underneath. Now heat was emanating through the trunk and Tore felt the steady feeling of thawing throughout her body.

Tore scooped all of the pine needles towards the back of the log near the mountain wall. They would make good insulation under her fur tonight. Tore was tired.

She spread her fur over the needles and brewed some tea before falling asleep. Tore soon found herself warm and dreaming.

She was a little girl again and her father had just returned from a raid. She could see him coming towards her with open arms and a smile spread across his bearded face. He reached into his bag tied around his waist, hanging over the blue and brown striped pants he wore, and pulled out a small parcel wrapped in leather and tied with cord.

Tore saw herself, eager and happy reaching out and accepting his present. She was sitting on the ground, and Ulf was telling her to get up out of the dirt; but she was too excited about opening her gift. Her father watched her tugging at the cord, and the piece of leather finally fell open on her lap. Two silver pins! She would have the best apron among all of the children now! Tore saw her child hands turn them over and closely look at them. Silver dragon heads, scrolled and carved with such intricate care that they looked as if they came directly off of a ship's mast and stern! The dragons were covered with tongues of fire, and wore fierce, protective expressions. Tore felt her little arms grasp her father's neck as he heaved her off of the ground and into his embrace. She remembered the musky smell of his hair, and the wet fur smell of his robe. Most of all, she remembered the kiss of his chapped, sea-salted lips against her cheek. How she had loved her father. He was young and strong then. Now he was gone. As reality began to sting, Tore tossed in her sleep. Tore dreamed of so many things from her past and from her present. As she slept, her dreams took her to places far away and close to home. Suddenly, she was back inside of her huge tree again, but she was not alone. Coming towards her on huge, magnificent horses were a troop of beautiful women. Maidens -- lovely to look at, but wearing fierce scowls. Who were these women flying towards her on magical horses? Tore watched as her dream self sat up quickly and move farther back in the tree somewhat frightened. But why was she scared?

Tore now knew who the maidens were...they were the Valkyries... Odin's troop of maidens who harvested the worthy slain warriors for the ranks in Valhalla.

But why were they here? She wasn't a warrior! She wasn't even a man! Surely, they could see that! Why were their horses flying right up to the opening of her tree? The maiden closest to her, the one in the lead position, seemed to wave a dreamy, misty hand towards Tore in a trance-like way. The dream Tore cowered in the back of the tree, and the sleeping Tore felt a pang of shame for her other self's cowardice. What did the maiden want?

Dream Tore called out to her. There was no response, just the slow, almost musical way the maiden waved her arm and somewhat pointed towards the cowering Tore. Then they were gone.

Tore woke up. She looked around her tree, breathing heavily and sweating profusely. Had the Valkyries really been here, or was it just as it seemed...a dream? Tore shuddered at the thought of immortal beings being so close to her that she could see them. Certainly, it had to be a dream! A crazy dream at that! What would Odin's Valkyries want with her? She wasn't even a warrior! And what had they kept pointing at? What did they want? Tore looked in the area where the maiden had continued to wave at...the sword? Did they want the sword?

Tore frowned. Why would they come for a sword? It must be something else...but what?

Tore was puzzled and now couldn't sleep. The storm was still raging outside and a significant amount of snow had heaped itself up in a drift inside of the trunk. The drift had almost completely covered the entrance of the trunk, leaving only about a foot where Tore could see out. When this storm quit she was going to have to do some serious digging to get herself out of this mess. Tore sighed. It seemed like her "simple" journey to the next shire was becoming more and more a complete failure...but what other choice did she have? She couldn't go back home, and she had nowhere else to go. She had to keep going on her planned mission, at least until Ulf finally came home. If he ever came home. Tore slapped her knee. "Don't think about that!" Tore said aloud. "He's coming home. He has to!" Tore realized the pathetic tone her voice rang with. Ulf was her only salvation and right now she didn't need to let herself think anything could change that. She had to think positively.

"Now, drink some tea and go back to sleep!" Tore told herself sharply.

Tore did just that.

The ground moved. Trembling at first, but then more violently. Tore rolled over, dreaming. A loud crack filled the air.

Tore was awake! What in Hades was that? Crack!

The sound ripped through the air again.

Tore was now aware of the trunk around her moving. The cracking sound was coming from the end embedded in the mountain. It sounded and felt like the trunk was being ripped from its century old resting place by force.

Suddenly, Tore was thrown to the other side of the trunk. She caught herself on her forearms. The trunk was moving! Tore quickly snuffed out the fire, lest she be thrown onto it and burned alive.

She struggled to see out of the end where the snow was, but the view from over the drift was quaking back and forth with an incredible fury.

What was happening? Tore wished this too was a dream, but it wasn't. This was real. Something or someone was moving the trunk that she was sheltered in, and they weren't doing a nice job of it.

Slowly a foul stench wafted in through the small opening in the trunk. "Agh!" Tore said loudly. Never before had she smelled such a reek.

The trunk was given another massive heave, and another loud crack seared through the once peaceful air. The smell was stronger now. What was it? Tore couldn't place it...it smelled animal, but not exactly. Besides, what sort of animal had such an overpowering stench about them? Tore couldn't think of a single one that smelled this badly, not even dead and rotting!

Suddenly, she heard a great, snot-laden snort. By the gods! Tore thought wildly, what was that? She crawled towards the opening of the trunk for a better view and to get away from the end that was being wrenched out of the mountainside...she steadied herself in the quaking trunk to look outside.... Suddenly, a powerful blast of ice hit the drift.

Tore was flung backwards in a flip. She staggered up, and saw that the entire end of the tree had been frozen solid. The ice had to be inches thick for Tore couldn't see through it at all.

Tore positioned herself defensively in the center of the trunk. Going to each end was now out of the question. In a grabbing motion, Tore snatched her bearskin bag and all the belongings that she could catch as they flew by. She shoved these into her bag and held onto it frantically. Her existence depended on the contents of this bag...she couldn't lose it!

One end of the trunk was frozen shut by the ice outside. The other end was being forced splinter by splinter out of the mountain wall. Tore was casually tossed back and forth like a child's doll with no power to stop whatever it was, and no idea what it was out there doing this.

Tore sat and waited for the next jolt. There it was. The old trunk heaved and groaned and a sprinkling of snow sifted in from the outside. Whatever it was out there doing this, was succeeding. The trunk was starting to give way. All at once, Tore realized that the thing outside might be after her...a Frost Giant? Tore wondered. Tore didn't know if one Frost Giant would have the strength to rip this ancient tree from the possession of the mountain. She didn't hear anything that remotely sounded like a man of sorts, and she heard no armor, or swords. Surely, a Frost giant would've tried burning her out or hacking his way through the brittle wood with his sword.

The sword! Maybe it was a Frost giant after her sword. The Valkyries had wanted it, (Maybe, Tore added to herself mentally), Why not the Frost giant too? What if it were a Frost Giant's sword? Tore pulled her sword out of the scabbard that was now tied securely on her belt again, and looked at it. It had no markings that would indicate a giant of any sort. It looked like a man's sword to her. Tore thrust the sword back into the scabbard and braced herself for another blow.

The tree cracked and groaned again. More snow fell through the cracks, but it was pouring in now. Frost giants don't snort like that, Tore thought to herself. They probably smelled as bad as whatever it was out there, but that snort was nothing like anything she had ever heard described before.

The tree swayed again. More roaring snorts. It sounded angry as if the task of yanking the tree out of the mountain was more difficult than whatever it was out there had first imagined.

The tree stopped moving. Tore breathed hard. What was she going to do once the tree was free from the mountain? It was going to be free, enough of it had already splintered and cracked that the trunk was weak enough now that it wouldn't be too much longer until it was free.

What then? Tore's mind raced with plans that she half- way devised and then chunked due to the fact that she had no idea of what she was dealing with out there. If it were a god, there would be no point trying to escape.

With an ear-piercing crack, the tree finally left its mountain mother. Tore flew forward with a force she had never known before. The tree rolled viciously in the snow, now free from its stone home. Snow and ice fell in upon Tore who laid stretched out on what was the ceiling in her tree shelter, bracing herself for yet another jolt. It came just as expected. The tree was lifted off of the ground and hurled through the air as easily as an archer lets loose his arrow from his bow. Tore's hands found a hole in the wood around her and she held on for dear life. Her bag swung heavily every which way, and kept hitting her in the head. Tore looked down and saw that her sword was still firmly in place in the scabbard at her side.

What now? The tree stopped flying and came to a body- jarring halt in a deep snowdrift. The smell was gone now. Whatever had tossed this massive tree as if it were a child's toy must be far away now. Tore stayed in the tree. If the thing wanted her, maybe this was a trap. Maybe the thing was standing far enough away, and down wind so Tore would crawl out in hopes of escape. Well, she wasn't going to fall for that cheap trick.

Tore scurried to the center of the tree trunk and squatted down, resting. She hadn't lost any of her possessions thanks to her quick thinking and quick reflexes. Tore peered inside of her bag. Some things were a little wet, as the pot used for boiling water hadn't been quite empty; but other than that things were no worse for the wear.

Tore breathed a little easier now. She didn't know how long she would have until the thing outside would give up its plan...if, of course, waiting for its prey to crawl out of the tree was its plan. Tore had no way of knowing since she didn't know what the thing was that was out there stalking her was.

Tore thought long and hard and finally arrived at a bone-chilling thought. What if the creature outside was a White Dragon? Tore shuddered. She had never seen a dragon, but she had heard the tales ever since childhood. They were known to exist in out of the way places, and the gods knew she was in a very out of the way place at this time.

"Think, Tore, think!" Tore told herself softly, not wanting to draw attention to herself hiding in her solid, but not indestructible tree.

White dragons lived in caves. There were caves, lots of caves near-by. White dragons had breath that when directed at any object could freeze it solid...just like the entrance to the tree had been before it had been ripped out of the mountain.

Tore thought hard trying to remember anything else she knew about white dragons. The only other thing she could come up with was that they were evil and greedy; but then again, what dragon wasn't?

Tore sighed. Her plan had seemed so simple at the onset. Walk to the nearest shire, and masquerade as a man until Ulf got home. She hadn't planned on any of this. The storms, losing her way, winding up the gods only knew where, and now...a damn dragon!

The ground trembled slightly, and then it began to shake more violently. Tore's heart began to pound inside of her chest choking off the pumping of her lungs. Whatever it was out there, and Tore prayed to Sif it wasn't a dragon, it was coming back.

Tore dug her hands into the hole nearest her to hold onto in the event the tree was once again sent soaring. The quaking stopped for a moment, and Tore became aware of the foul-smelling stench that had returned. It had to be a white dragon.

Tore held her breath. Maybe the dragon would think she wasn't there anymore; but Tore thought to herself, if it was a dragon then it could prob-

ably smell her.
  Both ends of her wooden fortress were open and exposed to the elements. An ear-splitting roar sounded and suddenly an immense, snotty snout appeared at the end of the trunk. It was sniffing strongly for her scent and it had found it. The snout disappeared again; followed closely by the deafening roar Tore had heard minutes before.
  Before her, Tore could see the gigantic white-scaled dragon's body shimmering in the faint sunrays. Huge taloned feet were planted deeply in the snow, and pearly wings hung around the dragon's body like gauzy silk. A foot moved and stamped in the snow. It roared again.
  If the dragon stuck its mouth in here, it could freeze her where she stood. Tore looked behind her as if planning her retreat. She knew she wouldn't get far. She would either die fleeing or die on her feet like a...like a man, Tore thought and laughed.
  Tore waited and wondered why the dragon hadn't already sprayed her with his icy breath. Maybe it wanted to play with her some more before finishing her off. Tore's thoughts raced uncontrollably through her mind. What should she do? What should she do?
  She decided she'd rather be frozen to death and die instantly, then to be ripped to shreds piece by bloody, gory piece and die in agony. Tore held on firmly and waited for the dragon to act.
  The dragon paced noisily outside of the trunk. Snot- gorged snorts and roars blasted the once serene forest over and over again as the frustrated dragon decided what to do next. Tore wished it would hurry up and decide its next action. The suspense was going to kill her first.
  The dragon stuck its snout back in the trunk. "This is it!" Tore said aloud to herself. The dragon withdrew its snout
and snorted again. Tore sighed loudly. Now what was it doing? Whoosh!
  Tore found herself hanging by her fingers from the hole in the tree trunk, her bag once again flying around beside her yanking hard on her shoulder. The tree trunk was being held straight up in the air now, and the dragon was trying to peer in through the narrow opening to see her hanging there. Tore looked down past her feet to the end of the trunk and saw an enormous steel blue eye staring back up at her. Crystal clear lashes framed the cold eyes as they blinked in apparent amazement at the size of the cornered prey that held on so frantically inside of the protective tree trunk. The tree fell with a devastating thud. Tore was now hanging diagonally. The tree had been tossed into the forest, and other trees had hung it up so that it couldn't hit ground again. Tore scampered up and back to the center of the trunk and grasped the

tree again. This dragon was playing with her, just like a cat does a mouse. She wondered how long she would have to keep preparing herself for death, before it finally came.

Tore was soaked with sweat. Her heartbeat so hard it made her chest hurt. Her lungs hurt from breathing the cold air. Her hands were bloody and sore from digging into the wood to hold on for dear life. She was painfully aware of splinters jabbing under her fingernails, but knew with her mittens on she wouldn't be able to hold on. Tore also noticed that she had urinated on herself some time after all of this flying about in the air had begun. She was cold, she was wet, and she was scared to death.

Tore hung there, breathing heavily, waiting for the end. She didn't want to die. Not yet, not this way. She thought of her brothers and her father...saw them lying there bloody, headless. She thought of her poor dead mother. To die meant seeing them all again, but to live. To live! She wanted to live. There was still so much she wanted to do in her life! So much her brothers would never get to do, or her father would never see her do. She didn't want to die a death with no honor, to die in vain, like her brothers and her dear father. She had to live for them. Their deaths had to be avenged. She had to stay alive to make sure Ulf avenged her family. She had to stay alive so Ulf would have a family.

She didn't want to die. Tore felt like screaming. Why was this dragon here? What did it want with her? Had she disturbed it in some way? What cause had she given it to hunt her down and eat her like some form of rodentia?

The trunk was being clawed at from the outside. The grating of the dragon's talons against the wood was an eerie sound. The wood was old and brittle; it wouldn't stand up much longer.

"Aahh!" Tore screamed as a talon ripped through the side of the trunk with ease.

The dragon outside would shred the tree until there was nothing left and Tore would have to come out.

"Aahh!" Tore screamed again as another claw popped through the ancient wood.

Her time was running out quickly. Chunks of the side of the tree were falling away exposing more and more of the inside to the dragon's grasp.

"Sif?!" Tore screamed out in pain as a talon ripped through the side of the trunk and sliced her leg. Tore saw the leg of her pants oozing, dying her pants blood red.

"Sif?" Tore screamed, but her screams could not be heard over the dragon's angry roars.

"Sif!" Tore cried again, "If ever I needed you, it's now!"

Sif had protected her all of her life. Would her goddess bring her this far to let her feed some hungry dragon? Tore winced in pain as she tried to push herself back farther against the trunk's inner stonewall.

All at once the forest was bathed in a silvery flood of light. A heavy, deafening silence hung over the woods. Tore could see the dragon turn its head and look towards something close by. It roared.

From her perch high above the ground, in the trunk still held aloft by the massive dragon, Tore could see it too.

The form of a beautiful woman dressed in silvery white, skirt flowing out around her as if she was walking on air…a blinding flash of a sword held high above her head as if battle ready…The last image Tore saw before hitting her head on the trunk that had once again been heaved aside, was of long, flowing, golden hair dancing on the cold winter wind…the hair of Sif, Tore's ever faithful goddess.

Chapter 6

Sharp, piercing pain brought Tore back to her senses. Dazed, Tore looked around her surroundings. Obviously, she had slipped out of the tree as it was being hurled for the last time by the ferocious dragon, that was now, thank the gods, no where to be seen.

Tore sat up slowly.

"Aaah!" She cried in pain and reflexively clutched her leg. The dragon's claw had done a good job lying open the flesh on her thigh. Tore ripped the leg of her pants above and below the wound in order to get a closer look at it. It was a clean cut, not bone deep, but definitely deep enough that it was going to leave quite a scar. Quite a convincing battle wound. Battle with a dragon. Tore laughed despite her pain. There had been no battle. Just a hungry, angry dragon that had her trapped like a rat in a hole. If it weren't for Sif there would be no tale to tell at all. Perhaps all the stories of battle and heroics were like this one. No bravery at all, just the intervention and the blessing of a god or goddess at just the right time. Tore smiled thinking of all the tales she had been weaned on. What if they all had been embellished to favor the man in the fight? She laughed again, but searing pain soon changed her smile to a grimace. She had to tend to her leg. Luckily, her bag was still securely wrapped around her arm. Tore found a shirt and tore it to strips. She bound the wound tightly. She would have to wait until she found sufficient shelter to do anything more with it. Tore moved away from the blood soaked snow she had been lying in. She had to get up and get out of this weather. Her safe and secure haven had been tossed aside somewhere out of her line of vision.

Tore used her sword to help her push herself up and out of the snow. There was a gigantic boulder in front of her that she would have to climb over to get back to the mountain wall. Tore struggled and cried out in pain, as she heaved herself up and on top of the jagged boulder to get to the other side.

Once on top, Tore leaned on her sword and rested. New blood was seeping through the bandages that she had crudely fashioned for herself. She had to sew that wound shut before she bled to death.

Tore looked across the land. There before her lay the dragon. It reeked more now than before and Tore could see why. Across its belly was a tremendous gash that revealed all of the great beast's guts and gore. The stench rising out in a misty trail of rotten steam filled the area with a putrefying odor. Tore felt ill.

She leaned over and vomited. Wiping her mouth with the back of her sleeve, she watched as her own bile and gore slid down the other side of the boulder and slopped off in chunks onto the snow beneath. Tore gasped in the air and tried to hold her breath as she struggled painfully down the boulder to the ground before her; but, she was too weak from exhaustion, cold and pain to hold her breath for very long and soon her body had to breath in the foul air. Tore fought the urge to vomit again and scampered as quickly as her leg would allow around the massive slain corpse of the great white dragon that had been cut down by Sif's sword.

Tore clung to the mountain wall as if she half expected a cave to just open up before her. She paused and surveyed her surroundings and started to back off in the right direction. She couldn't go very far before her leg would require attention, but she had to try.

After about half an hour, Tore found a small cave. Dizziness was setting in, and she knew she would only have a little time until she passed out from loss of blood. She crawled into the cave, dragging her leg gingerly along. Quickly she started a fire, shoved some snow into her pot, shoved some more snow into another pot, and jerked her pants off.

Wadding the soiled pants up, she thrust them under her leg as a sort of prop. From her bag, she produced a clean pair of pants for later, some more shreds of cloth and a sewing packet.

Tore carefully untied the bloody strips and threw them into the fire. She picked up one pot of boiling water and set it on a rock to cool. Tore looked at the bloody, grizzly mess of flesh that stared up at her. This wasn't going to be much fun.

Tore tested the water in the pot and decided it was good. She poor the hot water over her leg to wash off the blood so she could have a better view of the cut.

She winced and grabbed her leg above the cut. She rested her head against the cave wall for a moment and breathed hard.

Slowly, she threaded her needle and reassured herself that she could do this deed for she had no other choice. Sif wasn't going to come down here and do this for her.

Tore pinched the sliced flesh together tightly. She cried out loudly. Stitch by stitch, she pushed the needle through her flesh, dreading that popping feeling of flesh beneath her needle each time it went through to the other side. She stopped half way through to take a swig of mead. Not too much as to lose her senses; just enough to warm her innards and calm her nerves some. The cut was a long one. She sewed flesh to flesh from her hip to her middle thigh. She was fortunate it was not deep and no muscle was sliced. Just the flesh, but that was enough to hurt and slowed her down on her journey.

Tore brought her leg up somewhat and leaned over and chewed the thread off. She stuck the needle into the leather of the pouch and reached for the mead again. She was feeling faint. Tore found her fur and drew it out of her bag, wrapping it around herself. She found the dried meat and added it to the brewing pot. When the meat had softened while she was resting, she removed the pot from the embers and sat it on the rock to cool Tore made herself as comfortable as she could, added some more wood to the fire, and drank down her broth. Drawing the fur closer, she drank more mead and fell painfully asleep.

As Tore slept, two days and nights passed with the goddess Sif standing guard over Tore.

Tore became aware of someone or something softly nudging her awake. At first, her mind played tricks on her and she imagined she saw Arne standing over her telling her to get her lazy hide out of bed and start breakfast before their father awoke; but, then she remembered the lifeless body of her brother and chills woke her from her slumber.

Chills and a warm hand.

Tore sat up slowly, careful of her leg, and looked into the most beautiful face she had ever seen. Sitting before her, legs crossed, golden hair flowing over and around the strong shoulders, sat Sif in her full glory. Tore was speechless, vaguely aware that her mouth was moving, but no words were coming out.

Sif smiled and then laughed loudly.

"Are you frightened?" Sif asked still laughing.

Tore thought about that for a moment, and then, peacefully concluded that she was not.

"No. I, I, I'm not. Though I think I should be." Tore found the words at last.

"And why do you think you should be?" Sif, so humanly poked at the fire aimlessly.

"You're Sif." Tore said matter of factly.

Sif laughed again.

"It is I that should be afraid of you!" Sif leaned back against the cave wall illuminating it with a pulsing silver glow.

"You? Be afraid of ME?" Tore laughed this time.

"You're the one who keeps running into misfortune." Sif smiled slightly.

Tore nodded her head sadly. "True...but I do not wish it to be so."

Sif laughed again. "You've been making me work very hard lately!"

"I'm sorry. I, I..."Tore looked downward ashamed.

Sif reached out and gently patted Tore's good leg. "It is good to work, is it not?"

Tore smiled at Sif. "You must be so busy."

Sif leaned back again and shrugged, golden hair rippled off of her shoulder and down her back. "There are things here and there are things there, but I am not so busy."

Tore laughed. "I am glad."

Sif laughed at that too. "I know you are! If it weren't for me, you would be churning around in the gut of that dragon about this time!"

Tore squelched up her nose just thinking about the stench of that dragon.

"He smelled awful." Tore gasped.

"Smells. He's still out there." Sif pointed over her shoulder.

Tore squirmed to find a comfortable position for he leg, and because she was nervous in the presence of a goddess.

"You are wondering why I am here?" Sif asked Tore.

"Yes, but I didn't think it was for me to ask." Tore lowered her eyes humbly.

"You may ask me anything. You are ever loyal. Few mortals have honored the gods as loyally as you have done me all of your life...however short it has been." Sif smiled warmly.

Tore smiled gratefully. "Why did you save me?"

"Which time?" Sif laughed.

"Any of them!" Tore said seriously.

"I like you." Sif said simply.

"So, if you didn't like me, I'd be dragon food?" Tore asked slowly.

"If I didn't like you, you'd be dead in that chest your brother stuffed you into." Sif leaned forward balancing her upper body on her knees, poking the fire.

"Oh." Tore said knowingly.

"But, you're not dead. You're here and you're alive. Most mortals would want me to ask other gods to heal your wound." Sif seemed puzzled that Tore didn't ask for such a favor.

"Most mortals would, but that would dishonor the blessings that you have already given me. The cut is a small price to pay for your gifts." Tore said sounding much older than her young years.

"You are very wise. Your father taught you well." Sif nodded approvingly.

"There is one thing I would ask." Tore said softly.

Sif wore a look of anticipation.

"Are my brothers and father well?" Tore said slowly.

"They are well." Sif smiled, secretly amazed at this girl who graciously thought of others and not herself.

Sif looked into the pot sitting near the fire. "Do you have tea?"

Tore's eyes opened wide. She didn't know that gods or goddesses cared to consume mortal foods.

"Are you so shocked that I drink tea? Did I not kill a dragon? Is drinking tea much harder?" Sif laughed.

Tore smiled. "Yes, I have tea." She quickly picked up her pot, knowing she'd have to struggle out of the cave to get snow.

Sif seemed to be one step ahead of her and casually lifted her hand in a slow wave. Snow appeared in the pot right before Tore's eyes.

Tore stared wide-eyed once again.

"Thought I'd make you walk?" Sif smiled and leaned against the cave wall again.

Tore waited until the water boiled and then poured it over the leaves in her cup, which she gave to Sif, and in the other pot she sipped from herself.

Sif drank the tea slowly almost as if she had never tasted it before.

"Have you ever had tea before?" Tore asked between sips.

"No." Sif savored each drink, tasting the robust flavor of the leaves.

"Be careful not to drink the sludge at the bottom. It's horribly bitter." Tore pointed to the dregs at the bottom of her own pot.

Sif peered into her cup and stopped drinking when she came to the murky mud at the bottom.

"Your tea is good, but this is not why I am here." Sif put the cup down on the rock near the fire.

"It is a serious reason?" Tore asked a bit frightened.

"It is." Sif toyed with her pin.

"Does it have to do with the dragon?" Tore asked fearfully.

"That and much more; but, I do not wish to have you guess a riddle. I will tell you everything…and you must listen to every word carefully." Sif admonished.

Tore nodded her head furiously to show Sif that she understood the importance of her visit.

Sif took a deep breath, which made her seem so human to Tore who often wondered about the gods, goddesses, and their habits.

"I have bad news." Sif began. "Your sword…"Sif pointed towards Tore's new found sword that lay beside her sleeping fur near the fire. "It has brought you some trouble."

"Trouble?" Tore didn't understand what Sif meant; her sword hadn't brought her any trouble, not yet anyway.

"The clearing you entered was a burial site of a great warrior." Sif stroked the scabbard absently.

"But there was no mound or markings whatsoever." Tore frowned.

"The sword was the marker." Sif said simply. "And, when you took the sword from its resting place you defiled the grave of the warrior Rognvald the Victorious."

Tore knew this was not good. "I should put the sword and scabbard back then?"

"No. It is far beyond that now." Sif sighed.

"I don't understand." Tore was puzzled.

"Rognvald the Victorious was his favorite warrior." Sif said slowly. Suddenly it all made sense to Tore. She had pissed off the God of Justice.

"Did Tyr send the dragon?" Tore nearly whispered.

"Yes." Sif nodded. "Tyr buried Rognvald with his own two hands."

"Buried by a God?" Tore said in disbelief. "He must have loved him so."

"Very much so." Sif said sadly. "It was a great blow when Rognvald was slain. Tyr even tried to blow the life back into him, but even that was out of a god's hands."

"Tyr couldn't give Rognvald his life back?" Tore's eyes were wide with amazement. She had always believed that the gods could do anything.

"It was not to be. Even a god cannot change a man's fate." Sif continued. "When you disturbed Rognvald's burial place, Tyr grew angry and sent the White dragon to kill you. Tyr felt that justice would be served if death visited you, a girl, who dared to violate the sacred burial of a great warrior."

"I didn't know!" Tore wondered how the God of Justice could punish her for ignorance. She wouldn't have taken the sword if she had known it was a burial marker.

"Tyr is too angry to listen to reason." Sif smirked.

"Then Tyr is not very just!" Tore snapped.

"Sssh, girl!" Sif glanced over her shoulder towards the entrance of the cave as if she expected Tyr to be standing there observing this whole conversation. "Watch your tongue! What if he hears you? He is already angry with you, and the wrath of a god is not a light thing."

Tore hung her head shamed. "I am sorry."

Sif smiled. "There is more."

Tore looked back up into Sif's kind and beautiful face. "Tyr wanted you dead. When I killed the dragon he was angered even more." Sif sighed.

"So, is he still going to kill me?" Tore felt her heart began to pound more viciously than before.

"It depends." Sif smiled. "I made a bargain with Tyr."

"A bargain? What kind of a bargain?" Tore suddenly realized that this bargain would involve some sort of action on her part. Bargains with gods always did, and she knew that even if Sif liked her as much as she claimed she did, no god or goddess was willing to shoulder the responsibility for the outcome of a bargain without the mortal doing his part. Usually, the god failed to include the mortal in the decision making process as well.

Sif leaned forward, her face glistening in the firelight.

"Tyr wanted you dead. I told him that you did not deserve death, that you were a loyal and worthy mortal. Tyr asked if you prayed to him. I told him that you prayed to me." Sif smiled reassured. "But, then Tyr laughed at me and asked why he should care that a mortal girl was so devoted to me and not him. He had a point."

Sif pulled at her dress and shifted her weight onto her other buttock. "I asked Tyr if there was anything you could do to atone for your violation of Rognvald's burial site." Tore leaned closer to the fire to more clearly see Sif's face.

"At first, Tyr laughed and mocked me, calling me a foolish woman, comparing me to mortal women; but, I took offense to this and drew my sword. Tyr stopped laughing." Sif laughed now, "I don't know if it was fighting me he was afraid of, or fighting me and then my husband because he fought me in the first place. Thor can be very protective even though he need not be." Sif smiled.

Tore found this revelation touching, the gods were very similar to mortal men and women in their feelings for one another.

"At any rate, Tyr grew more serious when he saw that I was determined to bargain for your life. That is when he proposed the agreement." Sif's face had a serious expression.

"This agreement involves action on my part? To atone for my ignorance?" Tore asked worriedly.

"Tyr doesn't care about your ignorance. He only cares about Rognvald the Victorious' grave being defiled." Sif pointed at the sword again.

"The agreement was simple." Sif smoothed her apron. "You must prove yourself worthy of Rognvald the Victorious' sword. If you do so, you will live. If you fail to demonstrate your worthiness, you will die." "How will I prove this worthiness?" Tore was puzzled. "In battle." Sif answered shortly.

Tore's eyes bulged and her mouth dropped open. "In battle? But, I'm a woman!"

"And, yet, you are dressed in man's clothing." Sif smiled and jabbed at Tore's good leg.

"Then men will believe me? That I'm a man, I mean?" Tore stammered.

"They will." Sif reassured Tore.

"But, battle? How, I mean, when? Will you help me?" Tore found all of this new information mind numbing. She had so many questions that she wished Sif would answer for her. Sif laughed. "How like a woman to ask so many questions!"

Tore blinked hard, and swallowed the next question that had been hovering on her tongue waiting to come out.

"I can't tell you anymore. To help you too much would dishonor my part of the bargain. I have given my word that you are worthy of Rognvald's sword, woman or no. It is up to you to not make a liar out of me." Sif laughed.

"If I prove myself worthy, in battle," Tore found that those words came slowly for her, "Then, Tyr will forgive all and allow me to live out the rest of my days free of his vengeance?"

"Yes. All will be atoned for and the sword will be yours. Until then, consider the weapon a loan from Tyr." Sif started to stand up.

"That's it? I mean you're going now?" Tore started up after Sif, but pain jolted her memory back to the current state of her health and she slumped back into the reclining position she had been in earlier.

"I will be with you, Tore. I'm not deserting you, if that's what you fear. For now, I have other things to attend to." Sif walked towards the mouth of the cave. "Do you have other wounded girls resting in caves that need your attention?" Tore laughed.

Sif turned and faced Tore again, and laughed heartily. "Your humor will help you survive, Tore Nordahldatr." "Will I know the way to the shire?" Tore asked concerned.

"Rest here for a week. I have brought fresh meat and wine." Tore grew aware of a mound of animal carcasses and a leather wineskin that she had somehow not seen earlier during their visit. "After a week's time, continue on your journey. I will guide you to the next shire by that nightfall. After that, your destiny is in your own hands." Sif smiled and stepped outside in the snow. "Thank you!" Tore called towards the shimmering figure of her loyal goddess, as Sif walked off through the woods and into the realm of the gods.

Tore leaned her head back onto her sleeping fur. She had sat and shared tea with a goddess, her goddess, her Sif. What would father have said? Tore smiled thinking about her father.

One week. Tore had one week to gain her strength back before setting out on her venture. Sif had said that her destiny rested in her own hands. Tore wasn't so sure of that. She wished Sif would have told her what that destiny would be, but then again, maybe the gods didn't always know.

Tore closed her eyes and concentrated on the warming, blanket of heat that penetrated her skin and lulled her off to sleep.

Chapter 7

A week had passed since Tore's encounter with Sif. Her leg was healing nicely, though it still had far to go before it would be whole again. Tore thought that if she could find lodgings in the next shire, she could hole up for awhile until her leg was totally healed.

Tore packed her belongings carefully. It had been nice to stay somewhere safe for more than one night. She felt rested and confident that she was up to the bargain that Sif and Tyr had concocted; besides, she wasn't going to let Sif down. If Sif had trusted and believed in her this much, the least she could do was give her all to prove she was worthy of Sif's devotion...and of Rognvald the Victorious' sword.

Tore strapped the sword in its scabbard around her middle, and slung her bag over her shoulder. She had smoked some of the animal meat that Sif had given to her, and eaten quite a lot of it. It had been good to taste fresh meat again; and, it had done her body good. The wineskin was empty. It had been good wine.

Tore kicked the fire into ashes, and then emerged from her cave. She felt renewed and a new vigor was stirring inside of her urging her on to her destiny. Whatever that destiny happened to be.

Tore started walking aware of Sif's guiding tug. She walked for a few hours easily for the weather was good, and the winds blew lightly if not at all.

Soon, Tore could see the waves of the great Swan Road coiling themselves around the jagged rocks that framed the fjord. She walked downhill, to the shore. A huge, unfinished ship stood on its braces farther up the beach. Winter must have taken her builders off guard. There was about four feet of snow that had drifted into the massive ship, and timber and building supplies were stacked neatly under a large piece of leather. Wouldn't be too long until spring came again, and the men could finish this great boat.

Tore had never stood this close to a longship before. It was massive. It's high sloping sides, even unfinished, were far out of her reach. This ship was well built. Each nail was perfectly cast, not misshapen like some cheaper nails she had seen before. This ship must belong to a wealthy man.

From where she stood, she could see the rooftops of the shire peering at her from over a wooden fortress type wall. Her father had told her that people living near the coast had taken to building large fortified walls around their shires in order to protect them from seafaring pirates...or other Vikings from Dane land and the likes.

Tore trudged up the beach, past the chunks of ice that had formed here and there, and towards the town's gate. It was open and bustling with merchants and traders of all types.

This was a large shire. It would be easy to blend in and get lost in this shire. Not like her home, where everyone knew everyone else. She wondered if there was a principal family here, or did everyone just do their own thing. Surely, there must be a Jarl in this shire.

Tore wandered into the walls of the shire. She became acutely aware of the smell of smoked herring, and came to a street vendor who was hocking steaming, smoked herring wrapped around a stick.

Tore produced a piece of silver and the merchant all too happily snatched it up, and shoved two pieces of herring towards her on their own sticks.

Tore unwrapped the fish that was coiled around the wood, tossed the stick on the ground, and hungrily devoured the food.

She was amazed by all of the sights. Her father and Ulf had done their best to describe all of these activities to her, but words could not describe all that she witnessed. There were foreign traders whose skin was the color of bronze, some darker. There were men with strange rolls of rag tied around their heads. Men and women with strange markings and tattoos on their bodies. All of the merchants sold or traded from tents, and small wood stalls. There were plates, and pots and pans of every design. There was glass and jewelry of all colors and shapes and textures. There were fabrics, and furs...so many things all crammed into this merchant area of the shire.

All around her people crushed in, great crowds of people all curious to see what they could bring home with them. Living here must be a marvelous thing.

Tore walked up onto a scene that she didn't quite know what to make of it. About twelve men were gathered around a platform of some sort. On it was a beautiful young girl with dark long hair. She was a little plump, and her eyes were wet from crying. She stood there so quiet.

Tore pushed her way to the side of the group so she could see what was going on. Apparently, this was a slave girl brought back from some shore raid for sale. The man on the platform had said some foreign word, indicating that her people were of some tribe or family called 'Celts'. It had an odd sound to it, and Tore mentally said it again and again.

The men were laughing, and since Tore had been lost in thought she missed the joke. She laughed anyway, so as not to stand out in the group. So far, no one seemed interested in her, which meant that none questioned her gender in this group.

The man on the platform lifted the girl's dress over her head exposing her bare breasts and dark mound to the eyes of the men. Tore felt a pang of pity for the girl, and also felt her own face grow red with embarrassment. She hoped none of the men noticed. They didn't. They were too enamored with seeing the poor girl stripped naked in public.

What came next was of even a bigger shock to Tore. The man on the platform dropped his pants to reveal a massively engorged, bobbing penis, with which he grasped and tugged on much to the glee of the audience. He grasped the girl by the shoulders and jerkingly pushed her to the bare wood below them. Roughly, he parted her legs and thrust his hideously huge organ into her, pumping and grinding in a noisy frenzy. The men made obscene gestures and a few not so discreet soldiers among them, grasped at their own rock hard members and yanked away, not peeling their eyes from the slave seller and the poor girl who stared up at the sky as if she wanted to die.

The man pulled his dripping shaft from her, and smiled a toothless grin. The other men clutched hands of gold and waved their bids wildly in the air. The slave seller smiled, and pointed excitedly towards one taller man in the back of the group. The man came forward amidst the jabs and heckling of the more unfortunate bidders, and grasped the girl by the arm. The slave seller took his gold, and tossed the girl her roughly woven shift. The man led her off into the crowd. Tonight, she would live the whole nightmare over again in a different man's bed.

Tore sighed. Poor girl. She wondered what sort of people these 'Celts' were to let one of their daughters go off alone into this land. Didn't they fight for the ones they loved? Tore thought these places far across the whale road must be horrible lands.

Tore continued on in her search for a lodging house. Surely, with this many merchants and traders there had to be some type of an inn around. Sure enough, at almost the same instant she thought her thought, she turned the corner to face a large wood structure that had rooms to rent.

Tore negotiated with the keeper on a price and when satisfied that she had bargained well, the keeper showed her to the room.

It was simple. A small cot and a flat-topped iron studded chest were the only furnishings in the room. There was no window, and the door barred from the inside; which, after witnessing the event she had seen in the slave seller's market, came as a welcome addition to the door.

Tore sat down on the edge of the rope-strung cot. It was better than the floor of a cave, but she didn't feel quite as comfortable being here among these odd people and so many foreigners.

Tore had her story down pat, and decided to pass herself off as a scop, or a gleeman as some wished to label the local story teller. Everyone loved a good story, and Tore knew all of the lore by heart. She had often entertained the children and grown-ups alike with her renditions of the famous battle tales of the gods, and the friendlier versions of creation and such. She should be able to earn some bread and mead, and occasionally some silver telling a tale or two.

Tore poured some oil into the light pot that rested on the chest. She trimmed the wick with her dirk, and lit it. The room was almost too dark to see her own hand without it. Tore laughed, the keeper probably kept it this dark so the tenants couldn't see the size of the rats that they shared their beds with!

Tore felt that the thought of sleeping sounded comforting. She had had an exhausting and sometimes troubling day exploring the boundaries of her new world; and there would be so much more to do tomorrow. Tore checked her leg and rebandaged it with the remaining strips of cloth left from the original shirt she had ripped up. Tomorrow she would have to look for a cloth dealer and get some fresh cloth to bind her wound in; but, for now, she would sleep.

When Tore woke the next morning she could hear the loud clangs and bangs of traveling peddlers and the normal noise from the street. The market place was already abuzz with people, and Tore didn't need a window to know that. The walls in this lodge were so thin she could practically hear the words in people's passing conversations. Tore felt a sense of renewal, of hope. For the first time in a long time, she felt like there was hope for her and hope for her existence.

The first thing she needed to do was to somehow establish herself in the community around her...perhaps a friend. She didn't know anyone outside of her own shire, or family for that matter. Hablok Bloodaxe had been to her shire a few times, but women were usually hurried off like they were some type of embarrassing family secret or something. For Tore, simply meeting a new person would be a difficult task. She would use her stories to gain acceptance from the people around her. If she stayed in the marketplace, most of these people would be just passing through. They wouldn't be related to the Jarl who lived in a more secluded area of the shire with his large family. The marketplace had built up around this family due to the port and the wealth available to traveling merchants. Tore had to work her way into the inner circle, into the Jarl's world. She needed a family until Ulf came home. More importantly, she had to find a way to get the training she needed to become a warrior. Without a family, she would have a hard time doing this. If she was to fight in battle, she must have a side to be on first!

Tore knew that all of this would fall into place in time. It better had, or else Tyr would send some other surprise for her. but, if that happened she would be dead. There would be no more chances. This was her only chance.

Tore dressed herself and fastened her traveler's cup onto her belt along with her sword and scabbard. This cup had been her father's...his kuksa. It was finely carved from birch and it had a double-fingered handle to make drinking easier. She rubbed her hand over it for reassurance. It would come in handy to take the coins people would give to her for her stories.

Tore left her room and went to the dining area in the great hall. She paid for some gruel with a bronze coin, and ate it hungrily. It paled in comparison to the smoked herring she had bought yesterday in the marketplace, but it would do for breakfast. At least, it filled that gnawing hole in her belly.

Tore thanked the cook and went out into the cold street. A little snow had settled from the night, but mostly the dirty, packed snow from before filled the shire. There was a steady breeze coming in form the sea, and people laughed loudly around her. Women, with children tugging at their aprons, were shopping for fruits and house wares, men were trading furs for more important items like spades and picks and a knife or two. All around her were sights and people of the like she had never seen before. She wondered at what point would she stop being so amazed; and hoped that her amazement was not so obvious to those around her. Tore looked for an established scop in the marketplace, but found none.

She wondered how one goes about setting themselves up as the local scop. She decided to find a place where people seemed to be congregated, eating or talking, or simply mulling about, and then just start telling stories in a loud expressionate voice. Hopefully, people would gather to hear the tale.

Tore found a spot near a large boulder that looked as if it was once used for chaining prisoners or slaves, but the chains were old and rusty from lack of use. Tore climbed atop the boulder and perched herself where she would be visible to those who passed by. She put her cup down at her feet and searched her brain for a good tale to tell.

Tore stood tall an cried out in the lowest, loudest voice she could muster, "Come all and gather round me as I have a story to tell about the great goddess Frigga, her husband, the god of all things, Odin, and their beautiful son, Balder."

Tore saw a few faces turn her direction. A few mothers handed their children a coin or two and shoved them in her direction. A few older men hobbled over to the boulder and leaned on canes, or sat down on the rocks and logs that were scattered about.

Tore took on a more animated expression and continued. "The son of Odin, Balder, was pure and innocent. In all ways was he the representation of beauty. All of the gods loved him and lavished him with praises and attention. but none loved Balder more than his mother, Frigga."

Tore kept herself from smiling as she noticed the growing group that was gathering around the base of her stone. Many children were there, but adults too were coming. These people were in sore need of a good story. Good, Tore thought, because she had a lot of stories to tell!

Tore cleared her throat, and sucked in a cleansing breath of cold air. "Frigga loved her son so much, that she came up with a plan."

She could see a few people leaning in closer to hear her more clearly. She continued, "Frigga wanted to make sure that no ill ever befell her beloved son. So, she came up with a plan to protect him always."

"Frigga went to each thing on earth and required each thing to swear an oath that it would never harm her son in anyway. Balder was so beautiful and flawless that swearing this oath was not a hard thing to do. Everything and everyone loved Balder for he was so good and pure."

Someone in the crowd sneezed and coughed. It was cold, but the story was good…so they stayed. Tore surveyed the expressions on the faces around her and went on with her story, "Frigga finally believed that every thing had sworn the oath. So, she held a lavish banquet for all of the Gods in Balder's honor. In the midst of the banquet, Frigga had Balder stand in the center of the room so that every God and Goddess could throw things at Balder and show that nothing could harm him."

Tore shifted her weight and lowered her tone. "But, Alas! Frigga did not know that Mistletoe had refused to swear the oath; but, Loki, that troublesome traitor knew and he had a plan too!"

Soft murmurings rippled throughout the crowd. Tore wore an expression of sadness as she continued her story, the crowd now hanging on her every word. She was amazed how few people had heard this tale of long ago. "Loki loved to stir up trouble. Loki loved to hate. Loki knew of Mistletoe's refusal to swear the oath that Frigga had demanded from all things. He had gathered up a bundle of mistletoe and crept his way into the hall where the banquet was being held. He knew he could not stay long, for he would be recognized and ousted. For no one like Loki and the trouble he caused."

Tore gestured dramatically and spoke loud and clear so all could hear the conclusion of her tale." Loki spotted Blind Hoder. He made his way through the crowd and up to Blind Hoder's side. He gave Blind Hoder the bundle of mistletoe and asked Hoder to throw it at Balder. Loki then slithered out as quickly as he could."

"Blind Hoder thought it all part of the festivities and he happily threw the bundle at Balder." Tore paused long enough to cause her audience to grow a bit antsy, and then she leaned in closer and lowered her voice sadly.

"Balder died instantly. He was escorted into Hel...separated forever from the mother and father and all things that loved him so." Tore acted sad as if that was the end of the story, but then she raised her chin and continued. She could hear the crowd growing quiet again.

"But, sadly, this is not the end of my tale...The Gods were angered and saddened by the loss of their beloved Balder and they went to Hel and demanded the return of Frigga and Odin's son; but, Hel was not so accommodating."

Tore shook her head emphasizing the shame of it all and kept on. "Hel agreed to release Balder on one condition. She demanded a single tear from every living thing on Earth. Then and only then would she allow Balder to leave."

The crowd seemed happy. Tore could see the visible anticipation in their faces and felt encouraged. "Every thing loved Balder so the Gods thought that this was an easy demand to meet...But, Alas! Loki was not finished with his troublesome ways yet! He had yet another act of mischief up his sleeve. Loki disguised himself as a Giantess. When it came time for her tear to be collected, Loki, pretending to be the Giantess, refused to cry. Without that single tear, Hel would not release Balder. Still Loki refused to cry."

Tore saw the worried looks on the people around her. "The gods were angry. Because of this one Giantess (for they did not know that it was really Loki) their beloved Balder would have to remain forever in the clutches of Hel. They were furious. Disasters plagued the earth. Fire ripped over the world and devoured the human race…and Balder, the lovely, pure and innocent Balder, remained forever a prisoner in the palace of Niflheim in the depths of Hades with Hel."

Tore saw a tear streak the red face of a young girl near her. The old people hovered near to each other exchanging whispers and sad nods. Tore saw that she had evoked powerful emotions in the hearts of her audience. She had told a good story.

People put coins in her wood cup as they left to go about their business. One person sat down a plate of food and a cup of hot tea. Tore thought this person was very polite. She hungrily ate the food, and the steaming tea warmed her from the inside out. She was very appreciative of the meal.

Tore gathered her coins and put them in her purse, which was attached to her belt. Sensing a shadow falling over her, she turned and looked up into the face of a very handsome man about Ulf's age. His features were striking, riveting. Then Tore remembered all to suddenly, that she had to be a man, not the woman who would seduce such a fine specimen of a man. She nodded her head in manly fashion, and went on dropping the coins into her purse.

He was quiet. He stood there and watched her for a minute before speaking. "That was a powerful tale." He said shortly.

Tore nodded again, not sure of what to make of his friendly gesture.

"I have oft heard of Loki and his evil ways, but never of this Balder you speak of." The man said slowly.

"Balder is only one of many Gods." Tore tied her purse securely and pushed it into the folds of her shirt.

"Do you know more about our gods?" The man asked excitedly.

"Yes. I know many tales. I have heard and learned them since I was a little…" Tore paused, catching herself and then continued, "Boy at my father's knee. Old warriors tell many tales."

"Your people must share more than mine do. We hear only a little about the gods. Most of those tales only have to do with battle." The man said softly.

"And there is something wrong with battle?" Tore raised her eyebrow.

"Certainly not!" The man said loudly.

"Good then!" Tore replied.

"Do you have a name, gleeman?" The man asked her.

"I am Eirik Graafell. Some call me Eirik the Silent." Tore pointed at her chest as she introduced herself. Her new self that was.

"The man smiled a crooked smile. "You are not so silent."

Tore laughed.

"I am Brock Thorvaldsson. My father, Thorvald is the Jarl in these parts." The now identified man said nodding at Tore.

"You are very important then?" Tore asked.

"Not so important. I am one of many sons." Brock shrugged his shoulders.

"Every man should feel important." Tore responded.

Brock laughed. "You come from strange people!"

"I come from good Norse stock such as yourself. My people must be more verbal than your kin." Tore put her hands on her hips like she had seen her father do plenty of times while speaking to other men.

"Then why is it you are called Eirik the Silent?" Brock laughed.

"It is because of my voice. I do not care to speak often, for my kin mock my voice." Tore said quietly.

"My father would not care about your voice! What good is a voice in battle? Only a man's skill in combat matters in battle. I believe your kin tell too many stories and fight little!" Brock laughed and slapped Tore on the back hard. She fought to keep her balance.

"My people are warriors too." Tore said with a biting edge to her voice, which signified that she took offense by this unintentional insult. One should never jest about the fighting capabilities of another's kin.

Brock caught the sting and quickly said, "Of course they are. Why else would they have such knowledge concerning our gods? I am sure your kin are great warriors."

Tore nodded, acknowledging this informal type of apology.

"Where are your kin?" Brock asked.

"Dead. They are all dead. That is why I have made my way to this shire to start a new life for myself." Tore said coldly.

"So, you are alone then? This must be hard. I see that you are about my age in years. Do you not long for the companionship a warm hearth brings with kin gathered around it?" Brock said sadly.

"Yes. But, my kin are not like Balder. They do not have gods asking for their return." Tore brought the conversation back to her former story.

Brock smiled his crooked smile again. "I must go now. Maybe I will hear you tell another tale sometime?"

"Maybe." Tore nodded and watched Brock turn and leave.

Tore had things to purchase and went towards the market thinking about Brock and his strange gesture of friendship towards a young man he did not know. Tore returned to her room still dwelling on the odd feelings that this Brock Thorvaldsson had evoked within her. Such a stirring he caused in the pit of her stomach! Such pounding he caused her heart! Tore was saddened. He could never know her secret. Never know at all. No one could know what hid beneath these clothes and lurked inside this brain of hers. No one. Not ever. Her life depended on her ability to keep a secret; and, she had never revealed a secret before. A little ting like a pounding heart wasn't going to make her tell all now.

Tore told stories for the next few days. Always at the same spot, so that people began to recognize the large stone as the story spot and would wait around hoping to hear the next tale. Tore would look out into the faces of the audience. Sometimes she would see Brock. Other times she would strain and look for him, but he would not be there.

On the days that he was there he would often stop by to talk with her after her story was over. He liked her tales. He would go home, he often told her, and tell his father the tale he heard in the market. At first, according to Brock, his father had berated him for hanging about leisurely in the streets of the market. People would think he had nothing worthwhile to do! Then as the days passed, Old Thorvald himself became enthralled with the stories that Brock would retell around the night fire. Brock would always insist that he couldn't tell the tales half as well as Eirik. Tore grew used to hearing her new name, and each time she heard it spoken, she began to think of herself more and more as Eirik Graafell, or Eirik the Silent. It became more natural for her each day that she had to keep this charade. Yet, she longed for the day that she could be Tore again. Plain old Tore. She could be herself and not have to worry about how she acted, or what she said anymore. She wouldn't have to constantly fear that someone was growing suspicious of her true gender. She could just be Tore. Tore Nordahldatr. That's who she longed to be. Then she would remember Ulf, count the days, and snap back into whatever conversation she had mentally left to pursue her usual daydreams.

Brock seemed to enjoy her company. A few times they had shared a meal together, or a drink of mead. Brock always left her silver instead of the bronze coins that most people tossed into her cup. She knew that he wanted to be friends. He liked being with her. Tore would often wonder if Brock sensed something, but then she would push that out of her mind. Of course Brock suspected nothing…and any man that would entertain thoughts of affection or attraction towards another man, well that was unthinkable. So, if Brock sensed anything at all, he would shake it off, quite confused. Tore could be sure of that.

No, she was only friends with Brock. That was all she would ever be, but she allowed herself to dream of Ulf's return and of her confession to Brock of her true identity. That was another thing she would never be able o do. If Brock were ever to find out her true gender, it would be an outrage to him and all the men she had encountered. A woman masquerading as a man! Unthinkable! Tore knew she could only be friends with Brock Thorvaldsson, but when she went to sleep at night...the thoughts she entertained were a far cry from the actions of friends!

Chapter 8

The weather was starting to improve. It was evident that spring was near. Ice melted a little more, people were out and about a little more. In general, the whole land seemed to be more alive than before. All of these things were clear signs that spring was just around the corner.

Tore, or Eirik as she had grown used to being called, was half way through a story when she spotted Brock looming behind the crowd that was gathered before her. News of her story-telling talent had traveled far and all sorts of people were eager to hear, in person, a story from the gleeman, Eirik the Silent Graafell. Most people felt it odd that a gleeman would also be known as someone or another the silent, but, once they heard Tore's girlish voice, understanding spread across their face. Usually there were a few elbow jabbings from newcomers, or the expected snickering just after she began to speak...but, soon all were mesmerized by her wonderfully woven tales and they forgot the strangeness of this "man's" voice.

Brock was standing behind a particularly bedraggled man. Tore nodded in his direction. She wanted to smile, but she had to constantly remind herself that men didn't go around exchanging smiles all that much...so, she learned to nod her acknowledgment instead.

Brock had heard this story before. Not with the crowd, but one night while they had been drinking mead. He had asked her to tell him a story, so she did. It was also handy to use stories to cover for her lack of discussion concerning her own family. The less she had to make up concerning that issue, the less there would be to get trapped in if she slipped up a lie.

She finished her story and nodded at the people as they expressed their likes and dislikes, all the while watching them toss bronze coins into her wood traveling cup. Once in awhile someone would toss her a silver coin, but Tore knew that usually if there was silver in her cup then Brock Thorvaldsson was somewhere in the crowd. Brock waited for her audience to clear away before approaching her.

He nodded at her in a type of silent greeting. She nodded back.

"I like that story." Brock said as Tore sat on a log and counted her coins.

"Did you like it better the first time or this time?" Tore asked.

"Were they different?" Brock raised an eyebrow. "Only slightly. Sometimes I see the audience growing restless so I spruce things up a bit." Tore laughed. Brock made a disapproving face. "You shouldn't change the stories."

"Oh, I don't change the essence of the story. I just add more details and try to make it more exciting. Or, well, like today...there were more women in the crowd, so I tried to add more about women and the duties of a woman. If there had been more men, then I would have left the story how it is." Tore tied up her purse and tied it to her belt.

"Women have such short attention spans." Brock said matter of factly. "It is good that you are able to keep them entertained too."

Tore, feeling her face grow hot with anger, looked down at the ground. Somewhere she heard Arne and Ubbe laughing at her for having to control herself in the midst of that last comment.

Brock asked if she had eaten yet, she hadn't. So, they went over to a stall that was serving herring and some form of thin gravy. Sitting on a log together, they began discussing a new sword that they had each seen in the market the day before.

"Those other swords are fine examples of craftsmanship; but none compare to the sword you wear at your side." Brock pointed to Tore's sword.

"Yes. Mine is a fine sword. It carries an expensive price though." Tore said, fondly caressing the scabbard. If only Brock knew the price this sword carried!

"I wish I had a sword half as fine as that one." Brock pointed again. "Mine is a good solid sword, but nothing compared to yours."

"It isn't the sword that makes the difference anyway, Brock. It's the man behind the sword that fights the battle." Tore echoed her own father's words.

"You must have had great teachers to be able to wield such a sword. My arms are twice as big as yours, yet you carry a sword made for a giant!" Brock shook his head.

"I have no dealings with giants." Tore said suddenly. It was a known fact that all Gods and Goddesses hated giants. She wasn't going to leave any doubt in Tyr's mind that she too hated giants.

"Of course not." Brock said quickly.

"Nor do I. I only meant the size of the sword...oh, never mind." Tore laughed.

"Not important." Brock laughed too. "If only you were my brother. We think so much alike."

"Have you been having quarrels with your brothers again?" Tore asked.

"Eirik, all I have is quarrels with my brothers. The latest one has to do with you. It seems that they are jealous of our friendship." Brock picked at a frayed seam in his pants.

"What does your father think of your friendship with an orphaned gleeman?" Tore laughed.

"He thinks it's good that I create comrades so easily. He says it's always good to have a friend to watch your back." Brock laughed heartily.

"Your father is a wise man!" Tore licked the fish oil from her fingers.

"I suppose that's why he's Jarl." Brock kicked at the ground in an attempt to get something, dung of some type, off of his boot.

Tore and Brock sat there for a little while watching people come and go.

"Father was interested in having you come to dinner one night in the great hall, and tell us a story." Brock said as if he suddenly remembered.

"I would like that." Tore said. "It would be nice to share dinner with a family again."

"Father thinks the women would like it. Most of them don't get out too much. Not that they aren't allowed. They just have so much to do." Brock was still kicking at the ground. Tore saw a stick nearby on the ground and picked it up. She handed it to Brock, who in turn began digging at the shit on his boot.

"Most men say that women don't do anything at home." Tore said, and then laughingly added, "Except gossip and think of ways to hassle their husbands." Brock laughed. "Thank the gods I have no such wife!" Tore laughed too. "Thank the gods I have no wife at all!" Tore had to consciously keep herself from smiling. She was amazed at how easily that had rolled from her tongue. She was beginning to think like a man now.

Brock seemed relieved when he finally managed to dig all of the shit from his boot. He was a neat dresser and was obviously agitated when anything concerning his appearance was less than perfect.

Tore wondered if Brock knew when she was supposed to come to dinner. She would make sure she had an especially good story lined up for this event. She wanted to do her best to impress the Jarl. She needed to be battle trained, and this was the man who would supply that need. She had to do her best to get under his skin. It would have been a lot easier to do if she could use her womanly charms; but the fact of the matter had always been that most men found her to bold and outspoken for a woman.

The sky was starting to darken. Brock stood up and Tore did the same.

"I had better be heading home now. I will talk to father more about your coming. I am sure he will be anxious to hear your tales soon. He said that when he was younger there were more gleemen about then. Now, he says, there are few who know the stories of our gods. He looks forward to your visit." Brock nodded towards her.

Tore nodded back. "I hope your fire is good tonight."

Brock nodded one last time and left.

Tore stood there watching him go. She wanted to cry out after him. Don't leave! Stay here with me! Brock had awakened within her feelings that she had only dreamed about and heard other women talk about. She had thoughts about him that she had never entertained about any other man ever before in her life. She suddenly was aware of the coldness in her bed; of the emptiness she felt each night when she crawled between lonely furs, and rose to a cold room. How she wanted to feel him in her arms, pressed against her flesh. She wanted to keep him warm and happy...but how could she ever do that? She was a man to him. A brother, just like he had said. Nothing more.

Tore sighed and went back to her rooms in the lodge house. She had decided to move to a room with its own fireplace. The innkeeper had said it would cost her more, but what did she care. She had money enough to afford a fireplace of her own. At least this way she wouldn't be so cold all of the time.

Tore packed up her stuff and followed the innkeeper to her new lodgings. This room wasn't much bigger than the one she had been occupying, but as she had said, it did have a fireplace. The innkeeper quoted her the price for firewood per day, dumped an armful in the wood box and left.

Tore laid out her fur on the rope-strung cot and put her belongings in a chest at the foot of the cot. She hung her sword and scabbard on a peg in the wall, and hung her clothes up beside her weapons.

She had brought a bucket of water up with her to try to wash herself. It had been days since she had last bathed. She had been afraid to do so for fear of discovery. She dipped her rag into the cold water and sponged at herself before the fire. Here she was who she really was. A woman. She felt like she was protecting some horrible secret. Tore laughed. If only everyone knew the truth! How foolish they would all feel! And that, is precisely why they can't ever find out, Tore thought to herself.

She wrung out the rag and hung it before the fire to dry out. She felt better now that she was clean. She used the remaining water to clean all but one set of her clothes with and spread them out on a bench that she had dragged before the fireplace to dry.

Tore sat down on the bed and wrapped a fur around her tightly. She was lonely. This little, dark room had no character, and did little to stir her imagination. She leaned over and lit the wick in the whale oil lamp on the crude little table beside her cot. She needed to take up some type of man hobby to do in her spare time. She hadn't had this much time for so long. At home, there had always been chores or dinner to do...or favors for a mother with a bunch of noisy children. Here, there was only herself. Food was bought already prepared. Dishes were returned to the innkeeper's wife in the center of the hall. There was so little for her to do once she came in from telling her tales outside.

She needed a family. A place to belong again. Somewhere where she had duties and functions that made her feel vital again. Like she was needed and loved. Here, she was just here. There was nothing to do, and even if there had been something to do, there was no one to appreciate it. She was alone. It was moments like these that made her all the more aware of how she ached for companionship...ached for love. Ached for Brock.

Tore leaned back against the rough wood wall and pulled her legs up close to her body. She looked down at herself, just a shapeless form of fur and a head sticking out at the top. She laughed.

"Tore what are you going to do with yourself now?" She whispered to herself.

Tore tossed another log on the fire and curled up on her cot. It seemed she went to bed earlier than she did at home, and feeling more tired even though she had actually done less. She determined that the stress and strain of the secret she kept and of the constant feeling of pervading loneliness wrecked far more havoc on her spirit and body, than her daily chores used to. She never thought she would think this, but she would rather be a woman any day, than the man she had to pretend to be.

Tore went to sleep thinking of her brothers, her father, and of Brock. She might not be able to have him in life, but in her dreams she had no secrets to hide.

When day came again, Tore found herself going through the motions of life without any real feelings at all. She told her stories as best as she could, trying not to reveal the depression she was feeling. As far as she could tell everyone was satisfied with her tales and her personal feelings hadn't affected her story telling abilities.

A couple of days passed, and Brock hadn't shown up at any of her tellings, or to talk with her afterwards. Tore began to feel isolated from the world. She had felt like she had a friend with Brock, someone to count on and lean on, and not be so totally alone...and now, she hadn't seen him for a time.

She rationalized that he had duties to perform, and that maybe he had curbed his visits to the marketplace in an attempt to pacify his quarrelsome older brother; but it wasn't like him to turn his back on a friend, no matter how new that friendship might be. She reasoned that whatever it was that kept him from the market, must be important.

When a week had passed, Tore found herself almost too depressed to drag her lousy carcass out to the big stone where she told her tales. When she finally got there, a crowd had already been mulling about restlessly for a time. She took her place and hurriedly began a story, but it didn't have the enthusiasm her other stories had. She almost didn't even feel like she was even telling the story. It was as if she was looking down on herself, watching her mouth spit out the words of the story with no thought whatsoever. Then she saw him. Brock was smiling in the back of the crowd. Not the usual nod, but a smile.

Tore found herself rushing through the story, cutting out details that she suddenly decided were no longer necessary to the plot of the story. She ended it with gusto that she had forgotten she was capable of, and could barely even wait for the people to finish depositing their coins in her cup, before heading over to see Brock. She fought the urge to go running over to him as a girl might, she had to remember to be a man. Always be a man. But, oh, how she wanted to run to him, throw her arms around him, and kiss him! Then again, she wanted to scream at him for daring to leave her so alone all of these days! Her reactions and thoughts were those of a woman's, a lover's, not a brotherly friend. Tore had to take a moment to compose herself before she actually spoke to Brock. She didn't want to appear overly affectionate!

Brock spoke first. "I am sorry I have missed so many of your tales. Father had important tasks for me to accomplish for him this past week."

Tore nodded. "It is understandable. I know that family must come first." She wanted to scream at him, and strike him with her fist. You left me all alone! She wanted to cry out. "My brother, Jens...his wife divorced him." Brock said slowly, almost ashamed.

"He quarreled with her as well then." Tore said simply.

"Jens quarrels with everyone. Even himself." Brock said in an exasperated tone. "Geira, my sister, says that Gormflaith has another she wants to marry."

"Gormflaith is Jens' wife?" Tore asked.

"Was Jens' wife." Brock corrected her. Tore laughed.

"You find this amusing?" Brock raised that eyebrow of his.

"No. No. Of course not. But, you do have to admit, if anyone had it coming to him, it's your brother Jens." Tore said slowly. "What does your father think about all of this?"

"He thinks it is shameful that a man can't keep his woman happy enough to keep her." Brock turned and looked over his shoulder at a gaggle of odd sounding musicians that had gathered across the marketplace.

"Are there many divorces here in Tunsberg?" Tore asked. She didn't remember overhearing about any since she had arrived here in this shire.

"Not many. But then again, I only pay heed to information having to do with my own kin. The market place is full of travelers who I care not about." Brock shrugged.

"Your father must care about the travelers since they are under his watch." Tore reminded Brock.

"I suppose you are correct." Brock said.

"I am always correct." Tore laughed and pointed to the food stall. Brock followed her lead.

"You sound like a woman!" Brock laughed.

"Do I?" Tore laughed hard.

She purchased some hot tea for herself and Brock got a flagon of mead.

"You drink a lot of tea." Brock noticed.

"It soothes me. It's also good for my throat from telling all my tales." Tore said blowing on her tea to cool it.

"So, Eirik the Silent is silenced by his own talking." Brock found the irony amusing.

Tore laughed at him and then leaned against the wood beam that supported the thatched roof of the food stall, and watched a funny little group of ragged musicians.

Brock watched them too. "Where do you suppose they are from?"

"I don't know. Are they what people call, Muslims?" Tore asked.

"I don't know. I am not quite sure what one of these Muslims are like." Brock studied the musicians a little closer.

Tore drank her tea and wiped out her cup, letting it dangle from the leather cord that kept it attached to her belt. Brock was doing the same.

"I spoke with my father." Brock said peering into his cup to make sure it was cleaned adequately.

"Does he still want to hear a tale?" Tore tried not to sound too excited.

"Oh, yes." Brock said happily. "I promised him that he wouldn't be disappointed."

"I hope I don't make a liar out of you." Tore said concerned.

"I have never heard a story that wasn't good come from your lips, Eirik. You are a master at your craft. You tell tales that make one feel like they are part of your story." Brock looked strangely at Tore. She looked away, feeling strangely uncomfortable with his penetrating glance. It was almost as if he knew something.... but what? Certainly, nothing, Tore reassured herself.

"He asked me to invite you to our fire tomorrow night." Brock said and then added," And he says to bring your appetite, for his wife, Ymma, is a fine cook!"

"I could certainly do with a good meal! The innkeeper's wife makes food fit for a horse!" Tore laughed. "Tell your father I accept his invitation gratefully. I will be there."

"Good. I will bring you to our hall tomorrow night, then. For now, I must attend to some business father has here in the market." Brock nodded to Tore who nodded in return. He went off in the direction of the leather tanner's stall, and Tore resumed her position on the stone. Already she felt better. She hadn't been abandoned then, quite the contrary. Tomorrow night she would eat with a real family again.

That night, Tore sorted through her mental store of stories for just the right one to make a good impression on Thorvald tomorrow night. There were historical stories as well as mythological stories. One was about King Sveigdir, an early Norwegian king who got so drunk on mead that one night he ran after a particularly annoying dwarf, and then just vanished into a boulder, never to be seen again. That was a good story, but sometimes people wanted to know where King Sveigdir went to, and it was hard to explain that he just disappeared into that rock and no one knew where he went.

There were stories for children, for warriors, for women and for old people. She needed a story that all would find fascinating. She thought back to her own family and which story appealed mostly to everybody. She remembered the story about man's creation. Ulf would tell that to her when she was a child. Their mother had told it to him, and now, she would tell it to Brock's family. She was sure that they would enjoy it.

The next day seemed to fly by more quickly than any day had in a long while. She actually had something to look forward to that night besides eating her fish gruel and letting her thoughts wader in front of her fire alone. Tonight, she would be with other people! Tore didn't remember how long it had been since she ate her night meal with other people.

As promised, Brock showed up at her inn. The innkeeper came to tell her he was there. Tore pulled her fur cape around her to keep out the cool night air, and went outside to meet him. Brock nodded in greeting. Tore did the same in return.

"My family is anxious to hear your tales tonight." Brock said on the way to his family's hall.

"I am anxious to share my tales with your family." Tore replied. She was nervous too, but she didn't tell Brock that thought.

Brock seemed unusually quiet for the rest of the walk to his family's hall. Tore figured he was nervous at the prospect of introducing his kin to his new friend, this stranger, this orphan called Eirik the Silent Graafell. Tore was glad he was nervous too, that way she didn't feel all alone in her anxiety.

When they reached the massive hall, Tore felt a pang of homesickness. Although, her kin didn't have a hall quite so big, the general style and feel was the same. The wood and stone structure was long in length and narrow in width. She followed Brock through the low, wood door and down a step onto the sunken stone floor.

Already around the fire, his kin sat eating and talking. At the far end of the smoky hall sat an enormous throne-like chair, and in it was seated a man of great stature and age. She noticed his lame arm and the fire that still burned in his eyes. She knew this was Brock's father, Thorvald. He was a man that exuded great power. He was used to having his way, and getting everything he wanted. Tore had always had good perceptual capabilities and she could read Thorvald like a book.

Brock nodded to various family members and walked, with Tore on his heels, straight to his father to properly introduce the guest that he had brought with him tonight.

"Father, this is Eirik Graafell. Also called by the name, Eirik the Silent. He is the gleeman I asked you to welcome to our fire tonight." Brock nodded to his father then to Tore.

Thorvald nodded in return. "Why are you known as Eirik the Silent, if you live as a gleeman?"

Tore cleared her throat. It was an honest enough question. "It is my voice that makes me silent at times." She touched her throat in a gesture.

Thorvald raised his eyebrows in much the same manner as Brock often did, as soon as Tore had spoken. He understood now why he wouldn't want to speak. Poor man was cursed with the voice of a woman!

"What injury did you receive that makes you speak so?" Thorvald was curious.

"There was no injury. My voice has always been so. As was my father's before me. I choose not to speak often and thus I was labeled so." Tore sounded convincing enough.

Thorvald held out a carved wood bowl full of hazel nuts and offered some to Tore. "I do not judge a man by his voice. You are welcome at my fire, gleeman."

Tore took a handful of hazel nuts and nodded. "I thank you."

Brock led her away to a bench and handed her a bowl of fish and bread. She took it and ate hungrily. Brock was saying something to his stepmother, and soon brought his own meal back to the bench where Tore was seated.

"Ymma was asking if I knew what tale you had in store for us tonight." Brock smiled at his mother who was looking their way. "She also thinks you are very pretty for a man."

"Pretty?" Tore almost choked on a piece of fish.

"She does not mean it offensively." Brock frowned at Tore. "She has a different way of looking at faces. She says that you can tell the condition of a man's heart and soul by the shape of his face and the depth of the color of his eyes." Brock dipped his thick brown bread into the oils and juices of the fish in his bowl.

"She is very wise?" Tore asked and then added, "For a woman?"

"For a woman, ja. She knows much." Brock spoke very respectfully of his stepmother.

"My mother died when I was young." Tore said, noting that this actually was true, not just another part of her great scheme.

"As did mine. We are like brothers in this sense, ja?" Brock asked with fish oil smeared on his upper lip.

Tore's first instinct was to lovingly wipe off the oil that had deposited itself on Brock's face, but she dropped her hand to her lap and nodded in agreement at Brock's question. They did have things in common.

Once the meal was completed, Brock's family spent some time talking and catching up on the day's activities.

Thorvald was standing at the end of the hall. Gradually, the hall grew quiet.

"We have a guest amongst us tonight." Thorvald's voice boomed in the echoing hall. "He brings with him knowledge in the form of stories. He is a gleeman, some call him a scop."

Thorvald paused, a trained public speaker.

"Our gleeman shares our meal tonight in exchange for a tale. Lend him your ears as he will open your minds to things and places you have never been to."

Thorvald sat down.

Tore wasn't quite sure what she should do.

Brock nudged her and whispered, "Go to the fire and begin."

Tore was grateful for the instructions. She rose and in her best manly gait strolled to the fire. She turned and sort of bowed and nodded all at the same time towards Thorvald, acknowledging him as the head of this family. She then turned and faced the majority of the family, with the exception of the few women who were hustling and bustling in and out of the benches refilling mead cups, and offering more bread and honey to the children.

Tore cleared her throat and began. "Long ago, before time began, there were no men in the land." She waited for the expected giggles to subside and then continued.

"There were no gods or goddesses, men or animals." Tore heard the murmurings of wonderment and continued, "All that existed were the elements. From the elements grew a giant named Ymir. Ymir was alone and so he created creatures from himself."

"From one armpit, he birthed a son. From the other armpit, he birthed a daughter." Tore paused. "But, these two children were not enough for Ymir."

"Ymir rubbed his feet together and made a six-headed giant. And still, Ymir wanted more." Tore took a drink of tea that Brock had instructed his stepmother to bring Eirik. She nodded at Ymma thankfully and continued.

"Now, Ymir had in his possession a cow. This cow often fed him. One night, the cow was licking a block of ice. From the block of ice, the cow licked a god into being."

"Who was this god?" A boy called out and was hushed by an older sibling sitting near him.

Tore smiled at the boy. "Who was this god? Who was this god? This god was Odin. The cow licked the block of ice again, and Odin's two brothers were made."

"Odin and his brothers were not happy with how things were going. They did not like the way their father, Ymir, ran things so they killed their father." Tore paused.

"From Ymir's body they brought creation. Ymir's flesh made the earth. His bones formed the mountains. His skull formed the sky."

"What about his blood?" Another boy called out.

"Ah. His blood. His blood was the most important of all. His blood formed our seas; and, in this bloody sea most of the race of giants that had come from Ymir himself, drowned."

"But, that is not all." Tore took another drink of her now lukewarm tea, and cleared her throat. The room was smoky and dark making it hard for

Tore to see most of the faces; but she could see Brock sitting over there by the fire: His face tinted orange by the flickering flames.

"No, that is not all. Odin and his brothers thought it best to create a new race of beings to populate the earth that had been freshly made from Ymir's flesh. So, they shaped the first two humans, a man and a woman, from two pieces of driftwood. And, Odin named these humans, Askr and Embla. The first man, and the first woman."

Tore looked around at the faces that she could make out through the haze and went on. "It is from Askr and Embla that all mankind has sprung. And this is the story of how man as created long before time began."

Tore nodded and crossed the floor to where Brock sat. The room was silent for a moment and then erupted into a loud frenzy of clapping and approving hoots.

Thorvald was standing again.

The room grew quiet as the old man stood, demanding the attention of all present.

"We thank you gleeman. Your tale has taught us new things. I heard that story as a boy, but not so well told." Thorvald smiled. "Tales like that should be shared more often. You are welcome at our fire anytime, gleeman. Let it be known that as of this moment, Eirik the Silent Graafell is to be seated at our fire at any time." Thorvald rather dramatically waved his arm in a commanding gesture of power.

Family members nodded and whispered. A few grumbled, as there are always the dissenters in every family. Brock slapped Tore on the back.

"Well done, Eirik. You did not make a liar out of me!" Brock laughed.

Tore grew aware of the women and children scurrying off to the far regions of the house. Only the men were left. The events that she had pondered for so long were happening now. She was alone; in a hall full of men who also believed she was a man. If she had been her old self, Tore, the woman that she was, she would have been packed off to the other side of the house just like all the other women had, yet, here she sat one of the men around a man's fire.

Thorvald dragged his massive chair closer to the circle of men. They discussed all sorts of things, from weaponry to women, to battles to outrageous prices demanded by local merchants. Tore felt herself being more and more accepted by the men around her. They didn't seem to object to her being a stranger. It was almost as if Thorvald's words had made her a part of this family.

Thorvald talked to his sons loudly. Brock explained that sometimes Thorvald's hearing came and went, so he yelled louder than would be expected. The old man had survived numerous injuries in countless battles. Many men would not have survived even on of the wounds that Thorvald bore scars of, but Thorvald was a warrior and a leader. He would not die, because he had warriors to lead and a family to guide. It was his duty, and so he lived on despite the odds.

Tore felt a growing respect for this aged warrior. He was a proud man, and a proud father. She felt the weight of his hand on her arm.

"Eirik the Silent?" Thorvald asked, turning to Tore.

"Yes, Thorvald?" Tore studied his grizzled old face.

"My son tells me you are without a family. That you are an orphan?" Thorvald had been thinking about this all night.

"Yes. Brock speaks the truth. I am alone in this world." Tore suddenly felt guilty for lying to this revered man who commanded and deserved her respect.

"My son, Brock, is a good man. A good man who will someday be a good leader." Thorvald watched Brock talking with some other men.

"But, what of Jens, surely he…" Tore was cut off by Thorvald.

"Jens. Jens. Jens is not a leader. Brock, Brock has a quality about him. He is able to judge men and find the good ones. I did not doubt his word when he told me of you." Thorvald said quietly. "I knew you must be a man of great substance if my son was to have formed such a close alliance with you so quickly."

Tore felt flattered, but only nodded.

"That is why I have reached a decision. Brock does not know of this decision. I only decided this thing tonight while listening to you share your knowledge with my family." Thorvald picked at his decaying teeth with the end of his eating knife. "You have a gift that my family can benefit from. I need knowledge like this shared with my kin. You, on the other hand, need a family to train you in the ways of battle. Brock tells me you come from a family of warriors." Thorvald paused.

"Since you no longer have a family, I will take you as my son. I will train you so that your fathers before you can be proud of the warrior their son will become. You will learn side by side with my own sons. Brock will have you for his brother." Thorvald said these things as if they were law.

Tore was overwhelmed with gratitude. This is what she had hoped for, this is what she needed. This is what she had to do in order to fulfill Sif's end of the bargain with Tyr.

"I am grateful, father." Tore added the last with mixed emotions. It was odd to call another father.

Thorvald smiled. "Go. Tell Brock that on this night, he has a new brother."

Tore smiled, nodded and crossed the room towards Brock.

Chapter 9

Tore went about her new found career as a gleeman with the new enthusiasm she had gained that night around Thorvald's fire. To belong somewhere again, that was what Tore had longed for. She felt she had a family once more. Each night she ate her night meal around Thorvald's fire...always sitting next to Brock. Thorvald often joked about how close the two were. Brock and Eirik seemed more like brothers than did Brock and his own blood brothers.

One night around Thorvald's fire, Tore decided it was time to return to her room back at the inn. She had said her goodbyes to Brock, and his younger brother Claus with whom she had been sitting, and went to pay her respect to Thorvald and ask for his leave to return to her lodgings.

Thorvald was already sound asleep and snoring loudly in his big chair at the end of the hall. Tore stood there in front of the old, yet strangely powerful man for a moment, not exactly sure if she should wake him or not. She decided to let him sleep and turned to leave.

Thorvald snorted awake behind her. "Leaving without saying goodbye, boy?" He snorted and wheezed.

Tore spun around and faced Thorvald, who was now pushing himself up straight in his chair.

"I didn't want to wake you, father." Tore addressed him as she usually did, the way he had asked her to address him. "Nonsense. I'm an old man;

I have plenty of time to sleep! Off so soon?" Thorvald smiled slightly at Tore. "I am tired. Ymma's cooking is so good, all a man wants to do afterwards is sleep and dream about the food all over again!" Tore laughed.

Thorvald laughed too. "She does wonders with herring." He stated as if it was the first time he had considered the matter.

"I will return tomorrow night." Tore nodded at Thorvald.

"Why must you live in the inn?" Thorvald asked suddenly.

"I have no where else to live." Tore stated.

"I have rooms to spare. All of my sons have their own private rooms. Most households have to share sleeping quarters, but not so in my house. I have extra rooms. There is no point in your tossing good silver towards that lazy, drunken innkeeper when you can live under my roof as my son, at my expense." Thorvald waved his arm around to emphasis the amount of space to be found in this massive dwelling.

"I, I, huh..." Tore began, "I don't know what to say. Your offer is so generous."

"Say you'll pack up your belongings tomorrow and move into my house where I can train you and feed you, and make a proper warrior out of you. I will do it as a favor to your dead kin." Thorvald reached out and took Tore's hand and patted it kindly, fatherly.

Tore was nearly overwhelmed. Here she was a total stranger and Thorvald, the Jarl of all of Tunsberg, was asking her to live as his son. She felt guilty for hiding so many truths from him, for making him believe that her little charade was true.

"I accept your offer, father." Tore said at last. As long as she had her own room, there was little to fear that anyone would find out her secret.

Thorvald smiled. Tore had apparently made him very happy. "Then it is settled. I don't know why I hadn't thought of it earlier. Tomorrow I will send Brock to fetch you...from now on, you will only have to tell stories around this fire, our fire, the fire of your family." Thorvald waved his hand towards the fire.

Tore smiled and nodded. "Until tomorrow then, father." "Goodbye, son." Thorvald smiled and leaned back in his chair.

Brock followed Tore to the door. "What was all of that about?" He asked.

"Your father has asked me to move here. He has given me a room and wants to train me along with you and your brothers to be a proper warrior." Tore said smiling and pulling her fur over her shoulder. She stepped outside and noted that soon she would no longer need such a heavy fur to walk around at night with.

"Did you accept his offer?" Brock asked.

"Of course. I don't think many people turn down any offer made by Thorvald, do you?" Tore laughed. Brock let out a very loud sigh of relief.

"You knew he would ask me then?" Tore cocked her head inquisitively to the side.

"I suspected it. He has muttered such things before. He likes you, and misses you here with the rest of us during the day. Some days, all he talks about are your stories. It makes Jens jealous." Brock looked at Tore.

"I don't think it takes much to make Jens jealous." Tore had gotten to know Jens, and liked him no more than Brock did.

"You're right there." Brock nodded. "I'll see you tomorrow?"

"Your father is sending you to help me bring my belongings here." Tore said. "He told me I wouldn't have to tell stories to strangers anymore. Just to his family. No, he said to my family." Tore smiled.

Brock laughed. "That makes you happy?" "I have wanted a family again for a long time." Tore said seriously.

"Even one as troubled as mine?" Brock asked incredulously.

"It is no more troubled than the average family." Tore smiled again.

"Don't take offense at this, but you should try to not do that too much." Brock pointed at her face.

"Do what?" Tore was puzzled.

"Smile." Brock said while smiling.

"Why not?" Tore frowned.

"It makes you look like a girl. Like Ymma says, you are pretty for a boy." Brock laughed.

"You're making fun of me." Tore said gruffly.

"I have to, you know." Brock laughed. "If you're to be my brother then I must start treating you like one. Not like a friend."

"And you can't be friends with your brothers? I was friends with mine...once." Tore said sadly.

"You are right. I can be both friend and brother. I just have no experience in doing so." Brock turned and looked over his shoulder towards the hall door. "Sometimes, I don't even want to be brother to some of my brothers, none the less a friend." Brock's voice took on a sad edge to it.

"Well, I will be the brother you want to be brother to." Tore slapped Brock on the back, hard, the way he often did her.

Brock laughed and nodded at Tore as she turned to return home.

Home. Tore thought about that for a moment on her way to the inn. She had never really thought of her room at the lodge as home. No, home was something she no longer had; at least, until Ulf returned. If Ulf returned.

There was that unpleasant thought was again. It lurked there in the back of her mind; ever ominous, ever waiting to creep back out into the open, to make her face the possibilities, make her face the prospect that Ulf may never return. That she might be here, alone, for the rest of her life. Tore smiled to herself. She wasn't alone anymore. She had a family.

A family that thought she was a man. How long could that last? How long could she live among people day in and day out without them growing suspicious? Without anyone doubting her lies? She had gotten herself in deeper now and there was no going back. Either she would pull this off, or die trying. Either way, she would die by Tyr's sword if she failed to prove herself worthy in battle...she had to get to a battle first. She was one step closer to that anyway.

Tore made her way to her room. Lit the whale oil lamp, and threw some logs on the smoldering fire. She paid extra to have the innkeeper's fat, pimply son come and keep her fire going during the day, so it would always be warm for her return, but it was seldom burning when she returned at all of the odd hours she often returned at.

Tore unlaced her boots and set them before the fire. She sat down on the fur laid before the hearth and took off her shirt. Slowly she unbound her breasts, unwinding the strips of fabric that kept them pinned close to her chest bone.

"Aaa." She let the gasp of relief ease out of her mouth slowly and quietly. She thanked the gods daily for letting her be small breasted. She couldn't even begin to imagine the agony she would constantly be in if her breasts were any bigger than they were now. She hurt all of the time from the sheer pressure of the bandages. She was fortunate there wasn't much more to have to bind down. The strips of cloth had cut into her skin over her ribs and under her arms. She found some seal lard and rubbed it into her skin where the cloth had chapped and chaffed her raw and red. It felt better. Night was the only time she felt comfortable, she was afraid that living in Thorvald's house she would have to keep her breasts bound even at night. What if someone was to come into her room while she was sleeping?

Tore hadn't thought every detail through about living under Thorvald's roof; but what else was she to do? She had to be trained to fight so she could go to battle. To learn to fight she must be in a family of warriors. To do this meant living under Thorvald's roof. She had to just pray to Sif that Sif would look after her enough to allow her secret to go on undiscovered.

Tore went to sleep that night with a troubled mind. She tossed and turned fretfully all night long imagining the horror of discovery and the cruelty of the punishment she would undoubtedly receive. She imagined that they would leave her out on a mountainside to freeze, or throw her overboard from a ship into the sea...much like the custom of dealing with unwanted babies.

The next day, Tore packed up her belongings and stacked them in piles on the cot. She was amazed with how much she had accumulated since first arriving in Tunsberg. When everything was neatly tied up into bundles, she went to the central hall for some breakfast...and to wait for Brock.

Brock came in long after Tore had finished her oatmeal. She took him to her room and together they carried her bundles to his family's home.

Brock turned to Tore. "Father said that he has spoken to some friends of his who have agreed to teach us the finer art of battle skills."

"When do we start?" Tore seemed anxious. Brock raised an eyebrow, he wasn't too thrilled about having to spend too much of his time with a handful of aged warriors who somehow managed to survive this long. He also thought he was already pretty good with a sword and the battle-ax, so he questioned the entire need of more training.

"Soon." Brock answered. "You are looking forward to battle, ja?"

Tore felt a pang in her stomach. Actually, she thought, it was the last thing she wanted to do, but she had to do it because her life depended on it...there was no choice in the matter. "I want to be a great warrior. Don't you?" Tore thought up a typically male response.

"Doesn't every man?" Brock said sort of sarcastically.

"This training, what does it involve?" Tore asked.

"We will be taken to a military camp where there are only men. No women to distract us from fully concentrating on developing our skills. There we will learn how to master all of the weapons. I don't think you'll need to worry about sword skills." Brock pointed towards Tore's sword.

"You say this often, but you haven't actually seen me use this sword." Tore laughed.

"I am confident you are a master." Brock laughed too. Brock took Tore to the room that Ymma and some of the other women had cleaned for her. It was similar to the room back at the inn. It was narrow with a fireplace at the end on the outside wall. Alongside the wood wall, was a roped cot with a thick fur spread over it. At the head of the cot was a small table with a lamp, and at the foot of the bed, in front of the fireplace was a large wood chest. The wall across from the cot had wood pegs driven into the wood for hanging clothes.

Tore opened the big chest and dropped several of her bundles into it.

"Come," Brock said setting the rest of the bundles onto the cot, "You can unpack later. Father is waiting for us in the hall."

Brock closed the wood door behind them and they went down the long, narrow hallway that led to the main hall, where Thorvald was sitting, as always, in his big chair.

Jens, Havelok, Claus, Johan, and Ingolf were all there too. Geira, Brock's sister and Ingolf's wife, was sweeping the wood floor around the seated men. When Brock and Tore entered the room, Thorvald signaled that the men needed to talk and Geira left quickly. Tore silently felt sorry for her.

Brock and Tore sat down on the bench next to Ingolf. Thorvald turned to Tore and smiled.

"Eirik, my son!" He bellowed.

Tore caught an angry expression on Jens' face as she turned to acknowledge Thorvald.

"I thank you again, father, for your acceptance and your generous living space!" Tore nodded while she spoke. Thorvald's face exploded into a mask of a million wrinkles. "I am glad you are happy. I wish that all of my sons were as happy, and as easy to please as you are, Eirik." Thorvald turned and cast a glance towards Jens who sat with an intense scowl etched upon his face.

The conversation that followed contained Thorvald's plans for his sons, Eirik included, for the future. Not far from Tunsberg there was a military camp called Tostig. Thorvald meant for all six of his sons to go there. Constant training and the companionship of tried and true warriors would promise that his sons would come out top-notch fighters.

Tostig meant many things to all of them. To Jens it meant no women. For no women entered any military camp so as not to serve as a distraction, or to sap a man's strength that should be used to practice battle skills. To Havelok, Claus and Johan it meant leaving their father's home and their mother's watchful eyes...and their new girlfriends. To Brock and Eirik it meant a chance to prove their manhood in a world where manhood rested primarily on the ability to fight and stay alive; but to Tore it meant the constant nagging fear of discovery by an entire camp of men. She would never grow used to that ever-present fear.

Thorvald sent them off that night with nothing but the clothes on their backs and the swords in their scabbards strapped onto their waists. A military camp was no place for the luxuries of home.

When the men arrived at Tostig it was daylight. They had traveled most of the night and were hoping for some rest as soon as they were shown to their sleeping quarters...but the more they saw, the less rest they knew they would get. As they were being led through the tall, wood gates, Tore looked around and marveled at the place that would be her home for the next few months. She thought about the cozy room that Ymma had shown her to back at Thorvald's dwelling...she never even got to sleep in it! Everything was happening so fast. One moment she was thinking she was moving in with Brock and his family to share her stories around their night fire, and the next moment she found herself being carted off to a harsh military camp with Brock and his four brothers. One thing she could say about Thorvald, he didn't waste anytime getting things done.

Tore and the others were marched past several long wood buildings. Even the roofs were wood, not the usual wood and thatch and stone that she was used to. The path below them was made out of wood planks, sanded smooth much like the side of a ship. Carts and men alike moved easily over these plank streets. The hulk of a man, who was marching them along, stopped in front of one of the buildings and shoved the large wood door open, revealing a large hall that spanned out before them. Along the wall was a row of cots. There was a fire in the middle of the room and crude benches lined the other wall.

A thousand worried thoughts raced through Tore's mind. She would have to spend night and day with men. They had no other clothes, so that wouldn't be a problem. If she needed to bathe she hoped she would be allowed outside of the camp's walls to find a stream...maybe she could say she needed the fresh air or something. The only real problem could be her woman's time. She had long ago cut up rectangles of sheep's wool still on the skin to use for her time. It raised no questions if found in her possessions, because she could just say she used the rectangles to clean her sword. She had a few tucked into her purse on her belt. She could probably scrounge up some more sheep's skin if needed.

Tore sat down on the cot directly before Brock's. It was full of fleas.

The hulk of a man who was serving as their guide, or warden as it seemed, laughed hysterically. He seemed to find the men swatting at their arms and legs an amusing spectacle.

"That'll be yer first task. Take them furs out and shake them down." The man was still laughing.

Tore looked at Brock who in turn was looking back at her with disgust. Shaking down furs was women's work. Tore shrugged and struggled to peel the rotted old fur from the cot. Most of it fell apart in clumps. She grimaced and looked over at Brock whose fur was in pretty much the same condition as her own.

Claus cursed. "How in bloody Hades are we supposed to sleep on these ragged pieces of filth?"

Tore smiled, but hid her grin behind her arm. He sounded like the spoiled child that he was. Brock frowned and made a face in Claus' direction that said to shut up.

The hulking warden laughed uproariously again. "Out with you!" He pointed outside. Brock and Tore lugged their furs outside, with Jens close on their heels.

"I never thought father would send us to be tortured!" Jens whined.

"He wants to make men of us." Brock laughed.

"I am a man already!" Jens growled, eyeballing Tore with contempt. "Not like your storytelling girlfriend over there!"

Tore's head snapped up from her fur shaking adventure. Even though she wasn't a man, she took offense to Jens biting remark as torridly as she would have if she had, in fact, been a man. The only thing for a man to do in the case of his manhood being questioned was to fight.

Tore whipped her sword from her scabbard before Brock or Jens for that matter, had time to respond. She threw herself to the ground, rolling on her shoulder, up and over in a violent somersault, springing up onto her feet, in front of Jens shocked face. Before Jens could even reach for his sword, Tore had him pinned on the ground, with her blade pressed to his neck. Her arms flexed as she steadily held her sword calmly on Jens' flesh, revealing the tough, sinewy muscle that bulged there.

"I will not harm you brother." She hissed, spittle flying from between her teeth, "For you do not know what you speak."

Jens looked up into Tore's face, back to the steel blade that was coldly and heavily pressed against his neck, and pleadingly towards the other four of his blood brothers.

"I spoke foolishly!" Jens said shakily, who was shocked to find himself in this position once again.

The burly, hulk of a man who had turned his back to talk with another man of the camp, turned around to see Jens lying flat on his back, one leg askew, his hands grasping the end of Tore's blade; and, Tore with legs spread, blade pressed firmly on her brother's neck.

"Whoa! Now is not the time for fighting, man!" The hulk walked towards Tore.

Tore's glance cut into Jens sharper than any blade could as she eased off and let her sword hang loose at her side. She stood there like that with all the men staring at her, and then she casually slid the sword back into her scabbard, drew her legs together, and smiled.

"We have furs to shake." She said steadily as if nothing out of the ordinary had occurred.

The hulk stood there a little dazed and then hustled Jens back to his work. Jens scampered back to his feet, knocking dirt off his clothes wildly with his hands, and resumed his fur shaking, keeping one eye on Eirik.

Brock watched Eirik shake out his fur. Eirik moved faster than any man he had seen. His kin had taught him well. How much better a warrior would he become in this camp?

The first lesson of the next day, involved running. Simple, uncomplex, exhausting, run until you drop, running. The hulk of a man, who now had a name, Egill, treated them as if they were slaves. He ran them and the other young men from other shires until some of them frothed at the mouth like horses. Running built endurance, that's what Egill said.

Tore never before felt so tired. Even on her journey to Tunsberg when the elements and the gods plotted against her, she did not feel as tired as she did now. The fact that the furs were still crawling with fleas did not matter that night when they were finally allowed to crawl onto their cots in sheer exhaustion.

The days passed by quickly. There were new weapons to try, new techniques to master. Some things Tore knew, some she remembered from watching her brothers and uncles and cousins practice, some of it she had learned play fighting with Ulf. And, she was good. She amazed her teachers with her quick learning. She was good with a bow and arrow, good with a knife, but best of all the men with her sword. Only the mighty battle-ax eluded her. She was adequate, so Brock said, but adequate was not something Tore liked to be. She wanted to be the best. Egill told her that many men disliked the battle-ax and preferred, like her, their swords. Besides, with sword skill as hers, who needed any other weapons?

Jens was the same old Jens. He hated and distrusted Brock, always feeling like this number two son was living to usurp his birthright; but, lately, he had grown to hate this Eirik Graafell even more. This serpent had slithered his way into his father's heart, and his brother's heart. Eirik was fiercely loyal to Brock, and Jens resented loyalty to anyone but himself. Jens didn't know when or how he would make Eirik pay for the humiliating scene he had caused outside of the longhouse that first day in camp, but he would make him pay. Some day when the gods smiled upon him and not upon Eirik.

Tore was amazed at how long they had been in Tostig. Her woman time had come and gone three times, each causing her a panic that she would somehow be discovered. Somehow she had managed to find a few private moments every day to tend to her body's needs. It hadn't always been easy though and a few times she was sure someone had noticed, but no one had.

After the months had passed, the men of Tostig felt that the sons of Thorvald had mastered all that they could teach them without an actual battle. They were to have a banquet with Thorvald and all of the other fathers from the surrounding shires that had sons in training here. Thorvald arrived with arms outstretched having heard that his sons had ranked best in nearly every category. He also noted that it was Brock and Eirik who bested Jens every time. Thorvald could sense the hostility between his sons, as the tension was thick enough to be cut.

Tore did not tell the story that night. An old, grizzled warrior who was missing an eye, an arm, and most of his teeth related a battle tale that raised the hairs on the arms of all the newly trained men. Mead flowed freely, but Tore was careful not to drink more than one flagon full. She must keep her senses at all times. She had a tendency to talk too much and cry when she was drunk, and crying wasn't exactly a manly thing to do. Especially from a man who had just bested about forty men in sword skills!

Someone in the crowd proposed a fight between Eirik and a man named Kalf, who had been second to Eirik in sword skills. Tore felt frightened to fight in front of Thorvald. Maybe she wouldn't be so confident under Thorvald's practiced and watchful eyes but she could not get out of this entertaining spectacle without looking the coward. Besides, Brock was there cheering her on. If he had faith in her, then she would have to have faith in herself. She valued Brock's opinion more than anyone else's. She wasn't sure if it was because she respected Brock as a warrior and friend, or if it was because she was falling deeper and deeper in love with him as each day passed.

Tore was half shoved, half escorted to the center of the hall amidst roaring laughter and whooping cheers. Kalf paced in front of her, knowing that he would lose. The event commenced with each man giving a good show of his skill and talent with their swords but just as nearly everyone present suspected, Eirik soon had his man. With one quick swipe he had managed to send Kalf's sword flying, and Kalf stood before her empty handed. Tore, or Eirik smiled.

She nodded at Kalf and the room burst into applause. Kalf nodded in return and melted into the crowd behind him. After all, this hadn't been his idea!

Tore realized that all eyes were on her, and that Thorvald had proudly come to stand by his son. The room grew quiet for a moment to allow Tore a chance to speak as was customary in these events. Tore held her sword above her head, holding its point with her other hand.

"Tonight, all of you have seen the skill of my sword. Because it is a good sword, a sword that will always seek out and find my enemy, I will name it

Gungnir!" Tore called out loudly.

The crowd began to laugh. Not at her voice this time, but at the haughtiness of the name she had chosen.

Thorvald slapped her on the back with an incredible force for such an old man. Tore was thrown forward and had to catch her balance with her leg thrown out in front of her.

"Perhaps, son, your pride makes you choose such a name that you could never live up to!" Thorvald laughed loudly.

Gungnir was the name of Odin's spear. Odin's spear always sought and found Odin's enemies.

"No, Father. My sword will always find my enemy!" Tore shouted over the laughter of the crowd. She went to lower her sword from above her head where she had been showing it to the crowd, but as she lowered it, Thorvald had been reaching up to touch the sword. In a flash, blood was drawn in a trickle on Thorvald's hand. Thorvald recoiled reflexively, but then seeing it was merely a scratch began laughing even harder than before.

"Perhaps your sword is not Gungnir if it cuts your own father!" Thorvald laughed, as did the rest of the hall. "You should give it a new name!"

Tore smiled as Thorvald slapped her on the back again, but something deep down in Tore's gut stirred and quaked uneasily. Gungnir always found its enemy. Why had her sword cut Thorvald? Tore smiled weakly, but out of the corner of her eye she spied Jens.

Jens glared at her uneasily and turned and faded into the crowd. Tore shivered. Did Jens feel it too?

Chapter 10

On the way home, many things raced through the minds of all of the young men. Welcome thoughts of clean clothes, clean beds, and good food flooded their minds. The easy pace of life would be welcome soon.

Brock had other puzzling thoughts beating at the sides of his skull. He remembered nights when he would lay awake looking at Eirik sleeping soundly, not snoring and snorting like the other men. Just peaceful slumber. Brock was often amazed at how beautiful a man could look. There in the firelight, he would look at the softly etched features on Eirik's slim face. The squared jaw of a young man, but the delicate eyebrows and huge eyes of a woman. Eirik was an enigma. Brock often felt goose bumps jump up on his arm whenever Eirik touched him…what was this feeling? It scared Brock. For feelings such as these about another man were unnatural! How could he think another man beautiful? Brock realized that maybe it was time he found a woman. Perhaps he was spending too much time with his beautiful friend and it was confusing his brain.

Yet, remembering how Eirik would softly sigh during sleep, and Brock's heart would beat wildly, sending deafening blood roaring in his ears, he thought he might already be in love…but with a man? Of course, no one would ever know these troubling thoughts that hung in Brock's mind so heavily. Brock glanced over at Eirik's beardless face, sweating as they all were on their trek back home.

Brock had thought Eirik's inability to grow a beard odd at first, until Eirik had explained it as some family freak trait. His great-grandfather had been called Canute No Beard. Brock no longer thought it strange. It bothered Eirik sometimes, just as his voice did; but Brock always encouraged Eirik by reminding him of his sword skills or his talent for weaving a good tale. Eirik was a good friend, and he had never done anything inappropriate to encourage these wild, abnormal thoughts in Brock's mind.

That was it; Brock determined silently, he would find a woman. That must be it. Jens was forever taunting him about not engaging in more sexual pursuits. Maybe for once Jens was right. Having a woman might dispel these wicked thoughts.

Ymma greeted all the men with open arms. She could tell that her boys had become men. This was one reason she was reluctant to let them go to Tostig; she knew how they would come back.

The women had prepared a hot bath in each of the men's rooms. Tore closed and locked her door behind her, stripping at once out of the crusty and dirty clothes that had become her second skin for all these months. She unbound the filthy strips of cloth binding her breasts and almost gasped from pain at the sudden release of pressure. She wondered if her breasts would ever retain their natural shape after all of this was over.

Tore slid down into the tub. The hot water felt good rippling over her skin. She soaked there for a long time, listening to the sounds throughout the house. Tore wanted to be alone. Tore was awakened by a sound coming from beneath her window. She looked down in the water and saw that her skin had shriveled up like an old woman. She must have fallen asleep in her bath. What was that noise?

Tore dried off and dressed. She crept to the wood panel that pushed open for a window, and cracked it so that she could look outside to where the sound was coming from.

It was Brock…and Amalie, a girl from Tunsberg. They were between Tore's lower wall and the stable wall. Some of Amalie's clothes were tossed on top of a nearby stone, and Brock's striped pants were down around his ankles. Tore sucked in her breath. She felt like an axe had just hit her.

Amalie's fingers were dug deep into Brock's thighs, as they both ground away at each other in noisy pleasure. Tore watched, her heart breaking. Brock seized Amalie's rump, and jerked her over onto her stomach.

Tore wanted to close the window, to retreat to the security of her dark and quiet room; but she couldn't. She couldn't peel her eyes off of Brock and

Amalie. It should be her, not Amalie, down there sighing with pleasure underneath Brock…but, Brock thought she was a man. It would never be her, with Brock, like that.

Brock grunted. Both collapsed on the ground, smiles and whispered words exchanged between the two of them. Tore had never felt a hurt so deep in all her life. Suddenly, it felt like someone had stuck a knife right into her heart. She closed the window and bolted it absently.

Sitting on her bed, she leaned against the wall and stared up at the ceiling. She wanted to cry, but the pain was so deep that no tears would come. There was a knock at the door.

"Eirik?" It was Tova, Brock's sister. "I've come for the bath water." Tova shifted around outside of the door.

"Just a minute." Tore unbolted the door.

Tova came in; nervously glancing at this odd man her father had permitted to live with them. She opened the window, propping it open with the stick that was hanging next to it, and began scooping the water out. She went to toss it outside the window, when Tore cried out suddenly. "Wait!" Images of a doused Brock and Amalie filled Tore's mind.

Tova turned around quickly, water still in hand. "What is it?" She asked.

Tore looked out the window, but there was no one there anymore.

"Nothing. I'm sorry. It's nothing, go on with your work." Tore frowned and lay down on the bed, staring up at the ceiling while Tova worked.

"You don't talk much." Tova said to Tore after awhile. "I talk when there is something to be said." Tore answered in a typical manly fashion.

Tova laughed nervously. "Do you like it here?" She asked.

"Yes." Tore answered shortly.

"Aren't you afraid of Father? He terrifies me." Tova said while laughing.

"You shouldn't be afraid of him. He loves you." Tore said thinking of her own father.

"I never thought about that before. I don't ever speak with Father that much, except to ask him if he needs anything." Tova continued scooping water from the steel tub.

"You should try to talk with him more. He loves all of his children. You're lucky to have such a father." Tore said slowly.

"Brock tells me that your father is dead." Tova said quietly.

"All of my kin are dead." Tore replied. "I'm sorry." Tova said softly. "I hope our family can help you be happy again."

"Is my sadness that obvious?" Tore asked. "Yes. Except when you're with Brock. Then your whole face lights up!" Tova laughed again with her high, girlish twangy laugh.

Tore smiled. "He is a good friend...and brother." Tova smiled too. "Yes, he is a good brother." Tova finished scooping out the water and dried the tub.

She lifted the tub up onto her strong, young shoulders and nodded goodbye, closing the door behind her. Tore thought back at how many times she had done the same task for her father and her own brothers. Lifting tubs and other heavy things had helped build the muscles that were so important to her survival today. Who would ever have imagined the need for those muscles that she now had? Tore laughed quietly.

Tore heard Ymma ringing the bell for the night meal. She double-checked the flatness of her chest, and the tightness of the two braids that hung from the sides of her long blond hair, and closed the door behind her. Going down the narrow hall, she met up with Brock. Tore swallowed hard. She couldn't ever let him know how she felt. "What's wrong with you?" Brock sensed the uneasiness around Eirik.

"Just woke up. Haven't quite shaken off the sleep yet!" Tore replied, hoping that it convinced Brock. Brock looked convinced.

"I'm starving!" He said.

"You? I could eat an entire horse!" Tore laughed. "Well, I think you'll have to settle for fish!" Brock smiled.

Jens grudgingly moved over so Brock and Eirik could sit down at the table next to him. He eyeballed Eirik evilly, and shoveled in the food. Havelok began relating his latest sexual conquest in much detail to the rest of his brothers. The rest chimed in with their victories. Brock boasted, it seemed to Tore, the most. At the mention of Amalie's name, all of the other brothers grunted with delight. They too had had her. Brock seemed disappointed.

"What? Brother, you thought you were the first one to dip your stiff bone into Amalie's honey pot?" Jens asked elbowing Claus. "There's not a man here who hasn't tasted of that sweet, dripping cunt!"

Brock frowned. Tore shifted uncomfortably on the bench. "How 'bout you, story-boy? You fucked Amalie yet? She has teats like a cow? Eh?!" Jens laughed loudly, as did the other brothers. Brock sat quietly by Tore's side.

She cleared her throat. "No. Can't say that I have." Tore thought for a moment that had she been a man and had been with Amalie, she would never have said so for Brock's sake. He must feel terrible.

"Can you say that you have had any woman?" Jens growled with bawdy laughter.

"Those of us who know we are men, don't need to go around telling about balling women to prove it." Tore said, then grunted for emphasis, swung her leg over the bench, and got up, leaving.

Jens said something she couldn't hear, and hooted with raunchy laughter as she went to take her dish to Ymma. Tore went outside and sat on a bench in front of the hall. Brock joined her.

"You shouldn't let Jens get to you like that." Brock said after awhile.

"He seemed to get to you, too." Tore reminded him. Brock sighed and leaned back against the wall of the hall, looking off towards the market.

"Jens obviously feels the need to prove his manhood more than the average man. What does he have to hide?" Tore laughed.

Brock was quiet. That sounded like his own feelings. He had sought out and fucked Amalie just to prove to himself that he was normal...that these feelings for Eirik were nothing but comradeship, brotherhood, and friendship. "Some men have that problem." Brock said simply. "But, not you?" Tore looked Brock in the eyes hard, and unwavering.

Brock felt that uneasy feeling again. It was almost as if Eirik's blue eyes bored right through to his soul. "Not me." Brock said, and then spit.

"Then that makes two of us." Tore laughed to break the tension. She didn't want Brock to wonder what she was thinking.

Brock kicked at a rock and then got up. "I think I'm going to go ahead to bed. I'm tired, and it feels like we haven't slept for years!" Brock yawned. "Good idea." Tore wanted to add, I'll join you, to the end of that, but she caught herself.

Brock and Tore got up and made their way to their own rooms. Sleep didn't come easy for either one of them that night.

The next day, Thorvald announced that they would be heading out on a raid soon. He was going down to examine the langskips on the beach, and wanted his sons to come with him.

The men walked down to the beach. Two massive langskips were being built, nearly finished. There would be 120 men in each boat. Sixty of those men were from Tunsberg alone. Tore had only been right up alongside of a longship once or twice during her whole lifetime. She had watched them on the sea, but never sat foot in one. That was for a man and his warrior companions. The ship was enormous. There were places for their sea chests that would double as the rowing benches. The sides had slots carved into the wood for each of their shields to protect them while they rowed. The archers would sit in the stern. Tore ventured away from the group over to where the massive serpent head was being painted. The head was already finished, but the craftsman was finishing up the tail. Tore knew that these pieces were made to be detachable so they could be removed once the boat reached home shores again. This was so Norway's guardian spirits wouldn't be scared away.

"Fine work, ja?" The craftsman broke Tore's train of thought.

"Very fine work. Your painting is magnificent. I don't even think a real sea serpent would be able to tell this wasn't real!" Tore started to touch the massive serpent head. "No. No." The man said quickly. "It isn't dry yet. You will smear the paint!"

Tore apologized and returned to the group. Thorvald noticed that Eirik had returned. "Admiring the serpent, ja? That man is the best there is at carving and painting."

"It is a wonderful job, Father." Tore smiled. "Well, worth the gold you must have paid."

"Gold, ja! Much gold." Thorvald laughed. Tore went up to the side of the ship and ran her hand along the smooth sides. Workers were busy erecting the tall, sturdy masts. Silently, she wondered what the sails would look like. She had seen a lot of different types from time to time out on the sea. There were checkered sails and striped sails, and many others that were both colorful and practical. Tore was thinking about all of this when she was aware of Thorvald standing near her.

"What are you dreaming about, boy?" Thorvald cocked his old head to the side inquisitively.

"I was wondering what the sails are going to look like." Tore shielded her eyes from the sun peering up at the masts being erected as they spoke.

"Ah, interested in the finer details! That is what makes you such a good storyteller. Most men don't bother." Thorvald smiled and nodded. "The sails will be white with red stripes. They're being made right now by women in the market."

Tore nodded, trying not to smile. Then she switched moods. "Father, are you coming on this raid?" She asked suddenly aware of how old Thorvald was and the slim odds he might return alive.

"I wouldn't let you boys go off and have all the fun without me!" Thorvald laughed loudly.

Tore frowned.

"I know what you're thinking, boy. Don't. If I die, I die. Better to die with my sword in my hand, then to die in my sleep like a woman!" Thorvald growled, but not too menacingly.

Tore nodded. "You speak the truth." She said simply. She wanted to say that she had known a lot of women who hadn't died in their beds, peacefully; but she held her tongue. In fact, most of the women she had known who were dead had died horrible, painful deaths in childbirth. Men often forgot that birthing a child could sometimes be a battle too.

That night around the night meal, once the women had left, Thorvald discussed more of the details for the shore raid. They would go to a place called East Anglia. Tore wondered where Ulf had gone, and if he was still there. Thorvald had mentioned that many raiding parties chose to stay through the winter months if the conditions were right and the women were plentiful...but they would be coming back as soon as the raid was accomplished. Slaves and loot was the primary reason for this raid. More and more traders began coming to Tunsberg, and there had been less and less to trade lately.

Thorvald seemed younger and happier in the glow of the fire. The approaching raid seemed to give him a rush that he had not felt for years. He had waited until his sons were old enough that they could sail with him into battle and into glory, and finally this day had arrived. He paced around with a new found vigor rather than sitting in his chair like he usually did each night.

Thorvald raised his hand suddenly, while his sons were talking, and they all hushed in mid-sentence. "I have gifts for you, my sons."

Thorvald smiled and went to the far corner of the room. He dragged a pallet behind him that was heavy with six leather-covered bundles.

"There is one for each of you." Thorvald waved his hand over the mysterious packages, indicating that they should each pick one up.

When they untied the leather cord that held the leather coverings over the gift, the hide fell away to reveal brand new shields. Each of them was identical. The men looked at each other and smiled. Thorvald stood, hands on hips, watching approvingly at the joy he had brought to his sons, now all holding sturdy, new shields.

Tore ran her hands around the round, wood shield. There were metal rivets all over the front and wood ribs for strength on the back. The whole shield was black, covered with leather, and had metal rimmed along the edge. It was heavy, and sturdy.

Jens grumbled something barely audible to the brothers. Thorvald grunted, and then asked, "Something is not to your liking, as usual, son?" Thorvald scowled at Jens. "It is fine." Jens said slowly.

"But, not fancy enough for your tastes? Is that it, boy?" Thorvald had this way of reducing a man to a mouse with one change of his tone.

Jens touched his shield and said nothing. "I suppose you had hoped for one of those gaudy yellow and red painted numbers? Or some other fancy painted shield?" Thorvald looked at the pleased looks his other sons wore; there was never any pleasing Jens. He had been difficult since birth. Thorvald sighed.

"No, father. This is exactly what I wanted." Jens said with his teeth clenched.

"So, now you lie to your father as well as begrudge the gifts I give you?" Thorvald sounded a bit angry, but Tore reasoned that everyone, including Thorvald, must be used to Jens typical ungrateful attitude.

"Yes, father. You are correct. I would have chosen a more colorful shield. Your tastes are plain." Jens shrugged. "My tastes will keep you alive." Thorvald cleared his throat and then continued, "Do you want everyone on the coast of East Anglia to see you coming with your pretty, colored shield? You young men think nothing of practicality today!" Thorvald grunted.

"It is a fine shield, father. Sturdy, strong...better than a painted fancy shield." Claus nodded energetically. "I am glad my other sons agree with me." Thorvald smiled.

"One of them is not your son." Jens growled casting a glaring expression Eirik's way.

Thorvald knit his eyebrows close together. A look crossed his face that scared Tore nearly to death. She felt her heart quicken and a knot bulge in her stomach as she watched Thorvald's anger unfold.

"I decide who my sons are and who they are not!" Thorvald boomed. "I suggest you keep that in mind, Jens." Jens snorted. He knew that he was the eldest son, and therefore had his position in life sealed and protected by fate...only death could steal it away from him and that was not going to happen. Jens also planned on not taking this ugly shield into battle. He would simply purchase his own if it meant avoiding this ugly leather creation his father expected him to carry.

Jens' comment seemed to put a damper on the rest of the night. Thorvald retired early and promised to discuss the raid in further detail in the morning. They had plenty of time before he planned to shove off.

The next morning came all too quickly. Tore had restlessly tried to sleep, but visions of Tyr and his anger haunted her. She had spent most of the night pleading with Sif to protect her in whatever lay ahead. There was no going back; Thorvald had a plan to take them directly into the thick of things. Men! They were so driven by greed and amassing wealth. Tore couldn't see why she had ever wished she were a man...now that she was living as one.

Tore pulled on a pair of striped pantaloons and went through her ritual of binding up her breasts. She had mastered breast binding to a tee. She had the best technique down and it was doubtful now if anyone would ever be able to tell that she was a woman. She just had to trust Sif that her secret would be forever protected.

Thorvald was waiting to take them down to the beach again. He was overzealous in his preparations, but better to be over prepared than caught short. Tore and Brock walked along with a few of Brock's younger male cousins. "Eirik!" shouted Snorri, Brock's ten-year-old cousin. Tore looked in the direction of the voice. Snorri stood legs apart, a smile on his baby face, and a large stick in his hands ready to challenge Eirik to a round of play fighting.

Tore smiled.

"Come on! What are you waiting for?" Snorri taunted.

Tore laughed and held her hand out for the stick that Snorri's little friend, Sweyn, was standing by ready to provide.

"Feeling brave today, Snorri?" Tore called out against the salty sea wind.

"I feel brave everyday, Eirik!" Snorri laughed and lunged forward, jabbing towards Eirik's mid-section. Tore decided to let Snorri have some fun. She could easily put him on his little backside, but that would take all of the fun out of playing for Snorri. Besides, Tore could remember her brother and father playing with her much like this, when the other men weren't around of course. Play fighting taught boys valuable skills they would later need in battle; the boys rarely knew that though.

Snorri tried to take out Tore's legs, but she averted his stick by jumping high in the air. Her body in motion, half off the ground, Snorri then tried to thrust his stick at her on her way down; but, to no avail. Tore had barely landed on the sandy soil, when she brought her stick down in a swooshing arc and took Snorri's legs out form under him swiftly. Snorri was face down in the dirt before he even knew what had happened. He raised his dirty face, smiling a broad smile.

Tore laughing, stuck out her hand to help him up.

Brock came up behind them.

"Tried to take on the best again, huh?" Brock tousled Snorri's hair, knocking the sand out.

"I almost won too!" Snorri laughed.

"You did put up a pretty good fight, for awhile." Tore laughed.

Sweyn tagged along faithfully behind them. "Tomorrow, will you fight me, Eirik?"

"Tomorrow is a good day to die then, Sweyn?" Tore laughed.

"Oh, no!" Sweyn looked horrified. "I only meant to play!"

Tore laughed and slapped the boy between the shoulder blades. "Of course you did! I'm just teasing!"

Sweyn's face broke out in a relieved smiled, revealing his missing front teeth. He beamed from ear to ear.

Brock laughed. "You have a way with kids."

Tore and Brock stopped and watched Snorri and Sweyn run up ahead on the beach between the workers and the traders who were wandering around trying to rout up some more business.

"Naw, not really. I just treat them the way I liked to be treated when I was their age." Tore shrugged and jabbed the stick that she still had in her hand deep into the sand.

"A lot of people forget how it was when they were children. Maybe that's why you're such a good story teller." Brock scratched at his beard.

"Everyone likes stories, not just children." Tore laughed.

"I suppose it's the child in us that cries out for the story to be told, Ja?" Brock smiled.

"Maybe." Tore smiled back.

"Hey, I thought I warned you about that." Brock pointed to her face.

"I've been working on it. I caught myself a couple of times when I was talking with your father. I wouldn't want him to think I look too pretty!" Tore laughed.

"I don't think Father cares what you look like. All he cares about is how well you use that sword, and trust me, he loves how you use that sword!" Brock pointed to Tore's sword hanging at her hip.

Tore looked seaward as her mind raced over thoughts she wished she wasn't thinking. She would love to see how Brock used his sword, she thought to herself, and then suppressed a smile…though it wasn't the sword at his hip she was interested in, more like the sword of flesh that hung between his legs. Tore looked at Brock finding it slightly amusing that she knew what she was thinking about, and he was standing there, boots covered in sand, hands shielding his eyes from the briny wind, thinking she was a man.

Tore snapped her head in the direction of the market. "Let's go see if there is a new story teller around."

Brock shrugged. "Nothing else to do."

The market was full of the usual traders and merchants. Looking around, Tore could see why Thorvald wanted to get a new crop of slaves in here. There weren't too many being offered, and the ones that were available were girls who had apparently seen better days. Most of them weren't even girls any longer, and had long ago lost that virginal glow that so many men preferred. No doubt Thorvald had visions of breaking in a whole bunch of new girls in preparation for the market. Tore shivered. She couldn't think of many things more horrible than to be kidnapped from the world you know, and dragged half an ocean away to be raped and enslaved by a people you only feared. Nothing worse except being woke up in the middle of the night to hear your whole family being slaughtered like goats.

Tore shook that thought out of her head. Didn't do her any good dwelling on the past. She couldn't' go back and change those events. She didn't even know who had killed them. She only knew that she had to stay alive, but in the process of staying alive, she might just go and get herself killed.

Brock said something that she didn't hear.

"Are you listening to me?" Brock asked.

"Huh? What?" Tore turned her attention back to Brock.

"I said, do you want to get some mead?" Brock laughed at his friend's daydreaming capabilities. "I sure as Hades hope you don't fucking go off dreaming like that when we're shit deep in battle."

"We aren't going to any battle. We're going off to steal women, children, and gold." Tore said sarcastically.

"Well, you have to fight in the process." Brock laughed at Eirik's sudden seriousness.

"I suppose so." Tore shrugged. "And, no, I don't want any mead, but I'll go with you to go get some."

Brock nodded and they sought out the stall. After knocking back a flagon of mead, Brock wiped his mouth on the back of his hand. "Well, now what?"

"I think we should see if your father needs our help with anything." Tore bit on her bottom lip, tearing it to shreds of chapped and dried skin that just hung there.

"He probably has everything under control. You know father, he pays everyone imaginable to do every task imaginable." Brock looked around the streets.

"Just the same." Tore tilted her head towards their dwelling signifying that they should go home.

Thorvald was sitting on the bench outside of the main hall when they arrived. He was spitting on his sword and rubbing in a handful of sand for polish, when he noticed that Brock and Eirik were approaching.

"What are you up to?" He said between hocking up great globs of mucus filled saliva.

"We walked up through the market." Brock said sitting down besides Thorvald.

Tore could see the resemblance immediately. Thorvald was the exact picture of Brock in his old age.

"Did you finish what you meant to accomplish on the beach this morning?" Tore asked.

Thorvald grunted. "Sails are nearly finished. Should be, I paid enough for them to have been finished months ago."

Tore fingered the braid hanging on the right side of her head. "Are they fine sails then?"

"Best that my gold could buy!" Thorvald laughed.

"That doesn't guarantee that the sails are fine, father." Brock laughed and looked at Tore.

"No, it doesn't. You are wise, son. But, these sails are fine. Most of the preparations are finished." Thorvald stopped rubbing at his sword for a moment to look at his son. "All that is left to do is the sacrifice."

Brock looked down for a moment. He hated this custom. In some parts of Norway, it was entirely disused. He wished his father would let go of some of the old ways, at least on this one issue.

Thorvald studied his son for a minute, and then looked at Tore. "Eirik, what are your views on the sacrifice?"

Tore cleared her throat. "Well, father, my tribe stopped that practice long ago…mostly due to the fact that slaves are hard to come by."

Thorvald nodded in agreement to this statement.

Brock looked at his grizzled father. "It is said that Hablok Bloodaxe is opposed to the sacrifice as well."

Thorvald hooted with laughter. "Son! The Bloodaxe is probably a bleached skeleton on some beach by now. What care I for what Hablok Bloodaxe feels!"

Brock thought about that for a moment. The wergild that was served not too long ago came to mind as all too solid proof of his father's feelings towards the authority of Hablok Bloodaxe; but, of course, he didn't bring it up as it was a subject that one did not discuss ever again once it was carried out.

"So, both of you are against the sacrifice?" Thorvald asked.

"Would it matter if we were?" Brock asked hopefully.

Thorvald thought for a moment and then matter of factly replied, "No. But, it does matter that you have had the courage to be honest with me. Your sniveling brothers would have agreed with me out of fear, and Jens would have disagreed with me just for the sake of disagreement."

Brock smiled slightly. "I never know when Jens really agrees or disagrees with you father. He just wants to contradict you for the sake of establishing some type of power."

"Power? Power!" Thorvald struck his sword into the dirt suddenly. "That boy knows nothing of power. Jens knows nothing about mostly everything, but then, I don't have to tell either of you two that, do I?" Thorvald jerked his sword back up from the dirt and held it up to the sunlight studying it closely.

"Jens hates Eirik." Brock said shortly as if this was the first time anyone had ever noticed Jens' attitude.

"It is good to have your enemies close where you can watch them." Thorvald snorted.

"I don't wish him to be my enemy." Tore said quietly.

"Very few men choose their enemies, Eirik." Thorvald looked into Tore's face kindly.

"How do I make him not my enemy then?" Tore asked.

"That is not for you to try. Jens has made his choice. Jealousy and petty rage are his motives, but nevertheless, he has made his choice. Just remember that hate has a way of destroying the hater in the end." Thorvald slid his sword into the scabbard resting by his side on the bench.

"I will remember, father." Tore nodded, trying not to smile.

Brock watched Eirik's expressions. He wondered what Eirik was thinking in that story filled head of his. Thorvald seemed to have a tender spot for Eirik, one that Brock found touching as much as Jens found resentful.

Thorvald got up slowly, but then turned back to Brock and Eirik. "A warning, to both of you. Jens is your brother, ja?"

Brock and Tore nodded.

"He is your brother, but that is no reason to trust him. Jens is like the angry sea wave that reaches out to pull your ship under black waters. When we sail, and when we reach our battle site, keep Jens where you can see him. A dagger in the back in the middle of battle is an easy way to rid yourself of brothers you do not want." Thorvald looked sad for a moment, and then turned and went into the hall.

Brock and Tore sat silently, stunned by the words their father had issued. Both had entertained these thoughts, but neither of them ever thought Thorvald himself would warn them of Jens potential treachery.

Brock looked down at his leather boots, fiddling with a leather lace. "Never did I imagine I would hear my father say that."

"Neither did I." Tore said pushing down the lump in her throat.

"Do you think that Jens would really try to kill one of us?" Brock said incredulously.

"Why just one? Why not take us both out?" Tore raised her eyebrows.

"Wouldn't that look suspicious?" Brock laughed.

"Jens thinks he's indestructible." Tore stated.

"Either way, it's an eerie thought." Brock got up from the bench and touched his scabbard absently.

"Well, we've been warned." Tore wondered if Jens would be Tyr's weapon against her.

"And it's a warning I'll not soon forget." Brock shook his head and then added, "Oh, I forgot, I'm supposed to meet Amalie tonight."

"Again?" Tore said the words before she had a chance to think about them.

"Ja." Brock laughed.

"I thought after everything your brothers had said that you wouldn't want to see her again." Tore held open the door as they went into the hall.

"Shit. I don't care what they said. It's a long boat ride to East Anglia, and she is as good as they claim." Brock smiled.

"It's only a month to East Anglia." Tore laughed.

"That's one month longer than I like to be without a woman!" Brock laughed again.

"That sounds more like Jens talking than you." Tore pulled up a bench to sit on.

"Why don't you come with me? Amalie has a friend, Helge. I'm sure she'd like to wish you a good trip!" Brock chuckled.

"I have my chest to pack." Tore said.

"You're much too serious about women, you know? You aren't married yet, why keep yourself in some sort of self-made prison?" Brock could understand Eirik's hesitations concerning women; he just wished his friend would lighten up once in awhile.

"Maybe later." Tore smiled. "I want to make sure I don't forget anything."

"All you really need is your sword, and your…sword!" Brock grabbed his crotch.

"All I need is Gungnir." Tore touched her scabbard. "I don't want women who are fucked at sword point."

"Interesting point." Brock laughed.

"Have a good time." Tore nodded and headed in the direction of her room.

Brock felt bad for being so anxious to go see Amalie, slut that she was. "You're sure you don't want to come?" He called after Eirik.

"Positive." Tore called over her shoulder.

"I could bring them here." Brock tried one last time to include his friend.

"You go have a good time." Tore stopped before heading towards her room. "Tell the girls hello for me."

"Oh, I will, brother! I will!" Brock laughed and got up from his bench.

Tore turned and went up to her room. She closed the door behind her and she couldn't help but feel mildly ill at the thought of Brock and Amalie together again. She loved him. She wanted him. If ever in her life she wanted to be a woman it was now...but, now, she had to be a man. Ironic, wasn't it? Tore punched the feather filled pillow on her bed, and cursed.

Would he ever be hers? Tore fought back the tears. She would not cry over a man. In the end, most men weren't worth it. Tore squeezed her eyes shut and blocked out the image of Brock mounting Amalie. It was a scene she hoped she would never see again, and wished she had never seen in the first place.

"Oh, Brock!" Tore sighed and lay on her back, staring up at the cold, black ceiling feeling lonelier than she had for a long time.

Chapter 11

It was still dark when Tore and the others made their way to the beach where the langskips awaited. Thorvald had decided to offer the sacrifice to the gods directly before setting sail. Some of the men had objected to this, wanting instead a larger, more elaborate celebration; but, Thorvald was aware of the rising influence of this new religion called Christianity and didn't want to make any trouble before setting sail. So, it was decided the sacrifice would be before dawn. Tore sat on a gnarled log before one of the fires. The air was chilly and smelled of salt and seaweed.

Somewhere across the beach, she could see a man being led in chains towards the central fire. She had never actually witnessed a sacrifice, but she had heard of them being offered. Her tribe wasn't all that active in the slave trade, so there weren't always extra people to do away with no matter what the price a god was asking.

Through the smoke from the fires, and the steam from the waters, she could barely make out the man's face. He was young, not much older than herself or Brock. He wasn't a big man; even if he had been there would have been no chance for escape with the heavy chains that bound his wrists and ankles. She wondered if this foreign man knew his fate yet, or was he simply suspecting more beatings and more humiliation at the hands of his captors. Brock was quiet next to her on the log. Tore could tell by the expression on his face that he wasn't one hundred percent approving of this ritual, but he wouldn't say it. Brock whispered something to her that she didn't catch. She made a look that said she didn't hear him, so he leaned in closer.

The feel of his breath on her ear made her hair stand up on her arms and neck. Her heart beat more rapidly, and she suddenly found breathing difficult.

"I said, he's a warrior. For a Strandhogg, they only sacrifice warriors, or those caught fighting." Brock whispered.

"I've heard of girl slaves being sacrificed at these things.... before a Strandhogg, I mean." Tore whispered back. She had heard that it didn't really matter what the gender of the sacrifice was. It was the sacrifice offered before the shore raid that was the only important element of the whole ordeal.

"Sometimes. Only when there aren't any male slaves or captured enemies." Brock said and then leaned away, still watching the man in chains who was standing near a fire with an inquisitive look about his face.

Tore was quiet. What was there to say? Her chest was being loaded onto the ship; her weapons were sharp and waiting in their sheaths and scabbards for whatever task their owner might need them for. In an hour or so, she and Brock and the rest of the men would be in these ships headed off to East Anglia.... a land she had never known about until Thorvald described it to her. Essentially, she was terrified. For one month she would be trapped aboard a ship with forty or so other men...trapped in close contact with men who thought she was a man and wouldn't hesitate to kill her if they found out the little scam she had pulled off making them all look like fools. Tore looked at Brock and wondered if he too would want her dead if he knew her secret. She loved him so much, and she knew that he loved her too; but, not in a lover's sense. He loved her as a brother, as a confidant, and a friend. There were no dreams in his mind of touching her soft flesh, of feeling her under him, of touching her hair in the moonlight. There were no dreams of them together at all, because Brock thought she was a man.

Tore sighed. Brock looked at her and knitted his eyebrows closely. "I don't like it anymore than you do." He muttered.

"I didn't say that I disapproved." Tore wasn't sure what her position should be on this tradition. "Oh." Brock said now raising his eyebrows. "I assumed you would."

"I don't know how I feel on the subject. Never seen it before." Tore said while holding out her cold hands before the fire.

"Well, you're going to now. Look. Here comes father." Brock stood up.

Tore saw Thorvald coming in a pair of brightly striped pants and a steel helmet. The nose guard that jutted downward from the brow of the helmet made Thorvald look much more menacing than he already did.

Another man jerked the man in chains up and over towards Thorvald. From behind Thorvald, stepped another man, a man they called Horik the Black for his dark hair. Brock looked at Tore who was staring intently upon Horik the Black. Brock knew that Eirik didn't know that Horik was the man who would offer the sacrifice.

"You do know what the Bloodeagle is, don't you?" Brock whispered to Tore.

"Yes. I've heard it described." Tore said quietly. "Many men are sickened by it at first." Brock said slowly.

"I know this too. Don't worry about me, Brock." Tore smiled at him.

Horik the Black came forward and recited an ancient saga praising the battle feats of long dead warriors, and of the goodness and graces of mighty gods. He pulled from his heavy leather belt an axe and held it high for all to see. The crowd of men hushed immediately and stared, transfixed at the weapon in Horik's hand. The light cast from the flickering fires bounced off of the newly shined axe blade and made it look more like a shimmering diamond, than a weapon of destruction. This was not a household axe used for cutting wood. This was a smaller version of a battle-axe, used for killing.

Tore watched the blood-hungry expressions on the faces of the time-weathered warriors. Now she understood Brock's disgust. These men were so excited about the preeminent death of this chained man, that they could barely contain themselves. When Horik had pulled the axe forward and raised it high above his head, many of the men had drawn their swords and brandished them high as well. They called out in chanting form, loudly and lustily.

Brock sucked in his breath as two men led the chained man towards a large boulder that had been rolled here for this purpose. The chained man was just now beginning to realize what fate had in store for him. Now he began to struggle for the first time. The two men wrapped the chains around the boulder and tested to see if the chained man was secure, then they stepped back into the crowd. Horik offered more prayers and turned his attention towards the now weeping man. Brock looked down on Eirik. "You don't have to watch, Eirik." Brock said quietly. Tore noticed that indeed there were quite a lot of men who were looking down at the ground now, rather than directly towards the man chained to the rock.

Tore only looked at Brock and said nothing. She needed to know what sort of people she was among...what sort of person she was.

Horik stepped aside as another man emerged from the darkness. The man bent over the chained man and cut his skin from his breastbone to his pelvis. Blood spurted up over the man as he made his cut. Tore swallowed a large lump that had welled up in her throat. She could see Brock looking down at his boots.

Next, Horik, grinning dementedly, approached the bleeding man and began chopping at the man's ribs, separating them from the poor victim's spine. The chained man screamed in agony the whole time. Tore now felt too stunned to look away. Her eyes were hooked to the man on the rock, she couldn't make herself move…and it seemed as if she hadn't breathed for an awfully long time.

The crowd cheered. Horik inserted his massively hairy arms into the screaming man's innards and yanked out the man's lungs through the wounds. The lungs hung there, like bleeding crimson wings, pulsing over the man's butchered body and over the gray of the rock.

Tore gasped for air. The lungs pulsated and quivered. The man screamed and gasped, until finally he could scream no more…and then he died.

It was quiet.

Tore found the power to move once again, and Brock looked up at the bloody mess chained on the rock before him. Tore was sure that she had never seen anything so barbaric as the event she had just watched. Not even the slaughter of her family had matched the purposed and well-planned murder of this man. This sacrifice.

Tore prayed to Sif. She hoped that this sacrifice would not be in vain. She prayed for their safety, but most of all, for her own protection. Sif did not answer.

Tore turned her back on the gruesome picture and watched as Brock did the same. Everything seemed like it was going in slow motion…voices sounded far off, the waves seemed to stand still. The odor of blood and sea mingled together and seeped their way into Tore's hair and clothes. Welcome to battle, a tiny voice inside of her said.

Brock crossed the beach without a word. The men were boarding the ships now. Other men would clean up the bloody mess on the beach before people were up and about and could see such a spectacle. Thorvald grumbled and fumed about the days when he was a child and it was not uncommon for such a sacrifice to be offered for less important things than a shore raid. He wondered out loud what this world was coming to if a man couldn't even practice his traditions anymore. Another man argued that in this Christianity, people had sacrificed the son of a god, had nailed him to a wood cross and pierced him with a sword…. was there a difference? Thorvald and the man continued to gripe and groan as the other men found their places in the boats.

Tore and Brock sat side by side in silence. What was there to say after that? Words would not come for either one of them, so they thought it best to simply stay quiet. There would be plenty of time for talk later. Tore felt the oar before her. She was glad her hands were already calloused and worn from work and training. She knew that shortly her hands would be bleeding and painful enough.

The horn was blown, and each man grasped the oar before him and pulled. The sails were hoisted, and the ships were slowly inching their ways out to sea.

Tore heaved with all of her might. The other men on her oar did the same, and slowly, Tore could feel the rocking motion of the boat on the waves and the gentle propulsion forward caused by their rowing. She was between Brock and his brother Claus. Claus, unfortunately for him, had the seat next to the side of the boat. Occasionally, a salty spray of seawater would rise over the shields on top of the ship's side, and cover him with water. A few times, Tore got sprayed too. She more than once uttered a silent prayer to Aegir beseeching him for their safe passage over the swan road they were traveling now. Tore hoped that the sacrifice the other men had offered Aegir, the god of sea and storms, would be sufficient enough to allow them to once again set foot on land safely.

As they rowed out of the great fjord they passed by a rocky waterfall that flowed beautifully off of the cliff behind them. It was a beautiful site to behold, but no sooner had they seen it then they had rowed past it. Along the sides of the boat, Tore could see the rocky, forested splendor of her home, Norway. Would she ever come home again? Tore only prayed that the answer would be yes. What man would want to leave such a beautiful land as theirs? Did Ulf ever have these longings when he was far away in a distant land, on some other distant shore, far from his native homeland and everything that he was used to?

Tore pulled the goatskin mantle around her shoulders closer and readjusted the silver snake shaped pin that held it there. She sighed and once again took hold of the oar and rowed. By the time they got to East Anglia, her muscles would be twice their present size and no doubt very sore. She wondered how men were able to jump directly from the boat and to shore to raid and fight, after having rowed for so long and so sorely. Maybe some of that fervor was simply exaggeration. Maybe they really did make camp before stealing out to rape and plunder.

Tore's helmet began to bother her after a few hours. She had purchased an elaborate helmet for herself and one for Brock. The helmet was in the shape of a boar's head. The nose guard was a wide one, and occasionally, Tore felt like she was going cross-eyed from having looked around it for so long. Brock had complained of a similar feeling but reasoned that they would get used to it after a few days.

Even with her goatskin mantle, and fur-lined boots, the water sloshing continually around her ankles made her cold and irritable. The rowing made her shoulders ache, and she found out that she had never really been tired before this. Tore looked over at Brock who looked as if he was on the verge of sleep. She nudged him softly to bring him to.

"Damn. Did I fall asleep?" Brock muttered. "Nearly. It's been about ten hours. Maybe we should start taking longer shifts, it looks like the other men are doing that so more people can rest." Tore looked at Claus to see what he thought about her idea.

"Sounds good to me. I have to piss again." Claus mumbled from under the lambskin he had pulled up over his face to protect him from the constant spray of stinging salt water. "Again?" Brock said laughing. "You sure you aren't a pregnant woman?"

Tore laughed.

"I drank a lot of mead before setting sail. Father said it would help calm my worries." Claus got up rigidly and scooted past Tore and Brock.

At the back of the ship, a small partition had been erected that held a large iron bucket to serve as a type of toilet. Most of the men just pissed over the edge of the boat where they were rowing, but nature called in other ways too. Tore was glad that some men were modest and demanded the partition. It made things easier for her. Since she had so many clothes on, mantles, and other skins for warmth, it was easy for her to squat over the iron bucket and relieve herself without fear of discovery. The skins hung all around her concealing her nakedness from any eyes that might be watching. She only hoped that in a week or so when her woman time hit, that she'd be able to tend to her needs without being discovered.

It was almost night. Tore knew that when anchored the men made sort of makeshift tents to hover under for warmth, but no mention of setting anchor had been made. She assumed that meant they would continue rowing into the night. Most of the navigation was done by the sun with a lot of sailors, but the navigator that Thorvald had among his tribe was adept at both navigating by the sun and the stars; so, no time would have to be wasted setting anchor as soon as the sun retired for the night. This made for quicker traveling time, but unfortunately it meant more rowing.

Tore had eaten several strips of dried herring, but she found herself ravishingly hungry once again. She tried to avoid the mead that constantly was in circulation. Mead was a dangerous thing to her for many reasons, although it did have a warming effect on her body. It caused her to have to pass water more than usual, and she wanted to cut down on her chances of discovery if possible. It also made her tired. She was already dead tired, even with the short naps that she was able to catch when her shift was up. Visions of roasted meats and gravies kept dancing around in her head teasing her and tormenting her mouth juices. She could almost smell Ymma's stews and soups!

One thing she could also smell was the stench from the spilled iron bucket that had toppled over when they had hit the last big wave. It was up to the men to dump the bucket when they noticed that it was growing full; but, the men were more apt to think that it wasn't full yet and that the next person could dump it.... only, no one was dumping it. She could hear Horik giving a loud order that from now on the bucket would be dumped by every man regardless of how full the bucket was. It was bad enough to have freezing cold water sloshing around their feet, shit and piss made the whole area intolerable.

On the third day, Thorvald decided that come nightfall they would anchor so the men could get some real sleep. He had noticed the decreased speed of the boat and the obvious haggardness of the men. Tore kept rowing with this goal in mind. Sleep. Real sleep. Well, she thought to herself, as real as real could get cramped up on this sea chest with no bed except her hudfat. She had made her own hudfat. Tore remembered Ulf having given her an old and worn out hudfat many years ago. He had primarily used his as a skin bag for possessions, instead of a sleeping bag. Ulf was more of the rugged and tough sort who felt that being comfortable was some odd form of weakness. Not her! She relished the idea of burying herself deep in the warmth of her hudfat and sleeping like a baby! It seemed like years, not mere days, since she had slept in her warm bed back at Thorvald's dwelling.

Brock took a swig of water from his water skin and continued rowing. Tore didn't feel like making conversation so they rowed in silence. Claus griped bitterly about having to row for so long and about Thorvald just now deciding to set anchor at nightfall.

Brock told him to be silent. Tore was a little more tolerant of Claus' complaints. Brock was growing more irate and cranky from having to be so cold and cooped up for so long in such a tight place. Tore felt like she was caught between two feuding bears. She found herself having to smooth over comments made by each of the brothers in order to avoid a major showdown right here in the boat.

"Hey, you two. Save it for the raid, huh?" Tore finally snapped at both of them. Brock raised his eyebrows, obviously he had no ideas of how annoying he and Claus' bickering had become.

He smiled. "Are we annoying you, Eirik?"

Tore nodded and kept rowing silently.

"How much longer till nightfall?" Claus asked.

"I don't know. Everything seems out of balance somehow out here. I'm still a little seasick." Tore wiped the sweat off of her brow with the back of hers sleeve and kept rowing.

"There's a sundial in the stern of the ship." Brock stated.

Claus nodded.

The three of them continued rowing without saying much. They were all just biding time until the sun went away and the moon came out of hiding. Sleep wasn't too far away now. With this thought, Tore was able to find renewed strength to continue her rowing.

When night finally fell, the men were visibly relieved. Men gathered in clusters after the anchors had been let down. Tents were erected and groups of men huddled together under them exchanging conversation and food. Under their tent, Claus, Tore, and Brock pulled out their hudfats from their chests and huddled close together for warmth. No talking here, only the desire to sleep soundly. If sound sleep on a rocking ship was possible. Tore shut her eyes and listened to the conversations of the timeworn men around her. They were used to these conditions and some even seemed happy to be here. Somewhere in the boat she heard the voices of drunken men singing an old song and the beating of a hand held drum that some man had decided too valuable to leave behind. The soft beat of the drum and the slurred singing of the men lulled her to sleep and despite the wet wood around her and the awkwardness of having one leg pulled up close to her chest in order to accommodate her sea chest, she found she was falling into a deep and welcome sleep.

Morning broke with a glorious sky full of colors and clouds. The sheer beauty of the world around her, and the strength gained from sleep made everything seem more exhilarating and exciting than it had even been when they first set sail. For the first time, it really dawned on Tore that she was at sea. She was a woman, sailing as a man, in a langskip, as a Viking warrior! The concept nearly proved overwhelming. It slowly sank into her brain, as she awoke and watched the men around her stretching and resuming their rowing positions. Thorvald would be sounding the horn shortly that would signify they were pulling anchor and sailing once again. Someone was filling cups with warm tea. Tore passed her wood traveler's cup down the row and it came back brimming with steaming tea. The pungent odor livened her senses and she drank it heartily, washing down the bread she had been gnawing on. Brock and Claus were folding up their hudfats and punching them down into their sea chests. Tore was one step ahead of them, and already ready to row. Brock and Claus were more like their old selves. Tore was glad; she was tired of being their mediator.

On the tenth day, Tore had to deal with the awful realization that she had begun her moon cycle. Ordinarily, her woman's time was uneventful; but finding a way to deal with her personal needs while trapped on a boat full of men was going to be a challenge. She finally arrived at a plan that seemed to work. Most of the men slept heavily at night if they were anchored. On nights that they took shifts and kept sailing, the ones who were awake rowed in a type of comatose state, so one lone man going to relieve himself at the back of the ship didn't draw too much attention. Tore had realized the first night when she emptied the iron bucket over the side, that the piece of lambs wool that she had used to absorb her bleeding had not sunk, but floated on top of the water. Tore had held her breath hoping that no one would see it and wonder what it was. The next time she was more careful. Tore took a bronze coin from the purse at her belt and used a piece of cord to tie the soiled wool around it. This time when she tossed the bucket of piss out, the lamb's wool sunk right away. No more worries. No one would be able to detect a thing. Her clothes were loose enough to camouflage any accidental leaking, and she wasn't afraid of anyone smelling dried blood on her. Everyone on this ship reeked to Valhalla. They were all in need of baths...badly! The ship smelled worse due to spilled urine and feces, rotting food, and the occasional puddle of vomit that occurred due to overindulgence in mead or wine. Tore was pretty sure she'd be okay. Luckily for her, she had a short moon cycle. She whispered to Sif for protection and tried not to think of her body's involuntary functions.

Another week had passed and Tore found herself with the others anchored at sea with a clear black sky, and millions of tiny stars twinkling like gemstones in the sky. Out here rocking up and down, it was peaceful. The men were either sleeping or talking quietly. Some were dreaming of all of the things they hoped to loot, or the women they hoped to discover and keep for their own. All dreams that would come true at someone else's expense. Tore sighed. She was wiping her sword blade slowly. Watching it reflect the small flame that Brock had lit in a whale oil lamp. Brock was working on mending part of his leather belt that had somehow gotten caught on something in the boat and ripped. He was all thumbs, but Tore didn't relish the thought of mending anything so she let him work at it himself. After all, she wasn't a woman to just come running and fix his every little problem at his beck and call. Tore stifled a laugh. Actually, she was a woman, but that didn't change how she felt about sewing!

Brock cursed as the whalebone needle pierced his thumb and drew blood. Reflexively, he stuck his thumb in his mouth and sucked at the blood.

"Damn needle." He muttered and continued sewing.

"You need a wife." Tore smiled and said.

"Like I need a sword in the gullet." Brock looked up for a moment and answered sarcastically.

"Hmm. Why don't you ask Claus to do that? He's pretty handy with needles. I saw him mending the fishing net for your father the other day. He did a pretty good job of it." Tore held her sword up straight in front of her and studied the polishing job she had just completed.

"You still calling that thing Gungnir?" Brock asked without commenting on Tore's suggestion to seek Claus' assistance.

"Ja. Why? Don't you like the name?" Tore slid the sword slowly back into its scabbard.

"I like the name. I'm just not too sure you should name a sword after Odin's spear, that's all." Brock stopped his mending for a moment.

"Does it frighten you?" Tore raised an eyebrow.

"Eirik, you know that there is little that frightens me." Brock growled.

"I know that there is much that you pretend does not frighten you." Tore laughed.

"You talk too much." Brock twisted his bottom lip and continued to struggle with his mending.

"Ja. I forgot. That is why they call me Eirik the Silent Graafell." Tore laughed.

"I've never known you to be so silent. They should call you Eirik Talks Too Much Graafell." Brock laughed.

"There you are in a better mood now. Almost done with your belt?" Tore asked, eager to blow out the lamp and get some sleep.

"Almost." Brock said, and then turned his head towards a noise on the right side of the ship.

"What's that?" Tore asked getting to her feet.

"I don't know. I was just going to ask that myself." Brock said and then was thrown forward by an incredible bump.

"Aahh!" Tore yelped and grabbed her sea chest to steady herself as the ship lunged to one side sharply.

"What in Hades is that?" Claus woke up from his dozing and was tossed into the side of the sea chests suddenly.

Tore and Brock tried to make their way to the front of the ship where men were gathering. There was that noise again!

It was an eerie noise. Sort of like a high piercing screech. Like a dying bird, or a trapped animal. It was loud, and whatever it was it was coming from whatever had happened to hit their boat.

Brock grasped the aide of the ship and peered over into the dark, murky waters. The moon cast a pearly glow over the water that rippled around them. Bump! Brock fell backwards into Tore who caught him. She held her breath. Brock had fallen directly onto her chest. Would he notice anything there? It had been so long since she had been able to check the condition of her bindings. She had hoped they were still tight and snug. They felt tight; damn near killing her with pain they were so tight.

Brock struggled to his feet, thankful that his friend was there to keep him flying across the boat into the gods only knew what.

"What did you see?" Tore asked.

"Couldn't see a fucking thing! Just water." Brock hissed.

The men in front of them were making a loud commotion. Suddenly, Thorvald emerged from the crowd and attempted to calm them.

Someone cried out, "It's a sign!"

Another voice chimed in fearfully, "The gods are angry!"

Thorvald raised his hand and his voice. "Steady yourselves, men. If the gods are angry it is not for anything we have done. All of us are worthy men, doing the biding of the gods! Remember our sacrifice!"

The men had their heads together whispering and hissing quietly. Thorvald was right. Thorvald was always right. What was this in the water then that threatened to capsize their ship?

Suddenly, it was in front of them, water rose from the depths of the ocean high above the sides of the ship. Water sprayed out over them, even into the ends of the ship. Tore cupped her hands t her eyes to keep out the water and peered up into the night sky.

"Great Sif protect us now!" Tore uttered out loud.

Brock looked at her and back at the black, shiny creature that had emerged from the dark depths of the sea. "Great Aegir!" He prayed and looked terrified towards Eirik.

"What in Hades is that?" Claus hung on to the back of Tore's loose shirt like a frightened child.

The creature before them let out an ear-shattering wail again. They clutched their ears. Visions of shattered wood and drowning men filled Tore's head, as a thousand thoughts rushed and collided with one another. Was she the cause of this creature being disturbed from its sleep? Ws her presence, a woman's presence, causing all of these other men to lose their lives? Granted no one knows on board the ship, but she wasn't quite so arrogant to believe that she had fooled all of the gods too! Surely, Tyr wouldn't' play so dirty! He had to let her at least try to prove herself worthy in battle. To kill her before she even got a chance would not be just...and he was the god of justice; surely, he would give her the chance before killing her! And these other men! It wasn't their faults that she had been able to blind them to the truth and convince them that she was man. For this did they deserve to die?

Tore silently evoked Sif's protection over and over again in her head. All around her men were praying to their gods, and cursing quietly under their breath.

The creature wailed again, and then leaped into the air and plunged back into the blackness of the water around them. The wake the creature left caused the boat to lash back and forth furiously for several minutes. The whole ordeal had seemed like hours, but the creature's emergence had in fact only been a matter of minutes. Once the creature disappeared under the inky waves, men ran to the sides of the ship in an attempt to see if it was truly gone. About a half an hour later, everyone was still quiet, nearly afraid to breath.

It was no surprise to any of the men, when Thorvald hoisted the anchor and set sail in a hurry. Even the mighty, fearless Thorvald had never encountered such a creature. Sea serpents were plenty, but this creature was nothing like anything he had ever seen or heard about before. Hel, herself, must have let this creature loose to terrify those who crossed its waters.

Tore was actually glad to be rowing. It seemed like all of the men were rowing with a newfound strength and making remarkable time. The ship sped along the waves quickly. Tore prayed that the creature they had awakened had once again settled back to sleep. She hoped she never had to encounter such a creature ever again in her life. However short her life might prove to be.

Tore sighed quietly. Battle. She knew what it would be like, but as Thorvald had once said around their fire one night, you don't truly know what battle is until you find yourself knee deep in guts in the middle of it. Tore thought about her sword, where she had discovered it, and wondered what path her life would have taken had she not taken the sword from its resting place. Would she still be going through all of this? Would she have ever met Brock? Tore reasoned that the gods must have ordained all of the events in her life so far, because everything had fit so well into the puzzle. Her family's deaths, the discovery of the sword, the pact wit h Tyr by Sif, her masquerade as a man, being accepted by Throvald's clan, and now here she was aboard one of the most majestic langskips ever to set sail, heading for East Anglia to prove herself worthy in battle for her life.

Most of these men were thinking of their own personal gain. Tore knew in order to be allowed to live, she must not only fight, but fight gallantly, bravely, loot mercilessly, and prove to Try and all of the gods in Aesgar that she was indeed a worthy warrior. Sif had pleaded for her life, and Tore considered it her duty to prove Sif was speaking the truth in claiming that Tore could in fact prove herself a might warrior regardless of the fact that she was a mere mortal woman.

Tore not only had to do this for her life, but she had to do this for all womankind. She had to prove that a woman could have the same instincts, the same reflexes, and the same skills in battle that a man could. In fact, the more she thought about it, she had reasoned that women could probably make better warriors than men given the chance due to their overwhelming maternal instincts to protect their own. Tore arched her back, and breathed deeply. She wondered when they would finally be off of this stinking ship.

As the days passed, that thought crossed her mind daily. Then came the sound of the horn, and the cry from the helm of the ship. "Land Ho!"

Chapter 12

Tore let go of the oar in her hands and stood up. All over the ship, men were doing the same. The coast of East Anglia was rocky, but not like the coast of her homeland. All over were lush green fields and hills. Atop one green hill was a large stone building. She could see men gesturing towards the building and knew this would be one of their targets. Wherever there was a dwelling of this size, there must be smaller dwellings around it that would depend on the protection of the massive stonewalls that the larger dwelling provided.

Brock had gone to the helm to address his father. He returned with more information. It seemed that this stone building was a type of temple for the Christian gods. There would be plenty of gold there, but not many women. Thorvald had encountered these types of buildings several times before so he knew the general layouts of the huge structures. They always proved easy targets once the door was brought down, which sometimes could prove difficult.

The boat was brought to shore and anchored. One by one the men leapt over the sides of the ship and onto the sandy shore. Tore knew that she would have to draw blood soon. This was only the beginning of Tyr's test. She would have to kill innocent people and seem to enjoy it while she was doing it. If she had to kill, then kill she would; and, she would leave no doubt that she was a worthy warrior. She and her sword, Gungnir! This would be her time to prove her sword's worthiness of its new name...a name Odin had chosen for his mighty spear. Should she tempt the gods with such a bold name? Tore had little to lose; as things stood now she might not have that much longer to live anyway.

Tore secured her weapons, looped her shield's straps over her shoulder, pushed her helmet firmly down on her head, and jumped onto the shore. Brock followed her, stopping for a moment to wait on Claus. Tore suddenly knew that in order to survive; this waiting on other people stuff would have to be stopped. Every man was out there for himself. Those who hesitated to look out for others ended up dead. Tore had no intention of ending up dead...even if it meant losing Brock.

Brock and Tore gathered around Thorvald along with all of the other men. High up on the hill, Tore could see a blur of action going on. They had been spotted. The heavy wood door that barred their way into the huge stone structure was being closed. She could see people arriving too late to be allowed inside the protective walls, and they were outside beating against the door and crying out. Tore said a prayer to Sif. She prayed that she would never find herself in such a vulnerable position. Tore looked up to the massive stone structure with the ragged people wailing at its doors. No one showed them mercy. The door stayed shut.

Tore suddenly realized that the men had not exaggerated claims of having gone straight from the ship to raiding. The mission, as explained by Thorvald, was to loot, rape, capture any slaves needed, gather some fresh food, and ship off as soon as possible. They would head up the shore to another village and to the next, until the ships were full. Then they would return home.

Brock raised his eyebrows and looked around him. He wondered how many dead men they would leave on this foreign soil and prayed to Odin none of his brothers would fall. Or his father, whose age was an apparent negative factor in this whole raid.

Swords were brandished high around them as Thorvald led the cheer to charge mightily and fearlessly. Tore banished all guilty thoughts from her head about innocence, unarmed people, and all the like. She had to kill to live, and kill she would.

Caught up in the fervor, she raised her sword high and cheered along with the other men. Brock stood there watching her as if for the first time. He was here, and he would fight; but, he would not like it nor would he pretend to enjoy it. Thorvald banged the back of Brock's shield with his fist and growled. Brock smiled. His father was in his element here on this soil that would soon run thick with blood.

Thorvald raised his sword and pointed towards the stone building. "Bring me gold!" He bellowed and his cry was met with furious cheers.

The men were off and running towards the stone building. The door was strong and would not budge. From inside, Tore could hear the prayers and cries to these Christian gods. She wondered whose gods would be stronger today.

A huge tree was felled in a matter of minutes. The men grasped the incredibly large trunk on either side and heaved it into the massive wood door. Splinters and cracking noises followed.

The men backed up again and made another running pass at the door. Again, splinters and wood flew. Grasping the woody trunk with both hands, Tore found her footing on the grassy terrain and prepared to run at the door again. This time the door could not hold. It had to buckle under the impact of the battering ram. The men ran. The door caved.

The warriors flooded into the structure, some were cautious taking cover from whatever enemy they might encounter, some charged on ahead fearless of their weaker foe who cowered somewhere in the belly of this stone beast. Tore saw a winding, stone staircase and decided to try there. She ran quickly, her feet pounding dully on the stone floor, her shield pounding sharply against her back. She came to a small door and kicked it in. Cowering in the corner was a fat man in a brown bag-like robe. He was bald and grotesquely obese, but that didn't interest her at all. What did interest her was the massive jeweled covered object he held in his fat hands. She approached in a mad dash and amidst his pleas and cries in his foreign guttural tongue, she ran him through, and caught the large paper and jeweled object as it fell from his grasp.

She heard loud thumps of running feet behind her, and she swooshed around ready to fight whoever it was coming... but it was only Brock. Brock looked at her, and back at the bleeding fat man on the floor who bled like a stuck pig in the puddle where he died. Brock looked back at Tore and into her hands, which held the jeweled book. Tore shrugged and dumped the book into her hudfat strapped to her back.

Brock seemed a bit dazed at first, then turned and left the room. Tore stormed up the stairs to the next door that she had seen. This was easier than she had planned.

Thorvald had been right; so far Tore had not encountered any women. Just a shit load of morbidly obese men in ugly, dirty brown robes. Most of them shit themselves in fear and begged for their lives in their odd language, and more than once had uttered a strange term. "Norderne", that's what they had called her. She had no idea of what it meant, but she was sure they were calling her that because more than one of them had pointed directly at her and cried Norderne before she rammed Gungnir through their fat guts.

Only one man had put up a fight. He was thinner and had more hair than the rest. He had gone for a knife, which Tore discovered, had made her blood boil, and his death more the challenge. She would actually get to fight for a change, instead of simply killing a cowering lard ass in some stone corner! The man lunged at her with his pathetic blade. A blade so small that she had seen children who possessed larger knifes than the one this man hoped to save his own life with! Tore had fun toying with this man who fought so weakly, and so verbally! Finally, she had tired of this mouse and took his head with one strong slash of her sword. Blood sprayed over her as she pulled her arm back and let it fall to her side. She wiped her face with the back of her arm and then took the purse of gold that he had strapped to his belt, and with one strong jerk yanked off the large silver cross that hung from his neck on a leather cord. On her way out of the room, she kicked his head out of her way and into the corner. It was hardly a fight at all. She lifted her sticky boots off of the stone floor for a moment. Blood was oozing everywhere. It wasn't just coming from the headless man she had just sent to Hel, but it was running in torrents over the stones from all directions. Her boots were covered in the port colored muck. She looked down at herself, and thought, her boots weren't the only things covered with blood and gore...she was drenched in the stuff.

Tore heard the horn blow. She looked up from her blood soaked self and toward the sound of the horn. It was time to regroup at the ship. She secured her hudfat, and made her way back downstairs through the bloody halls, and over the bloody floors. The men had their hudfats full, and all were smiling. None were hurt, and Tore could see the glee on Thorvald's face as his watchful eye scanned his men for injuries.

Brock caught up with her as she was attempting to wipe the blood from her forearm and face. The piece of cloth she was using was already saturated, and instead of wiping herself clean, she had only succeeded in smearing the blood around making the whole mess worse. Brock grimaced.

"What did you get?" Tore asked without looking up from her task.

"Nothing much." Brock said watching her distastefully. Tore glanced up and noticed how clean Brock was. Obviously, he had not fought with as much relish and gusto as she had.

"You didn't kill anyone, did you?" Tore asked suddenly. Brock frowned. "Of course I did."

"You don't have to lie to me, Brock. It's of no matter to me if you kill or not." Tore flung the piece of cloth onto the ground. "Your father might not be too pleased though." "Hel can have my father." Brock cursed. "You don't really mean that, brother." Tore slapped Brock on the back and led the way to the ship. "I don't understand how you could kill those people like you did. You seemed to enjoy it, Eirik!" Brock whispered. Tore thought for a moment. "I suppose I did." Brock furrowed his brow and squelched up his mouth.

"Won't your father be proud of me though?" Tore said grasping her hudfat and pulling it in front of her so that Brock could see its bulging seams.

"Good for you." Brock muttered.

"There will be another chance, Brock." Tore said seriously.

"What if I don't want another chance?" Brock snapped.

"Come, Brock. You and I both know that you will be a great leader someday. You must prove yourself worthy of these men. You have to do it for our future." Tore said while climbing aboard the ship.

Once seated on their sea chests, Brock turned to Eirik and said, "Jens can have the future."

"We both know, as does your father, that Jens will get himself killed long before he is in control of the tribe!" Tore got up and dumped her loot into the chest before retaking her seat.

Brock growled something to low to be discerned. "How much of the loot do we give to your father?" Tore asked Brock.

"Half of everything." Brock said absently. "We wait till we get home, right?" Tore asked while taking up her oar.

"Ja. Unless you get yourself killed. In that case, all of your loot goes to father." Brock dumped his few objects into his chest, and sat down.

"Seems fair enough." Tore laughed.

The men around her were singing joyfully. Thorvald gave the command to sail. They could take the next village before nightfall, and then anchor for the night.

"Anchor's up!" The cry went out and the ships pushed off once more onto the sea. The waves were choppy and the ship banged back and forth with a vengeance. Brock mumbled and muttered to himself distainfully. Tore was absorbed in her own thoughts, absently rowing rhythmically to the beat of the drum being beat in the helm.

It was taking longer than expected to get to where Thorvald had planned. The place in which they were going was called, by some, Orkney. It had a strange sound to it, as did all of these Angle names. Tore no longer felt the pain in her arms that she had when they had first set sail. She felt like she had been rowing all of her life, and she had the arm muscles to prove it.

Thorvald had called a meeting with his top men. Tore could see them huddled together speaking softly. Apparently, there was some sort of dispute over when and where to set anchor. None of them wanted to miss an opportunity to get their greedy hands on all that they could; and, the lack of women at the last stop had fueled their quest to a feverish pitch. Tore smiled to herself. Men! Gold, food, and pussy! That was all they mostly thought about, and not particularly in that order either. The more time she spent among the world of men, the more she found herself awed that she had ever wanted to be one of these creatures!

Thorvald walked between the rows of men and talked freely of the new plan. They would camp off of the coast of this place called Orkney, and go ashore as soon as the sun broke. They would be permitted to light whale oil lamps only under their tents, so the lights would not be that noticeable. The first villages wouldn't produce much gold, but there would be an ample supply of fresh captives for slaves...that meant primarily, women and children. Most of the men would be slaughtered in the fight.

The real challenge would be a well-fortified manor located more inland than were the villages. Thorvald approached Brock and Eirik and inquired into their success. Brock feigned enthusiasm as Eirik, proudly, opened his sea chest to show Thorvald all that he had amassed. Thorvald seemed pleased and whacked Tore on the back sharply, before continuing on among the men.

Brock sneered at Tore.

Tore raised her eyebrows and asked, "What is it, brother?"

"Nothing. Seems that you and father both have a taste for blood, that's all." Brock growled.

"You don't approve at all, do you?" Tore cocked her head to the side.

"No. I think it's all very pointless. All of these men have plenty back home. I don't see the reason we need to sail all the way here to take what few belongings or family, these miserable people have." Brock picked at his teeth with his fingernail.

"You're getting soft on me, Brock Thorvaldsson!" Tore laughed.

"And, I don't know if I know who you are anymore! Eirik Graafell!" Brock answered spitefully.

"Sure you do. I'm still the same old Eirik. Just battle tried now. We had to face it sooner or later, you knew that." Tore wiped her runny nose on her bloody sleeve and continued rowing. She absently wondered how long it took blood to dry. "Ja. But, I had hoped for the later, not the sooner." Brock sighed.

"You'll get used to it. When you are Jarl, you will not have to sail if you choose not to. Just think about that if it makes you feel better." Tore smiled.

"You always manage to find the positive angle to everything, don't you?" Brock laughed.

"One of my many talents!" Tore laughed with him. When night fell, they had just neared the coastline of Orkney. Tore could barely make out the shoreline from where they set anchor. They didn't want to move in to close for fear of being spotted and losing the element of surprise. Raids went a whole lot smoother when the victims were unsuspecting. It was also easier to land ashore if no arrows were whizzing by their heads. Most of these poor villages didn't have archers, but one could never be too sure of what they were going up against. Surprise was your best friend.

Brock wasn't in a socializing mood and remained rather quiet. Claus chatted nervously. Tore curled up against her sea chest and spread a fur over herself to keep out the cold. She ate a little food, and preferred to go to sleep. She watched in the dark as Claus stared into the nothingness around him and Brock slept restlessly in a ball. Thoughts of cowering fat men and blood-curdling screams jammed her mind and chased away sleep, so she just laid there, breathing shallowly somewhere half between sleep and awake waiting for the dawn.

By the time the sun had bothered to wake up and poke its rays up over the horizon, Thorvald and his ships were already casting anchor on the shore of Orkney. Armor-clad men spilled over the edges of the ship and made their way to the slumbering village that would just be stirring in order to tend to their morning duties. Tore drudged through the mud towards the circle of thatched hovels that served as these unfortunate peasants homes. Already, as if in slow motion, men were dragging women and girls out of their homes and raping them in the mud. As she passed one hut, Aksel the Good, flung a girl about fourteen years old towards her with gusto.

"The young ones are the sweetest of all, Eirik!" He had his hands full with the fourteen year old's sister who only looked a year or two older. As he rammed his rod into her hungrily, Tore stood by clasping the younger sister oddly. The girl beneath Aksel, now covered with so much mud and muck that her original features were barely discernable, screamed and kicked painfully. Aksel seemed spurred on by the fight and flipped her over and plunged his huge bulge into her arse hole, pulling it out and jamming it back into the bleeding mess he was making of the poor girl. The other girl was too petrified to move and hung there limply in Tore's grasp. Aksel looked up long enough to laugh at Eirik.

"What'ya waiting for boy, fuck the peasant pig!" Aksel dug his nails into the now exhausted girls backside and continued to fuck her with a seemingly eternal strength.

"I don't want women who answer to swords of steel." Tore stated bluntly.

Aksel got up, kicking the bloodied girl away, and roughly grabbed the younger one, who now stared ahead blankly deep in shock.

"By the gods! That leaves more for me then! Go, steal some chickens! I got a sword of flesh to polish here!" Aksel threw the second girl down and remarkably rose to the occasion to plug her full of flesh, as she lay motionless beneath him, a deathlike trance settled on her face.

Tore watched for a minute or so, and then went to scavenge what food she could find. She gave herself credit for getting herself out of that one.

Tore managed to find a few scrawny chickens and some roots that weren't too badly spotted. After looking through a few filthy huts for whatever might be of some value, she headed back towards the ship and met up with Brock along the way. This village was a waste of time, unless of course you wanted to consider the free fucks and the slaves they would take aboard. Tore decided that this must be Thorvald's bonus gift to the fuck hungry warriors aboard ship. A little gold here, a little cunt there. It all added up to a higher level of morale among the men.

"Not out ravishing the beauties of the Orkneys?" Brock asked sarcastically.

"Don't like the concept." Tore shrugged.

"You'd rather kill than rape, is that it?" Brock questioned.

"At least when you're dead no memories are left to haunt you, no scars are left to remind you of your pain, and no bastard of mine is left to grow up fatherless." Tore stated quietly.

"Now, he gets moral!" Brock threw his hands up and laughed.

Tore laughed as well. "Do you suppose we will wait till tomorrow to take the manor?"

"I think so. There's a storm moving in. Weather would be against us if we went this afternoon." Brock pointed towards the blackening sky with his sword.

"Seen Thorvald yet?" Tore looked around at the ragtag bunch of men that had returned already. Many were still off having their jollies with whatever was left of the women and girls.

"Yes. He was over there near that fire cooking a chicken." Brock pointed again.

"Well, let's go join him." Tore started towards the fire when Brock grasped her sleeve.

"Let's stay here, and build our own fire." Brock frowned.

"You don't want to face your father?" Tore asked quietly.

"You know I don't. He'll want tales of bravery and of me rutting in the muck like some wild boar…I don't have the stomach to lie to him, and I can't tell him the truth." Brock sighed. "You cant tell him much either in the rutting aspect, Great Hunter of Chickens!" Brock jabbed at the chickens hanging from Tore's belt and laughed.

"You're right. We'll make our own fire. But, I bet he still makes a visit before night is out." Tore stated.

"We'll deal with that then." Brock began building a fire and dragged a large piece of driftwood over to sit on.

When night began to creep up on them, Brock and Tore were still picking the roasted meat off the bones they held in their greasy hands. The men were abuzz with excitement and were still fucking away at the poor girls they had dragged back and chained to the boat to take home as slaves. Thorvald had inspected a few, and waved them into the boat. Some of them were too beautiful and valuable to let these fiends fuck to death. The ones being chained inside the ship seemed to sense that a more horrific fate waited for them. They would never touch the soil of their homeland again.

A fur covered Thorvald made his way to his son's fire. Brock stood up to greet his father by clasping arms heartily. Tore stood up and prayed to Sif that Thorvald didn't make such a big deal out of their refusing to rape the local women. Vikings with a conscience! Now, that was a first!

Thorvald had with him another man that Tore seemed to remember seeing once or twice before. Who was he though?

"Brock, Eirik. This is Hablok Bloodaxe. Hablok, my sons." Thorvald spoke loudly so that all who were near could hear that the chief was here among their raiding party.

Tore nearly gasped. Hablok Bloodaxe! Was Ulf nearby? Oh, great Sif! What would happen if Ulf saw her? Tore sucked in the air around her quickly. Perhaps he would not recognize her at all.

"Come on, boy!" Thorvald bellowed to the daydreaming Eirik, "Greet your chief!"

Tore had been so terrified that she hadn't even heard Brock greet Bloodaxe, and here she was standing staring at him as though he was some sort of freak or something.

Hablok Bloodaxe laughed. "Petrified with fear, are you, boy?" He grasped Tore's arm strongly and smacked her on her shoulders. "Bony shoulders! What are you feeding these men, Thorvald?" Hablok laughed loudly.

Thorvald laughed again.

Tore gathered all of her courage. "Hablok Bloodaxe, I heard that you were on a raid these past years...no one knew your fate."

"You heard correctly. My party got split up and I am searching for the other half. It has been longer than I ever imagined being away from my family and home. Some of my men have even abandoned me to live here among these peasants!" Hablok growled unpleasantly.

Thorvald changed the tone of the conversation. "Tomorrow we will be joined by Hablok's numbers to attack the manor with more strength! The gods have smiled upon us to allow us to fight with the Bloodaxe himself!"

Brock nodded. Thinking to himself, he knew how his father really felt. His father had made decisions without Hablok Bloodaxe's consent that could very well have serious repercussions on all of them. They had slaughtered Nordahl and his sons, and Athelwold's family with a fury, so as not to have to take the blood price instead of their lives. Brock seriously doubted his father would discuss such a decision or matter with Hablok now, before the raid on the morrow.

"Tomorrow, I will bestow gifts on those of Thorvald's men who have fought most bravely." Hablok looked around at the men who were going about their business, some unaware of his presence in their camp. "Your name, Eirik Graafell, has been mentioned."

Tore raised her eyebrows. "I am sure there are much braver men and more seasoned men than I that deserve your praise, chief Bloodaxe."

"Such modesty from one so young! Such unnecessary modesty! Be proud of your abilities, Eirik!" Hablok shook a fist in the air to emphasis his position.

Tore fought to recoil in fear. "Yes, I will be."

Hablok said something to Thorvald that was too quiet for her to hear, and then they nodded and left Brock's fire. Tore looked up at the dark night sky and listened to the loud thunder that was beginning to crack and roar above them. The rain wouldn't be too far behind that roar.

Brock audibly let out all of his breath in one loud gust. "Thor's hammer! I never thought we'd see him again!"

"Nor I!" Tore gasped.

"You've met him before?" Brock asked amazed.

"Once when I was a little…eh, boy. He came to my shire with many men." Tore decided that she shouldn't reveal that her brother Ulf was with one of Hablok's parties. As much as she longed for her brother, she had no intention of seeking him out if he was here. An action such as that could have deadly results. Tore had no reason to believe that her own brother would spare her life for her blatant violation of the codes that men and women alike lived with for centuries. A woman in battle! That might surpass any feeling of tenderness Ulf might possess for his younger sister. She could die by the very hand that she hoped would save her. Mighty Sif, let him be with the other lost party! Tore prayed earnestly in her head as she hovered near the fire lost in her own thoughts. As Tore sat pondering her fate, a deafening crack filled the sky and the black, ominous clouds began emptying themselves of the water they held. Brock pulled his fur cape up and over his head. Tore did the same. This was going to be a long, dreadful night.

The next morning, the wet and shivering men woke to a clear sky. The storm that had hit so suddenly had done its business and then left. It was also clear from what Tore could tell, that Ulf was not among the men in Hablok Bloodaxe's party. Ulf was taller and more handsome than most men, and he would have been easily spotted, so if he was still alive, he was undoubtedly in the party that had gotten lost.

Tore gathered with the rest of the men who were brewing thick black coffee and slurping it down with caution. Brock was jittery, obviously dreading the task before him. He knew that he couldn't continue to escape his duties. Tore watched him as he silently prayed to his gods, and she did the same.

Hablok was approaching the center fire, and the men parted on either side to let him through. Close on Hablok's heels came Thorvald, who wore a grimace that smarted from having to play second to Bloodaxe. Thorvald didn't like having to share his spotlight with anyone, but what choice does a man have when you stumble upon your own chieftain out here in the middle of nowhere!

Hablok Bloodaxe stood before them, a massive giant of a man. Even Ulf paled in comparison to the huge hulk of a man that Hablok was. No wonder why men flock to him as a leader of most Norway! He was almost god-like in stature, and some said that he fought with the strength of twenty men. Tore was sure some of that had to be exaggeration, but she could see how it could easily be believed.

Hablok climbed upon a large log that someone had scrounged up the night before. He raised his sword high in one hand, and his battle-axe high in the other. The crowd of men hushed instantly, and all that could be heard was the lulling sound of lapping waves against the shores, and the creaking of anchored ships as the waves slapped their sides.

Brock looked at Tore with a blank look that she could not read. She wondered what it meant, and was wondering when Hablok began to speak. He rambled on about some old battle, that had a few gods thrown in for spice, and he recanted some deeds he had witnessed in battles throughout his years. Then he moved on to the required praise of Thorvald and the men who fought under him, of their fighting so far and the wealth they had amassed after two short raids. He personally thanked Thorvald for the girl that he had been presented with last night, and made a few rank sexual jokes before pulling her bloody head out of a bag he wore at his side. He held the wretched girl's head up by her brown tangled hair for everyone to see, then he went on to explain that after he had fucked her to a bloody pulp, he had offered her head to Odin for protection of himself and his men in the conquest of this heavily fortified manor.

Tore looked at Brock, who wore an expression that said he had somehow expected this sort of behavior, and she smiled a half smile of encouragement.

Her head snapped back to Hablok when she realized that he was talking about her and her actions in the first raid in East Anglia. He waved his arm in her direction. Tore felt Brock shoving her forward towards Hablok. Tore suddenly found a new meaning for the word terror.

Hablok was all smiles as he handed Tore a large ring. It was a present, a reward for her skill in battle. He went on to say how it was rare to find such abilities in a man so young. He credited Thorvald for his wise teachings and example to follow. Tore realized that Hablok Bloodaxe had no idea that she wasn't Throvald's blood kin at all. Facing the crowd, she could see Jens leering at her through the throngs of dirty men. He glared at Brock, and back at Tore. Tore had never known such hatred in all her life, and this ring seemed to seal Jens hate with a new purpose. Jens wouldn't rest until Eirik was dead. Tore wondered as she held her ring up for all to see, if it would be she who would have to kill Jens one day.

Chapter 13

Tore blended back in with the rest of the crowd as Hablok Bloodaxe continued presenting awards to the men that Thorvald had selected for such honor. Surprisingly enough, none of his own sons were among those honored. Brock wasn't surprised however, and acted strange when Eirik was. Half of the time, Brock had watched Jens just cower in a corner waiting for the horn to be sounded that would allow them to regroup at the ship. Thorvald couldn't have been very happy with his own sons, at least there was Eirik to take off some of the pressure.

Brock turned to say something to Eirik, but he was gone. Where did he go? They weren't finished with the ring giving yet. Brock looked around him and searched the blood covered, dirty men's faces for Eirik's, but could not find him. Slowly, he made his way out of the cheering throngs of men and went to look for Eirik.

There he was, behind a tree.

Brock stepped over a few large rocks and made his way over to the large, gnarled tree that Eirik was crouched behind.

"Hey! I wondered where you were!" Brock said as he circled the tree and stood before Eirik. Eirik recoiled like a snake and quickly hitched up his pants. He wore a look of mingled surprise and terror. "You aren't afraid to kill, but when someone sneaks up on you while you're shitting you jump like a frightened child!" Brock laughed loudly.

Eirik frowned and pulled the drawstring tight on his pants, resecured his belt, and stood there speechless. "What's wrong, shit out all of your words?" Brock continued to rib his friend.

"I didn't know I needed permission to crap." Tore was genuinely angry this time. She didn't have to pretend to react like a man; she had almost been discovered. Tore breathed hard. It was bound to happen sooner or later. She had really been shocked that someone hadn't stumbled upon her earlier than now, but it was still startling all the same. Brock continued to laugh.

"No. You don't. Just didn't expect you to sneak off like that after the big ring ceremony! Look! They're not even done yet!" Brock pointed off towards the shoreline where the men were gathered, their cheers floated to them on the breeze along with the smell of salty sea air.

"I had to go. Didn't see much opportunity for it in the next hours." Tore answered shortly. She was still trying to recover from the terror that had attacked her when she realized that Brock had been watching her. He obviously hadn't seen anything, or else he would have let on. He would have to have let on...he would be totally shocked if he had discovered that she wasn't a man at all, but a woman. Brock raised his eyebrows. "Are you still mad?" "I don't like being snuck up on like that." Tore answered and stood on the hill watching the men cheer. "Sorry. Isn't like you were doing anything the rest of us don't do too." Brock laughed again. He really had pissed off Eirik. Eirik was normally so even tempered, why so touchy now?

"Well, don't do it again." Tore grunted. Brock started to get angry at Eirik's relentlessness. "I didn't mean to offend you, brother!" Brock growled and then stomped off back towards the other men. If Eirik wanted to overreact to such a petty incident, then he was damned if he was going to stand around and listen to it. He had shit in front of men all of his life and had never paid much attention to it, why would Eirik think otherwise? Brock suddenly felt his old feelings creep up. Did Eirik think something was odd about the feelings between them too? Did Eirik feel that unusual charge between the two of them that he felt? Brock cursed and spit on the ground. He had tried everything he could think of to try to banish those thoughts back home. He had fucked, and drank, and cavorted with all of the known tramps in Tunsberg just like the rest of the men to prove himself every bit of the man that he knew he was...and now this! Did Eirik suspect him of loving men in the manner that a man loves a woman? Was he afraid of Brock's actions? Brock didn't know how to handle this. He couldn't really go up to Eirik and discuss this whole thing. If Eirik did think that Brock loved men more than women, then to bring up the issue would be embarrassing for both of them. If Eirik hadn't even thought of these things, and Brock was to bring it up, then that would be even worse, for it might look as if Brock did love men and not women. Brock cursed again. Maybe Eirik just liked to shit alone. Maybe there was nothing more to it. Brock sighed. What were these odd feelings he had though. He had hoped that all of the fucking back home would have erased them from his mind, but every time he brushed against Eirik, or whispered low against his ear in the night to keep from waking others, there was something in the air that raised the hairs on his neck and arms, and made his heart beat like it did when he touched a woman.

Brock took his knife from his belt and held it up to the sunlight. He had to vanquish these thoughts from his mind. Pain would erase these thoughts. Brock held his hand before him and slashed his knife across his own palm.

"Great Thor!" Brock cursed, and clutched his crimson stained hand against his chest. The pain seared through his body and brought tears to his eyes.... and wiped all of his thoughts from his head.

Eirik was suddenly behind him. "What happened to your hand?" He seemed concerned. His voice was tender, caring. Brock felt as if he might go suddenly insane. "I cut it." Brock bound it with a strip of cloth he ripped from his shirt and said nothing more. Eirik stood in front of him, with arched eyebrows and a questioning expression, but said nothing. Brock watched as Eirik turned to the group of men on the shore. "It is time." Eirik turned back to Brock who finished tying up his hand.

"Yes, it is time." Brock found within himself a new fire. He would kill, and kill, and kill. He would put these man-loving thoughts out of his mind once and for all. If the dripping wet cunt of a peasant slut didn't do it, then the dripping warm blood of one would. Brock raised his sword high in his right hand, and ran screaming a battle cry to Thor all the way towards the group on the shore.

Tore stood there for a moment, wondering what had suddenly gotten into Brock, and then shrugged and chased after him with her sword brandished high and her lungs crying out the same lusty battle cry.

The men stealthily crept through the forest and to the manor. Tore peered through the foliage at the dwelling. It was large like the first stone structure they had raided, but it had a different design to it. She could tell this building was designed for living in, not just praying. Might as well be a functional building, Tore thought to herself, the fortified building those fat Angles used for praying in protected them as much as did their Christian gods. Tore scanned the stone building as the other men were doing the same. She could see archers positioned along the top of the stone walls. Someone had obviously survived the attack on the village the day before and had warned the inhabitants of the manor.

Thorvald cursed from behind a tree somewhere. Hablok was none the merrier himself. This complicated matters to be certain. Tore wondered if they would turn back and pillage other surrounding villages instead; but she kept quiet. Brock crouched behind a bush and was studying the walls. According to the men who had scouted the place out, there were two gates, both large and wood, like the one at the Christian temple. However, there was also a smaller gate, made only for wagons delivering stable supplies to the stable of the dwelling. This gate wasn't as strong as the others. Thorvald and Hablok argued quietly about what approach to take. As they were mildly squabbling, Tore was suddenly startled by the blood-curdling cry that rose up next to her. As she snapped her head in Brock's direction, she had no time to say anything as she and the other men watched Brock go running towards the manor, sword raised, screaming and yelling uncontrollably. Tore was frightened. Brock acted like he had berserker in his blood. What had driven him so mad? The other men, thinking this was the signal to charge did so...Thorvald and Hablok stood, amazed at their plans falling apart before them, and then without much other options joined in the charge.

Arrows buzzed past Tore's head like angry hornets. She barely escaped the point of one, having ducked in the nick of time to watch it bury itself in the trunk of the tree where her head should have been. She frowned. Did Brock make it to the manor? Or did an arrow fell him before he could fight?

Tore knew there was no time to think about Brock or Brock's fate, for right now her own fate was hanging by a thread. This was like no other raid they had been on. This wasn't like taking the treasure of a fat man, or slamming a sword through the gullet of an old woman...this was battle. Archers on the rooftop kept her focused on the door before her. They battered the door until it gave, and were happy to discover once inside the gate that their men had also been successful barging through the smaller gate on the stable side of the manor. Tore ducked inside of a doorway as she caught her breath, it was a good thing they had run into Hablok Bloodaxe's men or they would never have escaped this battle alive.

Sucking in a great mouthful of air, she swung herself around out of the doorway and back into the thick of things. She found a small door and managed to kick it in. Summoning to some other men around her she quietly crept up the stairs that the door had revealed. She could hear the clamor and clang of swords and shields through the heavy stonewalls. The winding staircase was dark and dank, groping along the wet, slimy wall she wondered where it was leading her. Up ahead was a door. She laid her ear against the wood, and listened. All was quiet. She yanked open the door which revealed a long corridor full of other doors. The men flooded the corridor and began yanking open doors, and kicking in others that had been locked from the inside. Tore began to hear the screams from those once locked inside. Tore spotted an unopened door and rammed it with her shoulder. It didn't give. She rammed it again, and this time the lock shattered along with wood and weak metal. Inside, cowering in the corner was a very beautiful woman, and her children. Two boys, and a girl. The woman was pushing them behind her skirts in a protective stance. For a moment, Tore stood there, legs spread, sword held high, and looked into the terrified face of this beautiful woman. She would fetch quite a price on the slave block. Tore laughed. She felt no pity for such a weak woman who didn't even have a single weapon to defend her children with. This was no mother! Tore saw a golden tasseled cord that bound heavy curtains at the window. She jerked the cord from the curtains, and approached the woman who was too terrified to even scream. The woman backed away from her shaking her head no and babbling on in that annoying gibberish these people called a language. It was different from the tone of the fat Angles back in the Christian temple; but it was annoying all the same. She looped the cord around her neck, and with the long tasseled ends, bound her hands behind her. Then, Tore dragged the pretty mother over to the heavy door, and tied her to the door latch. Tore then turned back to the children. One of the boys in a moment of bravery took from beneath his tunic a wood chest and opened it to reveal the gold inside. He then pointed a trembling finger towards his mother. The child was negotiating with her, Tore realized and laughed. He wanted to trade the gold for his mother. Poor naive boy! Tore nodded and the boy approached her with the chest of gold. He handed her the chest and stepped back a step, as if waiting for her to cross the floor and release his mother. The beautiful woman tied like a dog to the door, was pleading frantically in that language Tore was growing more and more inclined to hate, she was motioning with her head for the boy to stand back. The boy looking towards his mother didn't even see the sword that Tore swung around and popped off his head like a grape with. The other boy and the girl, now covered with their brother's blood, dropped sobbing to the floor, and the pretty mother tied to the door, went limp. Tore cut down the other little boy, and turning to do the same to the little girl, she suddenly froze. Memories of her own brother's deaths flooded her mind. Tore choked for a moment. Spotting a smaller closet in the corner, she grabbed the sobbing little girl and pushed her in. The woman tied to the door, now awake, looked at Tore with a disbelieving stare that changed to relief. The little girl was spared. Tore put her finger to her own lips in an attempt to motion the little girl, not more than five, to stay quiet. Then she closed the closet door, crossed the floor to the woman, untied the cord from the door, and jerked her to her feet. The woman kept her eyes on the closet door dragging her feet, until the room was out of sight. Tore told her fellow warriors that the last two rooms were clear, and they believed her. Tore didn't know exactly why she had hid the little girl, but if the gods had spared her, then maybe she owed the gods a life in exchange. In any case, the woman she had tied up behind her, seemed to look at her in a different light and wasn't quite so uncooperative now. Tore dragged the richly clad woman to a safe spot. It was evident by the number of slain men not of her people that the manor would fall in no time at all. There was a long line of tied up women next to a wagon full of children that had also been tied up. Tore knew she should tie the woman to the wagon and rejoin the fighting, but something inside of her told her to protect this woman from something that she wasn't sure of what exactly. Thorvald came from the stable, and walked towards Tore with a look of amazement on his face. He seemed to recognize the lady tied up and sitting at Tore's feet. He pulled the woman up by her velvet sleeve and grabbed her delicate face with his two war- worn, blood-smeared hands. He peered into her face and laughed wickedly. Then he turned to Tore and smacked her hard on the back.

"Boy! You went and got the Lady of the manor herself! The fighting will stop now!" Thorvald bellowed something and then swiftly turned and yanked the decorative headpiece off of the lady. Then he jerked the large medallion from her neck, leaving a welt behind where the gold chain cut into her flesh. She gasped and flinched, unable to shield herself with her tied up hands.

Thorvald called for a man standing near, and pushed the items into his hands. Thorvald then pointed to a spot higher on the wall and sent the man off to deliver some sort of message. Within minutes, the clang of shields and swords came to a screeching halt, and a bloody, weary man emerged from behind a heavy door. He approached Thorvald with a look of beseechment on his face. The woman tied up at Tore's feet suddenly began to wail again, and was shaking her head at her husband, who seemed to be consoling her with his eyes.

Tore knew this was the chief of the manor. She didn't know what title he bore, or if he was a king, or what; but, she did know that this woman at her feet, he loved dearly, and he was willing to give up the fight for her. He was approaching Thorvald with his arms open in a sign of surrender. The woman sobbed louder and frantically moved around in the bloody straw she was sitting in.

Thorvald's head was jutting out in a haughty manner. He knew he had won, and one of his sons was the reason why. Tore suddenly knew why her instinct had led her to keep this woman away from the raping hoards of her fellow warriors.

The man took off the ring on his finger and handed it to Thorvald as if relinquishing his authority. Thorvald accepted the ring, and then drew his sword. The man's eyes grew wide as if to question the appearance of the sword. Thorvald laughed and then with a mighty swoop, brought the sword down on the neck of the man who dropped into the straw with both of his arms stretched before him in a pathetic attempt to protect himself. His head, half severed from his body, hung limply, and his body fell in the shit and blood covered straw. The woman at Tore's feet choked on her sobs, and fought to go to him. Tore looked into her face, and felt the pain that it reflected. She dropped the gold cord and the woman crawled to the body of her bleeding husband. There was no where for her to escape to, Tore saw no harm in letting the woman hold her dead husband's body in grief. Thorvald looked at Tore oddly, and then shrugged. What did he care if Eirik decided to allow the woman a moment of pity? He hadn't pitied her enough to let her children live, and he hadn't pitied her enough to kill her before she could be raped before every man here…and that is exactly what Thorvald had decided to do with her next.

The men gathered with the rest of the captives. Thorvald yanked the woman from her dead husband's side, and ripped the bodice of her gown straight down. Then he did the same to her skirt until she stood naked before all of the men. Thorvald wasn't too old that he couldn't do what was required of him by his men…and he planned to enjoy this fair creature. He yanked his wrinkled manhood from his pants and stroked it mockingly. His men cheered. The woman backed up in terror, stumbling and then falling on top of her dead husband's body; and it was there, that Thorvald shoved her down and split her legs with the strength of a twenty year old and sunk his throbbing sword of flesh into her scabbard.

Jens found the whole scene thrilling. How many times in a man's life do you get to see the great lady of a manor, fucked on top of the body of her own dead husband? Tore watched with a blank look on her face. She knew that Thorvald wouldn't kill her. It was too satisfying to know that a great lady would be a slave for the rest of her life. There were plenty of other wenches to kill if the taste for blood was unquenched.

Suddenly, from behind, Tore heard a quick movement and a cry. She jumped into fighting stance, sword whipped around in a defensive position. From behind a blazing wagon, a man sprang and charged Tore ferociously. His sword clanged with hers in midair where she held it, the muscles in her arms bulging under the strain. This was a strong warrior who was trying to protect the wife of the man he served. Tore heaved his sword off of hers and stepped back, circling the man as he did the same around her in anticipation of her next move. Brock drew his sword in a protective manner...Just in case. Tore saw the look in his eyes asking her if she needed help. Tore shook her head no. This was her chance to prove to Tyr that she was worthy of her sword.

The man was an excellent fighter, trained and battle scarred. His face was a patchwork of scars from previous battles, and his temper fueled a fire that Tore had not had a chance to fight. Until now, it had mostly been women, weak men, and children. The warriors she had fought had been no match for her training or zeal to succeed; but this man was driven by the spirit of vengeance for his lord's death and for the humiliation and shame of that dead man's wife. Tore had not experienced the strength of a warrior spurred on by anger and revenge.

The man side stepped a blow to the mid-thigh that Tore had attempted. He went for her legs. She leaped in the air, avoiding the blade. She noticed that the group of men around her was growing, pressing in around her, just waiting to lend a hand to their fellow warrior should one be needed. Tore wanted this to be a man-to-man fight, not a bloodbath. She had to show her skill, her true worth to Try and Sif.

Glancing up to the rooftop, she saw two figures in full battle attire, swords flashing in the sun, looking down on her and the man she was fighting in the dirty, straw strewn courtyard. She could tell by the way the sun bounced off of the silver clothes of the woman, that Sif had brought Tyr to witness this battle in person.

Snapping her attention back to the cursing, sweating man, Tore breathed loudly. She stood ready to take whatever the man had left. The man plunged headlong with his sword, crying out and missing his target. Tore had stepped aside without a moment to spare. The man cursed and spat, and thrust forward again, this time grazing Tore's upper arm with his blade. She winced and out of the corner of her eye saw Brock move a step forward.

"Just tell me when!" Brock cried angrily to Eirik who was refusing to let any man help him here in front of everyone. Damn man was going to let himself get killed out of pride. Brock knew that Eirik was no match for this warrior. Eirik did not answer.

Tore watched the man as he jostled his sword form one hand to the next so quickly that all she could make out was a blur of steel. He was playing with her, toying with her like a cat does a mouse. Tore felt the anger boil up to her face. This man was making a mockery of her fighting abilities in front of her fellow warriors! Tore charged madly at the man, screaming a primal sound, thrusting at his mid-section with all of her strength. The man backed up and hit the wagon side where the women were tied up, now shrieking and screaming, and clamoring over each other trying to get out of the way of the fight. The man inched his way away from the wagon, his eyes locked on Tore's eyes, never blinking, never leaving hers for a moment. He seemed to be hatching a new scheme…a new plan to defeat her.

Somewhere in the crowd a gasp was heard at the same instance that Tore's back met the stonewall behind her. The man had pinned her like a trapped animal. So, that was his plan. Tore had to think fast. There was nowhere for her to go now, and the man was coming at her slowly, his sword pointed in front of him ready to run her through. Either she cried for help like a coward and died by Tyr's hand, or she died on the end of this man's sword like a stuck pig. Tore looked around her frantically, trying to stay calm. She watched the man creeping towards her purposely slow, laughing, knowing that even when he killed this Viking scum he had so skillfully trapped in the corner, he too would be dead by the hands of these filthy beasts hovering close watching the spectacle. Tore saw the man look down at the body of a dead man he had accidentally kicked, in the blink of an eye, Tore saw her escape. Suddenly thrusting her sword into its sheath she reached towards the side of the wall and grasped the huge black iron sconce that was secured there. Flipping herself up and over the head of the man in a perfect upside down arc, feet first, she landed in the straw behind him, and swung herself around with a loud swooshing sound, sword back in hand ready to meet its foe. The man shook his head, startled that his victim was no longer before him, and then turned clumsily to see this evil Norderne standing behind him with his sword ready to kill. The scar-faced warrior's eyes were wide with terror. What sort of a man fought like this? Unfortunately for him, he never got the answer to his question, for as he hesitated, Tore brought Gungnir down with such great force that the man's body was nearly split in two. A great spurt of blood, like a crimson fountain, sprayed over Tore and the men close enough to the now, very dead man. Tore shielded her eyes against the sun, and looked up to the rooftop. Sif had raised her sword in congratulations, and Tyr smiled in acknowledgement of her deed. Then in a silver flash, they were gone.

Tore shook her head, as Brock came running up to her, followed closely by his father and Hablok Bloodaxe. She seemed dazed by the sudden disappearance of her protector and Tyr.

Hablok and Thorvald both were visibly impressed, and speechless. Thorvald happily smeared the blood around on Tore's face breaking out in uproarious laughter. Tore laughed at his spunk and spirit.

Brock embraced her, holding her for what seemed like a long time until Thorvald pried him off of her.

"I thought you were dead for sure Eirik." Brock whispered.

Thorvald bellowed his laughs and clasped Tore by the arm. "Men will speak of this fight for years to come, my son! Today you showed us single-handedly what it means to be a warrior!"

Tore felt as if she might blush. "I did nothing more than what any others of you would do if your life depended on it."

"There's that modesty again!" Hablok slapped her on the back knocking her forwards a few inches. "Thorvald you must tell me how you train such fine warriors!"

Thorvald led Tore and his sons and the other ragtag group of men back towards the camp, as the other men saw to the rounding up of the new captives. After all of the captives were secured, they would come back to this great manor and spend the night in its finery until morning when they would set sail.

Tore didn't like all of the added attention she was receiving from the men and Thorvald. She had only fought to prove to Tyr that she was indeed worthy of his faithful warrior's sword. Now, she had all of this to contend with. Maybe this was all part of Tyr's plan. Maybe there was more than just fighting to prove. Tore listened absently to the babblings of the men around her and braced herself for the occasional slaps on the back by whoever was congratulating her now. She really longed for sleep and food, and a quiet moment to thank Sif for her protection.

Sitting on the long in front of the fire, Tore remembered the little girl that she had shoved into the closet in that room upstairs. The men were planning on returning to the manor for a night of celebration. She had to insist on that room if she was to continue to protect the little girl. Tore had another idea. Somewhere in her heart she felt a sort of compassion for the beautiful woman who had been publicly raped and shamed, and who had to watch as Tore murdered her two sons. Tore would demand to have that woman, a load of food and wine, and the room where the girl was. She would give the grieving mother one more night with her little girl before they set sail the next morning.

Tore exhaustedly told Thorvald her desires. Along with a torrent of sexual innuendo and sexual jokes, Thorvald all but promised his prizefighter the moon. Enough food for an army was sent to the room, along with the woman, now freshly dressed in another opulent gown that someone had brought her from her own wardrobe.

Someone had cleaned up the bodies and blood of the slain children, and chained the weeping woman to a chair. When Tore entered the room, the woman only turned her head slightly, as if to acknowledge the fact that she was to be raped again by the champion Norderne fighter she had watched in the courtyard.

Tore cocked her head and looked at the woman. She crossed over towards her, and unfastened the chains. The woman stopped weeping so loudly, and rubbed her wrists where the shackles had been. She sat back in the chair and watched Tore oddly.

Tore walked over to where the food had been sat on a massive wood table, and motioned to it with her hand letting the woman know she was welcome to eat. Tore then went to the small closet, and opened the door. The small girl was huddled inside in a pile of papers and clothes. Her tear-streaked dirty face wore a hollow, detached look. Tore pushed the little girl gently towards her mother. The mother stood up weakly and clutched the little girl to her bosom.

Tore turned away, unable to communicate with the woman and busied herself with eating. The woman and the little girl huddled together in the corner where Tore had made them a kind of makeshift bed on the floor.

Tore began putting bread and some less perishable foods in baskets, and other containers that she could find inside of the closet. Under the questioning eye of the woman, Tore filled a large crock up with water from her bath and put it into the closet as well. Tore stripped the warm blankets from the bed and lined the floor in the closet like a nest. She then motioned for the two to crawl in, and bolted the small door behind them.

Tore took a long bath, soaking away the months of grime and filth, and blood, both hers and other people's. When she was thoroughly clean and had rebound her breasts with fresh strips, she dressed in clean clothes and felt like a new person.

Tore then unbolted the little door and motioned for the woman and her daughter to come out if they liked. Tore lay back on the bed and watched the woman watching her strangely. She wondered if the mother was aware that the girl would have to remain hidden in the closet tomorrow and that she would have to come with her attackers. Tore wondered if the mother realized that this barbaric warrior was giving her a last farewell with her child.

The woman sat in a velvet heap on the floor, in the corner, with her daughter, who had fallen asleep in her mother's lap. Tore looked up at the ceiling, her hands behind her head, aware of the penetrating stare of the young mother on the floor. The woman said something in a soft tone of voice.

Tore sat up and looked at her.

The woman spoke again, louder as if trying to make herself understood.

Tore shook her head. She didn't understand a thing the woman was saying to her. The woman tried again, and then sighed.

Tore smiled at her. The woman nodded and smiled back. She then settled back against the wall, and stroking her daughter's dark hair, went to sleep. Tore laid there for awhile watching the mother and daughter sleeping and wished there was some way to keep them together. She knew that even if they were taken as slaves together on the boat, even if the child did survive the journey home, she would surely be separated and sold later. No, she would have to stay here.

Tore sighed. There was no point in racking her brain for some new plan. Even with her new favored status, Tore knew that her wishes would only be granted to a limit. Keeping a foreign mother and child together would be an odd request that would be looked upon as some form of weakness, or pity that would be unacceptable in a warrior of her degree. No, the best chance for the child's survival would be to hole her up in the closet and let fate decide if her own people would find her before food ran out and death caught up to her. What chances of survival the woman had, was even a riskier chance. Even if she survived the journey home in the slave ship, there was no guarantee that she would survive very long in the slave market or with her new owner. It was apparent that this woman had never worked very hard in her life, and she appeared to be quite delicate. If she didn't get fucked to death first, then she surely would died from bring overworked. Tore only wondered how peacefully the young mother would come with her tomorrow when dawn broke. Surely, she had to understand that by making any sort of scene she risked the life of her last remaining child. Tore wondered what life would be like never knowing the fate of your child. Always thinking about her, but never knowing. Maybe she would die soon so she wouldn't have to think about it anymore. Tore sighed again. This would be a long night that she would care not to remember as long as she lived.

Tore uttered a prayer of thanks to Sif, and then asked Sif to watch over this foreign girl child. Tore didn't know if her gods could watch over a child of a foreign god, but it didn't hurt to ask.

When dawn broke, Tore hurriedly shoved the little girl into the closet. The little girl went willingly, obviously unaware that she would never see her mother again. Tore thought that the girl must think this some sort of a game they were playing, and when Tore put her finger to her lips to signal quiet, the little girl copied her. The mother, holding back tears, kissed her child firmly on the cheek, and giving her a small ring, closed the closet door for Tore.

Tore smiled at the woman. The woman wore a determined look on her face and walked in front of Tore to whatever fate she would endure. Tore picked up her sword and belongings and they left the room. Once in the outside courtyard, Tore watched the young mother glance over at the lifeless body of her beloved husband who still lay sprawled in the straw where he had died. Tore saw the wince of pain in the woman's face, and then the woman looked away. As the men were gathering, hoots and rank laughter were aimed at Tore as if to confirm her manhood in her spending the night with this beautiful woman. No one but the woman, the child, and Tore knew the truth. The woman hung her head in mock shame, and Tore caught a slight smile from the woman as she looked towards this warrior who had spared her child. Only they knew the secret. Tore paraded the woman in front of the other captives, and then chained her up with the other women beside the boat that would take them home ahead of the rest of them. The other boats were headed towards an island called Shetland. Brock came up from behind and nodded a morning greeting.

"So, did you find the beautiful lady agreeable to your palate, brother?" Brock smiled and bit an apple.

"Yes, I did." Tore lied.

"What happened to your not wanting a unwilling woman who must answer to a sword of steel?" Brock laughed again.

"Who said anything about her being unwilling?" Tore smiled, she was getting pretty good at this game. Brock laughed loudly. When he laughed, he reminded her of Thorvald. The truth of the matter was, that last night, while lying in that warm, dry, comfortable bed, Tore had longed to be back aboard the stinking, wet, cold ship huddled next to Brock for warmth. She had dreamt of his musky smell, and the feel of his thigh pressed against hers as they slept. She had longed to have him in that big bed last night.

Brock was stretching his arms above his head, seated on his sea chest before their oar, when Tore came aboard. She had been held back because Hablok Bloodaxe had wanted to give her a battle axe with an image of a dragon etched into the blade as a gift for her gallant fight yesterday. Tore unceremoniously dumped it into her sea chest and sat down beside Brock. Brock laughed.

"So, Hablok's gifts mean so much to you?" He laughed again.

"They mean only what I can sell them for in the market when we reach home." Tore laughed and cracked her knuckles. Brock reached across Tore's chest to examine something on the oar, when Tore threw her hands up protectingly and recoiled backwards.

Brock stared at Tore oddly. "Did I harm you, Eirik?" Brock wondered if he had somehow scratched Eirik or hit the cut on his brother's arm.

"No, no." Tore stammered fearfully aware of her sudden and unexplained reaction.

"Did I hit your arm?" Brock asked concerned.

"No. It's nothing. Just jumpy, that's all." Tore laughed praying that Brock would just let it die.

"You're sure?" Brock looked at Eirik strangely.

"Positive." Tore looked down at the oar and rubbed her hands over it absently.

Brock screwed up his face in an odd expression and then shrugged. Eirik had been jumpy lately. What was his sudden aversion to bodily contact? Brock fought the old feelings that he felt coming up again. He couldn't go on slicing up the various parts of his body in order to wipe his thoughts clean. He had to learn to deal with his insecurities. Besides, right now, he was thinking about Eirik's insecurities, not his own. Why had Eirik been so intent upon privacy, and not being touched lately? It was as if the close quarters of the ship were starting to wear on him, Brock had heard of that happening before.

Tore breathed slowly, trying to calm herself. She had almost blown it again jumping out of the way like that. Brock was going to get suspicious if she kept this type of behavior up. First the incident behind the tree, and now this. For the god's sake, he was just reaching for the oar! Tore fought hard to calm herself. She moved her thoughts on to Tyr. She had proved herself a worthy fighter, would Tyr let her be now? Was it enough? How would she know? Would Sif tell her? Hundreds of questions poured through her mind, as Tore sat waiting to start rowing. She was looking down at her boots, lost in thought, unaware of how intently Brock was studying her.

Brock watched Eirik sitting there thinking. What he wouldn't give to hear what thoughts were going through his new brother's head. There was something up with Eirik, what was it? Brock felt something stirring inside of himself, a gut feeling, an intuitive sense, something unexplainable about Eirik...watching Eirik now, Brock was sure that Eirik held the answer to that secret, whatever it was. Brock took hold of the oar in preparation for rowing, he would unravel this mystery...there was more to his brother, Eirik, than met the eye. This, Brock was sure of.

Chapter 14

Tore leaned against the side of the ship, and looked over into the water, watching the trail of disturbed waves ripple out behind them. Somewhere a sea gull squawked and screamed, and the sky was a constant dreary gray.

Tore, along with the other men, were headed to a place called Shetland. Some of the men called it the Isle of Shetland, the name didn't matter really...it was what they hoped to gain on Shetland that counted. Already one ship laden with new captives ripe for the slave market was on its way home. Tore wished she could be on that ship. Months at sea had wearied her and she longed again for the comforts of home and the welcoming rocky crags and cliffs of Norway. The constant drizzle of misty rain that they had encountered here in this foreign land was depressing to say the least. Tore would take the harsh, stinging wind and crystal white snow of Norway any day.

The people they had "met" here were cowardly and pathetic. Even the ones who fought back were no match for the power and barbarism that they encountered. Tore and the rest of the men were trained fighters...there was no contest in slaughtering a defenseless farmer and his undernourished family. Tore was growing tired of it already.

There had not been as much gold and treasures as anticipated by Thorvald or any of the other men. Thorvald had reasoned that these people along these areas were now all too accustomed to bands of raiding men and if they had any valuables left, were more clever at hiding them then they had years before.

One night over a flagon of mead, Thorvald had moaned about the glory days of raiding warriors. Apparently, he and the older men believed that soon their way of life would be extinct. The influence of these Christian gods was growing and violence and raiding more and more discouraged by the year. To Thorvald this painted a bleak picture of the future. What sort of Norway would Norway be without the battle-tested tradition of sailing and raiding? Where would revenues come from? Surely, the warriors of Norway wouldn't settle down into the lazy, unadventuresome life of merchants and trading! Tore listened to all of Thorvald's ramblings with a keen sense of interest. What would her homeland become? Tame, fettered, a new world that only children would understand? For them, life had always centered around men setting sail, fishing, and women tending to the chores that absent men could not perform. How would a culture so based on war and warfare, continue without the act of war? Tore scratched at the lice in her hair. They had picked it up in some filthy squalored hovel in one of the villages plundered. Now, everyone was scratching and itching.

Tore sighed. Looking into the water, she snapped back to the present. They were close now. Tore wondered if somehow she could escape having to fight in this mission. She had tried so gallantly to prove to Sif and Tyr that she was worthy of Gungnir. Hadn't she done enough already? Tore walked back to her sea chest and sat down, resuming her rowing.

Brock rowed on with a blank stare set on his face. "Hey, brother?" Tore poked him on the shoulder. He stirred.

"Hmm?" Brock mumbled, looking at her with a tired expression.

"Take a break. Claus and I can handle it for awhile." Tore yanked back on the oar and leaned forward with it in a steady fashion.

"Sure?" Brock mumbled again, lost in his own thoughts. "I'm sure." Tore smiled. Rowing and rowing out here, day by day, over and over, could turn monotonous causing most men to retreat into their inner thoughts for long periods of time.

Tore rowed on. She wanted to find a quiet place to rest and talk to Sif, but she needed to row. Brock was so good about making herself and Claus take breaks; Brock had that protective brotherly thing that forced him to watch out for his loved ones even if it meant overtaxing himself in the process. Tore tried to make sure that Brock got an equal amount of breaks. If she left it up to absent- minded Claus, Brock might not even get a chance to piss.

Tore tugged on the oar repeatedly. Her thoughts ran back to her childhood, and all of the ways she tried to prove she was every bit as valuable to her father as were his sons. She saw now, that Nordahl never questioned her worth...that he loved her just as much as he loved his boys, and maybe even more. All of these years she had wanted to be a man...and now she was one and wanted to be a woman again. Tore smiled to herself, how ironic life was.

Brock came towards her drinking a cup of tea. He handed her one as well, and she gulped down the lukewarm mixture quickly, still rowing awkwardly with one arm. She tied the cup to her belt and continued rowing.

Brock smiled. "Did you even notice that your cup was missing?"

"No, I didn't." Tore laughed. "You're getting to be quite a good thief."

Brock drank the rest of his tea, dumping the dregs onto the bottom of the ship and retying his cup to his belt. "I thought you might want something to drink, and since they were brewing up a pot over the lamp up there, I managed to snag your cup as you were rowing. I thought you knew." Brock laughed some more and sat down on his chest ready to row again.

"Nope. You were pretty sneaky. Rested now?" Tore smiled at Brock and rowed.

"Yes. Quit smiling so much." Brock smiled and tugged the oar.

"Sorry. That last break I took made me feel more relaxed. All this rowing was starting to get to me there for awhile." Tore said with a straight face.

"Me too. I'll be glad when we get all of this shit over with and go home. The initial excitement wore off months ago!" Brock sighed.

A loud snore jilted both of them in Claus' direction. He had fallen asleep and was slumped against the side of the ship; his arms limp at his sides.

"Wake that lazy beast up." Brock pointed at Claus. Tore laughed and kicked Claus hard with her boot. Claus snorted and jolted, and opened his eyes, suddenly aware that he had fallen asleep at his oar. He clumsily grasped at the moving oar and tried to resume his duty as if nothing had happened.

"What's wrong with you? Aren't we giving you enough piss breaks?" Brock laughed at his younger brother. "I just fell asleep, that's all. This rowing is getting old." Claus was ready to head home too.

In fact, as Brock looked around at the other men on the ship, they all seemed a bit restless and bored. Thorvald was the only one who really seemed to still enjoy their trip. Brock was glad that his father was having a good time, however, because as things were this would probably be Thorvald's last great journey across the Swan Road.

Brock was glad that this stop was their last planned one. After their tasks in Shetland were completed, they would head north homeward. Brock would be glad to be back in his warm bed at home.

Tore could hear the navigator talking to Thorvald. His voice was loud and the wind carried most of what he was saying to her clearly. They were almost there. They would set anchor at night and the next day they should arrive at Shetland some time in the afternoon.

Tore felt a sense of relief. They were almost done and would be heading home soon. Once home, perhaps Tyr would release her of her debt...or not. Tore wondered if perhaps Tyr had not felt she had proved herself worthy and her days were numbered and few. She shook her head. She would not think about that right now, there were more important things to think about than wondering what or what not the gods were up to right now.

When night fell, the anchors were cast, and the men huddled in groups under their tents. The soft glow of whale oil lamps fluttered dimly from outside of the tents. Tore ducked back under their tent, she had gone to relieve herself under the protective cover of darkness.

Tore leaned her head against her sea chest and sighed. She tried talking to Sif, but the words wouldn't come. She was tired and sea weary. She just wanted to go home. Sleep was just out of her reach, when she was aware of a silver glow all around her. She felt the presence of Sif and her eyes widened in anticipation.

"Sif?" Tore called out.

"I am here." Tore heard the soft, low voice of Sif who sat near her, slowly stroking her own silver sword. "Is it Tyr?" Tore stammered, unable to complete her thought.

"Yes. Tyr has sent me to congratulate you in your success so far. He wishes for you to fight one last great battle, then you will be free to live as you choose." Sif purred.

"And Gungnir?" Tore asked.

Sif laughed softly. "Odin thought you a bit haughty for choosing to name your sword after his spear...but, now he is honored."

Tore smiled weakly.

"You will be free to keep your sword." Sif nodded. "But, I must warn you Tore Nordahldatr. This next battle will not be as easy as the rest. You may not survive. You may die at the hands of your own kind." Sif frowned.

"Who do you mean? Thorvald, Jens? Or do you mean another mortal?" Tore felt a frantic feeling welling up inside of her.

"That is not for you to know. Even the gods do not know which path your fate will lead you. We must wait and watch just as you must wait and live." Sif touched Tore's white blond hair and smiled almost motherly.

"You will stay with me?" Tore whispered. "I am always with you, Tore." Sif smiled again. Tore smiled and began to thank Sif, when suddenly, as quickly as she had appeared, she had vanished. Tore woke up. Brock and Claus were sound asleep, and the boat was full of the sounds of snoring men, and the lashing of the waves against the wooden ship.

She breathed deeply. One more battle. Just one more. Sif had said that this might be the one that kills her though. Tore's stomach was full of knots. Would she live? And, what had Sif meant by one of your own kind? It was Jens Tore just knew it. He would try to kill her in the heat of battle. Up until now, they had not lost that many men, or sustained that many injuries; but Sif was forewarning a deadly battle. Tore wondered how many of her fellow warriors would ever set foot on Norway's soil again.

Tore wanted to warn Brock to be extra careful this time around, but how did she do that without making him wonder how she knew? He would be curious as to why Sif would appear to Eirik in a vision of sorts. Tore decided she would just keep her eyes open for any fatal danger when they landed on Shetland.

Tore felt her heart beating wildly. There would be not more sleeping for her tonight. Besides, dawn was not too far off now. In a manner of hours they would be stepping onto Shetland soil into the gods only knew what.

Soon, the sun spread its rays across the sky like a spider unfurling a web. The men were up, and ready to resume rowing. Thorvald had briefed them all on the plan of action, and when he estimated that they would land. Thorvald had also told them that parts of the Shetlands were already held by Norwegian and Danish Vikings. There were six islands, they would be attacking two. The others were already ruled by their countrymen. Thorvald expected little gold or other valuables, but promised slaves. There were, as he explained, a few more of those Christian temples that might yield a small amount of gold and other gemstones; but there were no promises.

As they neared the shore of the first island, Tore could see a rocky, cavy land. At first glance, it reminded her of home with its rockiness. Tore strained as they rowed closer. She could barely make out the crude, sunken dwellings that these primitive people must live in. This would be no fight at all.

Tore could smell the smoke in the air of the hearth fires of the Shetland people as the ship drew still nearer to the shore. Soon, anchors were cast, and the men were piling out onto the beach. Thorvald had been so confident that this would be an easy fight, that he had ordered the men to make camp first. After all, he reasoned, there was nowhere for these people to flee…it was an island. They might run to hide in the caves, but sooner or later, they would have to come out for food. Thorvald had plenty of time.

The thought of the people inhabiting this island having to constantly watch their loved ones pried away by the neighboring Norsemen on the rest of the Shetland, or Zetlands, as most called them, was disturbing to Tore. Sure, the other places they had raided were also used to the constant barrage from sea-faring warriors; but this was something almost evil. These people were trapped like animals on this island, leaving only to fish. They had nowhere to run or to escape to whenever any of the Viking bands decided to pay them a visit. And, yet, they had somehow managed to elude the Norsemen and remain independent. Tore wondered if maybe that was not by accident. Perhaps, this island was kept "free" so that the other Vikings could have a hunting ground. Or, maybe there was a special protecting god that loved the people of this island. This could be the battle that Sif had warned about.

Tore had one hundred grizzly thoughts bashing into one another inside of her head. Some of them she cared not to think about again. Others she couldn't help but think about. Sif's words did not fall on deaf ears. Tore replayed her conversation with the mighty goddess in her head over and over again. She hoped that she had not missed anything that Sif had said or warned her about. She did feel apprehensive about this island. Sif had promised a deadly fight.

Tore looked out over the hills covered with heather that was being whipped back and forth by the fierce winds that engulfed this island. She didn't see how neither this island nor its people could put up much of a fight. There were few trees to provide shelter, most of the land was plain, hilly, but with high visibility. Tore just didn't understand how these people could put up much of a defense against the weapons and the skills that she and the rest of her invading fellow warriors possessed.

It was quiet. So, quiet. Smoke curled out of the tops of a few of the stone hovels that were situated in a type of circle over on a hill before her. Yet, no one scurried from one dwelling to the next, or screamed a warning to any of the other inhabitants. Surely, they had seen them making camp by now. Tore caught a whiff of her own odor as the wind whipped around her with a powerful force. Her own stink was ghastly, if the people of this island hadn't heard them yet, they must have definitely smelled them!

Tore examined a bunch of nets that some fisherman had left on the shore. The people must be a lot like her own. Tore wondered if the years in which the neighboring Norsemen had been here, if some of the customs and ways of life had not rubbed off on the dwellers of this land as well. Surely, the Norsemen invaded this island frequently.

Thorvald was sharpening his sword. Tore approached him and sat down on the rocky beach beside him.

"Father?" Tore asked quietly.

"Yes, my son?" Thorvald looked up for a moment and then continued his sharpening.

"Is it not too quiet here?" Tore asked slowly. She didn't want to appear as if she was questioning his leadership in any way.

"It is quiet. Except for the howling of the wind." Thorvald said calmly.

"Is the quiet good?" Tore asked.

"I do not know." Thorvald seemed rattled a bit. Tore found this frightening. Nothing scared Thorvald. If the quiet that enveloped them had him apprehensive, this could not be a good omen.

"Do the other men sense it?" Tore asked hesitantly.

"Some. Most do not." Thorvald stopped spitting and sharpening for a moment and looked into Tore's face. "Most of them men aren't as intuitive as you are. But, the gods smile on you, Eirik."

"I hope the gods keep smiling on me, Father, for I do not like the quiet that I hear." Tore sighed and struggled to her feet in the rocks. She grasped Thorvald strongly on the shoulder with one hand and left.

She stopped a few paces away and watched Thorvald. He had set his sword down on his lap, and was looking out into the sea, listening. Tore suddenly knew that Thorvald would not leave this island alive.

Goosebumps raced up and down her neck and arms. There was an ominous stirring in the air that she could not explain. There was still no action from the hovels on the hilltop. No farm animals grazing, not enough smoke from the dwellings to indicate that all were inside waiting with baited breath for their attackers. Something odd was abounding here.

Brock came up to Tore and nearly whispered. That was something else that Tore had noticed. The surrounding quiet had also made the men talk in hushed tones as if they too were afraid of what was happening.

Brock whispered, "Did you speak with father?"

"Yes. He too feels it." Tore said shortly. There was no sense in going into a long drawn-out conversation about this; Brock knew what she was thinking.

"When do we attack?" Brock was uneasy.

"Thorvald didn't say." Tore sat down next to the fire that Brock had started and took a big swig of mead from a skin that Brock had passed her.

Brock raised his eyebrows. "You must be unnerved. You hardly ever drink."

Tore smiled and wiped her mouth with the back of her dirty hand. She said nothing.

Brock and Tore sat side by side, huddled over the fire that kept going out in the strong bursts of wind that kept coming off of the sea. They sat there, swords ready, waiting for the battle horn. A thousand hours seemed to pass before they noticed that Thorvald had gone over to the ship to do something.

Brock and Tore's eyes followed Thorvald. Thorvald stripped to the waist. All he left on were his pants and boots. He flung his cape, shirt, belt and scabbard into the ship. He stood there naked from the waist up, with only his sword in hand. No helmet, no shield. His aged body looked frailer without his clothing. He somehow looked smaller, and shorter than before. Brock looked at Tore questioning. Tore understood.

She pushed herself up with her sword and brushed the rocks from her pants. She turned to Brock and pulled him up by the arm. Brock still looked at her as if she held the answer for his father's unpredictable behavior.

"Today is the day he dies." She said shortly and walked off to the group of men that was growing impatient further down the beach.

The horn was blown. No one was expecting it. They had been lingering here for what seemed like so long, that now to hear the horn being blown, had caught them all off guard. It was sort of a rag-tag beginning to the charge that was the first indication that all was not right today.

Tore felt herself running, but she seemed to feel detached from herself, as if she was hovering above her own body watching herself run with her sword held high up the hill and towards the pathetic dwellings of the people of this island.

No people ran from the dwellings in fear to escape. Tore stopped dead in her tracks, as did most of the other men. Out of fear? Shock? The feeling was really rather unexplainable.

One man finally gathered up the nerve needed and yanked open the crude door on the first stone hut. Out streamed a line of Danish Vikings. Their battle cry was as chilling as their own had been moments earlier.

Tore suddenly realized that this was an ambush. These Danes had laid in wait, silently, in the crude, flea infested hovels of the island inhabitants all afternoon waiting for them to strike first. Tore snapped to attention and left her daydreams and sudden realizations behind as a tremendously huge sword came crashing towards her. Gungnir in hand, she met the steel with no time to lose. Tore grunted and sweated with all her might trying to keep that blade from taking her head. The man behind it was a stinking, massive man who laughed and drooled as he struck at her…but, he didn't see Thorvald, naked to the waist, blood streaked over his white skin, approach from behind and whack off his head with a massive iron battle axe.

Thorvald flashed Tore a look that asked if she was well and wished her the luck of the gods all at once, then he ran off towards another group of struggling warriors.

Metal clashed with metal, swords with swords. Screams penetrated the air, and all too many of the dead bodies that Tore kicked were her own men. Why were the Danes attacking them? According to Thorvald, the two Viking clans had ruled together on these islands for years. What had happened to cause this? Another man was closing in on her. She could feel his sweat roll off of his hands and onto her as he held his sword above her head. Tore watched him in his blood-smeared helmet, heaving and shoving trying to take her down. Remembering the dagger that she had gotten from an earlier raid in East Anglia, she whipped it out of her boot and thrust it deep into the fat belly of the warrior bearing down upon her. He dropped his sword and clutched at his belly. Then, as if realizing he had left himself vulnerable to further destruction, he reached gawkily for his dropped sword. Tore kicked it out of his grasp and kicked him in the head. She pointed her sword downward at the man now on his knees, and kicked him again. Now prone on the ground, the man's helmet, half off and half on, Tore thrust her sword downward again, running him through the throat. One hand clutched at his crimson throat, or what was left of it, and the other fat hand still clutched at the dagger buried deep in his fat gut. The man kicked around in the rocky dirt for a few minutes before Tore walked off leaving him to his gods.

Blood was everywhere. Not like in any of the other places they had been though, for this was the blood of her people. She looked towards the side of one of the stone dwellings and saw Johan slumped over. Tore ran to the building and knelt down beside Johan. He was already dead. A huge gaping gash across his chest and stomach revealed the work of a battle-axe that had found its target.

Tore let his shoulders drop back like she had found them, and then went to search for Brock. On her way, she stumbled over Claus's body. He had been chopped to bits and pieces. Only his face remained intact. Two of her brothers had fallen...how many more before the day was out? A pain that no weapon could ever make seared through her heart. Brock! What if Brock was dead as well? Tore felt like crying. She uttered a prayer to Sif to protect both herself and Brock and went blindly into the fighting hoard to search for him. She would not let him fall dead like his brothers, not if she could help it. She loved him too much, and if it meant sacrificing her own self so that he might live, she would do so willingly.

She looked frantically in all directions, but she could not find him.

Fearfully, she realized that there were fewer and fewer of her own men standing. Even the wounded were fighting. She had to find Brock. Where was he? She heard a scream that sounded like Brock's voice and ran to the direction it originated from. It was Jens.

Three men had cut him down and were sadistically severing his limbs one by one. Tore saw his eyes meet hers, and wondered if he would alert them to her hovering near this grizzly scene. Jens simply closed his eyes and died.

Tore retreated backwards quickly. She had to find Brock. They had to leave this place. They were being slaughtered like animals…slaughtered like all of the people in all of the places they had been to…like the two children that she had killed mercilessly.

Havelok came screaming from around one of the stone dwellings and dropped down before Tore. He held onto her ankles as if asking for help, but when Tore rolled him over, she realized he was beyond help. His throat had been slit, and blood and air were gurgling from his mouth and the gap in his throat. Tore felt a tear roll down her cheek. She looked up and saw two men coming at her with evil sneers across their faces. Would this be the day she died too?

Chapter 15

Tore braced for the powerful jolt of the sword that came down upon hers, the impact nearly knocking her off of her feet. She screamed and charged the man. He wasn't prepared for her blow. Tore assumed he had thought he had the upper hand and that she wouldn't dare fight back. His comrade moved in closer behind Tore as the other man got up from the ground where he had fallen in order to miss Tore's blow; but, he hadn't missed it entirely. Taking his hand off of his sleeve, the man looked down at the oozing scarlet stain on his hand, and then to the deep gash in his arm. This did not make him happy, and he signaled to his friend to move in even closer. Tore knew that she was cornered. She frantically moved her head back and forth in a vain attempt to locate one of her fellow warriors, but saw no one.

Suddenly, Thorvald came from behind a near-by hovel; his bad arm, remarkably useful, clutching a sword and his other grasping a smaller dirk. Tore watched in amazement as this aging warrior jumped onto the back of the man farthest from her and brought him down with only his dirk; but, with a price. Tore saw that among the many wounds that her bare-chested adopted father had already sustained, the man he had rid her of had managed to give him a good gash to the gut. Thorvald looked down at the body of the slain man, and then to his own mid-section. Tore grimaced. The other attacking man just watched in horror or awe, Tore wasn't sure which, as Thorvald slumped to his knees, his hands clutching at his bulging entrails.

Tore felt a tear roll down her cheek. He reached out his arm, and amid bubbling blood spittle, he addressed her as "Son." Then, Thorvald fell forward, still clutching his wound, and died.

Both Tore and her attacker stood there for a moment, watching this dying warrior...then, as if nothing had happened, the man snapped back to the task at hand and approached Tore with a new sense of triumph. Tore knew that the odds were now reduced, thanks to Thorvald's last effort.

The man was huge. Even with all of her training and skill, she was just no match for him. He had to be at least six foot five inches tall, and about 300 pounds. A massive man. He came at her with a sword that made Gungnir look like a child's practice sword...and he came at her laughing. "Your people shouldn't send boys into battle." He snarled in broken Norwegian.

Tore prayed and cursed with the same breath. She just kept backing up, slowly, steadily, her sword outstretched before her ready to use when the strike was made. From her left eye, Tore saw another Dane approaching. She was back to square one. Two against one, and she was growing tired.

Suddenly, she snapped her head to the left. The second Dane was rushing at her with a cry so terrible it could wake the dead. Tore pointed her sword in his direction, but before she could make any defensive moves, she felt herself flying through the air and landing in the mud.

Searing pain ripped through her body, as she realized that his sword had pinned her thigh to the ground. The man stepped forward and yanked his sword from her wound. She screamed in agony and clutched her thigh, rolling onto her side. Then, toying with her, he stabbed her ass sharply, and quickly. The other man hovered over her laughing sadistically as the attacking man did. The one man took out his knife and reached forward towards her face. Tore recoiled in fear. They were going to slit her throat as they had Havelok's.

The man laughed and grabbed at the blond braid on one side of her face and hacked it off, stuffing it in his shirt as a souvenir, Tore imagined.

Blood squirt from the wound in her thigh, as Tore tried to scramble to her feet, but couldn't. She collapsed in a semi-sitting, semi-laying position. The massive Dane laughed some more and then ran his sword through her side. Tore let out a blood-curdling scream and fought unconsciousness with every ounce of strength left in her body...which, she was becoming increasingly aware, was waning. Tore suddenly saw Brock and another man come from behind with swords brandished high. She slumped down to the ground, everything becoming a sea of black engulfing her where she lay.

Brock and Oskar the Fowler came around the building to see two massive stinking Danes chopping away at Eirik. Brock screamed and charged before Oskar had any idea what was going on, but he quickly sized up the scene and joined Brock in the fight. One Dane wounded Oskar, but Oskar was still on his feet and fighting. He took down the Dane, and then collapsed near his foe's body. The wound was a fatal one, and Oskar tried to staunch the flow of blood, but knew it was of no use. He lay back against the dead body of the Dane, and waited for the gods to claim him.

Meanwhile, Brock rushed the Dane that was hovering over Eirik and went a few rounds of sword fighting with him, until the Dane was finally caught off guard, and Brock struck him straight in the heart.

Brock dropped to his knees and scooped up his brother and friend. He looked around him quickly and saw that up over the hill there were some caves. Brock struggled up the hill and into the caves, where he laid Eirik's wounded and bleeding body on the ground. Cautiously, Brock went back to the opening of the cave and surveyed the scene below. They had managed to escape undetected. Brock sighed.

Ripping strips of cloth from his own tunic, Brock knew he had to stop Eirik's bleeding. There was so much blood covering Eirik's body that Brock could not tell where the bleeding was coming from. Brock ripped Eirik's pants leg up the seam to his hip, and laid back the blood soaked fabric. Brock gasped and reflexively recoiled backwards, looking in shock at Eirik's naked lower parts.

Eirik wasn't a man at all. Lying here, bleeding before him, was the body of a woman. Brock's eyes were wide in amazement, and his heart beat wildly from the shock. Slowly, shock gave way to anger.

"Damn you, Eirik! You lied to me! You lied to everyone!" Brock growled at Eirik's, or whomever this was, unconscious body that was still laying on the ground bleeding.

Brock was furious. He should just let this imposter die here in this cave, alone. Brock pushed himself to a standing position and began to walk out...but he couldn't.

He turned around and walked back to this person who he loved so much, whom he had trusted, whom he loved more than his own flesh and blood.

"Agh!" Brock punched his hand into his other hand in an angry outburst. Confusion surrounded his mind, and he found that he didn't know what to do.

"Brock." The person on the ground whispered weakly. Brock watched as his, or rather her, head moved slightly to the right, her eyelids fluttering. She was coming to.

Brock whipped his dagger from his belt and grabbed this woman by the hair. He yanked her head backwards, drawing up her throat. Her eyes, horrified, met his and locked there.

"I should kill you right here. I should kill you right now!" Brock yelled at her, spit flying from his mouth and spattering her cheeks and forehead.

Tore reached a hand up to his and weakly grasped it. She was too weak to fight, or to argue. If he was going to kill her, he might as well get on with it.

Brock leaned on the dagger that was pushed against the snowy whiteness of her throat. Why hadn't he thought of it before? This throat under his dagger, this long, beautiful graceful neck...this wasn't the neck of a man. This was a woman's throat. Then, as if a light was shining upon her body and he was looking at her for the first time, Brock saw her in a whole new light. How could he have ever believed she was a man? She was beautiful...and strong. A warrior...and a woman! Brock began to see the big picture and drew his dagger away from her throat in total awe at what she had accomplished. She had fooled all of them into believing she was a man! She had fought like a man, and rowed like a man, and behaved like a man! She might be a woman...but she was no ordinary woman.

Tore rolled her head away from Brock's staring eyes. He knew her secret now. She was dead. She might as well have been killed by those filthy Danes...at least that way, Brock would have never known how she had deceived him, deceived them all.

Tore moved her tongue around in her dry mouth, as if testing to see if it still moved. She quietly spoke, "So, you know." She looked back into Brock's blue eyes. "I know!" He snarled.

"Are you going to kill me then?" Tore said between coughs.

Brock was silent for a moment. "I should." Tore sighed, and stabbing pain brought her attention back to her wounds. Brock seemed to remember them as well, for without speaking, he moved towards her and began bandaging and tying off her leg above the wound to stop the bleeding. Tore felt a wave of blackness coming over her again, and allowed it to carry her off.

When she awoke, it was night, and Brock had started a fire and dragged her beside it. Her head was on something soft, and rolling her face to the side she realized it was Brock's lap. He was asleep. She lay there watching him sleep. How gentle he looked in slumber, the soft white lashes fluttering slightly against the reddened sea-stung skin of his face. Tore looked at the goldish blond beard that sprung from his face, and slowly extended her hand to touch it.

Brock opened his eyes and looked down into hers. All of this time, all of these feelings...he had known all the while somewhere deep inside of him, part of him had known. Brock caught her rough hand, in his own, his blue eyes blazing into her face. Then, he relaxed his hand and held hers there, in the air, above her face and close to his own.

Neither one of them spoke. It was as if all of their thoughts were already known by the other. All of their fears and wondering were exposed and open to each other...there was no need for words. Brock looked into her face as if for the first time, studying her eyes, her cheeks, her full lips. The closeness they had always shared, the feelings they had always fought to suppress...were all there, and now they made sense.

Brock cleared his throat and brought her hand to his chapped lips and kissed it. He leaned his head back against the cold, hard wall of the cave and looked into the fire.

"I don't even know who you are." He said at last, in a hoarse whisper.

"Sure you do. I'm the same person." Tore smiled slightly.

"Your smile." Brock smiled and laughed softly. "I knew you were too pretty to be a man."

Tore didn't say anything. She just lay there and looked at his face.

"What is your name?" Brock looked back down into her face.

She winced for a moment from pain, then took a deep breath. "Tore Nordahldatr."

Brock gasped. "By the gods!" He cursed. Tore frowned. Did he know who she was? Had he heard stories about her family? About her disappearance?

"You know me?" Tore tried to laugh, but coughed instead, clutching at her wound in pain.

Brock watched her writhe in pain for a moment, concerned. Then he brushed her hair from her face and leaned forward, pressing his lips against her forehead. He had always loved her. Eirik, Tore, whoever she was...he had always loved her. How could he tell her his terrible secret? Brock sighed. "Yes. I know you."

Tore frowned again. "But, I never knew you...before... before you knew me as Eirik Graafell."

"I knew of you." Brock corrected himself. Tore sighed. "You heard about my family then." Maybe she wouldn't have to explain so much if he already knew about her family's deaths.

"Yes, I know." Brock breathed heavily. Should he tell her? Was she able to handle the truth right now in her weakened state? Brock looked down at this wounded angel resting on his lap and sighed. Weak? This was the same person that had done a flip in the air to bring down an enemy...the same person who had bested every new warrior in the military camp...this was no weakling!

"I killed your family." Brock said slowly. Tore grimaced. She frowned and watched Brock's expression.

"What do you mean?" She said cautiously. "It was my family who carried out the wergild." Brock found the strength to look into her eyes once again. Realization crept slowly into Tore's mind as she put the voices together from her memories, with the voices she knew from her adopted family.

"You...you wanted to kill me?" Tore said blinking back tears.

"Not you specifically, since I didn't know you...as you...Oh, you know what I mean!" Brock said exasperated that he could not explain himself.

"You would've killed me if you had found me." Tore said tearfully.

"But, I never found you." Brock reminded her. "That's because you thought I was a man! And all this time, I've been living right with you...right with all of you!" Tore was crying, but then began to laugh a little hysterically.

Brock sighed sharply. "You're pretty clever." "I didn't know it was your family! I didn't know who wanted us dead! All I knew was what my younger brother had told me...and he never told me who the family was that wanted us dead!" Tore wiped at the tears on her cheeks ashamedly.

"You didn't know it was Thorvald and the rest of us then, the whole time you were with us? By the gods! You could have murdered us all in our beds!" Brock said feeling the impact more intensely now than before.

"Know? What would I know? Men don't tell women anything! I had to practically beg Ubbe to tell me what little he did tell me! I had no idea...I would never have lived with any of you...never have fallen in love with you...had I known!" Tore spat as she spoke.

"Woman, huh?" Brock laughed. "Sure, had me fooled."

"I meant before...before all of this." Tore waved her arm before him weakly.

"What was the last part of what you said? Fell in love with...who? Me?" Brock laughed again.

"Yes, you!" Tore punched him as hard as she could in the leg.

"Whoa! You might hurt me." Brock laughed. "Very funny." Tore said, still weeping.

"I think you need to get some rest. Who knows what tomorrow is going to hold for us. I want to try to make it back to the ships...if they've left any unburned." Brock said sighing. "I don't know how many men are left. I couldn't find father."

Tore felt the pain of losing her own father all over again. This man, this Thorvald, whom she had come to love as a new father, now he was dead...and he had killed her own beloved Father. Mixed emotions stirred within her, and Tore found that she was too exhausted to think about any of them right now.

"I saw Father...your father." Tore found that under this new reality, calling the murderer of her Father, Father, had an odd and unpleasant ring to it. "He died, saving me." Brock let out his breath sharply.

"Your brothers are also dead." Tore said softly.

"All of them? You saw them?" Brock asked in disbelief. "All of them. I'm sorry, Brock." Tore held his hand firmly. No matter what these men had done in the days before she had known them, they were still Brock's brothers, and she still loved Brock...as much as she didn't want to love him for what he had done, she couldn't stop her feelings.

Brock whimpered like a hurt dog for a moment, and then sucked in the air around him, quelling his rising emotions, refusing to cry.

"You can cry, Brock. It's okay." Tore said reaching up to caress his beard.

Brock looked away from her into the blackness of the cave, his eyes oddly vacant. "For a woman." He said softly. Tore knew then, that there were some things she could never change.

The next morning, Tore woke up on the ground with the fire next to her smoldering. He had left her. Tore felt a pang in her heart that was twice as painful as the wounds to her flesh. Brock had left her.

She struggled to get to her feet.

"I'll be damned if I'm going to let him go off and leave me in these God damned Zetlands!" Tore cursed and using her sword, hobbled to the entrance of the cave.

"Why in Hel's name are you up?" Brock suddenly came into the cave.

Tore looked at him startled, but stood there trying to maintain a false front of strength.

"I thought..." She began.

"You thought I had gone off and left you." Brock finished her sentence for her.

"Yes." Tore said and then lowered herself into a semi-sitting position painfully.

"We've been through all this other horse shit and you think that now because you're a damned woman I'm going to run!" Brock laughed. "It's going to take more than a woman to drive me away from you!" Brock laughed and helped Tore to the outside of the cave.

Tore didn't know what to say. Part of her was shocked that he was still here; the other part of her was embarrassed that she would have so little faith in him.

Brock walked to the edge of the rocky cliff that hung over the hill. He came back to where he had left her propped up against the rocks.

"It looks like all of those filthy dogs have left. I can see a few of our men moving around down there. There's a lot of men dead." Brock spoke as if he was briefing an entire army. "I think I'm going to take you down to that cluster of rocks there, and then go on by myself to survey the rest of the situation and the condition of the ships. I'll come back and get you when I've rounded up all of the remaining men." Brock turned back and faced Tore.

Tore felt the heat rising to her face in anger. "If you think that now that you know I'm a woman, you're going to start treating me like a damn weak dog, you've got another thing coming. I'll go with you to survey the ships, and I'll do everything else I would have done had you never discovered my secret!" Tore hissed.

Brock, propping his leg up on a rock, and leaning against his leg with his arm, bent over laughing.

"What? What is it? What's so damned funny?" Tore snarled.

"YOU!" Brock croaked between laughs. "You are what is so damned funny."

"Why?" Tore demanded.

"Tore, I really could care less if you're a woman right now. I've seen you fight, remember? Anyway…it has more to do with the fact that you can't walk." Brock straightened himself up still laughing.

"Oh." Tore felt embarrassed.

"Besides, the others don't know you're a woman. I don't think it wise that we let them know anytime real soon, do you? The others might not be as kind as I was with that dagger." Brock threw down a rock he had been absently clutching in his hand.

"I guess not. They're not in love with me." Tore said smiling.

"In love? I guess I am." Brock smiled.

"I used to dream about that." Tore fiddled with the bandage on her leg.

"I used to struggle with my feelings. I was afraid I was developing unnatural feelings towards you, towards another man. When you were a man." Brock stammered.

Tore laughed. "You mean all of that rutting and carrying on that you started suddenly doing, was a cover for the feelings that you were developing for me…the feelings you didn't understand?"

Brock shrugged. "I didn't understand it at the time. Part of me knew the truth about you, I guess."

Tore laughed. "That explains why you were so odd at times."

"Explains why I was odd?" Brock laughed. "What about all of the odd things you did? I thought you were the strangest man I had ever met!"

"Well, I was." Tore smiled warmly.

"Hey. I'd love to stand around here and chat some more, but I have to get you down to those rocks and on with the rest of the tasks at hand." Brock walked towards her laughing still.

"How are we going to do this?" Tore asked.

"I'm going to carry you to those rocks, then you're going to stay there until I come and get you." Brock said simply and hoisted Tore up into his arms.

Tore clutched at his neck and shoulders, burying her face in his chest. She sighed.

"Don't get too cozy there, someone might see us." Brock said in a whisper.

"Then why are you hiding me behind those rocks?" Tore laughed.

"You've got a big mouth for a woman." Brock said, stepping over a large rock in their path.

"My father used to tell me that." Tore said without thinking.

Brock didn't reply. An uncomfortable silence fell on them as Brock walked the rest of the way to the pile of rocks.

When they got to the rocks, Brock carefully lowered her down to the ground.

"You'll be okay?" Brock asked.

"I've got Gungnir, don't I?" Tore smiled.

"Yeah. Right." Brock smacked her on the shoulders like old times, and started cautiously down the hill towards the men.

The men were busy collecting their dead. They didn't have time to bury them, so they had built a massive pyre to burn them all together. Except for Thorvald. It wouldn't be fitting to burn Thorvald the One-armed with all of the other men. So, they had begun to dig a massive hole in the rocky earth to bury him like he should be buried. It was no easy task.

Brock arrived on the scene after these preparations were already underway. When emerged in the crowd, the men cheered. One of Thorvald's sons had lived to lead them. Brock approved of the arrangements for the dead. Two of the ships had not been burned. Only one would be necessary to carry the remaining warriors home in, so the other would be used to bury Thorvald in. They would dig the hole near the beach, drag the ship into the hole, and put Thorvald in it. The other men they would burn near Thorvald's burial site.

They would complete these arrangements and then they would set sail for home. Brock was issuing orders for this and that, when he turned his mind back to Tore. It was odd to think of her as Tore, not as Eirik. Even her

203

name sounded unfamiliar and foreign in his head. He hoped she was doing okay up there behind those rocks. He sent two men to get her.

Tore was half asleep and half alert when two of her fellow warriors approached her hiding spot.

"Eirik?" One of the men asked.

"I am here." Tore answered.

"Brock Thorvaldsson has sent us to bring you to the shore." The man said, and then they helped her up, down the rocky hill, and to the shore.

By the time they had gotten her there, her wound in her leg was bleeding again. Brock spotted the two men lowering her to the ground near a fire, and a group of other wounded men, and dropped what he was doing to rush to her side. He could tell she was in pain.

From somewhere, he had scraped up some mead and brought it to her in a wooden cup. Tore smiled and took the mead and drank it gratefully. It would help to dull her senses.

Brock threw a cloak over her and then returned to tending to whatever needed tended to. The morale of the men was low…they had lost more than half of their numbers, their leader and all of his sons, save Brock and Thorvald's adopted son, Eirik. Brock prayed to his god, Thor, that Tore's secret would remain just that…otherwise, vengeful, fearful men might reason that Tore had caused the bad luck that they had run into here on these islands.

By nightfall, most of the available men had taken more than one shift at digging Thorvald's grave. Brock, himself had dug on more than one occasion. A few of the injured men had even tried to help, but they weren't allowed to. They would need the men's strength for the journey home.

Brock walked through the group of dirty, grimy men towards the fire where Tore was asleep. She was alone. The men had built Brock a separate fire, now that he was Jarl, and had dragged Tore to it where she was now sleeping.

Brock sat down on the ground with a bucket of cold seawater and tried to scrub some of the dirt off of his face and arms.

Tore stirred. "Brock?" She asked in a whisper.

"Hmm?" He replied still scrubbing the dirt caked on his arms.

"Just checking to make sure it was you." Tore didn't move.

"It's me. Go back to sleep." Brock stopped splashing in the bucket of water for a moment to look in her direction, then resumed his bathing.

"What's happening?" Tore continued to speak.

"We're still digging Thorvald's grave." Brock looked over at her, through the smoky light of the fire and nodded in the direction of the grave.

"You must be tired." She said while smacking her dry lips together.

"A little. Don't worry about it. Go back to sleep." Brock moved closer to check her bandages.

"I think things have stopped bleeding." Tore watched him as he carefully examined her wounds, hovering over her to protect stray eyes with the wall of his own body.

"Looks like it. Did you get something to eat?" Brock pushed the one braid she had left out of her face.

"Hmm. A few hours ago. And you?" Tore was concerned that he was trying to do too much at once.

"I ate." Brock took the rag in his hand and wiped at Tore's dirty face with it. She smiled.

"Don't do that." Brock said quietly.

Tore struggled to sit up, but Brock pushed her gently back down.

"Stay down, you need your sleep." Brock pushed her down by her shoulders.

"I feel so helpless. You're doing everything for everybody. I feel like I should be helping you." Tore moved to sit up again, but pain made her cry out.

"Eirik." Brock said raising his eyebrows. "I need for you to get well. I need for you to sleep here, don't move and heal. You are all that I have left!" Brock touched her face briefly. "Don't you understand? I need you. You have to get better. You can't lose anymore blood." Brock frowned and looked her intensely in the eyes.

Tore fell back on the cloak and fur that she had been sleeping on. "I'm not going to die."

"Damned right you're not going to die. I'm not going to let you." Brock said firmly.

Brock sat there looking into the fire in silence.

"I don't hate you, if that's what you're asking yourself." Tore said after awhile.

"You should." Brock said without looking at her.

"I want to. But, I can't." Tore said truthfully. "I love you. Pisses me off to admit that, but I do." She sighed.

Brock turned his head to face her. "You do know, that I love you?" He whispered.

Tore smiled and put her arm under her head as a sort of pillow. "I had hoped you did. I prayed to Sif that you would."

"Sif? Does she have any involvement in all of this?" Brock asked.

"It's a really long story." Tore laughed.

"You'll have to tell me sometime. But, not now. I have too much to do, and you need some sleep." Brock pulled up the cloak over Tore's face to keep out the sea wind and cold. "I'll see you when you wake."

Brock got up, carrying with him the bucket of water, and disappeared beyond the light of the fire.

Morning broke the next day at the usual time, but no one woke Tore. She slept soundly through to mid-day, when someone nudged her awake and offered her some watered down wine and food. She accepted it heartily.

Brock was nowhere to be seen. She prayed he would return soon, because she had to piss something fierce and couldn't do it without his help. If he didn't come around real soon, she'd wet herself.

Tore drank the warm wine slowly. Sif had not returned to her since the last time they had spoken. Tyr had not killed her yet, so she assumed she had earned her sword. Tore didn't know why, but she had sort of expected some sort of closure to the deal, but neither of them had appeared, so she decided they figured she was smart enough to reach the right conclusions by herself. Just like a god to leave you hanging.

Brock stomped over to where she was laying; his boots caked with mud and dirt. Tore looked up at him.

"Eirik?" Brock asked with a sarcastic intonation to his voice. "How are you doing this day?"

Tore saw that there were other men with him, thus his greeting, "Better."

Brock turned and said something to the other men, who left them alone.

"I'm so glad you're back. I have to piss something terrible." Tore said through clenched teeth.

Brock laughed. "Where shall I haul you to?" He looked around for a private spot.

Tore pointed to a large rock down shore a bit.

"All that way?" Brock asked raising his eyebrows.

Tore touched her pants as if she was going to drop them right there.

"Okay! Okay!" Brock laughed, shaking his head. "I bet all of this has grown a bit old for you, hasn't it?"

"At times..." Tore held her breath as Brock heaved her to her feet and supported her body with his own. She gingerly walked, favoring her good side.

Tore took care of her business and was relieved when Brock took her back to the fire and helped her back onto the fur.

"There is some fresh blood. If it continues to bleed, I'm going to have to burn it." Brock said after checking her leg.

"Let's hope it stops bleeding. I don't relish the idea of a hot sword thrust on my wounds!" She sighed.

"Tomorrow, this time. We should be on our way home." Brock said and poked the fire.

"So soon?" Tore asked.

"The men are anxious to return home. You would be amazed at how fast they dig." Brock laughed. "We'll bury Father by nightfall."

"That's good." Tore said quietly.

"Tore, no matter what happened with your family, you knew Father. He wasn't all bad. He loved you." Brock smiled.

"Yes. He did. He had a kind heart, but he would have killed me without a second thought had he known the truth." Tore reminded Brock.

Brock nodded in agreement. "But, I won't." He said, and then got up. "I'll come check on you before the burial."

Tore nodded and watched him go. No matter what had happened with her family, she did love him. Love was the one thing she couldn't defeat.

Chapter 16

The fires were lit all over the beach. Brock had been reluctant to allow the men to light the fires for fear those blood-thirsty Danes would return to finish the job of killing them all off once and for all...but, the ceremony demanded that the fires be lit.

The ship had been dragged, pushed, and pulled to the pit they had dug. Usually, a great Jarl like Thorvald would have been buried with horses, treasures and slaves. All they could scrounge up were a few skin and bones horses that had already been killed in the attack by the Danes, some not so valuable trinkets left behind by the Danes, and one peasant girl that was dying fast due to her brutal rape and injuries. To say the least, the Danes had pretty much wiped out any possibility of Thorvald having a proper burial. One of the men had asked Brock why they didn't just push the ship out to sea and burn it; but, Brock didn't think the ship was seaworthy enough to float far enough out to do any good.

As Brock said the necessary prayers to Thor and Odin, and asked that they take his father to the halls of Valhalla where he would be a gallant warrior for all eternity, the men were hastily shoveling dirt back into the pit and over the boat and the screaming girl. Brock should have slit her throat or taken her heart out, but he couldn't bring himself to shed any more blood. Besides, he had said, she'll probably be dead before they actually have to bury her alive with the rest of the ship.

Already her cries were growing weaker as the men were pushing, throwing, and tossing dirt over the ship. Brock was standing with his back to the sea, his hair-blowing forward around his face. From where Tore lay on the litter the men had made for her, she could clearly see the deep frown marks etched on Brock's face. The prospect of leadership was not one he welcomed, but with all of his brothers dead, he had no choice.

Brock stood there watching the men cover the pit, his loose pants billowing out around him, hands on his hips, chin lowered. His thoughts went to Ymma waiting back home for news that she would not want to hear. Brock shook his head. There was no point dwelling on those sad thoughts right now, it would be another month at least until he had to deal with any of those events.

Brock looked over his shoulder in Tore's direction. What about Tore? When they got home, should she continue her masquerade as a man, or with him as Jarl would she be protected enough to return to her true identity? Brock didn't know what he should do about this situation. He had never observed his father having to deal with such a thing. Brock decided that he'd discuss it with Tore later on. For right now, and until they reached the shores of Vestland again, she would have to maintain her role as a man. Brock almost laughed, which brought him up a few notches from his somber mood. He had to hand it to her, the woman had spirit. There were very few men he had known with the courage that she possessed. She was braver than a hundred men put together, and a better warrior. Brock thought it a shame that she had to be a woman. A man like her would make a great leader.

Brock turned and made his way through the busy men to Tore. He fought the urge to touch her face, to push away that one stray hair that never stayed in its braid. She had been a good friend, a better brother, and she would make an excellent lover and wife. Wife. It was the first time that Brock had thought about that possibility. Tore probably wouldn't accept the role of wife very well. How could she be expected to fall back into a submissive role once she had tasted the freedom of a man's world? Brock sighed. The burden of leadership and of role model was a heavy one indeed.

"What is it?" Tore asked Brock.

"Hmm?" Brock looked at her but his mind was elsewhere.

"The look on your face, what are you thinking about?" Tore asked again, concerned.

"It's nothing. Just a hundred thoughts about nothing." Brock smiled at her and turned to check on the progress of the dirt shoveling men.

"We sail when the pit is full?" Tore asked. "Yes. The stars are bright navigation shouldn't be a problem. The men are anxious to get home. There's no point hanging around here any longer just waiting for those damn Danes to return." Brock crouched down and whispered to her, "Besides, the sooner we get our arses home, the sooner we can figure out what to do about you."

Tore smiled. "I'm sure you have some ideas." Brock laughed. He was glad she was able to relieve his mind of the tension he had been feeling. She really was the same old Eirik, just now with an extra twist.

All of Brock's brothers had been buried on the ship with their father. The other men had been buried as well. When all of the dead had been accounted for, and all of the living had been rested, Brock gave the command to load up the remaining ship. The men were more than eager to return home and wasted no time in assuming their rowing duties. They were going to have to work out some sort of shift rotation for rowing, since there weren't enough men to properly man the oars. There were plenty of wounded men, but unfortunately, a lot of those wounds were upper body, or arm wounds, which drastically decreased the numbers able to row.

Tore insisted on rowing, even though Brock argued it would make her start bleeding again. She said she'd take her chances and rowed alongside of him as they had for the entire journey. Tore let her thoughts go back to when they were just landing here on the Zetlands. They had so many hopes and soon those were all dashed. Now, she was glad to just have escaped with her life.

Brock continually tried to talk her out of rowing anymore, but to no avail. She was one stubborn bitch, he reasoned. She was right though in some of the fears she had that they had discussed, he was starting to think of her differently, as a, well, as a woman. This tended to cloud his memories of her abilities and limitations as a man. He suddenly found himself being more protective, more understanding, gentler, and all of the other characteristics that men generally reserved for women. He hated himself for doing it, because he had promised Tore that his attitude would not change simply because he now knew she wasn't a man; but, he couldn't help it. Years of custom were too ingrained in him to not slip back into the comfortable role of man and woman. Tore was a woman like no other he had ever known, and she really didn't fit into either role of man or woman. That left some unclear lines and definitions of how she should be treated. Tore insisted that she be treated no different than any of the other men aboard the ship, but Brock found it harder to treat her like the man she wanted to be, the deeper he fell in love with her.

When Tore finally collapsed from exhaustion, Brock was certain that her wounds would have to be cauterized. Blood was seeping through the cloth of her tunic and pants. Rowing had opened what little bit of flesh had closed. Brock heated his sword over a whale oil lamp until it was red hot, made Tore swig an enormous amount of mead and even some wine he had found, and then did the deed. Her screams ripped through him with a searing pain only equal to that which she must have felt when the red-hot steel touched her flesh. She passed out at the end, and Brock felt pretty close to that himself.

Keeping vigil over her slumbering body, Brock tenderly kept her covered from the cold winds. When he touched her his heart would beat a few beats faster. When he looked at her, a red hot searing passion equal to that sword now cooling against his brother's sea chest, welled up inside of him making him think and wish of things yet to come. He could only imagine what a woman as aggressive and untamed as Tore might be like in bed. He didn't even know if she had ever been with a man. Surely, a woman such as her must have already conquered the hearts and cocks of many men. Yet, Tore possessed a quality of innocence about her that would suggest that carnal love was foreign to her. Brock pulled the fur over her face, and smiled. Time would tell.

Twenty-eight days. It would be twenty-eight more days until Brock would be able to be alone with her. Even then, she'd be in no condition to test the waters so to speak. Her injuries were bad; it would take months for her to heal properly. He wondered if her passion was equal to his, if she'd be able to wait as long as was needed for her body to heal. Tore Nordahldatr, you are a mystery indeed, Brock thought to himself while looking down at her fur buried figure.

The next morning came quickly. Brock hadn't figured it would come upon them so fast. He was so tired from rowing that he had reasoned the night would seem endless. He looked around at the aching, tired men and stood up. He called for the anchors to be dropped so that the men could rest.

However, the anchors were too short. They were in too deep of water for a break. The rowing continued. What men could be spared were allowed a few short breaks, but most had to endure the pain and strain of constant rowing. There were few complaints that Brock heard. All of them wanted to go home.

At one point in mid-afternoon, two of the injured men had been discovered dead. They must have died in the night. Prayers were said, and their bodies dropped overboard. It was ghastly business, but dead men left to rot and putrefy on board ship would only drag more men to death with them. Better they swim with the fishes, then steal living men away. Brock watched the proceedings, and then ordered every man back to their rowing positions. Morale aboard ship was low. The Danes had taken all of the riches and bounty they had captured. The only form of compensation for these men would come from the sale of the slaves they had sent back in another ship prior to their landing in the Shetlands. A few of the men had wisely (although it had been a gamble at the time) sent a portion of their riches home on that slave ship; but, most had kept their loot safe with them in their sea chests.

Tore was stirring. Brock kept rowing, but also kept a watchful eye on his 'brother'. Sleep was good for her. Without proper rest, she'd never heal properly. Some of the other injured men were discovering this as well, and those of them who were anxious to do their part in the rowing, soon gave in to the pain of their wounds. Brock surveyed the ragged huddle of injured men and wondered how many more bodies they'd be flinging over the side of the boat before they reached the rocky shores of home.

Tore lay on her back, staring up into the heavens. She blinked. The sun was bright in her eyes, but warm on her skin.

Brock smiled. "So, you are awake, my brother?" Then he laughed slightly.

Tore looked around her as if for the first time, then she smiled. "I thought for a moment I was no longer on this earth."

"Oh, you're here alright. I'm not letting the gods and their Valkyries carry you away to join Father yet!" Brock laughed.

"The waves feel rough." Tore said struggling to sit up. "The wind has been picking up during the last hour. I've prayed to Aegir that he'll calm the sea. We've hardly the strength to row...we'd never last in a storm." Brock stretched his neck to look over the ship's side to the choppy waves beside them.

"Aegir has been good to us so far." Tore nodded. "I've prayed to Sif for our protection ever since we left the Zetlands."

Brock watched the oar for a minute then turned his attention back to Tore. "I think maybe you should give Sif a rest and pray to Frigga instead."

Tore frowned. "What would I want from Frigga?" Brock shrugged. "Oh, I don't know. I thought maybe you had been thinking about marriage for instance."

"Marriage?" Tore said while coughing. "What would I want with marriage?"

It was Brock's turn to frown. "I just thought..." He started.

Tore rolled her eyes. "I know what you just thought!" Then lowering her voice, "You think just because, well you know just because, that I would automatically be thinking about getting married?! Why?"

"Well, because you love me?" Brock asked. "I can love you and not have to be shackled to you like a goat." Tore lay back down, folding her arms across her chest.

"You confuse me." Brock said simply. Tore smiled where she was lying, and said with a slight laugh, "Good."

Brock laughed and continued to row. Tore stared at the clouds above, silent for now. Then she spoke. "I keep going over and over what happened in my mind, back in the Zetlands?" She looked over at Brock, who was sweating as he rowed, but he was listening, so she went on. "I mean, Danes! We were beat by Danes! For the god's sake, I can't believe a hoard of filthy Danes surprised and beat us! What would our ancestors think? To imagine, the Battle of Strangford Lough! We defeated those Danish cocks once and for all, and here they are attacking Norwegians again! And they beat us!" Tore said in disbelief.

Brock laughed. "You speak of Strangford Lough like it happened yesterday! It was in 877! A lot has happened since then."

"Nothing major." Tore grumbled. She hated it when men had to add their new sea knowledge to the knowledge she gained through listening to men around fires.

"Well, enough has happened all over that it's not just the Danes who are a threat to our way of life now. There's a lot of new enemies to fight, ones that didn't exist even fifty years ago." Brock stated. "Some of our new threats aren't even men with swords, there are new gods that threaten our gods. What could be more dangerous than that?"

"I know. I have thought of that too. In East Anglia, our gods were stronger though." Tore said matter of factly.

"But, one has to wonder how long it will be so." Brock said dismally. He knew this would be the last raid he would ever go on, and he was glad. There was a time when a man his age wouldn't even dare to think of being glad for never having to raid again, but the world was changing. There were many more options open then there were when his father was a young man such as himself; here, in the year 984, there were many more profitable and safer ways to live.

For the next few hours, Brock rowed in silence listening to the men around him, and the slap, slap of the waves against the wood ship's sides. Tore stared up into the clouds, and occasionally closed her eyes to rest.

Brock was confused. He had assumed that Tore would want to be joined with him. After all, she had professed her love for him, and he for her. What else was there but to be joined one with the other for all eternity? Was she just being stubborn or was she really serious about not wanting to marry him? He could see her point as long as she was unmarried. She was a free woman. Once she joined, or as she preferred, shackled herself to him, she no longer had a say in how her life was ran. Surely, she had to know that he wouldn't be a tyrant of a husband who would treat her as little more than a slave! If he wanted a slave, he'd buy one. He only wanted to share his life with this mystery of a woman who so passionately had him under her spell. He didn't know what to do! He was already going half mad from having to pretend she was still his brother, and a man. He wanted nothing more than to take her in his arms and shower her with kisses and caresses; but he couldn't. He thought he might go insane if he continued to dwell on her with his every thought.

How did she find the courage and the patience to maintain this false identity for so long? It had been three years now that he had known her and loved her as his brother and best friend. Three years that she had fought these same feelings that he was feeling now. How did she keep from going insane? It was wearing on him, little by little, tearing at his heart. He wanted her and he wanted the whole world to know that she was his; but the whole world thought that she was Eirik! It was all so maddening.

With all of these mad thoughts, the days began to slip into weeks. And soon, they were drawing near the end of their journey home. The men had a newfound sense of strength and increased their rowing with renewed vigor. Brock felt some of the cloud that hung over him starting to lift from his shoulders. Tore seemed much better, her wounds healing quickly. Most of the injured men had survived due to the care and attention given to them by their crewmen. Brock was impressed by the general pulling together of the men. Tore tried to attribute their successful journey home to his leadership skills, but Brock knew better than that. These were just men who wanted to see their families and homeland again. He had little if nothing at all to do with any of it.

Tore rattled the thought of home around in her mind over and over again. She knew exactly what she wanted to do the moment she set foot back on her native soil. She wanted to go straight to the temple and thank the gods for her safe return. Specifically, Sif and Tyr for allowing her to live and for finding her worthy of her sword, Gungnir.

A sound. What was it? It was clearer now, and loud. Overhead, they heard it again. There it was! Tore pointed triumphantly at the marvelous black bird that hovered over them squawking as if to welcome them home from their long voyage.

Brock stood up and watched it fly, his face lit up by the sun and by happiness. The men cheered. They were near land. Soon, they would be able to see the beloved cliffs of Vestland!

Tore weakly stood up, leaning against the ship's side, watching, eagerly awaiting the first glimpse of home. Brock smiled as he rowed. He knew Tore wished she could be rowing too.

There they were! Black, rocky, looming high above the sea, the cliffs of Vestland! A thick mist hung over the water and welcomed them home. Tore felt elated, like dancing! The men cheered wildly, and rowed frantically, wanting to get home.

"They're the most beautiful things I've ever seen in my whole life!" Tore whispered.

Brock smiled. Amidst the noise from all of the other men, he felt it safe to say to the woman he loved, "And, you're the most beautiful thing I've ever seen in my whole life."

Tore laughed. "You'll say anything if you think it'll make me marry you!"

Brock's face resumed its somber expression.

"I didn't mean to make you sad." Tore cooed.

"Let's not talk about this now." Brock feigned a smile.

Tore stretched her neck to see before them. Two men ran and removed the dragon's head from their helm so as not to scare Vestland's protective spirits away.

The beach sprawled out before them, busy people moving around like ants. Had they been spotted yet? They rowed in closer; Tore could see a crowd forming on the beach. They were home! They were home!

The ship rowed in and banked on the shore. The men, some with their sea chests on their shoulders, jumped overboard and ran to waiting family nearby. Faces, too many faces, searched the men coming from the ship, not finding the man they searched for. Brock and Tore stepped ashore. Tore fell to the dirt and kissed it. Brock pulled her to her feet gently by her arm. Ymma was waiting.

They could see her face as she smiled at them and then looked past them as if waiting for Thorvald and her other sons to come up behind Brock and Eirik. Yet, no one came. The questioning look on her face grew into a frown, she was growing angry.

"Where is your father, Brock? And your brothers?" Ymma grabbed his shoulders and shook him, still looking beyond him towards the now empty boat.

"They didn't make it back, mother." Brock said slowly.

Ymma's face went blank. "What do you mean, they didn't make it back?"

Brock gently removed his stepmother's claw-like grip from his shoulders and slowly held her arms at her side. "They are gone."

Ymma's bottom lip began to quiver.

"Thorvald and Jens, and Havelok, Claus and Johan. All of them perished in the Shetlands." Brock gulped. "We buried them properly, in one of the langskips, together. As they should be."

Ymma's eyes brimmed with tears. "All of them? All of them dead?" She mumbled.

"Let's go home, mother." Brock said, taking her around the shoulders and leading her home. He cast a glance over his shoulder, but Tore was nowhere to be seen.

Tore had stayed around long enough to be a support for Brock when he broke the bad news to his mother, but then she had left. She had to offer her thanks to the gods. She came up to the rectangular building made of stone and wood. Walking past the pillars carved in the form of human beings, she made her way to the front of the temple. Candles and lamps were lit casting flickering golden shadows over the images of the gods. The cleric stood quietly in the corner watching her every move.

"You have come to give thanks?" The old, gray-bearded cleric said in a hoarse and raspy voice, at last.

"Yes. I have brought gold." Tore produced a few pieces of gold that had not been looted by the Danes. She handed them to the gnarled and bent hand of the cleric.

"You want to thank Thor?" The cleric asked.

"Thor, and Sif, and Tyr." Tore said quietly.

"Odd choice for a man returning from battle." The cleric usually offered thanks to Odin and Thor. "Is this all?"

"No. I wish to offer a silent prayer to Frigga." Tore said suddenly.

The old cleric arched his eyebrows high. "Frigga?" He was baffled. "Odd choice, indeed!" He mumbled to himself, but offered the prayers to the first three gods then he turned to Tore and said, "Frigga will hear your silent prayer now."

Tore withdrew her sword and placed it before her on the stone floor. She knelt on one knee and bowed her head towards the statue of Frigga. Tore asked that the goddess guide her in the paths of love and family, to bring Ulf home, and to let Brock be hers regardless of a union or not.

The cleric cleared his throat to indicate that enough of his time had been taken. Tore looked up at him and smiled. Her smiled seemed to confuse him still further.

"My son. There is something unexplainable about you, may the gods go with you just the same." The cleric smiled and touched Tore's head lovingly.

Tore nodded and put Gungnir back in her scabbard. She nodded to each of the statues of the gods and goddesses, to the cleric, and then took her leave.

All through the streets towards home, Tore took in the familiar sounds and smells. She breathed deeply. She was home. Once at the door, she pushed open the heavy wood door, and entered the hall where she had talked with Thorvald so many times. That was before she had known the truth about Thorvald. It seemed like another lifetime ago.

Brock came out of nowhere towards her with his finger to his lips. "Quiet. Ymma and the other women are weeping near the fire."

Tore looked to the fire and saw them huddled together, wives, widows, women…weeping. She never wanted to find herself in such a situation.

Brock indicated that she should follow him upstairs to her room. It had been so long since she had slept in a real bed, and taken a real bath. She could hardly wait.

"Your bath is ready. I'll be back after I have finished with my own. We need to talk about some things." Brock smiled and kissed her neck. Tore touched his face, and smiled as well. She pulled his mouth to her own, and kissed him fully on the mouth. The kiss was long, deep, and promised things yet to come.

When they finally stepped back from each other, each was breathless. Brock fumbled around a bit with the door latch, before finally heading out and down the hall. Tore peeled off her ripped and bloodied clothes, and stiff, worn boots and with one quick slash of her knife cut the cloth that bound her breasts close to her chest.

She breathed deeply as the relief of from the constant pressure of the bandages on her chest welled up inside her and then permeated through her being. Tore tested the water with her foot, and then slid into the warm depths that welcomed her from the crude tub.

"Ah." She sighed and dunked her head under the enveloping warmness that beckoned her softly. It was so good to be clean again. To be out of those stinking rags of clothes. To feel like a person instead of an animal once again!

Tore laid there in the water, her hands and arms floating. It was quiet, so quiet. No waves lapping at the ship, no wind blowing through her ears. Just quiet. Tore reached up and touched her lips softly. The thought of Brock's lips lingering there still fresh on her mind. She smiled. How many nights had she laid in the bed in this room, wishing and praying for this kiss to happen? How many nights had she fought back tears and gagged on the pain in her throat? Now, all of that was gone. She didn't have to fight her love or passion for him any longer. He loved her, he would love her. They would love each other.

Tore must have fallen asleep, as was her habit while in a warm bath, for she heard footsteps outside in the hall, and whispered tones from sad women. There was a knock at her door, and she jumped to reach for her tunic.

"Who is it?" She asked.

"It's me." Brock answered.

Tore jumped out of the lukewarm bath, and dripping, made her way to unbolt the door. Brock came in with a whale oil lamp and set it down on the table near her bed.

"Still in the bath?" He laughed.

Tore looked down at the ground, and began to quickly dry herself off, trying to cover herself up as she did so. She felt uncomfortable under the steady gaze of Brock, looking at her naked body as if he were a starving man.

"I'm sorry." Brock said, suddenly aware of his heavy stare. He turned and faced the wall.

Tore clumsily slipped her tunic over her head and sat down on the bed. She had a towel in hand and was trying to sponge some of the dampness from her hair.

"You can turn around now." She said.

Brock pulled up the wood bench that was against the wall, and tilting his head to the side looked at her in a whole different light. Tore was very much a woman.

"I didn't think you were coming back. It has been so long." Tore said, combing her hair.

Brock watched her run the brush through her hair, as he had watched his sisters do thousands of times. It was all so clear now. He laughed. "How did I ever believe you were a man?"

"Gullible, I guess." Tore laughed.

"I guess." Brock shook his head.

"You aren't the only one who believed me, if that helps you feel better." Tore laughed and put the brush down on the table next to the lamp.

"Well, at least I wasn't alone in this trickery!" Brock touched her knee and flickered his fingers over her skin, stirring inside of her feelings that she had never had so intensely before.

"So, what do we do now?" Tore said, feeling as if she needed to gasp for breath.

"That's a good question." Brock smiled and withdrew his hand, toying with her.

"I mean, do I go on pretending to be a man, or do you want me to be a woman now?" Tore asked.

Brock laughed and moved to the bed. "Oh, I want you to be a woman now…as for later, we can talk about that later."

Tore felt her heart beating wildly in her chest. His hand was on her thigh. His arm encircling her waist. She felt her pulse quickening. Fear welled up inside of her, confusing her, she should be happy!

"Wait. Stop!" Tore said and wiggled out of his embrace. She ran to the other side of the room and gasped for air.

Brock laughed. "What is it, my dove? You aren't scared of me, not Eirik Graafell?"

Tore laughed but then added, "That's not funny."

"There's nothing to be afraid of, Tore." Brock got up from the bed and walked to her, taking her in his arms, and pulling her head close to his chest.

"But there is. There is, Brock." Tore sighed.

"No. There isn't. I love you. I would rather die than let any harm come to you." Brock held her tight.

Tore felt his heart beating as rapidly as hers. "Are you frightened too, then?" She said placing her hand over his heart.

"No. Not frightened, my dove." Brock looked down into her blue eyes and smiled.

Chapter 17

Brock tilted Tore's down-turned chin up, looking into her eyes. Tore had eyes more sapphire blue than the clearest and brightest sea. When he looked into those two gems, he felt as if he were looking into eternity. They pulled at his heart and tugged at his soul. Those eyes promised so much more than words could ever say...and all of those promises were being made to him.

Brock still hadn't gotten over the initial shock of Tore's not ever having been a man. Here was this incredibly clever, strong and skillful woman and she was madly in love with him, Brock Thorvaldsson, a man partly responsible for the inhumane slaughter of her entire family. What god was smiling on him right now to have made such a thing come true? What favor was he owed by some divine power to have swept such a woman off of her feet?

Tore reached for his face and pulled his strong jaw to her own. Her heart bashed against her ribs, her blood rushed through her body like the powerful waters of a waterfall. She had dreamed of this moment, of being in Brock's arms, of feeling his touch, his caresses...she never dreamed of being quite so nervous about the whole situation however. She was trembling...out of fear? She wasn't sure. It wasn't like anything she had ever experienced before. There was a rush of emotions, one flooding over the other before she had even had a chance to sort out the first. She felt dizzy, yet alert all at the same time. Scared, yet elated all at once. She could almost compare it to the adrenaline rush felt in that fleeting second before her sword first clanged with that of a new opponent, but this was different. No one was going to die here.

Tore found that her kisses matched Brock's with vigorous enthusiasm. She rather surprised herself at first, but with all things in her life she didn't see the point in holding back if enthusiasm got the job done better. Not that this was some sort of unpleasant task or something, quite the contrary; this was what every little girl dreamed about since the day she knew the meaning of the word "husband".

Brock pushed Tore's shift off of her shoulders, and kissed her neck, her shoulders, and her breasts. Tore uttered a slight moan as he rolled her nipple between his lips and sucked at them delicately. Brock slipped his arm under her legs and swept her up off her feet and laid her down gently on her bed.

He looked down into her face and smiled, brushing the stray hairs out of her face as he had longed to do as she lay sleeping on the ship so many times on their journey home. She smiled back and awkwardly tried to get his shirt off as he began to kiss her all over again.

Tore fiddled with the tangled ties on Brock's shirt, and couldn't get it untied. Brock stopped for a minute and laughed.

"Do you have problems with men's clothing often?" Brock laughed quietly.

Tore got the joke and returned his laughter, hitting him gently in the arm. "No! It's just that I haven't actually taken a shirt off of a man before!"

"Could've fooled me!" Brock was referring to her life as Eirik once again.

Tore stuck out her tongue and watched as Brock undid his shirt and dropped it in a pile next to the bed. "Now, where were we?" Tore murmured and returned Brock's kisses ardently.

His rough, sea-chapped hands felt oddly at home on her skin, as if they had always been there. Tore had dreamed of it about a million times, to her it had always been this way. Tore was aware of Brock's stiff member throbbing against her leg, as he moved all over her in ways she had only imagined. This wasn't the Brock she saw groping and fucking Amalie outside of her window so long ago. This wasn't the coarse and quick rut that men so often boasted of. Brock was relishing every inch of her body as if she herself was a goddess in human form.

She sighed as he moved her leg over to one side and moved his hand over her thigh and behind to her buttocks. At least he knew what he was doing, Tore thought to herself. It was comforting to know that one of them had some experience in these matters. All she knew about lovemaking was the gory details of rape and the sordid details of fucking a whore that she had heard from one too many braggarts aboard ship and around fires. This tender, loving side she knew little of... but she was learning fast.

Lost in her own thoughts, she suddenly grew aware of Brock hovering above her ready to thrust his bulging manhood into her. She gasped for a moment, fearful of what was to come. Reflexively, she clutched at Brock's shoulders, vaguely aware of raking his flesh with her fingernails in the moment of sharp pain that Brock unintentionally had bestowed upon her. She let out a small cry. She was no stranger to pain, but this was a new pain she had never before felt. How could something hurt and feel good all at the same time? Tore found it amazingly confusing. Brock stopped for a moment and looked into her face as if believing for the first time that she really had never been with a man before.

"What, you didn't believe me?" Tore whispered and smiled slightly.

Brock smiled and kissed her mouth passionately, then fell back into the steady rhythmic rocking of his body consumed in hers. Brock was careful not to put his weight on her hips, her wounds were still healing. Even though he knew she was a strong woman, he didn't want to be the cause of any unnecessary hindrance to her healing. In a way he felt a little guilty right now for even initiating their lovemaking, but Tore hadn't resisted. He was sure that had she not wanted to lie with him, he would have been the one to leave in pain.

Tore could feel the hair on his thighs rubbing on her smooth skin. She buried her face in his long hair and tried to concentrate on nothing but the rhythm of their bodies, but there were so many things to think about.

Above her, Brock groaned and his body jerked a little, before he exhaled a great gasp of air and collapsed, sweating and exhausted on top of her. Tore smiled to herself, feeling Brock all over her, and inside of her, and kissed his chest. Brock rolled over onto his side against the wall, and pulled up the fur on the bed. Tore lay in the crook of his arm, nestled up to his chest for warmth. She sighed.

"I never dreamed it would be like that." She said softly.

"What did you think it would be like?" Brock asked, not sarcastically, but genuinely curious.

"I don't know really. Rougher. Men talk like they rut like animals...I didn't know what to expect exactly." Tore ran her hand over the downy blond hair on Brock's chest.

"Well, are you pleased?" Brock asked, kissing her forehead.

"Hmm." Tore murmured. "Very much so."

Brock laughed. "I think I'll stay here tonight." Tore wanted him to stay, she wanted to wake up in his arms, but they still hadn't resolved her situation yet. She didn't want to bring it up and ruin the tender moment they just shared. She sighed and said nothing for the moment.

After an hour had passed, of Brock snoring steadily away, and Tore staring up at the dark ceiling, Tore gently nudged Brock awake.

"Brock?" She asked.

"Hmm?" Brock replied still not awake. She elbowed him harder in the ribs. His eyes popped open.

"Hey!" He snapped, then remembered where and whom he was with. "Oh, sorry." He smiled.

Tore laughed. "I didn't want to wake you, but in case you have forgotten, everyone else in the world still thinks I'm a man, remember?"

Brock rubbed his face and eyes. "I haven't forgotten." "So...what are we doing?" Tore propped herself up on one elbow and looked at Brock questioningly. Her fate was in his hands now.

"You're saying I should go?" Brock asked, not really wanting to make the decision.

"I don't want you to go, but if everyone still thinks I'm a man, won't it look a little odd to see you coming out of my room in the morning? Or did you have a different plan that you haven't told me about?" Tore kissed him on the lips.

"No, same old plan. I don't think you should let anyone know about you, not being a man, for a while. There are still too many men who would want you dead. Women too, maybe. When my leadership is no longer questioned, and no one challenges my authority, then it will be safe. Right now," Brock sighed, "Right now, I'm afraid Eirik Graafell must stick around a little while longer."

Brock smoothed Tore's hair and smiled. He half expected an argument, but he got none.

"You're the boss." Tore laughed.

"I never thought I'd hear that from you!" Brock laughed and crawled over Tore's body to get out of the bed. He fumbled around in the dark for all of his clothes.

He dressed, bent over and kissed Tore and then left. Tore rolled over and pulled up the fur to her chin, thankful she didn't have to leave her warm bed and make a trip down that wretchedly cold corridor. Tore sighed, smiled, and drifted off to sleep a very happy woman.

The next morning there were plenty of things to be done. Ymma was still not herself, and a lot of the other women were downcast and sad. Brock had a list of chores and tasks that he, as the new Jarl, was now responsible for. Among his own household worries, he had a list of community grievances and situations to take care of. He would have to see and hear a number of cases involving squabbles and disputes that had accumulated in their absence at sea. He wasn't too worried about fulfilling these duties. He had sat in nearly all of his life and watched his father dispense justice and rulings in these matters. He didn't doubt his own good sense to sort through the gritty details and rule justly and favorably. The only thing he was worried about, was how the general population would take to his being in charge now that Thorvald had been killed. There was no real rule of succession to an authority position such as a Jarl. The oldest son often took over for the father, but it was not unusual to be challenged by a neighboring warlord or have the chieftain replace the former Jarl's son with a more capable man.

Brock didn't have to worry about the later, since as far as he knew, Hablok Bloodaxe was still somewhere near East Anglia searching for the remainder of his sea party. The neighboring warlord could be a problem though. Due to Hablok's increasingly postponed arrival, petty warlords had rose to greater power and were stirring up trouble in the surrounding areas. Since there was no one to put them in check, their power and influence grew. So far, Brock had been lucky to learn, these bickering warlords had not interfered with Tunsberg. Thorvald had a fierce reputation for settling disputes and disagreements. Very few challenged his rule; but Brock reasoned, for how much longer would these feuding warlords afford him the same respect? How much longer would they fear Thorvald's former power now that his second son was in charge? Brock knew that trouble could begin brewing at any second, and he decided that he should have some type of plan ready should someone come calling.

These thoughts and more rattled around in his head as farmers and merchants came in and out of his hall to address their problems to him for his judgment. He sat in Thorvald's massive chair, feeling all the while like Thorvald was going to come in from the shadows and demand an explanation as to why his lousy arse was perched in his father's chair. Thorvald never came, and Brock continued to rule and settle the petty problems of Tunsberg clear into the dusk of early night. He hadn't stopped for food or beverage the entire time, preferring instead to get all of the hassles of ruling out of the way.

Brock sighed when the last farmer had come and gone. Now he knew why Thorvald always looked exhausted after a day of settling disputes. Brock had always assumed it must be easy to listen to the sides of the parties involved and then solely on one man's opinion, settle the dispute. He had assumed wrong. Justice was entirely in his hands, and that meant if he hadn't listened carefully enough or been given all of the correct facts involved that he was in danger of ruling unjustly, and that certainly was not how he wanted to start off as Jarl.

Thorvald had given him a pretty tough legacy to follow. He had ruled firmly and sometimes harshly, but justice was almost always said to have been done. Brock hoped to rule less harshly than had his father, but just as effectively. He could tell by the expressions on some of the people's faces that he had seen today, that his brand of justice was much more appreciated than was Thorvald's. That could be good and bad, Brock rationalized. If he was perceived as weak, he might not be feared, and if he was not feared than he was open to attack and destruction by one of the neighboring warlords just waiting to seize everything that Thorvald and Thorvald's father before him had established. Brock would be damned if he was going to allow that to happen. Tore approached Brock and handed him a flagon of mead. "You look beat." She said and sat down on a bench near the fire.

"I feel worse than I must look." Brock sighed. "What did you do all day long?"

"Well, I settled a lot of the household bills, and saw to some of the bills that Thorvald had left outstanding for the ships and cargo. There is also the matter of the slaves that were sold." Tore paused to see if Brock was listening, he was so she continued. "Since you were busy most of the day, the slave trader approached me to ask you to come look over your merchandise before he prepares to sell them." "You mean all of those slaves haven't been sold yet?" Brock had assumed that they would have been sold as soon as they got to Norway on the first ship.

"No." Tore took the empty cup that Brock was holding out and set it on the table behind her. "The slave trader, I can't remember his name, anyway, he said that Thorvald always personally oversaw the sale of all captured slaves."

Brock sighed.

"One more thing to do, huh?" Tore slapped Brock's knee affectionately. "Don't worry, I cut down half of your workload. I told the trader to go ahead and sell all of the children and what little men there were. I told him you'd decide on what to do next with all of the women." Tore arched her eyebrows and continued. "He promised me that all of the women were in better condition than they had been when they first arrived, said that he nor his men had touched any of them, and gave me a list detailing the extent of any injuries the women arrived with, and how they had been taken care of. There were a few that died on the journey here." Tore rested her boot on the hearth.

"You took care of all of this...and the bills?" Brock asked tilting his head.

"I didn't think you'd object to the help. After all, I am your brother, that gives me a little bit of authority." Tore laughed.

Brock shook his head smiling. "No, No, I certainly don't object. That leaves less for me to take care of. I have a whole list of other petty bickering to hear tomorrow. I doubt if I'll be able to get down to the slave market tomorrow. You might have to go for me." Brock slumped in his chair.

"Don't you want any of the women for yourself?" Tore asked feigning seriousness.

Brock laughed. "I think I've got all of the women I can handle, don't you?"

"Well, I'm somewhat biased, you know." Tore laughed. "So, you'll take care of the women tomorrow?" Brock asked relieved to have his load lightened a bit.

"Will do." Tore kicked a log that had somehow jutted out of the fire at an odd angle. Sparks flew up and smoke curled towards the hole in the ceiling.

"So, anything interesting today?" Tore asked watching the sparks from the fire.

"No. Just he took my damn goat, he fucked my damn daughter, shit like that." Brock shrugged. "Sounds fun." Tore laughed.

"Oh, you have no idea!" Brock sighed again.

That night after everyone had gone to bed, Tore heard faint steps creeping into her room. She hadn't bolted the door in hopes that Brock would decide to visit her again.

"You didn't knock." Tore said quietly moving over so Brock could get into her bed.

"I assumed you wanted me here." Brock smiled and laughed.

"You're pretty good at this decision making stuff." Tore laughed and put her arms around his neck, pulling him down for a kiss.

"You're full of piss and vinegar now, aren't you?" Brock kissed her and said playfully.

Tore just laughed and reached down under the covers, forgetting she had ever been shy about any of this…just the night before.

Settling all of the Tunsberg's squabbles took Brock nearly a month. Tore had tried to take care of the slave situation, but the traders were incredibly stupid and some troubles erupted. After another month, Tore was able to smooth all of those petty differences out, and the women went on the slave block at last. Brock was happy to get his portion of the money, and since fewer men had returned than had gone, there was more money for him that originally thought to be.

There was a knock at her door. Tore picked up the whale oil lamp and climbed out of her bed. She opened the door and peeked out. It was Brock. "Your door is bolted. How come?" He asked softly and came in closing the door behind him.

"Ymma was staring at me oddly this morning. I felt a bit uneasy." Tore shrugged and climbed back under the warm furs on the bed.

"What do you mean she was staring at you?" Brock asked while frowning.

"It's nothing." Tore didn't want to talk about it right now. It was probably nothing, just her imagination, but she didn't want to talk about it just the same.

"Then why did you bring it up?" Brock was a bit grouchy. He was starting to resent Tore's refusal to marry him, and he also didn't know how much longer either one of them could go on pretending they were brothers and not lovers.

"It bothered me. Sorry, wish I hadn't brought it up now. Just forget it, okay?" Tore snapped.

An uncomfortable silence hung in the room, as Tore got up to close the shutter. She had propped it open to let in some fresh air, but there was no need to take a risk someone walking below might overhear their conversation, or worse yet, their lovemaking.

Tore got back into bed. Brock watched her for a minute and then asked, "Do you think she knows?"

"I don't think so. I mean, why would she start suspecting things now? I don't know. She just watches me all the time." Tore sighed.

"I think, maybe Ymma thinks I've given you too much power, and that you might try to challenge my authority." Brock said after a moment of thinking.

Tore laughed. "That's ridiculous. I don't envy your power for a second. I've got everything I want right here." Tore grabbed at him under the covers.

Brock laughed and wrestled her down flat, kissing her until she begged for him to stop.

Ymma continued to watch Eirik for the next three months. Brock had been right in his assumption that Ymma believed that Eirik might try to usurp him. She had come to him one day and poured out her soul, saying that despite Thorvald's affection towards Eirik, that Brock should be careful. Thorvald, after all, was no longer here. Brock had reassured Ymma that Eirik was no threat. Ymma acted as if she was comforted, but secretly she continued to watch this mysterious son she had agreed to adopt.

Lately, something even more curious had occurred. Ymma couldn't explain it yet, but she was working on it. On more than one occasion, one of the women, or herself had been coming around the corner at night and had seen Brock leaving or entering Eirik's room. Ymma had confronted Brock on the one occasion and Brock had said that he and Eirik were discussing some of the day's events or rehashing old memories. She thought the explanation odd and Brock seemed uncomfortable when she had pressed him for information. Now, Ymma was even more curious as to what was going on between Brock and Eirik.

Just the other morning, for the third morning in a row, she had seen Eirik going off behind the stable, crouching over, and coming back towards the house wiping his mouth on his sleeve. When he got back inside, his face was sickly pale white, and food simply made him whiter. Had Eirik been a woman, all of this would have been simple to explain.

Ymma did not know of any man so prim as to hide his vomiting, and it was obvious that vomiting was exactly what Eirik was off doing behind the stable. Since he apparently didn't want anyone to know, Ymma fought back the urge to ask if all was well. Perhaps, he had contracted some odd foreign disease on their journey the past year. She didn't know what to make of it, but decided to ask Brock. He certainly would know if Eirik was ill.

Ymma found Brock pouring over a tablet etched with jagged runes. She cleared her throat, hating to disturb him while he worked. She could remember how Thorvald used to curse if anyone disturbed him, but Brock was not like Thorvald.

"Brock?" She asked hesitantly.

Brock looked up and smiled, laying the tablet down on the table before him.

"Mother!" Brock said happily.

"I'm so sorry to have bothered you…" She began.

"Nonsense! How can a mother be a bother?" Brock smiled one of his warmest smiles.

Ymma smiled back. "I was just wondering if you know if Eirik is ill or not?"

"Ill? I don't think so, why do you ask?" Brock frowned.

"Well, for the last three or four days, I have watched him sneak out behind the stable and vomit, only to return home white and trembling." Ymma wrung her hands nervously in front of her.

"You've been spying on Eirik?" Brock asked incredulously.

"Not spying. Just watching." Ymma suddenly felt bad for her behavior, but she couldn't help but look out for the people under her roof.

"I don't know of any illness that Eirik has. I'll ask him though. Don't worry about it, mother. I'm sure it's nothing." Brock smiled and picked up his tablet, subtly hinting to his mother that he needed to get back to work.

Ymma nodded and left.

As soon as Ymma had left, Brock set the tablet down on the table with a thud. Tore! Damn her! Why hadn't she told him she was sick! And, she had been right about Ymma watching her all of the time. It wasn't her imagination at all. Brock wondered what else Ymma knew. He did know that it was getting harder and harder for Tore and himself to restrain themselves in public, and to sneak around at night.

Where was Tore right now? Brock tried to remember where she said she was off to today. He had been busy counting up the past years' losses, when she had told him, and he hadn't really been paying attention to her. He couldn't remember. Besides if he went running out right after Ymma had addressed her concerns to him, Ymma and the other women, (for he was certain that Ymma and the other women must talk when the men weren't around); that Ymma would wonder why Brock was so interested. He might worry her further with his hasty actions. Better that he wait and ask her tonight.

Tore was down in the market fighting another wave of nausea. The rancid food smells and animal smells constantly churned her stomach and keeping food down was a constant battle more fierce than any fight she had ever fought with a sword.

She had come to collect the taxes that Brock had sent her for. She hated this job, as did Brock, but she was glad to ease Brock's burden somewhat. She now knew why Thorvald had paid men to handle all of these crappy little tasks. Brock, unfortunately, was more of a silver, and gold, and even bronze pincher than Thorvald was. He refused to pay men to do things that he and Tore could do for free. So, here she was about ready to puke her guts out all over the lower tax collector, collecting taxes to take back to Brock.

"You don't look too good." The fat, bearded man said to her while handing her a leather bag heavy with coins.

Tore grumbled something, and poured out the coins onto the tabletop to count the total.

"It's all there. Like always." The man said earnestly.

"I still have to count it." Tore said, they had this same conversation every month.

Tore counted it. It was off. There was gold missing.

"Where's the rest of the gold?" Tore asked.

"What do you mean? It's all there!" The man waved his fat arms about wildly, his voice raising a few notches.

"No. It is not. There is gold missing. Now, where is it?" Tore asked, not in a good mood to argue with this fat, smelly pig that liked his job a little too much.

"I, I, I told you…" He began, but before he could continue, he found Eirik Graafell's boot in his groin, and a sword at his throat.

"Now. Where is the gold? Or do I have to cut you from limb to limb to find it, you smelly man?" Tore hissed.

"I, I, I don't know what you're talking about!" The man clutched at a nearby table, trying not to lose his balance and fall in the dirt below.

"Maybe this will refresh your memory!" Tore swung her sword away from the fat man's neck and down on top of two fingers that were clutching the wood table next to them. Blood spurted from the severed fingers and the fat man collapsed into the dirt that he had been fighting so hard to avoid.

"Now then. Where is the damn gold?" Tore growled. "Or do I have to cut off something else?"

"No. No." The man wailed, clutching his bleeding hand against his grubby tunic. "It's here. In my boot." The man reached a bloody hand down and pulled a leather pouch out of his boot.

"You're stupid enough to steal from Jarl Brock Thorvaldsson and even stupider to actually have the stolen gold on your person!" Tore took the gold and put it with the rest that she scooped into the first pouch as she spoke.

"Yes. Yes, I am stupid." The man acknowledged still down in the dirt.

Tore was aware that the man had pissed himself sometime during their "conversation". "Thank the gods that I let you live, you disgusting man. And next time I see you, you had better have taken a bath!"

Tore turned and left the scene gruffly. Halfway home, she bent over behind a cart and vomited repeatedly. She couldn't hide this any longer. She was going to have to tell Brock.

Tore got back home and left instructions that she did not want to be disturbed. She peeled off her clothes and climbed into bed. She felt like shit. She was so tired, she felt like she had never slept before in her life. When Brock came in near midnight, she was surprised that she had been sleeping for so long. She jolted, startled by Brock's touch.

"Jumpy, aren't we?" Brock laughed.

"Oh. I'm sorry." Tore groaned. "I feel like shit, that's all. Gods, I've been asleep   forever!"

"I need to talk to you about something." Brock unbraided the two braids at the sides of Tore's head.

"I need to talk to you too." Tore rubbed her eyes. "Did you hear about the problem with the tax collector?"

"Huh. Yeah, the one with two less fingers now?" Brock smiled.

"Yeah. I know. It's not exactly your style of dealing with things, but I sort of lost my patience. It's not the first time that sweating hog has cheated you." Tore tried to sit up.

"Yes, yes I know. But, this isn't what I want to talk to you about. Ymma says she's been watching you." Brock said softly.

"I told you she was." Tore frowned.

"She also tells me you've been sick lately." Brock touched her face tenderly.

"That's what I wanted to talk to you about." Tore smiled weakly. She still felt bad.

"It is?" Brock raised his eyebrows.

"Yes. I haven't wanted to bother you about it, because you have so many other things to worry about, but it's gotten to the point where I can't NOT tell you about it anymore. " Tore sighed.

"What is this "It" you keep referring to?" Brock asked watching Tore's expression carefully.

"I'm pregnant." Tore blurted out.

Brock's mouth involuntarily fell open. He hadn't thought about that. How stupid could he be? Of course this was bound to happen sooner or later, why hadn't he thought about this? Brock sat there stunned into silence.

"Say something, Brock." Tore suddenly grew afraid.

"I don't know what to say." Brock said slowly. "I don't know why I am so shocked, but I am."

"But, you're not angry with me, are you?" Tore asked fearfully.

"Angry? No. Of course not!" Brock pulled her to him.

"It does make things more complicated for us however." Brock buried his face in her hair.

"I was hoping that Ulf would be home soon, so all of this charade can come to an end. I was thinking if Ulf was here, and people knew my reasons for what I've done, that all would be well. Now, I think that Ulf may never return, and that plan won't work. I don't know what to do, Brock." Tore ran her sentences together and had a panicky tone to her voice.

"We can wait a little longer for Ulf's return. If he doesn't return soon, then we must tell the truth. We don't have any other options." Brock sighed.

"We could go away from here." Tore frantically grasped his shoulders.

"Running away won't solve our problems. I have Tunsberg to tend to, remember?" Brock wiped the stray tears from Tore's eyes.

She ashamedly wiped at them herself. "I am so scared."

Brock laughed. "You? Scared? I never thought I'd hear those words come from your mouth!" Brock smiled at her. "Don't worry, we'll think of something. We have a few months until we are forced to take action. Let's try not to think about it until then, okay?"

Tore sniffed. "Okay. I don't know how long it will be until Ymma starts putting two and two together though. "

Brock stroked her hair. "Let's worry about that when it happens, okay?"

Tore nodded, but Brock wanting to postpone the inevitable wasn't going to make the problem go away. She had a baby growing inside of her and it was only a matter of time until both of her secrets would be known. She wished she could be more like Brock, but she couldn't just think about it later…this was her life they were talking about here, her life and her unborn baby's. She had to think about it now. Even if Brock didn't want to.

Chapter 18

Ulf scrambled up the helm of the war worn ship and held out his outstretched arm downwards for the grubby man at the bottom of the great serpent's neck to hand him the hammer. Slowly and steadily he pounded the wood pegs that held the serpent's head in place until one by one they fell out into his hand. He passed the pegs down to the man and firmly held the serpent's head in place. Two other men appeared beside the first one to receive the carved wood serpent's head being carefully handed down by Ulf.

Ulf grunted and heaved the heavy sculpted head down to the men waiting for it. Ulf took a minute to catch his breath and then shimmied down. The serpent's head was removed, and with no time to spare for the black, craggy cliffs of Norway were looming beyond the mist welcoming them home.

Ulf stood there, one leg resting on the ship's side, his cloak rippling out behind him over the steady wind that blew against them. The men in the ship rowed with all of their might anxious to touch the soil of Norway after so long.

"Ulf Nordahlsson!" A man's voice barked over the waves.

Ulf knew the voice well, it was the voice of his chieftain, Hablok Bloodaxe, and he turned and went towards the voice. The mist grew thicker the closer they got to shore. Ulf wondered if anyone would even see them coming into the fjord.

Tunsberg was far from home, but Ulf had planned to take a week or so to rest up before returning to his family. He had been gone for years now and he would need some time to himself to get his bearings and readjust to walking on solid ground. The last thing he wanted was to be swamped by his family's millions of questions, even if they did mean well and miss him. He just wanted to be alone in silence. Privacy was very hard to come by in a warship.

Then there was Pasha. Pasha of Ghazni to be exact. He and Ulf had developed a close bond over the last few months. It had been Ulf who pulled this friendly Turkish prince from the swirling black waters of the sea. His ship had been raided by a troubling pack of Danes and everyone else on board had been slaughtered. Miraculously, Pasha had survived. It had been night when Hablok's langskip had pulled up alongside of Pasha's burning merchant vessel. Pasha had cleverly clung to a rope that was dangling from the burning vessel's side. Ulf remembered the condition that they had found him in and then reasoned that Pasha must have very powerful gods to protect him as they did. Had Hablok's ship not arrived when it did, Pasha would have inevitably lost his saving rope to the flames that engulfed the rest of his ship.

Ulf had been intrigued with Pasha from the moment he saw this copper colored man clinging to life in the freezing waters that bubbled and whirled around his flaming ship. Ulf was a good swimmer and had leapt overboard, dragging the man behind him back to the safety of Hablok's ship.

Pasha had managed to save three things from his burning ship: a bejeweled dagger with an oddly curved blade, a brilliant emerald ring, and a huge ruby. He had given the dagger to Hablok Bloodaxe as a token of gratitude, but Hablok refused it seeing how this man had so little possessions left. Ulf thought that this was an unusually kind gesture from his chieftain who did accept the emerald ring after much persuasion from Pasha in his broken Norwegian.

Ulf had told Pasha how he could use the ruby to buy a ship and crew to get back to his own home of Ghazni. Pasha seemed eager to arrange these plans…he had enough of the seafaring ways. Pasha was a strong Turkish prince who owned vast palaces back in his warm home where the sun shone more than it ever did here. Ulf had, in turn, told Pasha of the coldness and the customs of Norway. Ulf even told Pasha of the gods that watched over the warriors and asked Pasha to speak of his gods as well. Pasha believed his gods too sacred to speak of, so Ulf let it go at that.

Now, they were standing side by side watching the cliffs of Norway loom ever closer and Ulf was answering Hablok's rapid-fire questions pertaining to the crew, wind speed, and the condition of the anchors. Ulf could tell by the tired lines on Hablok's face that he was as eager to get home, as were the men. Sheer exhaustion had aged Hablok about twenty years, if Ulf had not known him so well, he would never have recognized this man as their once handsome chieftain; but, age and worry and the strong salt air of the sea could wither and leather a man. Hablok wore the scars of battle and age. Ulf secretly wondered how long his chieftain would last before being challenged by a younger and stronger man. The role of a leader could be a dangerous one in the wrong times.

The anchors were strong and the shore grew closer. Hablok nervously paced the ship's side in anticipation of docking. Ulf felt his heart beating fast even though he would have no loved ones waiting to welcome him home. It was more the sheer exhilaration of finally stepping foot back on his native soil that excited him; his homecoming would be twofold.

Pasha leaned as far over the ship's side as he dared. He wanted a closer view of Tunsberg. He had been through parts of Norway before on a previous trade route, but never had he been in this Vestland that they were going to. Ulf had described it to him as best as he could, but these Vikings weren't very vivid in their details. They were very descriptive in things having to do with battle and killing, but plain non-story oriented description was hard for some of them. Besides, it had been difficult for Pasha to understand all that he was being told. He only understood a limited amount of their language, and a little of a few other languages; but, these men weren't the scholarly, learning types who were acquainted with any other languages besides their own, so that cut down on the options for communication.

He was, however, a very quick learner and had picked up quite a bit of their language on the journey to Vestland. In fact, he had amazed these men with his learning abilities. Most of them were easily entertained though.

Pasha watched with eagerness as the men rowed closer to shore. He could now make out the faces of the people gathered on the beach who were waiting to see who this ship would bring home. Pasha was most eager to find out about the women of these people. In his other trips through this country, he hadn't had much contact with women. The ones he saw were as rugged looking as the men. He longed for the delicate beauties that he had left in his harem back home in Ghazni. If he were lucky, maybe he would find a foreign beauty to take home with him from among these white, golden haired people. If only there was a gem among these stones!

Ulf tapped him on the shoulder and pointed to the shore, but his words were lost to the gust of wind that had blown over them so suddenly. Pasha made a face that indicated he had not been able to hear what Ulf had said, when suddenly the ship jerked forwards, and then bumped up in the air. Pasha and Ulf both clutched at the side of the ship, and then steadied themselves when the ship came to a slow stop. That was earth beneath them! The ship scraped across the watery soil and then came to a slushy stop. People ran to the ship and waded on tiptoes, holding up the children so that they could see. He could hear their calls and cries, as the first of the men began to disembark and happily leap to the muddy soil beneath them. Men ran to the arms of their families, some simply stood there searching for somebody to come to greet them. Families waited for men who did not come, some sadly turning away. Then there were men such as Ulf, and himself, who lived in other parts and did not expect to find a familiar face waiting beside the ship to welcome them with warm and open arms.

Ulf slapped Pasha on the shoulders. Pasha returned the gesture. He owed Ulf a great debt for saving his life. He had so little to offer anybody, but he had made a blood oath promising to make it up to Ulf someday in someway.

Ulf and Pasha jumped over the side of the ship and onto the ground. Pasha took a minute to allow his head to stop churning and adjust to the solidness of the earth.

"Feel like you're still on the sea, my friend?" Ulf asked Pasha.

"Yes." Pasha answered and steadied the turban on his head.

"You'll find that you're head will stop that swishing around after a bit. Let's find something to eat." Ulf smiled a toothy grin.

Pasha continued to hold the sides of his head. His "great bunch of rags" as Ulf had called his turban, was attracting a lot of attention.

"They are looking at me." Pasha told Ulf.

"It's those rags on your head." Ulf laughed.

"It is more than that." Pasha watched the people stop to stare.

"Maybe it's your brown skin." Ulf said and then spotted a fish stand. "You think these people are staring. At least they've seen foreigners who come to trade in these parts. Wait until you get to my shire. It's much smaller, not on a port and we rarely have traders. People will really stare when we get to my home!" Ulf laughed.

Pasha was still clutching his aching head, but he laughed anyway. Although, he didn't understand why it was funny. Ulf bought some cooked fish and a pile of some sort of porridge or pudding. He handed Pasha a wooden plate and a wood spoon. Pasha watched Ulf jab at the fish with his own dirk that he had unsheathed for the purpose. Pasha did not have such a knife, so he scooped the fish up with the crude spoon the best he could.

Ulf had been welcomed to Hablok's home, but it was just as far away as his own was, so he had gratefully, but firmly declined. Hablok had offered to arrange for the local Jarl, who was the young Brock Thorvaldsson, to put him and Pasha up for as long as needed, but Ulf had assured Hablok that he had the money to allow he and his friend to stay at the inn, be it cramped and cold, for a short time. Ulf had no intention of cow towing to Brock Thorvaldsson, who was years younger than Ulf himself.

Ulf and Pasha went to the inn and requested two rooms. The innkeeper welcomed these seafaring warriors cheerfully. It would do his business good for his patrons to know Hablok Bloodaxe's own warriors protected them! He gave them the two best rooms in the inn, which wasn't much; but, after sleeping in a bag for years, anything even remotely resembling a bed was fit for a king as far as Ulf was concerned.

Both he and Pasha were tired and hungry. They continued to eat everything that the innkeeper's wife brought them. When Pasha had finally reached his bursting point, he and the rest of the occupants of the inn were amazed to watch Ulf continue on as hungry as when he had started! Ulf made a great deal out of being so hungry, and people were betting on how much he could eat far into the night. Pasha watched all of this merriment from the shadows, near the great stone fireplace. Since arriving in Vestland, his first impression had been of bone-chilling, skin-piercing coldness and it seemed he could not get warm. How he longed for the roasting powers of his golden sun!

When Ulf had finally tired of eating and drinking and singing, he staggered over to where his quiet foreign friend sat huddled by the fire. He drunkenly threw another log onto the fire sending a blaze of popping and hissing sparks to fly out and over the hearth. Pasha recoiled from the flames but laughed.

"You warm yet, Prince?" Ulf asked, slurring his words a little as he spoke.

"No. Does this place ever get warm?" Pasha said shivering.

Ulf laughed a deep, bass-toned laugh. "I'm afraid not."

Pasha groaned.

"You'll get used to it." Ulf sat down and held out his hands to the fire.

"I don't think I will ever get used to being cold." Pasha shook his head in fierce disagreement.

"You don't have to hang around down here for my sake. If you'd like to go to your room, the innkeeper will make you a fire there." Ulf laughed. "I have women to see!"

Pasha smiled from beneath his black mustache. "Did you say women?"

Ulf laughed again, louder. "We aren't so different after all!"

"These are not women that I would want." Pasha surveyed the manly looking, thick-bodied women that Ulf was referring to. "Are there no others?"

Ulf laughed some more and took an enormous swig of mead from the mead horn that he clutched in his massive hand. "These are not to your liking?"

"They are nice." Pasha lied, "But, I like them more, how do you say it, more beautiful?"

"Beautiful, huh?" Ulf laughed and slapped his knee. "You've been without a woman all this time on that sea, and you want beautiful?"

Pasha didn't understand what Ulf was saying. Hadn't he just told Ulf that beautiful was what he indeed wanted? Maybe he should tell Ulf what it is he wanted again.

"I love the beautiful women." Pasha smiled.

"By Hades, we all love the beautiful women." Ulf smiled, "But sometimes we love any woman at all!"

Pasha did not understand so he just shook his head. Ulf was too drunk to understand he guessed. "You have your," Pasha waved his hand slowly towards the women, "Women, and I will go to bed."

Ulf laughed. "I will go to bed too, my friend!"

Pasha nodded and smiled understandably. He stood up and went towards his room, the innkeeper on his heels to personally build the fire in his room. By this time, everyone had heard the story of how he was a Turkish prince who had been rescued by Ulf Nordahlsson, one of Hablok Bloodaxe's men. The innkeeper was eager to please this brown skinned prince.

The innkeeper lit the fire and the whale oil lamps in Pasha's room. He nodded and left the quiet man alone. Standing in front of the main hall's fire was Ulf Nordahlsson telling more tales of his adventures with Hablok Bloodaxe. The innkeeper paused to listen to some of the story, but there was this nagging thought in the back of his ordinarily not too bright brain, that was telling him he had heard something that would be of interest to Ulf Nordahlsson. If only he could remember what it had been! It might even be financially rewarding for him if he could remember the information and pass it along to Ulf, but he simple could not remember for it had been so long since he remembered hearing it. Maybe his wife would remember, he would ask her later on tonight.

That night, when the last of the guests had retired, the innkeeper woke his wife who was already sleeping. He recounted his inability to remember the tidbit of information he had overheard regarding Ulf Nordahlsson sometime ago. His wife was perplexed, she remembered nothing.

Sometime in the middle of the night, however, the innkeeper's wife, sprang from sleep, and violently shook her husband awake. She had remembered.

"I know it now! I remember! Wake up you dirty goat!" She shook him by the shoulders until he woke up and stared at her with an expression that showed how stupid he really was. She went on. "It was about Ulf Nordahlsson's family! And the Thorvaldssons! Old Thorvald the One-Armed and his sons kill off some of Nordahl's family over something to do with Nordahl's brother."

The innkeeper was now fully awake. By the gods, she had remembered! Yes! That was it! Nordahl and his sons had been killed, along with Athelwold the brother and his family. There had been something about a girl who had been sold into slavery. What was her name? No matter. They had their information now! The innkeeper punched the limp sack under his head and restlessly awaited dawn. There would be no more sound sleep for him this night. His heart was pounding too quickly for that. HE might be a rich man tomorrow! Or, the innkeeper shuddered, he might be a dead man for bringing bad tidings.

Maybe he shouldn't tell Ulf Nordahlsson. Maybe the bearer of bad news would only be in danger himself. Then again, if Ulf Nordahlsson were to find out that he had known and not told, the massive Viking might kill him for that too! No, he would have his wife tell Ulf. Surely, he wouldn't' kill a woman. No man of honor would kill a woman of his own kind simply for bringing bad news.

The next morning, Ulf was not up for along time. His friend, the prince, was up early. He did not drink strong drinks. Pasha wandered around some of the stalls outside of the inn, careful not to wander too far. He was able to protect himself, but he didn't desire any trouble. When he returned to the inn, it was past noon, and Ulf had only recently stumbled to the table for food.

"Sleep well, my friend?" Ulf asked between bitefuls of his fish soup.

"Very well. My head has stopped swimming at last." Pasha smiled.

"That's good. Have you eaten?" Ulf asked.

"Yes. I ate some Hair fish." Pasha nodded.

"Hair fish?" Ulf laughed. "What in Hades are you talking about?"

"Fish." Pasha knitted his eyebrows together. Had he said something wrong? "Fish that was cooked over smoke."

Ulf smiled. "You mean smoked herring!"

"Yes, Hair fish." Pasha nodded again.

"Her-ring." Ulf said slowly.

"Haa-rin." Pasha sounded out the word as close to Ulf's pronunciation as he could.

"Close enough." Ulf smiled.

Pasha watched out the open door as the people in the market buzzed around like busy insects.

The innkeeper's wife was hanging around them oddly. Maybe the old woman was one of the women Ulf visited last night, Pasha wondered. He pointed to her and whispered to Ulf, "Your girlfriend, yes?"

Ulf made a face. "That old dog?"

Pasha laughed. "You said sometimes you just want a woman. She is a woman, no?"

Ulf smiled. "She is a woman, but, ugh! Someone's grandmother!"

"You did not say that age mattered!" Pasha said rather matter of factly.

"I was drunk." Ulf laughed.

"Still, she is a woman." Pasha said again.

"I'd rather jerk my own pole than stick it into a wrinkled, gray horse like that!" Ulf laughed, and then grew quiet as the woman came to their table looking nervously around her.

Ulf looked up at the woman and smiled, "You want something?"

"I have news of your family." The old woman said slowly.

"Of my family? They live far from here, how is it that you have come across news of my family?" Ulf put down his spoon very much interested in what the grizzled old woman had to say.

"It is very bad news." The woman hung her head sadly.

"Bad news?" Ulf repeated the woman's last words.

"My husband fears that you will kill him if he tells you. That is why he sends me, a woman. A very poor woman." The old woman emphasized the last part of her statement.

"Is it money that you want then, old woman?" Ulf frowned. "Do you have news at all, or do you just want my silver?"

"No. No. I have news." The old woman stepped back in fear.

"Don't run away. I won't hurt you. Here." Ulf tossed two gold pieces on the table and patted the table across from him indicating that the woman should sit down.

The old woman's hand darted out from behind her apron and snatched the gold pieces hurriedly. Her hand disappeared back into her brown apron. She sat down on the bench across from him hesitantly.

"Well, old woman. I have things to do before dark." Ulf pushed his empty bowl away from him.

"It's about your family…" She started.

"Yes, we have established that fact. "Ulf said sarcastically, growing weary of the delays.

"There was some sort of dispute involving an uncle of yours, I believe." The woman looked at the table in front of her, too afraid to make direct eye contact with this huge man.

"Probably was Athelwold." Ulf said turning to tell Pasha, "He's always making trouble for someone."

"Yes. Yes. That was his name. Anyway, Thorvald the One-Armed and his sons killed Athelwold and his family." The woman sucked in her breath sharply.

"Killed him? I mean he was an arsehole, but killed him?" Ulf's eyes were growing larger and rounder as he spoke.

"This is not all." The woman said and then continued, "Thorvald and his sons, they also killed your father, Nordahl, and your brothers."

"Fuck me!" Ulf said and jumped to his feet, drawing his sword in anger. Pasha jumped up beside his friend not knowing what would come next. Ulf had the look of a crazed, wild man on his face.

"When was this?" He demanded.

"I am not sure. Years ago. Two. Maybe three years ago." The old woman trembled with fear. "More like three I think."

"You think? This Thorvald, he had the nerve to settle a dispute without the ruling of Hablok Bloodaxe?" Ulf shouted.

"Bloodaxe has been away many years. Many problems have come and gone since Bloodaxe has been gone from these parts." The woman visibly shook.

Ulf paced the floor, his sword in hand, like a caged animal. "You said my brothers were killed. What of my sister?" He thought of Tore, who must be a woman by now, and of how he used to play with her, teaching her how to protect herself in case something ever happened to her brothers. Ulf felt his face grow hot with anger.

"There was something about a girl. No one really knew what happened to her. I heard she was sold as a slave." The woman backed up and ran into the wall.

"A slave? My sister!" Ulf growled. "I will kill the men responsible for these things! These unjust murders of my kinsmen!"

Pasha had never seen fury such as this unfurled before. In his country there were many strong and powerful men who were capable of all types of evil and treacherous acts, but never before had he witnessed such uncontrollable, intense fury like his friend, Ulf now demonstrated. It frightened him to a point. He wasn't afraid of his friend, just afraid of what his friend could do.

Pasha looked into the eyes of his friend. Ulf looked straight at him, but through him. Pasha felt as if Ulf looked through him and through the wall behind him with those stabbing, clear blue eyes. The hairs on Pasha's arms stood up eerily.

Ulf stormed past him and towards his room. Pasha understood. Ulf needed to think. Rashness would not avenge the death of his kin.

Pasha sat alone in the hall sipping the sad excuse for coffee that he had been offered. He tried to put himself in Ulf's shoes. It was hard for him to feel the way Ulf did however. In his country, brothers killed their own brothers all the time in a fight for the throne. Sisters, well, they often were married off so young, that there had hardly been time to know them. Fathers, they died and were replaced with a brother. Really, the only family member that news like this would matter about would be his beloved mother. Mothers were revered in his homeland. Fathers were killed and deposed, but mothers never went away. Right now, so far away, his own mother ruled in his stead, taking care of his concubines, and managing his whole household. He would miss his mother. Pasha knew that Ulf's mother had died long ago, so his family meant even more to him. Pasha tried to feel the pain that his friend was feeling. He knew how it would hurt to find out that his mother had been murdered unjustly. This must be how Ulf felt now. Pasha knew one thing for certain. He would stand by his friend in his time of need. Ulf had saved his life, now he owed his life to Ulf.

Ulf stayed in his room throughout the night. Pasha thought it best not to have him disturbed and so instructed the innkeeper and his wife to allow Ulf his privacy.

What sort of things were haunting Ulf right now? Pasha knew what it was like to be haunted by the spirits of the dead. He had killed his older brother and his brother's mother, in order to assume control of the position he now held as Prince of Ghazni. There had been a bitter war that struggled on for years, until he finally slit his brother's throat in the tent of a whore. That had been different than this killing. This was how things were done in his country. Still, memories of his brother and himself as boys danced in his dreams. Bathing in the baths, swimming in the river, laughter and games. All these images and sounds haunted him in his sleep, and sometimes when he was awake too. The dead do not rest easy. Pasha sighed. Whose ghosts were taunting Ulf in that dark room of his?

Pasha retired to his own room. He had already done what he knew how to do. He had bought a man's loyalty and sent him out to spy information for him. In his country, spies were common things. Here, well, Pasha doubted they worked this way. In any event, the man had been given two days to gather as much information about this event as possible. Then he was to report back to Pasha. The man worked for the present Jarl, this Brock Thorvaldsson. He had also worked for the old Jarl before him, Brock's father, Thorvald the One-Armed. Thorvald was the man that Pasha felt Ulf wanted, but Thorvald was dead. Maybe Thorvald's ghost haunted Ulf right now. Maybe Ulf's gods were at war with Thorvald's ghost.

Pasha knew not how Ulf's gods reacted in situations such as this.

Pasha went to bed with a heavy heart. The man who had saved his life was now in danger of losing his own if he acted too rashly. It was up to Pasha to keep him rational. Tomorrow, he would visit Hablok Bloodaxe and ask his help. Pasha would go without telling Ulf, because, Pasha knew that men such as Ulf, too full of pride instead of intelligence, would not approach their leader for help. So, he would do it. Was he not a prince? It would be a meeting between leaders…and Hablok would do as he was told. Pasha was tired of dealing with the ignorance of these people. Everything was swords and blood here. Where he came from, killing was the last resort. There were many ways more terrible than death to deal with things. Pasha had many plans, but for now he would get a good night's rest so he could be of help to his friend tomorrow.

The next morning, Pasha arranged to travel to Hablok Bloodaxe's home. He sent a messenger who would return with whatever invitation or information that he could. Meanwhile, Pasha had to tell Ulf of his plans. He wasn't exactly sure of how Ulf would receive the news, since it looked as if Pasha had been making plans behind Ulf's back.

Pasha knocked on Ulf's door. Ulf had been cooped up in there much too long to be healthy.

"Go away." Ulf barked from inside.

"It's Pasha." Pasha said firmly.

"I don't want to see anyone right now." Ulf growled.

"You have two choices, my friend. Either you unbar this door and let me in, or I will simply break the door down." Pasha paused for Ulf's reply, and when there was none, he said, "Well, which is it to be?"

From inside the dark room, Pasha could hear the heavy sounds of footsteps coming towards the door.

He heard Ulf lean against the door. "I really don't want to talk right now." Ulf said through the door.

"I will break it down!" Pasha said loudly.

"Alright. Alright." Ulf gave up. Pasha listened to the bar being lifted up and then dumped on the floor beside the door.

Ulf opened the door and stood aside as Pasha came in to the dark, dank room.

"Did you forget how to light the lamps?" Pasha said sarcastically and taking a small piece of kindling from the fire, lit the lamp closest to him. He sat down on the wood bench against the wall.

"What do you want?" Ulf said with his head buried in his hands, hair badly in need of washing.

"What we do not bathe anymore?" Pasha leaned back against the wall and glanced over the dimly lit room. Things were strewn around in disorder. The bed had not been slept in. "Or sleep either, I see."

"I have other things on my mind." Ulf said not too pleasantly. "And, you can bathe if you want to, it has nothing to do with "we"."

"You sit here and cry!" Pasha jumped to his feet angrily. "What kind of a man are you? You sit here in this dark, smelly room and you cry! Nothing gets solved this way!"

Ulf reached for his sword, but was met all too quickly by Pasha's in mid-air.

"Now, you would strike your friend with your sword, too?" Pasha acted like he was shocked. Actually, he had anticipated this sort of animal behavior from Ulf.

"You insult my manhood." Ulf stood there, hovering over Pasha by a good foot, dangling his sword in one hand.

"I speak the truth." Pasha stood his ground.

"What in Hades do you want from me?" Ulf bellowed. "I have news." Pasha said and sat back down on the bench that he had been sitting on previously.

Ulf jammed his sword back in its scabbard, and lumbered back to the stool he had been sitting on in front of the fire. Pasha took this as a sign that Ulf was listening.

"I have paid a man who works at the Jarl's home to provide us with information. I call him a spy. I do not know if your people operate like my people, but this man could give us very valuable information." Pasha saw Ulf's eyebrows flicker up for a moment and continued. "I have also sent a messenger to Hablok Bloodaxe's dwelling to arrange a meeting with him concerning this situation."

Ulf grunted.

"Just because this dead Thorvald took matters into his own hands, is no reason for you to do the same. Hablok seems to respect you as a warrior. A good leader will not let his man down." Pasha waited for Ulf's response.

Ulf sat there in silence for a few minutes as if processing all of what Pasha had just told him.

"You did all of this for me?" Ulf said in a flat tone that Pasha could not read as angry or just curious.

"You were in no state to act, and action was required." Pasha shrugged. "I am sure, had you been in control of all of your senses, you too would have done what I have done." Pasha knew that Ulf wouldn't have thought as craftily as he had, but never mind.

Ulf grunted again. "I want to find my sister."

Pasha frowned. "I do not know how we will go about doing that. They say she was sold into slavery."

Ulf turned and looked at Pasha. "Have one of your, spies, find out who sold her."

Pasha shrugged. He'd try. "And if no one knows?"

"Find out." Ulf ordered.

Pasha nodded. "You won't do anything until you hear from the Bloodaxe, yes?"

Ulf dwelled on that thought for a minute, but then agreed. "I cannot bring the dead to life, but I can find my sister if I have to travel the world and seas to do so."

Pasha frowned again. "You might have to do just that, my friend."

Ulf grunted and waved towards the door in a semi-friendly way of asking Pasha to leave now. Pasha nodded and left the sulking man to his own thoughts. Now came the hard part. Now, they would have to wait.

Chapter 19

Tore sat carving at a picture of a bear that she was etching into a piece of bone. Brock had told her to stay out of sight as much as possible. She looked down at her belly. She could still hide her slightly swelling stomach under clothing, but at nearly five months into her pregnancy, it was getting harder and harder to cover it up. Brock was fulfilling his role as Jarl easier now than he had at first. He still relied heavily on Tore for advice and a shoulder to cry on. Tore felt like his wife, but without all of the dreaded housework.

Ymma kept a sharp eye on her constantly. That was one of the reasons why Brock had instructed her to stay out of the way. He didn't need any problems right now. His authority as Jarl was just getting established and few had challenged him. He didn't want any sudden uprisings.

Tore looked up from her carving at the exact moment that Brock came barging through her door in a huff. He slammed the door hard behind him. He paced the floor like a wild animal, his eyes crazed and far off.

"Brock? What is it?" Tore put down her knife and carving. Brock looked at her like a berserker, then punched his fist into his other hand.

"Are you going to tell me, or make me guess?" Tore laughed.

"This is not a laughing matter, woman!" Brock growled. "Oh, so, now, I'm 'woman'. This must be bad." Tore cocked her head and smiled slightly.

"Hablok Bloodaxe and his men returned two days ago!" Brock boomed.

"What? And, you've just found this out?" Tore moved forward to the edge of her bed. "How come you weren't told of this sooner?"

"I don't know! That's why I'm pissed! The fucking chieftain anchors in Tunsberg, and somehow I am not told! What's worse, the man left for his own shire, without so much as an invitation from me or my household, because I didn't know he was here!" Brock paced the floor maniacally. "That's not good." Tore agreed.

"There's more." Brock paused, looked at her, and then continued his pacing. "Your brother is here." "Ulf! Ulf's here?!" Tore jumped to her feet, but was pushed back down onto the bed by Brock.

"Yes, he's here with a friend at the inn in the market." Brock said while holding onto Tore's shoulders. "But, there's still more."

"More what? More news?" Tore asked. "What could possibly be more important than Ulf's being here?"

"Ulf wanting to kill me." Brock said quietly.

"What?!" Tore grabbed Brock's hands. "How do you know this? Who said such things?"

"One of my stable men was caught trying to smuggle information to Ulf's friend, a Pasha of Ghazni, who's staying with him in the inn." Brock said sitting down next to Tore on the bed.

"Pasha of who?" Tore arched her eyebrows. "What the hell kind of name is that?"

"Apparently, he is some copper colored foreigner. The information I have tells me that your brother saved this man's life when his merchant vessel was attacked by Danes." Brock told her what he knew.

"Hmm. Ulf must have thought there was gold in it for him." Tore said absent-mindedly.

"Whatever the reason, this man is fiercely loyal to your brother and it seems they are trying to gain information that will help them kill me." Brock said and then sighed.

"You found all of this out, but you weren't told that your chieftain was ashore?" Tore frowned.

"Unfortunately, my sources aren't always reliable. It's amazing what extra gold can make men do." Brock ran his hand through his long hair.

Tore sat there quiet for a minute. "What do you plan to do?" She said quietly.

"Wait." Brock said in a near whisper. "I don't know what it is your brother plans to do yet."

"Shouldn't we find out? I mean, we just can't sit here and wait for him to come kill you. I won't let him!" Tore grabbed Brock's arm frantically.

"What do you want to do?" Brock laughed.

"I have to see him." Tore said firmly.

"We don't even know if he knows that you're still alive." Brock said picking up Tore's carving to examine it.

"Then I must let him know. I won't let him kill you." Tore got up and started to dress.

"You think you're going there alone? Just like that?" Brock asked as Tore belted her scabbard around her waist and slid Gungnir into it.

"Yes. Just like this." Tore frowned as she realized her belt no longer fit around her middle.

"Here, give it to me." Brock held out his hand, and taking the belt from Tore, he pierced another hole in it so it would fit around her belly.

"Thank you." Tore smiled at him, messed up his hair, and kissed him fully on the mouth. "And thank you for not trying to stop me."

"Would it do any good?" Brock sighed. "No." Tore laughed.

"I didn't think so. Do you want me to send a man with you? Will you be safe?" Brock suddenly grew concerned for her safety, and that of his unborn child.

"I am a man, remember?" Tore laughed. "I'll be alright. Ulf's my brother. I don't fear him."

"I think you should." Brock said wearily.

"If I'm not back before morning, send a man to find me." Tore said quietly.

Brock took her in his arms and held her. "If you're not back before morning, I'll personally come find you."

"No!" Tore grabbed his face in her hands roughly. "Promise me you won't! It could be a trap to lure you to him once he finds out who I am." Tore hissed.

"I..." Brock began.

"Promise me!" Tore held his face firmly in her hands.

"Okay. I promise." Brock smiled and kissed her. There was no point in arguing with her now. If she didn't come back by dawn, he'd go after her anyway...promise or no promise.

Tore left the room, and nodded to Ymma on her way through the great hall. She was very aware of Ymma's suspicious glare as she opened the door and went outside.

Tore grabbed the nearest horse and rode into the market. Ordinarily, she would have just walked, but the horse would get her there quicker. She needed to see Ulf for a number of reasons.

Arriving at the inn, Tore tied her horse up near the side of the building, and then stomped inside the inn. A few heads turned to look who entered the hall, but most kept to themselves and to their eating. Tore surveyed the room expectantly, but found no familiar Ulf, and no dark man.

She looked around for the innkeeper. She spotted him, and he seeing her was filled with recognition. He remembered her as the man who moved up from a mere traveling scop to Thorvald's favorite son. Tore swaggered over to him, one hand firmly on the hilt of Gungnir. The innkeeper saw where her hand rested, and trembling wrung his hands in front of him. "Can I help you, Eirik Graafell?" The innkeeper asked as politely as his trembling voice would allow.

"I hope so." Tore growled. "I'm looking for a man who might be here. Actually, two men."

"There are a lot of men here, as you can see." The innkeeper waved his hand towards the eating men at the tables around them.

"The men I seek are not at these tables." Tore barked.

"I don't know if I can help you then." The innkeeper said hoarsely.

"I believe you can. I am looking for a man by the name of Ulf Nordahlsson, and a companion of his, a dark colored man named Pasha of something. You know who I mean?" Tore grabbed the man by his scruffy tunic.

"I, I,..." The innkeeper started.

"My name is Ulf Nordahlsson." A voice boomed from behind them, and a visibly relieved expression flooded the innkeeper's face. Tore slung him aside.

"Ulf Nordahlsson." Tore addressed him loudly and looked him up and down. He looked well. "I need to speak with you."

"Then speak." Ulf demanded.

Tore cast a nervous glance around her at all of the men in the hall, and to the strange, dark man who stood behind her brother. "What I have to say needs to be spoke of in private."

Ulf looked at Pasha and then back at this scrawny man in front of them. Pasha shrugged. Even if this man had been sent to kill Ulf, he would be no match for the two of them. Why not give the man the privacy he had asked for. Pasha nodded as if to say he thought it would be safe.

Ulf looked at the man in front of him. "Innkeeper, mead."

They stood there staring at each other while the innkeeper scurried to provide them with the requested mead. Then Ulf pointed to a hall, and said, "We will go to my room."

Tore started to the door, starting to quake in her boots. How was she going to say the things she needed to say? Once in the room, Ulf closed and barred the door. Tore turned quickly to watch him do so.

"This is in case you have something tricky planned." Ulf said and pointed at the bench near the wall. "Sit." Tore did as she was told. It had been a long time since she had obeyed anyone without a fight of some sort. "Now, what is it that is so secret that you have to tell me in private?" Ulf growled.

Tore didn't know how else to say it, but to just come out and say it plain and simple.

She smiled, and then said, "Ulf, it's me. Tore." Ulf stood up, accidentally sending the stool he had sat on flying backwards. He went over and grabbed the man by the shoulders and pinned him to the wall by his tunic. "How dare you come here and make jokes to me!" Ulf growled.

"No! Ulf it really is me! I had to dress like a man to keep from being killed! It's me, I can prove it!" Tore hadn't anticipated not being believed.

Ulf sneered, spittle dribbling from the corners of his mouth. "Then prove it."

Tore reached inside of her tunic and pulled out a ring on a chain. It was her father's ring.

"It's father's." Tore showed the ring to Ulf. "How do I know you aren't one of the swine who killed and robbed him?" Ulf hissed.

"It's me, Ulf, it's really me! I realize it's been a long time since you've seen me, but look at my face! Father always said that whenever he missed you, he'd simply look at me and feel as if you were home! Look at me!" Tore pleaded with her brother.

Ulf grabbed her hair and pulled her head back, dragging her closer to the fire to look at her face. It was as if he was staring into a mirror. It was his face, only softer somehow, smaller, feminine.

He let go of her hair and stood back. Tore picked herself up off of the floor, and shook her hair back out of her face. She stood there not sure of what to do next.

Ulf watched her. "Why do you have a sword?"

Tore sighed. "It's a hell of a long story."

"Well, I have plenty of time." Ulf growled still not completely convinced even if his eyes did confirm this man's story.

Tore sat down on the bench near the wall, and sighed. "Okay." She paused; Ulf and his handsome friend were staring at her intently, so she continued. "It started with Athelwold. It was said that he killed one of Thorvald's kinsmen. Athelwold denied it."

"The coward!" Ulf shouted.

Tore shrugged. "You know Athelwold. Anyway, Hablok Bloodaxe, as you are well aware of, had been gone for far too long. Thorvald didn't have the patience to wait for Hablok's ruling on the matter, so he took the law into his own hands. Because Athelwold was such a coward and a liar, Thorvald and his men killed all of Athelwold's family and ours." "How is it you are here?" Ulf snapped. "Father and Arne and Ubbe made me get into the chest." Tore stopped as she saw a glimmer of belief in Ulf's eyes. "The men that were there killed all three of them." Tore stopped for a moment, "They knew that I was supposed to be there so they tore the place up looking for me, but they didn't find me. I knew that they'd be looking for me, so I dressed myself in Ubbe's and Arne's clothes, packed a bag and planned to get out of there as soon as I could. I didn't know if the rest of the family would protect me or hand me over to Thorvald's men if trouble started."

Ulf nodded. "You did the right thing."

"I know I did." Tore stated bluntly, somewhat shocking Ulf at her straightforwardness.

"That doesn't tell me why there's a sword at your hip." Ulf said more gently now.

"Well, while trying to make my way to Tunsberg, I stumbled across this sword and scabbard in the snow. I took it not knowing who's it was." Tore sighed. "That's where the trouble really started."

"Trouble, what sort of trouble?" Ulf leaned his head to one side.

"Well, it turns out that the sword, I call it Gungnir..." Tore paused as Ulf snorted a half laugh. "The sword belonged to Tyr's favorite dead warrior, and I unknowingly took it from the dead man's grave." Ulf's eyes grew huge.

"Tyr was pissed. He sent a white dragon to kill me, but Sif intervened."

Tore scratched at her head for a second.

"Your Sif? The goddess?" Ulf asked incredulously.

"The very one. Anyway, she made a deal with Tyr to try to save my life." Tore was interrupted by Pasha.

"Why would this goddess want to save your life?"

Tore frowned. "She likes me."

Ulf made a face in Pasha's direction and Tore continued.

"Sif got Tyr to agree to a deal. If I proved myself worthy of the sword, then I could live. To prove myself worthy, I had to be tried in battle. To get to any battle, I had to be a man.... so, here I am. Eirik the Silent Graafell." Tore waved her hands in front of her.

"And no men know this?" Ulf shook his head in disbelief. "Only one. I proved myself worthy. The people in Tunsberg, and Thorvald before he was killed, believe me to be a man...and a great warrior at that." Tore stated.

"A great warrior, huh?" Ulf laughed.

"Thorvald seemed to think so. He made me his adopted son." Tore said bluntly.

Ulf jumped to his feet angrily.

"Sit down, Ulf, I'm not through yet." Tore remained calmly on her bench and pointed at Ulf's stool. Ulf stared at his sister who was sitting here barking orders at him. He was so shocked at her boldness that he sat down.

Tore nodded then continued. "I didn't know who killed father and Arne and Ubbe. I just knew that someone was trying to kill me. Anyway, I earned money by being a scop and that's how I met Thorvald."

Ulf leered at Tore as if she had purposely betrayed their family.

"Thorvald liked my stories and invited me to live with his family. Then he grew fond of me and adopted me as his own son with all of the rights of his blood kin." Tore took a deep breath and continued, "He trained me with the rest of his sons and we embarked on several raids in East Anglia, the Zetlands and Orkney."

"I was in East Anglia." Ulf stated as if that changed Tore's story.

Tore smiled. "I know. Well, I managed to prove to Tyr that I was worthy of the sword so he let me live, only after I had been wounded."

"You were wounded?" Ulf asked stupidly.

"Yes." Tore sighed. "I would have surely died too, had it not been for Brock. He saved my life."

"That still does not change what he did to our kin. He still must die." Ulf growled and shook his fist in the air.

"There's still more." Tore's voice cracked a bit, so she took a drink of mead.

"What more could there possibly be?" Ulf asked looking at Pasha as if he held the answers.

"I learned that it was Thorvald and his sons who killed our family, only after I had lost my heart." Tore sighed.

"Lost your heart? What in Hades do you mean? Stop talking riddles!" Ulf spat his words out hatefully. Tore suddenly saw a side of Ulf that she never knew existed. This was the bloodthirsty side that urged Ulf into battle after battle. She grew painfully aware that she would get no mercy here.

"I'm in love with Brock Thorvaldsson. I'm going to be his wife." Tore said simply.

"You'll be nobody's wife until I say so!" Ulf stood up angrily and faced the fire.

"I carry his child." Tore hissed.

"I don't care if you carry the spawn of a giant! I'm telling you I will not spare the life of this man! He is a coward and he must die!" Ulf punched the stone fireplace and loose mortar crumbled to the ground.

"He is no coward!" Tore was on her feet now; she drew her sword and held it in front of her.

Ulf turned his head slightly to look at his sister. He looked her up and down as if getting ready to buy her on the slave market. His eyes went from her eyes to her sword, and then back to her eyes again.

Slowly, a low, bass toned laugh eased its way up through Ulf's being and boomed from his mouth. He laughed and laughed.

"Don't mock me, Ulf Nordahlsson! I have killed mightier men than you!" Tore bared her teeth and spat.

Ulf laughed and then with a loud snort stopped. "You would kill your own brother then, for this, this Brock?" Ulf hissed the name out as if it were pure evil.

"I love him." Tore stood waiting to be challenged.

"And me, what of me, little sister?" Ulf said fondly.

"I love you as well." Tore said sadly. "But when I needed someone. You were not here. You were gone. Brock was here."

"Well, now, it looks as if you have yourself quite a dilemma here, don't you?" Ulf laughed and sat down again.

Pasha stood by watching this woman in man's clothing who was madly waving her sword around, and Ulf who was calmly sitting on his stool, picking his teeth with the point of his dirk.

"Put the sword down, woman." Pasha commanded.

Tore cocked her head and shot Pasha a menacing glare. "I don't take orders like you do, you brown dog!" Tore hissed and pointed her sword in Pasha's direction.

Ulf laughed again. "I think you're carrying this protective love thing a little far, don't you, Tore?"

Tore looked at Ulf. He had said her name. It had been so long since she had heard her own blood say her name. She lowered her sword.

Ulf watched her and shook his head sadly. "I have to kill him, Tore. I won't be labeled a nithing." Ulf said grimly.

"Everyone knows that you are not a coward, they will not speak ill of you for showing mercy." Tore pleaded.

"It is the only way. Surely, your love for this man does not cloud your better judgment. He killed your father, and your brothers! For the love of the gods, Tore, this man must pay with his own blood!" Ulf reached out to touch his sister's face, but she recoiled in disgust.

"It is for Hablok Bloodaxe to decide!" Tore stood up.

"We have already sent for Bloodaxe's decision on the matter. We are trying to arrange for a meeting." Pasha joined the conversation.

"Do you let this man speak for you now, brother? Have you lost your tongue in battle?" Tore said sarcastically.

"Eirik the silent Graafell is not too silent." Ulf laughed and looked at Pasha. Pasha seemed to find the statement equally amusing and laughed heartily.

"Laugh now." Tore nodded.

"Because of what? You will come and kill us in our sleep?" Ulf laughed again, but then narrowed his eyes and grew uncomfortably close to Tore, "That is what your lover does…kill sleeping men and women. Not me, and not Pasha. We are honorable men."

"So honorable that you will kill your own kin's father?" Tore didn't back down.

Ulf frowned and looked at her belly, then back at her face. "That was your doing, not mine!"

Tore put her hand on her sword again.

"Not done challenging me, child?" Ulf smiled.

"Would it do any good?" Tore said sadly.

"No. If the Bloodaxe wills it, I will kill Brock Thorvaldsson." Ulf looked down into the fire.

"And there's nothing I can do to stop you?" Tore asked.

Ulf shook his head slowly.

Tore turned to leave. Before she could unbar the door, Ulf had cleared his throat and turned to her and said, "The next time I see your face, Let it be the face of a woman."

Tore bit her bottom lip to keep from arguing, yanked the door open, letting it bang against the wall behind it, and left.

Pasha chased her down the hall, through the main hall, and out into the open air. "Your brother feels your pain deeply."

"What the hell do you know about my brother?" Tore turned and looked into Pasha's dark, chocolate brown eyes. She had never seen eyes so dark and enticing; they were almost hypnotic.

"I know his heart." Pasha said slowly.

"My brother has no heart." Tore swung her leg up over her horse and rode towards home. How much time did she have left? "Oh, Brock!" She sighed out loud as she rode away, leaving Pasha of Ghazni standing helplessly behind her.

Brock was waiting in front of the house when she rode up on the work worn horse. She leapt off and handed the rein to the waiting stable hand, a new one, and a man she had never seen before. Brock must have hired new people in order to protect himself from those who knew too much and could be a detriment to his safety.

Brock's face was one big question. Tore looked into his eyes and felt like bursting into tears. There was so much love in these twin pools of sapphire blue that stared tenderly into her own. How could she tell him what Ulf intended?

Tore walked quietly beside Brock inside the hall and to her own room. Once in the safety of her room, her door barred behind them, Tore broke down and wept.

Brock's arms were around her in an instant. To see Tore in such a state, frightened Brock. Tore was one of the strongest people, man or woman that he had ever known. To see her cry stirred emotions he never knew he had.

Tore clung to Brock as if Hel herself were trying to yank him from her grasp. Brock hushed her, and stroked her white blond hair.

"What is it, my dove?" Brock finally asked.

"Ulf is going to kill you." Tore said between jerking sobs.

"We won't let that happen." Brock chuckled.

Tore straightened herself up, and pulled back a little so she could see Brock's face. "No, you don't understand. He has gone to Bloodaxe over this matter, as your father should have done earlier. Don't you see? Bloodaxe loves Ulf dearly. He will rule in Ulf's favor!" Tore wailed.

"I don't think I've ever seen you quite so sad." Brock smiled and stroked her face.

"Did you not hear me?" Tore studied his face carefully.

"Fate is fate, my dove." Brock said simply as if resigning himself to his own death.

"Bullshit!" Tore hissed. "I won't let him do it!"

Brock laughed. "And what will you do? You with your big belly? Kill him before he kills me? You cannot kill your own brother."

Tore searched Brock's eyes for the answer. As if Brock knew a way to defeat Ulf, but wasn't telling her. Brock simply continued to stroke her cheek softly.

"I'll ask the gods for help!" Tore said triumphantly as if she had arrived upon the perfect solution.

"The gods again, huh?" Brock smiled warmly. "No gods will intervene in this matter. Justice is justice. My father ordered your family slain disregarding the laws of the land. If Hablok Bloodaxe rules those deaths unjust then I will be killed. No god will interfere with just laws, Tore."

"They have to!" Tore gripped Brock's arms firmly, desperately.

"You ask them. You see if they respond. Not even Sif will help you in this matter. I am quite certain of it." Brock said sadly.

"You act like you want to die!" Tore frowned.

"I don't want to die, but I don't want any harm to come to you either." Brock said and kissed her forehead. "If I fight back, you will most assuredly fight alongside of me, whether or not I want you to. I won't risk your life or that of our child's. Justice must be served, and if that justice requires my life...then so be it."

"You can't mean that!" Tore said angrily. "You just can't lay down and die for them."

"What other choice have I? I can't change the events of the past. I can't bring back your kinsmen." Brock shrugged.

"You can fight!" Tore raised her fist high.

"What good would that bring?" Brock shook his head slowly. "I must obey the laws. Thorvald didn't do that and look what it has brought us. I am not that kind of man. I will obey the ruling of my chieftain."

"Even if it means your own death?" Tore's eyes were wide with fear.

"Even so." Brock pulled her close to his chest and held her tightly.

"I dare not think of life without you, my love!" Tore whispered, tasting the salty tears that rolled into her mouth.

"Then don't. I am not dead yet." Brock laughed quietly and reached for the laces on her tunic.

Tore tried hard to concentrate on Brock's warm lips, but visions of death, funeral pyres, and bloody battles haunted her every thought. To be alone again. Without Brock's strong arms to hold her, without his warm hands to caress her. How would she go on? Her mind elsewhere, Tore felt her body respond to Brock's motions instinctively. At times she even felt as if she were standing by and watching Brock make love to her, as if she were in someone else's body. She felt his rough hands part her knees. Waves of elation spread over her like rippling water, bursting at last like the torrid spray of a waterfall. Only in his arms did she feel like a complete person. How could she go on knowing she did nothing to save him?

Lying next to Brock, feeling the tightness of the muscles on his thigh and arm, Tore let her thoughts drift into the future. She saw Brock's son, or was it a daughter, and heard her own voice explaining why it was the child's father had died before ever knowing the child.

Brock stared lovingly into Tore's face. Her expression was a far off one that spoke of great sorrow and grief for a woman so young. "Where are you?" He asked softly.

Tore blinked and looked into his face smiling. "Somewhere far away." She sighed.

"Am I there too?" Brock whispered, nibbling at her ear.

Tore choked back sobs. "No. Just me and your child."

Brock moved her chin towards him with one finger, and looked deep into her eyes. "Wherever you are, I'll be there too. You will keep me forever…in here." Brock placed his hand over her heart, softly brushing against her breast and hardened nipple. He kissed her neck and smiled.

Tore had never felt such utter despair. To lose Brock would feel much worse than losing her father or brothers. Those were different kinds of love, and they didn't sting half as bad as losing Brock would sting.

Brock pulled her closer to him and held her tight. Tore listened to the steady beating of his heart, wanting forever to remember the sounds of the blood rushing through Brock's body giving him life. How much longer would his life last? Tore fought back tears and fell asleep against Brock's chest.

Chapter 20

Pasha stood outside of the inn waiting for news from his messenger and spies. One by one they crept out of the shadows to pass him the bits of information they had been successful in obtaining. Some of it was totally irrelevant. Parts of the information gathered proved helpful. What Pasha really wanted to hear was word from Hablok Bloodaxe. He wanted a meeting for Ulf, or any decision that Bloodaxe cared to make.

Pasha grew weary of waiting. He paced back and forth feeling tense and bored. Occasionally a passing girl would distract him from his unpleasant thoughts, but none very successfully. Most of the girls in these parts, Pasha found to have horse faces and thick bodies. They had beautiful gold hair and creamy white skin, but other than that, he longed daily for the warm, inviting arms of his women awaiting him in his harem back home. Here, all the beautiful women were married! Ulf had tried his best at finding a woman to please Pasha for Pasha did not believe in pleasing himself with his hand or anything else for that matter. His religion forbade him from spilling his seed onto anything other than a woman. Ulf had laughed riotously when Pasha had told him this. Ulf had said that it was clear that none of Pasha's people had spent much time in langskips on the sea with a bunch of stinking men. There had been one woman that had caught Pasha's fancy, but he wasn't going to mention it to Ulf.

Tore Nordahldatr. Pasha had never met a woman quite like her. She had spirit. She was like an unbroken horse, ready to fight all those around her for whatever reason presented itself. Looking into her eyes, Pasha had noticed it. She had no fear of death. The speed and agility with which she had drawn her sword had amazed both he and Ulf. Though she had made a comical picture readying her sword to smite her brother...Pasha had never doubted for a minute that she would kill Ulf to save her precious Brock.

Brock Thorvaldsson. Pasha wished he could meet the man whose fate he was helping to decide. What a man he must be to capture and hold the heart of a warrior such as Tore. He must be a strong man to control the fire that Pasha had seen burning in Tore's eyes when she spoke his name.

Ulf had noticed it too. His little sister was no longer a girl. Even dressed in man's clothing, once her true identity had been revealed, both Ulf and Pasha kicked themselves for having been fooled. Just one look at her revealed the stunning rugged beauty that Tore possessed. She was strong and smart. She was a beautiful woman and a brave man. Tore had discovered the best of both worlds. Pasha wondered if she would ever be content with being just a woman ever again.

There was more to Tore than just a beautiful face that attracted Pasha. He was used to women who were submissive, quiet, and self-sacrificing. Women who hid themselves from all men except their husbands. Women who died without question if the husband deemed it so. Never in all of his days had he ever experienced a woman with the ardor and zealot nature that Tore possessed. To challenge her own brother! Not even in this Viking culture was that an acceptable behavioral characteristic! She defied the very standards of her own culture.

Pasha shuddered, as he grew aware of his hardening cock that swelled within his flowing pants. Just thinking of Tore aroused him. A woman like that would be a true conquest in bed, not like the subtle charms of the women in his world. She would be any man's equal. Pasha smiled and stroked his goatee. She would be a free woman once this Brock Thorvaldsson was out of the picture.

A man rode up on a horse wearing the colors of Hablok Bloodaxe. He reported that Hablok was awaiting their arrival to discuss the problem at hand. They were to ride out with the messenger immediately.

Pasha went into the inn to find Ulf. This was the news that they had been counting the hours of each passing day waiting to hear.

Ulf was sleeping in his room. Pasha pounded on the door.

"Ulf! Ulf! It is time." Pasha said still pounding.

Ulf staggered to his feet and unbarred the door, letting Pasha enter.

"What is it, man?" Ulf growled. He hated being awakened hurriedly.

"Hablok Bloodaxe has sent the messenger back. We are to ride out immediately to join him to discuss the situation." Pasha was throwing Ulf's belongings into his hudfat. Ulf grabbed the bag hastily out of Pasha's hands and finished the job. Pasha ran to his own room and did the same.

Ulf had secured two horses earlier in case this might happen. He had to pay too much gold for their use, but he had little choice. There were very few horses to be found.

Ulf and Pasha paid their debt to the innkeeper and graciously accepted a bundle of food the innkeeper's wife had thrust at them with an awkward smile. They climbed onto their horses and waited for the messenger to return from his meal. The whole waiting period from the time the messenger arrived until the time the messenger leapt back onto his horse took about thirty minutes. Ulf was glad that no time had been wasted. He was eager to put this matter to rest once and for all, so that he could return to his former life without any unnecessary distractions. He had been gone a long time, and he had not anticipated being troubled with so many difficulties when he had arrived.

The ride to the inn where Hablok waited took three days and three nights. They arrived early in the morning of the fourth day eager to talk with the chieftain and resolve this matter. Ulf wanted one thing and one thing only. He wanted the blood of the sole surviving son of Thorvald the One-Armed.

Hablok had more information that Ulf had even imagined he would. The moment Ulf opened his mouth to start explaining the situation; Hablok amazed them with his knowledge on the entire incident. The one thing that Hablok didn't know was the unexpected twist involving Tore.

When Ulf rambled off the entire tale of his sister's escape and her subsequent life as a man, Hablok raised his eyebrows into a very pronounced sharp V. He had never heard of such actions before. A woman pretending to be a man, and fighting as one. When Ulf told of the involvement of the gods in Tore's ordeal, his eyebrows continued to arch even further causing his eyes to take on an odd shaped appearance.

"And no one figured out that she was a woman?" Hablok asked in disbelief.

"No one. Until she was wounded. Brock Thorvaldsson discovered her lie when he was tending to her wounds. He hid the lie to spare her life." Ulf grumbled the last part of the sentence not wanting to paint the son of Thorvald in a pleasant light.

"Why didn't he kill her?" Hablok questioned.

"He almost did. Tore said he was going to slit her throat, but by then

Thorvald's son had grown to love her as a brother and he realized once discovering Tore's true gender that he loved her as a woman too." Ulf shrugged.

"And all these years, she's lived as a man?" Hablok seemed stunned by this revelation.

"Until a few days ago. I told her the next time she showed her face to me, I wanted it to be the face of a woman." Ulf took a drink from his cup that had been sitting on the table in front of him.

"Yes. There is no point in her continuing her disguise now that you have returned." Hablok nodded, agreeing with Ulf's decision.

"You are not angered by her actions?" Ulf asked hesitantly.

Hablok smiled and shook his head again. "I'm so stunned that any woman would have such courage that I am not angered at all. In fact, I'd like to meet this daughter of Nordahl."

Ulf laughed. "Father wouldn't have been surprised at all by Tore's actions!"

"So, she has always been full of fire?" Hablok laughed.

Full of fire. Pasha thought of Tore's face glowing against the background of the dancing fire, brandishing her sword in Ulf's room back at the inn. Those words captured the essence of Ulf's little sister. She was full of fire. Pasha smiled to himself, and watching her caused his man parts to burn with desire like he had never known.

Hablok turned towards Pasha who was sitting silently in the shadows. "So, Pasha of Ghazni. What do you think of Ulf's sister?"

Pasha leaned forward into the light of the fire. He looked at Ulf and back at Hablok. "I have heard tales of the many men she has killed. I have heard tales told of the many men she has saved." Pasha paused as if thinking over this question for the first time. "I believe she is a gallant warrior and a beautifully strong woman."

Hablok laughed. "A gallant warrior, huh?"

Pasha nodded fiercely. "I would not want to cross her in battle."

"Well, you don't have to worry about that. Tore won't be seeing anymore battles in her lifetime, isn't that right, Ulf?" Hablok narrowed his eyes as if to silently tell Ulf to rein in his wayward sister and bring her back to her rightful position as a woman.

"That's right, Hablok." Ulf smiled and raised his flagon high.

Pasha frowned. For some reason, he didn't believe either of the men. Seeing Tore with Gungnir held high, he believed there were a lot of battles left in the girl.

Hablok grew serious. He talked of Thorvald and his hastiness in settling disputes. He talked of a wilder time where chieftains often ended their lives at home in their beds through murder, rather than bravely on the battlefield. Now, things were different. There were laws, but men such as Thorvald still existed. Men who took it upon themselves to live by their own rules instead of those agreed upon by all. Hablok wanted to settle the matter with gold. Pasha knew that Brock Thorvaldsson must have plenty of gold. Ulf would receive a hefty sum; but Ulf wanted none of Thorvald's gold.

Hablok tried his best to persuade Ulf that gold was the way to go, but Ulf wouldn't hear it. It was his right to demand blood, and he wanted Brock Thorvaldsson's blood. An eye for an eye, a tooth for a tooth. Ulf had all the gold he wanted. He didn't have the head of the last son of the man who had decided the fate of his father, brothers and kinsmen.

Pasha thought the gold sounded like the better deal, but before he got the chance to discuss it with Ulf, his thoughts drifted back to Tore. With Brock out of the way, he would be free to woo Tore for his own. No, let Ulf kill this son of Thorvald. Ulf would get his revenge, and Pasha would get Ulf's sister. Never did the thought cross Pasha's mind that Tore would not want him. He had seen the ways that Tore had gazed into his eyes, he had held her there as if a rabbit in a trap. She had been mesmerized by him. He had seen the fire in her eyes. Tore was too much of a woman to love only one man. No, Pasha never doubted that Tore would be his. He just had to rid himself of the one she thought she loved so dearly right now. Time would take care of the rest.

Ulf's fist slammed down on the wood table. Pasha's thoughts came hurtling back to matters at hand.

"I want his life. Nothing less. Nothing more." Ulf growled.

Hablok threw his hands into the air. He had grown tired of arguing with Ulf. Ulf was, after all, justified in his demands. Hablok studied Ulf intensely, and then sighed loudly.

"He is yours." Hablok Bloodaxe said at last.

Ulf gripped Hablok's arm in a firm hold, Hablok likewise did the same. In this way they sealed their agreement. Ulf turned to Pasha and nodded towards the door. He had the decision he had come for.

Tore had no idea that her brother was meeting with Hablok Bloodaxe at this very moment. She was too busy trying on the new dress and apron that Brock had given her. It felt good to be back in a dress, pinning her apron to her dress with two gold dragon-shaped pins. Her long golden hair sprayed out over her shoulders, and down her back. It felt so good to have her breasts loose and unbound like nature had intended them to be. Tore laughed at herself. She could remember a day so long ago, when she had actually longed and yearned to be a man. Now all she wanted to be was the woman she was.

She ran her hands down her chest and over her swelling belly. There was no point in trying to hide it any longer. It had grown impossible to cover up anyway. Ulf had given her the freedom she had desired for so long. She could be herself again. Eirik the silent Graafell no longer existed.

Brock was telling the rest of the family the truth. He had conveniently omitted the part about her being Ulf's sister, however. He didn't want to place Tore in any danger after he was gone. He told them that he was sending Tore away to a safe place where no harm could come to her. He didn't mention that his life was soon to be cut short.

Tore came into the main hall slowly. Ymma watched her curiously, almost in awe of this woman who had been her son. When she saw Tore in her dress, with her belly protruding before her, a look of knowing swept over her face as if to say, how did I ever believe this was a man? Ymma had always known something was different about Eirik. She had just never been able to put her finger on it. Now, she had the answers. And everything made so much sense!

Brock walked up behind Tore and put his arm around her. He knew that already men were coming for him, but he said nothing to Tore. He didn't want Tore to know.

That night, he made love to her with the vigor that he had the first time his flesh met hers. He wanted to take this last memory of her with him into death. He wanted to forever remember their last embrace, the tenderness, the love they shared. He closed his eyes and pictured her as she was now, as she had been in the past, as she would be forever through all eternity in his mind. Her love would have to last him for an eternity.

He kissed Tore who lay sleeping soundly, one hand resting on her kicking belly, and went outside to wait for his fate.

He didn't have to wait for long. Ulf crept out of the darkness and towards him. Brock turned to Ulf and stared him in the eyes.

"What? Coward, you aren't going to fight me?" Ulf spat venomously, pricking Brock with his sword.

"No." Brock said simply and let his belt and knife fall to the ground.

"I am going to kill you, Brock Thorvaldsson." Ulf taunted him, wanting Brock to pick up his knife.

"So be it." Brock stood there waiting for Hel to claim his soul as her own.

"My sister loves you? You are a coward." Ulf hissed.

"A coward is afraid to die. I am not afraid to die." Brock lowered his voice. "Tell your sister that I love her."

Ulf felt his face grow hot with anger. "I'll tell her no such thing!" He bellowed and charged Brock, taking his head in one swift motion. His bloody sword chopped the air long after Brock's lifeless head rolled across the ground, and his headless body dropped into the dirt spilling the warm blood that had given him life.

Pasha grabbed Ulf's arm. "It is over." He said loudly to his friend.

Ulf madly cut the air as if he didn't hear Pasha. "It has ended." Pasha said again.

Ulf dropped his arm, dangling his sword in his hand, staring at the decapitated body of Thorvald's last son. It was over. It was over.

Tore heard a commotion outside, and heard the other women stirring throughout the house.

She sat up in bed. Before she even heard the screams of the other women she knew what had happened. Somewhere something deep inside of her had gone numb. She was engulfed by a horrid, empty feeling as if part of her had been ripped away and destroyed. Before her feet even hit the cold floor, she knew Brock was dead.

Tore went outside. Before her the women of the house surrounded Brock's body much like a wolf pack surrounds the carcass of their prey. The wails pierced the air. Shrieks rent the silence of the still night like a sharp sword cutting taunt silk. Tore clutched her bulging stomach and felt her knees quiver.

She had stared death in the face many times in the past. She had wrestled with death and won. To her death was an enemy that she had never feared for she had defeated it so many times. This time, peering down on the lifeless, headless body of the man she loved, knowing their bed was still warm from the heat of his body, death had beat her.

Her own brother had caused this pain. Her own brother had invited death to sup here tonight. He had claimed his rights and killed the father of his sister's child. His own selfish need for vengeance had spurred him on to kill the only man Tore had ever loved with all of her being. Tore gulped back the tears and sobs that tried to force their way up. She would not cry. She would not show Ulf her weakness. She would face Brock's death with the same courage she had faced his life with. And, she would never forgive her brother for Brock's death.

The women continued their weeping until someone's husband dragged them inside and out of the cold. Brock's body and head lay on the cold ground oozing the last ounces of life-sustaining blood. She was left there alone, and although she knew the feeling well, alone had never quite felt so cold. No one came to move Brock's body. Tore regaining her strength, walked towards her lover. Slowly, she picked up his head, staring at his beautiful face, that even in death shone so brightly. She tucked his severed head into his tunic, and picking up his legs began to heave his body towards the stable. She had to stop and rest every few feet. Her hand rested on her belly for a moment, feeling the life that Brock had put inside of her. She smiled, as she grasped each of his ankles and heaved again. She wasn't quite alone.

Tore covered Brock's body with a blanket and went inside the house. She walked calmly past the weeping women and to her own room. Weakly she crawled into the bed and pulled up the furs around her. She squeezed her eyes shut and listened. She could still hear the beating of Brock's heart against her ear.

The next morning, Tore was up and gone before anyone stirred. She had packed all of her belongings and left. There was nothing to keep her in this house anymore. Without Brock, the only meaning this family had was that of murderers of her father and brothers. Only her love for Brock had allowed her to push those grim details into the dark recesses of her mind. Now, she had no place under Thorvald's roof.

Tore rode her horse to the inn where Ulf and his friend Pasha were staying. She had no idea of what she would say to Ulf when she saw him. She didn't even know if she wanted to talk to him at all. The only thing she did know was that her place was with Ulf.

When she got to the inn, she awkwardly slid from her horse and tied it up. She struggled to sling her hudfat over her shoulder. From out of nowhere, Pasha appeared.

"Let me take that for you." Pasha extended his hand.

Tore eyed him suspiciously but was too tired and weak to argue with him. She handed him the straps to her hudfat and walked on alone. Pasha quickly was beside her again. He smiled at her but said nothing.

"Where is my brother?" Tore asked shortly.

"He will be happy that you look like a woman again." Pasha grinned.

"I could care less what the bastard is or isn't happy about. Where is he?" Tore hissed.

"In his room, of course." Pasha said sounding hurt.

What did the brown shithead expect, Tore thought to herself. Her lover had just been killed by her own brother, and he was making pleasant conversation in his thick accent. Tore cursed and pushed open Ulf's door, which surprisingly, was unbarred.

"Expecting company?" Tore growled and sat down on the same bench she had been sitting on during their first encounter.

"I thought you might be by early this morning." Ulf said and went back to crack the heavy wood shutter that was closed.

Tore sat there in numb silence. She didn't know what to say and she didn't feel like talking. Ulf sat before the fire and simply watched her with a look on his face that said he half expected her head to fall off or something freakish. Tore simply stared him back.

"Are you hungry?" Ulf said at last.

"Hmm." Tore said with mock interest. "The man kills the father of my child, but he's concerned that I might be hungry."

"Come on, Tore." Ulf raked his hand through his matted hair.

Tore raised her eyebrows, but said nothing.

"You know I had to do it." Ulf said and threw another log on the fire.

Tore still sat in silence.

"Aren't you going to say anything?" Ulf was confused by his sister's silence. He expected her to charge him with her sword or something.

"Is that my lover's blood on your arms?" Tore said with a near comatose expression on her face.

Ulf looked down at his arms and tunic. He was covered with dried blood. He hadn't noticed it until now. He had been too worried about Tore and too caught up in his elation over killing the murderer of his kin to care about his personal appearance.

Ulf grimaced. "Yes. It is."

Tore nodded, but said nothing further.

"That's a nice dress." Ulf tried flattery as if that would somehow dull the pain Tore bore.

Tore looked past him through the crack in the shutter into the street.

"I thought we might stay here for a few more months before heading home. Pasha is going to buy a ship so he can head back to his home. I promised him I would help him out in anyway I can." Ulf said very business-like.

Tore said nothing.

"After Pasha sets sail, we can go home." Ulf smiled.

"I have no home." Tore swung her feet off of the floor and lay down on the wood bench.

"Sure you do. Think of everyone who has missed you all o f these years, fearing the worse. Wondering what happened to you!" Ulf tried to sound comforting. "Why don't you lay down on the bed?"

Tore got up and walked to the bed. She lay down without a word, cradling her belly in her arms.

"There is still another matter we have to discuss, Tore." Ulf sounded concerned.

"Why wait. I know what it concerns. It's about my baby. Isn't it?" Tore said quietly.

"I'm sorry, but I can't have the bastard of that swine under my roof." Ulf said it so calmly one would think he was discussing what he wanted to have for dinner. "I think the best thing for everyone concerned would be for you to put the baby out to sea."

Tore had anticipated this comment so it didn't shock her.

"I want you to stay with me, Tore. I love you, you know that. " Ulf pleaded with her now. Maybe he actually did feel guilty about causing her pain. Tore doubted it.

"And if I choose NOT to kill my own child, will you kill it?" Tore asked in a monotone.

"I can't kill my own kin." Ulf said slowly.

"But a mother can?" Tore laughed.

"It's been done for centuries." Ulf shrugged. "It's the best way."

"I won't kill my child. I won't kill Brock's child. I love him and I love my baby." Tore rolled over and faced the wall.

Ulf sighed a long, laborious sigh. "You can stay with me until the child is born then. After that, well, you'll have to decide what you want to do."

Tore breathed deeply. Alone again. She had lost one family, gained another. Found one family, lost another. She would be damned if she would kill the child that kicked and moved within her. This baby would be the only true family she had left.

Tore fell asleep cursing Ulf.

When she awoke, it was Pasha, not Ulf who hovered over her like a protective older brother.

"You must eat something." Pasha said kindly. He had a bowl of fish soup and a cup of tea on the table against the wall.

"I'm not hungry." Tore said staring past him into the fire.

"Maybe just the tea, yes. For the little one." Pasha brought the tea over to her and sat on the edge of the bed next to her.

Tore smiled at him. Putting it that way gave her no choice. He tenderly cupped her head and raised her lips to the tea. She drank it. It was warm and it tasted good. She let her head fall back onto the bed.

"Thank you." Tore smiled.

"You have a beautiful smile." Pasha said softly.

"Brock used to say that." Tore said with longing in her voice.

"What else did Brock say about you?" Pasha said eager to know what he would have to compete with.

Tore laughed thinking about all of the happy times she and Brock had shared, many of them before he even knew she was a woman.

"He used to say such wonderful things." Tore said wistfully.

"He was a good man, then?" Pasha patted her on the hand.

"A very good man." Tore said decidedly.

"Then he will have a good baby." Pasha nodded his head as if his saying so made it so.

Tore looked at him strangely. "Ulf hasn't told you his plan for my baby, then?"

"What plan is this?" Pasha was surprised that Ulf had not confided in him on this issue.

"Ulf, my dear and caring brother, wants me to kill my baby." Tore sneered.

"Kill the baby?" Pasha said dumbly.

"Our people have a custom. If a baby is unwanted, the wrong man fathered the child, there isn't enough food, then the baby is thrown into the sea. Or left on a cliff to freeze." Tore said with a blank face.

"You don't want this baby?" Pasha knitted his brows together. He didn't understand. He thought Tore had been in love with this Brock.

"I want my baby." Tore said loudly. "Ulf doesn't want my baby."

Pasha nodded. Now, he understood. "What if you refuse?"

Tore laughed. "As if anyone refuses Ulf Nordahlsson!" But, she continued. "If I refuse, I must go away."

"Banished?" Pasha said with wide eyes.

"You could say so." Tore nodded.

"Where would you go?" Pasha held his palms up.

"I don't know, but it wouldn't be the first time I staked out on my own, you know." Tore smiled at Pasha's genuine concern for her well-being.

"Is there no one you can marry who would want your baby?" Pasha asked quietly. In his country, it was all so easy to marry a favorite concubine or lover to a friend. The friend usually agreed as a favor. What was one more woman added to his harem?

"All of the men in this country think like Ulf." Tore shook her head. "If something or someone isn't wanted…then kill it!" Tore threw up her hands in disgust.

Pasha sighed. He would take her and her baby, but it was too soon to offer such a thing. He didn't want to interfere with his friend and his sister, but he was falling in love with this tall, blond warrior faster than he ever thought possible.

"Don't worry." Tore smiled and touched Pasha's arm, "I'll think of something."

"I will speak to your brother. Maybe there is another way." Pasha nodded as if agreeing with himself.

Tore smiled. "Ulf must really listen to you. You have such confidence that you can persuade him."

"We are friends." Pasha said simply.

"Still, all of Ulf's life, he has done exactly what he wanted to do regardless of the consequences. If you really can make him listen, you truly are a valuable friend." Tore said while laughing.

"Sometimes, I feel like we are brothers." Pasha found Tore easy to talk to, as if he had always known her. Maybe it was because he knew Ulf so well, and Tore was so much like Ulf.

Tore sighed as she thought back on Brock and her relationship. "I know the feeling. You think to yourself, this is my friend, and then you find there is a bond much closer than what it means to be just friends."

Pasha nodded. "Yes. Sometimes, it is as if I have always known Ulf. Like I knew he was coming to save me as I struggled in the water. It was as if I was telling myself to hold only a little while longer so Ulf could get there to rescue me!" Pasha felt a kinship with Tore as well.

Tore nodded and leaned forward. "That's how it was with Brock. I used to think maybe I was just insane or something for feeling those feelings; I'm glad to know someone else has felt things like that too."

Pasha took a deep breath and took a chance. "I feel like I have always known you too."

Tore smiled a warm smile. "You are easy to talk to Pasha of Ghazni."

"Thank you." Pasha said while stroking his goatee absently.

"Now, I think I need to get some sleep. I can't very well figure out what to do with myself if I'm too exhausted to think. Ulf has at least agreed to let me stay with him until I have the baby. Kind of him, don't you agree?" Tore said sarcastically, chuckling a bit.

Pasha smiled and pulled the fur up closer to Tore's chin as if she were a small child. He picked up the cold soup and left the room.

Ulf had moved into Pasha's room so that Tore could have some privacy. He had been away too long to feel comfortable sharing a room with this woman he barely knew anymore.

Pasha entered the room and found Ulf deep in thought. He cleared his throat.

"Ulf, I have never asked you for anything, except that you help me get home." Pasha began.

Ulf nodded.

"Now, I ask you one last favor." Pasha paused for Ulf's response. There was only silence, so he continued. "I want you to let Tore's child live."

Ulf laughed. "You know nothing of our ways! I cannot do this thing that you ask of me."

Pasha frowned. "There is no other way?"

"I tell you what. If you can find someone to marry her and take that bastard child of hers, then the baby can live; but I'm telling you now. You won't find a single man willing to take her bastard in all of Vestland." Ulf laughed.

Pasha thought for a moment, and then running his fingers along his ebony mustache, he asked, "What if I want your sister?"

Ulf started to laugh, but then seeing the serious expression on his friend's face, grew stern. He raised his eyebrows, shrugged, and looked absently into the leaping flames of the fire.

Chapter 21

Pasha hovered over her like an overprotective mother hen. As Tore bit down hard on the leather strap in her mouth, Pasha smiled and cooed encouraging her every step of the way. The labor pains had started a day ago, but were coming harder and closer together now. Never in all of her wildest thoughts had she imagined childbirth would be so painful and long. She had witnessed birthings before, but she now realized, until she was actually the one shoving this small human being through part of her body that seemed three sizes too small for the task...she had never really witnessed a birthing before.

Pasha knew a lot about medicine and science. Over the past months, he and Tore had spent hours in the forests, and over hills searching for herbs and plants that Pasha said held secret uses. Pasha had been disturbed to find that many of the plants he sought out, simply did not exist in Tore's frigid, freezing world. Their worlds were so different. Pasha never failed to be amazed by the lack of scientific development of these Viking people. Weapons and warfare had been mastered to an expert level, but all else seemed unimportant to these bundled up people, who spent the majority of their lives huddled around fires and eating things made of fish.

"Agh!" Tore knelt down closer to the ground that she had been pacing, praying to Sif, Frigga, and any other goddess that might be listening to speed this child into the world. Pasha ran to her with more mead.

"If I drink anymore of that shit, I'm going to be too drunk to stand and have this baby!" Tore said shoving away the wood cup in Pasha's hand.

"But the pain?" Pasha again offered the cup.

"It is nothing I can't handle!" Tore grunted and tried to stand upright again. It was no use; the baby must be almost here. Tore reached down and felt between her bloody legs...she could feel the baby's downy hair and its tiny scalp.

"I can feel the head!" Tore shouted. Pasha readied a blanket to catch the baby in, as Tore leaned against the wall for support and pushed with all of her might. A wet, bloody baby slithered and plopped into the blanket that Pasha held below Tore. She nodded for him to hold the baby away from her as she struggled to heave the afterbirth from her aching body. A mass of bloody pulp slid out and fell in the bucket below her. Pasha cut the cord with a knife, and washed the baby off before the fire. Tore gingerly made her way to the bed and sort of fell onto it in obvious pain.

"Is it a boy?" She asked.

Pasha turned and smiled at her, "It is a boy!"

Tore smiled. She knew it would be. She laid her head back in the furs and reached for the tiny pink bundle that Pasha laid in the crook of her arm. She was a mother. A mother! Daughter, sister, warrior, lover...they all seemed so natural to her, but to be a mother? What did that mean to her? Tore shook her head as if trying to clear her thoughts. All of this was for real!

Pasha was pouring warm tea down her throat and rubbing the tiny downy head of the baby. Tore smiled. She was glad that Pasha had been here to help. He wasn't Brock, but then she doubted that Brock would have helped her have a child. That was woman's work. Pasha seemed to enjoy being a part of bringing a baby into this world.

She knew that Ulf was in the hall waiting to hear about the baby. She also knew that he was probably hoping the baby would be born dead. That would have solved all of his problems. Well, damn him! Tore thought to herself, and then whispered to her baby boy, "We showed old Ulf, didn't we?" Pasha turned and looked at her. "Did you say something?"

Tore smiled weakly, "I was just asking the baby boy here what we should name him."

"What about naming him after your father?" Pasha suggested.

"Oh, no. One Nordahl in this family was enough. No, I want him to have his very own name. One that only he has." Tore stared up at the ceiling and thought hard for a few minutes. "Harek." She said slowly, letting the sound of the name roll over her tongue.

"Harek?" Pasha asked. The name sounded strange to him, but then most of these guttural, harsh names in Vestland did.

"Yes. Harek. Harek Brocksson." Tore said quietly.

"I think you might want to keep that last part quiet." Pasha sighed and nodded towards the door that they both knew Ulf was waiting behind.

"You're right." Tore sighed. "Doesn't matter though, I'll have to leave soon anyway."

Ulf knocked on the door. "Is she well?"

Pasha opened the door a crack. "She is well." Ulf nodded and turned to return to his room. "He didn't ask about the baby." Pasha seemed shocked.

Tore laughed. "You thought he would? I'm surprised he even came to ask about me!"

"Your brother loves you." Pasha reminded her.

"But, not enough to love my child. Pretty thin love, I'd say." Tore sighed.

"Sleep now." Pasha brushed the blond hairs out of her face. "Sleep. We'll talk about all of this later." Pasha smiled and tucked the furs around her and her baby.

Tore fell asleep smiling. In her thoughts, she thought of how Brock used to gently brush the hair out of her face, much like Pasha had done. It didn't feel the same. She was sure that she cared for Pasha. He took care of her, watched over her, much like Brock did, but that passion was not there. Tore remembered making love to Brock and how they would go for hours consumed in each other's love, lost in each other's arms. Where had passion taken her?

Tore was sure that the next man she let herself love, would be a love based on intellect...not one rooted in passion. She wouldn't let her heart be broken ever again.

When she awoke, Pasha offered her some roasted fish. She was starving! Tore woofed the food down as Pasha held Harek, singing to him softly in his native tongue. His native language seemed so odd to Tore, but then she imagined her language seemed just as odd to Pasha. He had learned so much Norwegian in an effort to communicate with Ulf and her. Sometimes, he spoke so well that Tore forgot he had only recently learned the language.

She had so much to consider. She knew that Ulf wanted her to set this baby out, or toss him into the sea. Ulf repeatedly made his desires known. Tore had no intention of harming her child in any way, and she knew that she would kill whoever attempted such a thing. She didn't even want Ulf near her baby. Not that he had made any effort to try. She did not trust Ulf anymore.

Oddly enough, Pasha was able to maintain an equal friendship with both she and Ulf. How he was able to stay neutral was beyond her, especially knowing how vile Ulf could be; but he had explained to her that in his country awful things were done too. He had killed his own brothers to take the throne he now held.

Tore trusted Pasha with her very soul. She had told him things that she had never even told Brock. With Brock, there was always that family situation to avoid. It was hard to really bare her soul of her true emotions when dealing with and discussing the very people that Brock had helped to slaughter like animals; and, Brock had always been visibly uncomfortable listening to her if she tried. Pasha had no involvement in any of these dreaded dealings. He hadn't been there, wasn't a part of a rival family, didn't know the ways of her people... so, Tore found him objective and with few biases. He was fiercely defensive of Ulf, even when he knew what Ulf might be doing was wrong.

Tore ate the last of her food, and licked her fingers. She hadn't realized how hungry she had been. Harek was sleeping soundly, when Pasha put him back in her arms.

"Motherhood agrees with you." Pasha said smiling.

"Oh?" Tore laughed. "And, how can you tell that?"

"You are glowing!" Pasha touched her cheek and smiled.

"It's just the heat from the fire!" Tore said smiling.

"Whatever it is, it looks good." Pasha laughed. "I will leave you two alone for awhile. I have things to tend to of my own."

Tore nodded and caressed her baby's face. She wondered what business Pasha was up to now. He had been having a ship built for weeks, and the supplies he was gathering were mounting by the day. She didn't know how he did it all alone. Thorvald had many men working for him, and it seemed that he hadn't accomplished half of what Pasha had in the time that Pasha had...then again, Pasha wasn't ordering a fleet of warships!

Tore stared at the ceiling, wondering how long Ulf would let her stick around before he wanted her and her "bastard child" as Ulf referred to the baby, gone. Pasha had said before the baby was born, that if he had understood Ulf correct, Tore could remain with him until Pasha set sail and Ulf returned to his own shire. In other words, Ulf didn't want Tore to go home with Brock's baby. Tore sighed.

She had plenty of money. Brock had given her a lot of gold in case something were to happen to him...they both knew that his life would not be a long one with Ulf Nordahlsson around. She could stay in the inn until she felt better, and then stake out on her own. Staying in Tunsberg seemed an unwise thing to do. She would go somewhere else. Another port town perhaps. She liked the foreign traders and merchants...there was always so much new to be seen. The ships were constantly bringing news and goods too...of course, where there were ships there would either be warriors or fishermen.

It wasn't that she was afraid. She had done much more years ago when she was much younger and definitely less experienced in the ways of the world. She didn't need a man for protection...just for social acceptance. After everything she had been through in the past months she wasn't even sure that she wanted social acceptance either. Tore sighed again, this time louder.

The next morning, Pasha crept into the room not wanting to wake Tore or the baby; but she was already awake. Harek nuzzled her breasts and sucked hungrily. Tore smiled and nodded at Pasha as he closed the door behind himself.

"Up already?" Pasha smiled and produced breakfast on a tray.

"Seems odd being in bed this much!" Tore laughed. "Oh, thank you!" She cried when she noticed the food on the tray before her, "I'm starving!"

Pasha poured her tea into her wood cup. "I also have a gift for you!"

"A gift?" Tore looked at Pasha with wide, excited eyes, "You didn't have to get me a gift! You've done so much for me already!"

"No, I wanted to get you a gift." Pasha sat down on the edge of the bed and watched Harek nurse. "In my country, I always lavish gifts on my concubines and lovers when they have given me a child."

"You mean a male child?" Tore cocked her head and joked.

"No. No. I love all of my children. Sometimes I think that my girl children are more fortunate for they are not likely to be killed by their own siblings in a race to the throne. Most will live their lives out in the lavish splendor of one of my beloved friend's harems." Pasha pushed the small leather wrapped package at her.

"Do you have many concubines?" Tore asked. She had never had this personal a conversation with Pasha before. He discussed things in his childhood, minor political confrontations, and squabbles with his mother, but rarely did he share intimate details of his life in the harem.

"I have thirty." Pasha said after a slight pause that indicated he was counting them up to get the correct number.

"Thirty women?" Tore said and then felt her mouth drop open.

"Yes." Pasha laughed at her obvious shock. "That is a small number where I come from!"

"How many wives do you have then?" Tore asked expecting an even larger number.

"None." Pasha grinned. "I love the women that I have, but elevating one to the status of wife, often causes problems within the harem...or with my mother." He laughed again.

Tore liked the rich, resonating tone of his laugh and laughed too. "So, none of your children count as your heirs?"

"That's up to me." Pasha shrugged. "Perhaps, someday I will marry. I just haven't found a worthy woman."

"You sound like all women are bad!" Tore laughed and slid her finger into Harek's tiny fist.

"No, not bad. I do not know your word for what I want to say..." Pasha tried to think of how to describe how he was feeling, but he couldn't, so he changed the subject. "No matter. I saw Ulf this morning while examining my ship."

"Did he ask about me?" Tore noticed the obvious change in conversation, but went along with it.

"Yes." Pasha smiled.

"Well? Are you going to tell me what it was he said?" Tore laughed and placed Harek in Pasha's outstretched arms.

"Just asked if you were well." Pasha said looking up from the bundle he held.

"How considerate of him." Tore laughed. "You know, you are very good with babies! I feel so inadequate when you are around!"

Pasha laughed. "You are never inadequate in anything, Tore! You are an amazing woman!"

"Yeah, well, I've never seen a man who was so tender and interested in a baby before...and, Harek isn't even your baby!" Tore shook her head and got up from her bed to stretch.

"Not all men in my country are like me. I just happen to like children and babies. They make me remember when life was happy and carefree. I miss my own children." Pasha said with a gleam in his eye that bordered on a tear.

Tore was touched by Pasha's love for her tiny son. "Actually, Harek probably thinks you're his father. He hasn't known any other."

Pasha looked up and smiled from ear to ear. "I am honored for you to have said such a thing about me!"

"Are you so surprised? I don't know what I would have done without you all of these months, Pasha, my friend." Tore smiled warmly and drank some of the tea that Pasha had poured earlier for her.

Pasha was touched. Maybe she was falling in love with him; he would be satisfied with confidant and friend for now. If only he could tell her that he wanted to be Harek's father, but it was still too soon.

"I don't think many people would believe that this little white baby was mine! He's whiter than snow, and I am a copper kettle!" Pasha laughed.

Tore shrugged. "Nature often surprises women!" "Harek would be one big surprise in my land!" Pasha laughed again.

"I was hoping you'd go with me on a walk later on. I'm feeling restless. I need to get some fresh air." Tore ate a piece of bread dipped in honey.

"The pain is gone?" Pasha raised his eyebrows inquisitively.

Tore laughed. "I don't think the pain will ever be gone." She had much more than physical pain to contend with at this point. "I do feel stronger though."

"Very well. We will go for your walk later." Pasha handed the baby back to Tore. "For now, I must meet with a merchant."

Pasha turned to leave, but Tore's words stopped him. "Wait! I haven't opened your gift yet!" Tore smiled, she laid Harek in the bed, and picked up Pasha's gift. Pasha came towards her and watched as she untied the leather cords that held the leather wrapping in place. The wrapping fell away to reveal a beautiful emerald on a gold chain. Tore looked at it in amazement. She had never owned a gem before. "Oh, Pasha! It's beautiful! But, it must have been too expensive! You should have saved it for one of your...concubines." No matter how many times she said this word, it still sounded foreign and odd to her.

"No. I wanted you to have it." Pasha smiled and taking the necklace, offered to put it around her neck for her. Tore bent her head so that Pasha could put the gold chain around her neck.

"It's so beautiful. I've never had such a beautiful gift!" Tore reached up and felt the facets of the square emerald.

"In my country, gems such as these are plenty. All women of status have them dripping from their bodies and clothes." Pasha smiled.

"Your country must really be beautiful!" Tore said in a hushed voice. "I would really like to visit such a lovely land someday."

"You are welcome anytime." Pasha smiled. "It would be an honor to be your host."

Pasha's heart beat rapidly. She had shown a desire to see his world! Maybe persuading her to leave with him wouldn't be too difficult after all. He felt so in love with her now, that each day that drew nearer to his departure, he felt pangs of sorrow to have to leave her behind. However, if his plan went as scheduled, she would be on that ship as well.

The voyage home would be much longer that Tore's raiding trips had been. If he had decided to stop and trade along the way, there would've been many stop offs in many different countries. He could've sailed part of the way, then disembarked and gone ahead on foot and by horse. As things would have it, he would sail around Spain, through to the Mediterranean and on to Turkey. It would take about a year, if not more to reach his beloved homeland. This time, he would make sure he never went out adventuring again.

Ulf's knock brought him out of his daydreams.

"Pasha? Are you in there?" Ulf started this knocking stuff ever since the baby had arrived. He acted as if seeing the baby would burn his eyes right out of his head.

"Yes, I am here." Pasha went to the door and opened it.

"There is a man here who says he needs to speak with you about some smoked meats you are buying from him." Ulf said through the crack in the door.

Pasha nodded. "It is the merchant I told you I must see." He said to Tore who nodded in remembrance.

Pasha left the room. Tore wondered how Ulf had been able to suppress natural curiosity and not even take a peek at the baby. He was colder and stonier than she had originally thought. Maybe it was the only way he knew to control himself from killing her child. Tore shook her head in disgust. Whatever his problem was, she sure had been mistaken in waiting all these years for him to be her savior from all that was evil. He had only made her life more complicated.

Tore pondered these thoughts for a long time. All of those years thinking that Ulf would be this great hero who would solve all that ailed her, he would understand her love for Brock and set all things straight. She should have known better. Why had she been so naïve to believe that Ulf would be this tender, caring brother? He was a warrior, guiltless, feelingless. He was simply a trained fighter with no real mind of his own. He killed whoever he deemed necessary, and felt no remorse for his murders. Tore shook her head and laughed to herself.

Listen to her thoughts! She was a murderer just like her brother. Had she not killed without mercy, innocent children, women, men? Had she not trusted Thorvald blindly and fought for his gain? Had she not destroyed the peace and serenity of peasant's homes, and rammed the solid doors of the wealthy? She was no better than Ulf; she simply still had a heart. Ulf had been killing so long that he no longer had any senses or feelings. He simply did what he knew he should do. That was why he killed Brock. Revenge was his motive, regardless of her feelings. Ulf followed custom and eliminated the killer of his kinsmen.

Tore had known it would be Ulf's right to do such a thing. She just thought that he would spare Brock because of her feelings. He hadn't. Now, here she was alone, a mother, and her own brother wouldn't even look at his nephew. Was this child not part of her as well? Tore thought that Ulf could at least value that part of the child. He said he loved her as his sister, why then couldn't he accept her child as his nephew? Tore cursed and got up to wash herself with the water in the bucket before the fire.

When Pasha returned they went on their walk as planned. It was a beautiful day, with a clear and crisp blue sky. The air was fresh, with an occasional salty tinge as it wafted off of the waves in the sea. Pasha showed her his ship and the supplies he had stockpiled. He had spared no expense. Tore had given him quite a lot of gold and silver as payment for taking such good care of her. It had been hard to get him to accept it, but he finally did, saying that he would consider it a loan and that he intended to pay back every last piece. Tore told him not to be silly.

Tore felt comfortable with Pasha. He had a way about him that made her feel like anything could happen and he would know how to make it turn out right again. It was similar to the way Brock used to make her feel. She would hate to see him go. When Pasha left, she would be all alone again. All of these tender thoughts for this tender man, but Tore knew that he had another side to him as evil and deadly as her other side could be. They were both killers, as was Ulf. Maybe that was the kinship they felt, the bond they shared. Pasha and Tore killed when they had to, Ulf killed because he wanted to. There was a slight difference in the two, though very slight. The reason behind murder didn't make it any less than murder.

Days passed and Pasha began concentrating on the finer details of his journey. He grilled the men who had agreed to sail with him. He wanted no criminals or men who would not do whatever it was that was expected of them. He had no patience with laziness or whining. He gave orders and expected to be obeyed. They would be going to his land. In his land, he was a prince, not some copper colored foreigner that raised questions and curiosities. He was a prince and expected to be obeyed as a prince. He had boiled down this crew to men who wanted the adventure of sailing to a new and totally different world. Pasha promised each man his own home, and women too if they wanted them. Once they arrived in his homeland, if for any reason they wanted to return to Norway, Pasha had promised to try to find them a way home as soon as he could. He had warned them that a way home might not be for years though. Few people made such a journey as he had unwisely done. Few people had the resources to afford such a trip.

Tore was interested in the finer details. How they would navigate, how they would eat, where they would sleep. This ship was far different from the langskips that she had grown accustomed to. It was roomier, and the men did not sit in rows on sea chests to row the boat. There were more sails, and mechanical devices that Pasha himself had crafted for the most part. Tore wondered why Pasha's people sailed so little if they were able to come up with such convenient devices. Pasha had told her that most of their journeys were carried out on foot. Few liked the sea and the treacherous dangers it posed.

Tore was impressed by all that Pasha had accomplished. She touched his arm as he was explaining a few details to her, "I'm really going to hate seeing you go."

"Well," Pasha smiled and put his own hand over the one she had placed on his arm. "I still have a few more weeks yet."

Tore sighed. Together they walked to the inn. Ulf met them in the hall and quickly made an excuse to leave. The look on Ulf's face suggested that he resented his sister for taking his friend away. Even though Pasha remained neutral in Ulf and Tore's disagreements, Ulf felt betrayed by Pasha's concern for both Tore and her child. Tore understood Pasha's position and felt no anger or resentment towards his friendship with Ulf. For Ulf, it was not so simple. Ulf demanded sole loyalty. He did not want to share his friend with anyone, not even his sister; but as Pasha grew deeper in love with Tore, Ulf discovered that Pasha also spent more time with her instead of him. Sure, Pasha always invited him to come along, but why would he want to be accompanied by Tore and her bastard? Ulf would be glad when Pasha's ship set sail so he could return to his family and his shire. The problem with Tore was no longer his. She had chosen to defy his wishes; therefore once Pasha departed she was on her own. He had planned to allow his family to just keep wondering what ever happened to Tore. No point stirring up trouble. Tore was smart enough not to return to the shire ever again.

Days passed, and soon they melted into weeks. Tore knew that Pasha's day of departure loomed closer each day that passed. She didn't want him to go. She had come to depend on his security and comfort. She dreaded being alone again.

Tore stood, clasping Harek to her chest, on a high rocky cliff with only a few green patches here and there. It was her favorite place to seek solitude and peace. She faced the sea, her hair billowing out behind her, her fur cape flapping loudly in the wind. Sadly she watched the ships coming and going, knowing that tomorrow Pasha's ship would be one of those that were sailing out of the fjord never to return again. A single tear rolled down her cheek as she contemplated life without him, without anybody except her baby. How would she go on alone?

Pasha walked up quietly behind her and cleared his throat to get her attention. Tore turned around swiftly, startled by the sound. No one she knew came up here except maybe Ulf. She had to come to this place for peace and quiet ever since she had first come to Tunsberg, before Brock, and before Ulf came home. She had told Ulf about this place, even bringing him here once. Ulf must have told Pasha where to find her.

"Ulf told me you'd be here." Pasha said with a guilty tone as if he had intruded upon her privacy.

"I come here often." Tore turned and faced the sea again. "I like to watch the ships come and go."

"Do you miss it? Sailing, I mean?" Pasha stepped closer to her, looking out into the misty waters as she was doing.

"Yes." Tore sighed. "That part of me will never die."

"I leave tomorrow." Pasha said slowly and sadly.

Tore did not respond. How could words say what was so heavy on her heart.

"I was telling your brother that I was in need of a warrior for protection. Most of the men who agreed to sail with me turned out to be fishermen. So, I was looking for someone who was skilled with a sword. You never can be too sure what you'll run into out there on those waters." Pasha laughed nervously. "Especially considering what happened to me before."

Tore turned and looked at him. What was he trying to say?

"Anyway, Ulf said you might know of someone who would be willing to sail with me on such short notice. I'll promise the same thing to this person that I promised the rest of the men sailing with me: a home, security, my protection once we reach my homeland." Pasha shrugged as if what he was protecting wasn't much at all.

Tore suddenly knew that Pasha was asking her to come with him to his warm home so far away from Norway. He was asking her to sail to a better life where both she and her son would be safe and happy.

"I'd love Harek as my own son, Tore." Pasha smiled warmly. "I already do."

Tore stared at this man. Could she feel love for another man so soon after Brock's death? Part of her felt as if she was betraying the only man she had ever loved by loving Pasha; but, part of her knew that Brock would want her to continue to live, love, and fight. She would never love another man the same way she had loved Brock, but wasn't there so many different types of love?

Tore turned her face into the gusty wind and smelled the salty sea air. If she left Norway, who could say if she would ever return? This was her home, her people. Everything she knew and loved was here. Her heart beat in rhythm with the blackish waves so far below. She watched as the waves hit the rocks and sprayed sharply into the air. She missed the sound of waves slapping the side of a ship. She longed for the rocking motion of a ship on the waters. She missed sailing and the adventure of the journey. Tore watched Pasha eagerly watching her. She knew this man loved her and would take care of her. He was cut from the same strong cloth that Brock had been. His solid, calm temperament was a good match for her volatile, passionate one. She could have a good life with him.

Besides, Tore smiled at Pasha, she had never been one to turn her back on the impossible. She had never balked at an adventure. Waters or lands did not limit her gods; they would go with her and her son. What did she have to hold her here? Harek deserved a better life than what he would have if they stayed here in Norway.

Waves. Ships. Far away places. Tore reached out and took Pasha's arm and smiled, looking up into his enthralling brown eyes, she said, "When do we sail?"

Pasha clasped her hand in his and leaned over to kiss her warmly on the lips. "At dawn." He said simply.

Tore nodded again. "At dawn." She repeated and turned to watch the waves crash against the rocks far below this quiet cliff for one last time.

BIBLIOGRAPHY

Anderson, George K., Ed. <u>The Literature of England</u>. Vol I. 5th edition. ---: Scott, Foresman, 1968.

Balent, Matthew. <u>The Compendium of Weapons, Armour, and Castles</u>. Michigan: Palladium Books, 1989.

Benton, William, Pub. <u>Encyclopedia Britannica</u>. Vols. 8,10,16, 19,23. Illinois: William Benton Publishers, 1970.

Diamond, Robert E. <u>Old English: Grammar and Reader</u>. Michigan: Wayne State UP, 1970.

Gygax, Gary. <u>Advanced D & D Monster Manual II</u>. Wisconsin: Random House, 1983.

Harding, David, ed. <u>Weapons: An International Encyclopedia from 5000 BC to 2000 AD</u>. New York: St. Martin's P, 1990.

Heath, Ian. <u>The Vikings</u>. England: Osprey P, 1985.

Manguel, Alberto and Guadalupi, Gianni. <u>The Dictionary of Imaginary Places</u>. California: Harcourt Brace, 1987.

Norman, A.V.B. and Pottinger, Don. <u>English Weapons and Warfare 449-1660</u>. New York: Dorset P, 1985.

Ormand, Clyde. <u>How to Track and Find Game</u>. New York: Funk and Wagnalls, 1975.

Petersham, Miska and Maud. <u>Best in Children's Books</u>. New York: Doubleday, 1959.

Ward, James M. <u>Deities and Demigods</u>. Wisconsin: TSR Games, 1980.

Webster, Hutton. <u>Medieval and Modern History</u>. Nebraska: ---, 1925.

Scars Publications

Books

sulphur and sawdust
slate and marrow
blister and burn
rinse and repeat
survive and thrive
(not so) warm and fuzzy
torture and triumph
oh.
infamous in our prime
anais nin: an understanding of her art
the electronic windmill
changing woman
harvest of gems
the little monk
death in málaga
the svetasvatara upanishad
hope chest in the attic
the window
close cover before striking
(woman.)
autumn reason
contents under pressure
the average guy's guide (to feminism)
changing gears

Compact Discs

music: The Demo Tapes *MFV (Mom's Favorite Vase)*
music: The Final (MFV Inclusive) *Kuypers*
music: The Beauty & The Destruction *Weeds & Flowers*
performance art/spoken word: Live at Cafe Aloha *Pettus/Kuypers*
performance art/spoken word: Rough Mixes *Pointless Orchestra*
performance art/spoken word: Seeing Things Differently *Kuypers*
performance art/spoken word: T&T audio CD *Assorted Artists*
internet CD: Oh. Internet CD *Assorted Artists*
performance art/spoken word: Change Rearrange *Kuypers*
performance art/spoken word: Stop Look Listen *Kuypers*
performance art/spoken word: Tick Tock *5D/5D*
performance art/spoken word: Six One One *Kuypers*